Southwestern Writers Collection Series
CONNIE TODD, EDITOR

The Southwestern Writers Collection Series originates from the Southwestern Writers Collection, an archive and literary center established at Texas State University–San Marcos to celebrate the region's writers and literary heritage.

LONE STAR SLEUTHS

AN ANTHOLOGY OF TEXAS CRIME FICTION

EDITED AND WITH AN INTRODUCTION BY
BILL CUNNINGHAM, STEVEN L. DAVIS, AND
ROLLO K. NEWSOM

Requests for permission to reproduce material from this work should be sent to:
Permissions
University of Texas Press
P.O. Box 7819
Austin, TX 78713-7819
www.utexas.edu/utpress/about/bpermission.html

♾ The paper used in this book meets the minimum requirements of
ANSI/NISO Z39.48-1992 (R1997) (Permanence of Paper).

LIBRARY OF CONGRESS CATALOGING-IN-PUBLICATION DATA
Lone Star sleuths : an anthology of Texas crime fiction / edited and with an
introduction by Bill Cunningham, Steven L. Davis, and Rollo K. Newsom. —
1st ed.
     p.   cm. — (Southwestern Writers Collection series)
   ISBN 978-0-292-71737-4 (pbk. : alk. paper)
     1. Short stories, American—Texas. 2. Texas—Social life and customs—
Fiction. I. Cunningham, Bill, 1949– II. Davis, Steven L. III. Newsom, Rollo K.
(Rollo Kern), 1937–
PS558.T4L667 2007
813'.01089764—dc22   2007005813

For Nevin Cunningham and Drew Cunningham;

for Joe Davis and Mary Comparetto;

for Sylvia C. Newsom

CONTENTS

INTRODUCTION

Once upon a time, literary murders were largely relegated to British drawing rooms and California's mean streets. Hard-boiled heroes in Dashiell Hammett's San Francisco and Raymond Chandler's Los Angeles personified American noir, while British "cozies" circulated around the elaborate plots woven by Sir Arthur Conan Doyle and Agatha Christie.

On both sides of the Atlantic, a distinct sense of place has long been one of the chief pleasures of the genre. Yet only in recent years have mysteries expanded to include America's regional cultures, and now millions of readers are familiar with Tony Hillerman's Navajo country, James Lee Burke's New Orleans, and Carl Hiaasen's Florida.

Texas has always staked a large claim on the nation's imagination and its mystery literature is no exception. Hundreds of crime novels are set within the state, most of which have been published in the last twenty years. From the highest point atop the Guadalupe Mountains in West Texas to the Piney Woods of East Texas, from the High Plains of the Panhandle to the subtropical climate of the Lower Rio Grande Valley, mystery writers have covered every aspect of Texas's extraordinarily diverse geography.

The titles associated with Texas mysteries showcase many native elements: *Armadillos and Old Lace, Mucho Mojo, Bad Chili, Chile Death, Bordersnakes, Diamondback, Hot Enough to Kill, Texas Wind, The Mexican Tree Duck, The Sheriff and the Branding Iron Murders, Death on the River Walk, Houston in the Rearview Mirror,* and *Deliver Me from Dallas.* Even Texas's greatest real-life murder mystery—the assassination of John F. Kennedy—is addressed in several novels, one of which resuscitates Sherlock Holmes and brings him to Dallas in order to solve the case.

The typical protagonist in a Texas mystery novel was once easy to define—a wisecracking, improbably macho male. The wisecracks have remained, but a profound transformation has taken place in recent years. Texas women, long consigned to stereotypical supporting roles, have come on strong, infusing the genre with a new energy. Women detectives usually aren't as hard-boiled as their male counterparts, but they are plenty tough and courageous. Instead of using their fists or firing weapons, the women use their brains and powers of observation to solve crimes.

The growing numbers of female detectives are complemented by a dazzling array of vocations available to protagonists. Texas detectives once consisted of cops, lawyers, and private investigators. No longer. Now a private eye can also be a rock musician, funeral director, game warden, advertising executive, stand-up comedian, priest, English professor, fashion stylist, football player, herb shop owner, librarian, chef, birdwatcher, salvage boat operator, and lesbian forensic chemist. The range of occupations for Texas detectives is so boundless that there is even room among their ranks for a Jewish country-and-western musician and provocateur named "Kinky."

Despite this expanding diversity, one troubling aspect of contemporary Texas crime fiction remains—very few authors are African American or Mexican American. The situation will undoubtedly improve as the genre continues to evolve. In the meantime, many Anglo American mystery novelists have sought to portray Texas's cultural diversity in their work. Ethnic minorities often appear as major characters in novels, usually in the role of a sidekick to the Anglo American protagonists. The increasing Hispanicization of Texas is also making itself felt in the ethnic composition of some heroes and heroines. Bicultural and quasi-Hispanic elements are found in Jim Sanderson's Dolph Martinez, Nancy Herndon's Elena Jarvis, Allana Martin's Texana Jones, and Rick Riordan's Tres Navarre.

Several other factors distinguish Texas-based mysteries. One important element is the weather. Tornadoes, droughts, dust storms, flash floods, blizzards, and hurricanes appear periodically, but it's the killer heat that takes center stage. Detectives battle dehydration and sunstroke as they make their rounds. Even the hard-boiled types—the gutty detectives who seem to bounce right back from broken ribs and gunshot wounds—take great care to avoid burning themselves on the upholstery of their cars after they have been parked in the sun all day. Perhaps the most vivid description of Texas heat occurs in Rick Riordan's novel, *Big Red Tequila*. Riordan's protagonist notes that the temperature remained ninety-five degrees in San Antonio, even as the sun was setting. He observes, "The sun kept its eye on the city until its very last moment on the horizon, looking at you as if to say: 'Tomorrow I'm going to kick your ass.'"

In addition to the weather, Texas sleuths confront a variety of natural hazards: mountain lions, tarantulas, rattlesnakes, fire ants, alligators, mosquitoes, and killer bees. And then there are dermestid beetles. These flesh-eating insects live just a few miles north of San Antonio in Bracken Cave, which hosts the largest bat colony in the world. When a murder victim in J. P. Ripley's novel *Lost in Austin* gets dumped in the cave, the beetles reduce the body to a pile of bones within minutes. Same thing happens to unlucky bats.

As every Texan knows, the Lone Star State is susceptible to stereotyping. It's easy for outsiders to come in and portray over-the-top yahoos—racist redneck sheriffs and women with Big Hair. Some non-Texan writers have given in to those temptations, and clichéd portraits emerge in their books. It's also true that some native authors will exaggerate local color, engaging in what *Dallas Morning News* critic Jerome Weeks calls "the yee-haw factor." But, overall, the majority of Texas-based mystery and detective fiction presents an accurate picture, and mystery writers have created memorable portraits of Texas's landscapes, people, and social issues.

Crime fiction has received significant attention from academic scholars in recent years. Mysteries are taught in college classrooms, discussed at academic conferences, and analyzed in scholarly publications. Part of this trend is the result of an increasing emphasis on pop culture studies at American universities. But the mysteries also receive such attention because they take on cutting-edge social issues, addressing topics in ways more profound than the mass media, but less formal than statistics-laden academic studies. In Texas, mystery novels examine myriad issues: the role of illegal drugs in contemporary society, ethnic relations, politics, gender issues, corruption, religion, immigration, poverty, pollution, the nature of crime, and the roots of violence.

Texas mysteries also demonstrate that small towns are losing ground to America's mass culture. Bill Crider's Sheriff Dan Rhodes novels, set in fictional Clearview, are particularly adept at describing this phenomenon. In Crider's *Murder Most Fowl*, a local resident—who once owned a hardware store—stages a protest by chaining himself to the entrance of the Wal-Mart. The man is quickly arrested and hauled away, but his comments about the city's abandoned downtown linger long after the passage has ended.

Scholars have pointed out that the modern mystery novel derives in large part from the formulaic plots, themes, and characters that once ruled Western dime novels. This is hardly the most prestigious branch of the literary tree, and mysteries are regarded, rightly, as genre fiction. But increasingly, mystery novels are moving into literary terrain, becoming pulp free. The expanding popularity of crime fiction is a key to this evolution. With mystery novels dominating national bestseller lists and the shelf space in local bookstores, talented writers are becoming attracted to the genre. The result has been a substantial improvement in the quality of crime fiction. Many of the genre's best novels now contain hallmarks of what is considered "literary" writing: well-developed characters, innovative and lyrical use of the language, and an intellectual reach that considers complex social and philosophical issues.

In Texas, literary quality is evident in many of the state's best mystery writers. Several Texans have received the genre's major prizes: Mary Willis Walker has won the Agatha, Edgar, Hammett, and Macavity Awards. Rick Riordan has won the Edgar, Anthony, and Shamus Awards. Joe Lansdale received the Edgar, Jeff Abbott the Agatha, and Bill Crider the Anthony. Steven Saylor's *A Twist at the End*, although a mystery, received the Violet Crown Award for Best Novel from the Writers' League of Texas.

Other Texas mystery writers enjoy solid literary reputations outside of the genre. James Crumley, for example, is a Texas native whose first novel, a book about Vietnam titled *One to Count Cadence*, was published in 1969 and is considered a modern classic. Although Crumley's subsequent novels feature detectives, critics recognize that Crumley is a literary novelist whose canvas just happens to be crime fiction. There's also Rolando Hinojosa, who has won international prizes for his novels—some of which are mysteries—set in the Lower Rio Grande Valley. Hinojosa is among those who have roots as English professors at Texas universities. That list includes Susan Wittig Albert, Bill Crider, Clay Reynolds, and Jim Sanderson—whose first novel, *El Camino del Rio*, was a mystery, yet it also won the Frank Waters Southwest Writing Award.

Mystery writers from outside of Texas who have written about the state also enjoy reputations for quality prose. Nevada Barr's *Track of the Cat*, set in the Guadalupe Mountains National Park, won the Agatha Award for Best First Novel and the Anthony Award for Best Novel. Walter Mosley, who writes about East Texas in *Gone Fishin'*, is the author of the popular and critically-acclaimed Easy Rawlins series. Carolyn Hart, whose *Death on the River Walk* is set in San Antonio, has received multiple Agatha Awards and is one of the genre's most decorated writers.

In compiling this anthology of Texas-based mystery and detective fiction, we have focused more on the sense of place than the crime, and we've chosen excerpts that highlight Texas's physical and cultural geography. The mystery writers, like their detective protagonists, have probed beneath the surface of their surroundings, uncovering sometimes-unpleasant truths. While a very real affection for Texas exists in these books, the portraits will not always please boosters of the Lone Star State: there's rampant pollution along the upper Texas coast, wasteful water usage in West Texas, white racists in East Texas, gang activity in San Antonio, religious intolerance in small towns. This is not the stuff of glossy travel literature. Call it realism. And it's perfectly suited to crime literature.

Creating distinct geographical regions from the subtle variations in Texas's cultural and physical topography is a nearly impossible task, yet for the purposes of this anthology, we have divided the state into seven zones. The first section, "El Paso and West Texas," includes Big Bend and the rugged mountain ranges that arise from the Chihuahuan Desert. These wide-open spaces offer hundred-mile vistas and are what many non-Texans imagine the Lone Star State to be. This is the mythic Texas, and it is prime territory for murder mysteries. In fact, six of the selections are based in West Texas, more than any other single region in this anthology. "Austin and the Hill Country" is also a popular setting for mysteries, owing to the fact that so many of the state's writers live in Austin and the surrounding area. Hard-boiled noir is largely absent from this region, as the mysteries tend to reflect the Hill Country's attractive landscape. "Houston and the Gulf Coast" is hard-boiled territory, thanks to Houston's sprawling, anarchic energy and the Gulf Coast's tough and unsentimental terrain—no beach paradises found here. North Texas, as reflected in the mysteries set in "Dallas, Fort Worth, and the Panhandle," offers a different view of the state. The DFW metroplex is home to dozens of murder mysteries, yet, surprisingly, few of the books discuss the local geography. Perhaps this is a natural consequence of life in a prairie megalopolis where five million people live in adjoining cities. The Panhandle, in contrast, is rarely used as a mystery setting, but the novels based there vividly depict the local culture and landscape. "East Texas" contains vestiges of the Old South, and it has the highest concentration of African American residents in the state. Not surprisingly, race relations remain an important element of the mysteries set in this region. "San Antonio and South Texas" has a predominantly Mexican American population, a fact that is reflected in the region's literature, even if few of the writers themselves are of Hispanic descent. The last section, "Small Town Texas," looks at life in Texas's close-knit communities, which are often threatened by outside forces. Novels set in these towns often portray the intertwined lives of local residents, and thus are naturally more cozy than the hard-boiled works that predominate in Texas's metropolitan areas. We wind up the collection with "The End of the Road," where an excerpt from Mary Willis Walker's *The Red Scream* chillingly portrays how convicted murderers are subjected to Texas's ultimate punishment.

The thirty selections gathered in this volume represent only a small portion of the hundreds of mystery novels set in the state. We had to exclude many good writers, not because their prose is inferior, but because the sense of place evoked in their novels was not compressed enough to shine through in short excerpts. For those who wish to pursue further readings, we have created a comprehensive bibliography of Texas mystery fiction that is available online at: www.library.txstate.edu/swwc/exhibits/mystbib.html

BILL CUNNINGHAM, STEVEN L. DAVIS, AND ROLLO K. NEWSOM

LONE STAR SLEUTHS

PART 1

EL PASO AND WEST TEXAS

Track of the Cat

NEVADA BARR

At 8,749 feet, Guadalupe Peak is the highest point in Texas, crowning the Guadalupe Mountains National Park and the mountain range that extends north into New Mexico. The park was first proposed in the 1930s, but was established only in 1972 after a long battle with area ranchers.

Nevada Barr was a struggling writer when she took a job at Guadalupe Mountains National Park in the late 1980s. While on patrol in the backcountry, she developed the idea of creating a mystery series featuring a park ranger. Since then, Barr has published several novels set in America's national parks, taking her readers to locales such as Michigan's Isle Royal, Colorado's Mesa Verde, and Mississippi's Natchez Trace Parkway. Along the way, she has become one of America's most popular and critically acclaimed mystery writers.

Track of the Cat, set in the Guadalupe Mountains, is Barr's first novel in her series of national park mysteries. The book won both the Anthony and Agatha Awards for Best First Mystery Novel, and it introduced readers to amateur detective and park ranger Anna Pigeon. In the following excerpt, Pigeon is helping monitor the movements of mountain lions, which are protected in the park—much to the dismay of neighboring ranchers, who still resent the park's presence.

Nevada Barr's novel evokes both the grandeur and the intimacy of Texas's natural landscape, and here she provides a fine view of McKittrick Canyon, one of the Guadalupe Mountains' most spectacular features.

Anna sat down on a smooth boulder, the top hollowed into a natural seat. The red peeling arms of a Texas madrone held a veil of dusty shade over her eyes. This was the third day of this transect. By evening she would reach civilization: people. A contradiction in terms, she thought even as the words trickled through her mind. Electric lights, television, human companionship, held no allure. But she wanted a bath and she wanted a drink. Mostly she wanted a drink.

And maybe Rogelio. Rogelio had a smile that made matrons hide the hand with the wedding ring. A smile women would lie for and men would follow into battle. A smile, Anna thought with habitual cynicism, that the practiced hucksters in Juarez flashed at rich gringos down from Minnesota.

Maybe Rogelio. Maybe not. Rogelio took a lot of energy.

A spiny rock crevice lizard peered out at her with one obsidian eye, its gray-and-black mottled spines creating a near-perfect illusion of dead leaves and twigs fallen haphazardly into a crack in the stone.

"I see you," Anna said as she wriggled out of her pack. It weighed scarcely thirty pounds. She'd eaten and drunk it down from thirty-seven in the past two days. The poetry of it pleased her. It was part of the order of nature: the more one ate the easier life got. Diets struck Anna as one of the sourest notes of a spoiled country.

Letting the pack roll back, she carefully lowered it to the rock surface. She wasn't careful enough. There was an instant of rustling and the lizard vanished. "Don't leave town on my account," she addressed the seemingly empty crevice. "I'm just passing through."

Anna dug a plastic water jug from the side pocket of her backpack and unscrewed the cap. Yellow pulp bobbed to the top. Next time she would not put lemon slices in; the experiment had failed. After a few days the acid taste grew tiresome. Besides, it gave her a vague feeling of impropriety, as if she were drinking from her finger-bowl.

Smiling inwardly at the thought, Anna drank. Finger-bowls, Manhattan, were miles and years away from her now, Molly and AT&T her only remaining connections.

The water was body temperature. Just the way she liked it. Ice-water jarred her fillings, chilled her insides. "If it's cold, it'd better be beer," she would tell the waitress at Lucy's in Carlsbad. Sometimes she'd get warm water, sometimes a cold Tecate. It depended on who was on shift that day. Either way, Anna drank it. In the high desert of West Texas, moisture was quickly sucked from the soft flesh of unprotected humans.

No spines, she thought idly. No waxy green skin. Nothing to keep us from drying up and blowing away. She took another pull at the water and amused herself with the image of tumbling ass over teakettle like a great green and gray stickerweed across the plains to the south.

Capping the water she looked down at the reason she had stopped: the neatly laid pile of scat between her feet. It was her best hope yet and she'd been scrambling over rocks and through cactus since dawn. Every spring and fall rangers in the Guadalupe Mountains followed paths through the high country chosen by wildlife biologists. These transects—carefully selected trails cutting across the park's wilderness—were searched for mountain lion sign. Any that was found was measured, photographed, and recorded so the Resource Management team could keep track of the cougars in the park: where were they? Was the population healthy?

Squatting down, Anna examined her find. The scat was by no means fresh but it was full of hair and the ends twisted promisingly. Whatever had excreted it had been dining on small furry creatures. She took calipers out of the kit that contained all her transect tools: camera, five-by-seven cards with places for time, date, location, and weather conditions under which the sign was found, data sheet to record the size of the specimen, and type of film used for the photograph.

The center segment of this SUS—Standard Unit of Sign—was twenty-five millimeters in diameter, almost big enough for an adult cat. Still, it wasn't lion scat. This was Anna's second mountain lion transect in two weeks without so much as one lion sign: no tracks, no scrapes, no scat. Twenty of the beautiful cats had been radio-collared and, in less than three years, all but two had left the park or slipped their collars—disappeared from the radio scanner's range somehow.

Ranchers around the Guadalupes swore the park was a breeding ground for the "varmints" and that cattle were being slaughtered by the cats, but Anna had never so much as glimpsed a mountain lion in the two years she'd been a Law Enforcement Ranger at Guadalupe. And she spent more than half her time wandering the high country, sitting under the ponderosa pines, walking the white limestone trails, lying under the limitless Texas sky. Never had she seen a cougar and, if wishing and waiting and watching could've made it so, prides of the great padding beasts would've crossed her path.

This, between her feet, was probably coyote scat.

Because she hated to go home empty-handed, Anna dutifully measured, recorded, and photographed the little heap of dung. She wished all wild creatures were as adaptable as the coyote. "Trickster" the Indians called him. Indeed he must be to thrive so close to man.

Piled next to the coyote's mark was the unmistakable reddish berry-filled scat of the ring-tailed cat. "MY ravine," it declared. "MY canyon. I was here second!"

Anna laughed. "Your canyon," she agreed aloud. "I'm for home."

Stretching tired muscles, she craned her neck in a backward arc. Overhead, just to the east, vultures turned tight circles, corkscrewing up from the creekbed between the narrow walls of Middle McKittrick Canyon where she hiked.

Eleven of the big birds spun in a lazy whirlwind of beaks and feathers. Whatever they hovered over was hidden from view by the steep cliffs of the Permian Reef. A scrap of rotting carrion the size of a goose egg drew vultures. But eleven? Eleven was too many.

"Damn," Anna whispered. A deer had probably broken a leg and coyotes had gotten it. Probably.

A twelfth winged form joined the hungry, waiting dance.

"Damn." Anna pulled up her pack and shrugged into it. "You can have your rock back," she addressed the apparently empty crevice, and started down the canyon.

While she'd been sitting, the glaring white of the stones that formed the floor of Middle McKittrick Canyon had been softened to pale gold. Shadows were growing long. Lizards crept to the top of the rocks to catch the last good sun of the day. A tarantula the size of a woman's hand, the most horrifying of gentle creatures, wandered slowly across Anna's path.

"As a Park Ranger I will protect and serve you." She talked to the creature from a safe three yards away. "But we'll never be friends. Is that going to be a problem?"

The tarantula stopped, its front pair of legs feeling the air. Then it turned and walked slowly toward her, each of its legs appearing to move independently of the other seven.

"Yes. I see that it is." Glad there were no visitors to witness her absurdity, Anna stepped aside and gave the magnificent bug a wider berth than science or good sense would've deemed necessary.

Half a mile further down the canyon the walls began to narrow around boulders the size of Volkswagens. Anna scrambled and jumped from one to the next. Middle McKittrick was an excellent place to break an ankle or a neck, join the buzzards' buffet.

The sun slipped lower and the canyon filled with shadow. In the sudden cooling a breeze sprang up, carrying with it a new smell. Not the expected sickly-sweet odor of rotting flesh, but the fresh smell of water, unmistakable in the desert, always startling. One never grew accustomed to miracles. Energized, Anna walked on.

The walls became steeper, towering more than sixty feet above the creek. A rugged hillside of catclaw and agave showed dark above the pale cliffs. The boulders that littered Upper McKittrick were no longer in evidence. In the canyon's heart, Anna walked on smooth limestone. Over the ages water had scoured a deep trough, then travertine, percolating out of the solution, lined it with a natural cement.

Not a good place to be caught during the Texas monsoons in July and August. Each time she walked this transect in search of cougar sign, Anna had that same thought. And each time she had the same perverse stab of excitement: hoping one day to see the power and the glory that could roll half a mountain aside as it thundered through.

The smell of water grew stronger and, mixed with the sighing and sawing of the wind, she could hear its delicate music. Potholes began pitting the streambed—signs of recent flooding. Recent in geological time. Far too long to wait for a drink. Some of the scoured pits were thirty feet across and twenty feet deep. A litter of leaves and bones lay at the bottom of the one Anna skirted. An animal—a fawn by the look of one of the intact leg bones—had fallen in and been unable to climb out again.

This was a section of the canyon that Anna hated to hike, though its austere beauty lured her back time and again. The high walls, with their steep sloping shoulders sliding down to slick-sided pits, put a clutch in her stomach. Further down the white basins would be filled with crystal waters, darting yellow sunfish: life. But here the river had deserted the canyon for a world underground and left only these oddly sculpted death traps. Anna entertained no false hopes that her radio signal would reach up over the cliffs and mountains to summon help if she were to lose her footing.

She crawled the distance on hands and knees.

Even heralded by perfume and music, the water took her by surprise. Sudden in the bleak bone-white canyon came an emerald pool filled by a fall of purest water. The plop of fleeing frogs welcomed her and she stopped a moment just to marvel.

Aware of the ache across her shoulders, Anna loosed the straps and let her pack fall heavily to the limestone. At the abrupt sound there was an answering rattle, a rushing sound that brought her heart to her throat. With a crackling of black-feathered wings and a chatter of startled cries, a cloud of vultures fought up out of the saw grass that grew along the bench on the south side of the pool.

They didn't fly far, but settled in soot-colored heaps along the ledges, looking jealously back at their abandoned feast.

Anna looked to where they fixed their sulky eyes.

Saw grass, three-sided and sharp, grew nearly shoulder-high along the ledge beyond the pool. From a distance the dark green blades, edged with a paler shade, looked soft, lush, but Anna knew from experience anything edible in this stark land had ways of protecting itself. Each blade of saw grass was edged with fine teeth, like the serrated edge of a metal-cutting saw.

The sand-colored stone above it was dark with seeps of water weeping from the cliff's face. Ferns, an anomaly in the desert, hung in a green haze from the rocks, and violets the size of Anna's thumbnail sparked the stone with purple.

In the grasses then, protected by their razor-sides, was the carrion supper she had stumbled upon. Not anxious to wade through the defending vegetation, Anna reached to roll down her sleeves to protect the skin of her arms. Fingers touched only flesh and she remembered with irritation that, though, come sunset, West Texas still hovered in the cool grip of spring, the National Park Service had declared summer had arrived. Long-sleeved uniform shirts had been banned on May first.

Balancing easily on the sloping stone now that the drop was softened with a shimmer of water, Anna walked to the edge of the pool and entered the saw grass. She held her hands above her head like a teenager on a roller coaster.

The sharp grasses snagged at her trouser legs, plucked her shirt tight against her body. It matted underfoot and, in places, grew taller than the top of her head. Her boots sank to the laces in the mire. Water seeped in, soaked through her socks.

A high-pitched throaty sound grumbled from her perching audience. "I'm not going to eat your damned carrion," Anna reassured them with ill grace. "I just want to see if it's a lion kill." Even as she spoke she wondered if talking to turkey vultures was a worse sign, mentally speaking, than talking to one's self.

She must remember to ask Molly.

At the next step, stink, trapped by the grasses, rose in an almost palpable cloud. Death seemed to rot the very air.

In a sharp choking gasp, Anna sucked it into her lungs. Crumpled amongst the thick stems was the green and gray of a National Park Service uniform. Sheila Drury, the Dog Canyon Ranger, lay half curled, knees drawn up. An iridescent green and black backpack, heavy with water and whatever was inside, twisted her almost belly-up. Buzzard buffet: they didn't even have to dig for the tastiest parts.

El Camino del Río

JIM SANDERSON

Familiar to weather watchers as the nation's "hot spot," Presidio, Texas, is also one of the most isolated places in the country. Some ninety miles upstream from Big Bend National Park, in a rugged corner of the Chihuahuan Desert, this area was referred to by the Spanish as the *Despoblado*—uninhabited. This is the part of Texas people have in mind when they say that everything bites, pokes, sticks, or stings. The devil himself is said to live in a mountain cave overlooking the area.

Presidio's closest American neighbor is Marfa, a highlands town some sixty miles away and a world apart. Marfa has recently become a fashionable arts outpost; Presidio, meanwhile, remains a dusty border city, wrestling with an international boundary that divides two peoples who share a common landscape and culture.

This area is the setting for two highly regarded mystery novels by Jim Sanderson, an English professor at Lamar University–Beaumont. Sanderson's protagonist is U.S. Border Patrol Officer Dolph Martinez, a half-Anglo, half-Hispanic man whose dual ethnicity embodies both the cohesion and the divisiveness of this border region. Presidio is designated a "hardship" station by the Border Patrol. As such, agents who serve there are granted preferential status for transfers. Dolph Martinez is ready to move away, but then a series of murders compels him to stay in Presidio to uncover the truth about the crimes.

Riding back to Presidio on a motorcycle, I was cold. As I got farther south, to lower elevation, I warmed up. It was as if my blood had turned cold like a lizard's and now needed the desert heat. You don't have a choice here. Presidio is hotter than hell, Texans say. All summer long it has the daily state high and many days the nation's high. The heat, the dryness, mixed with the bit of humidity rising from the river, worked their ways into you.

The desert is not just about heat. It is about space, too. When you start tracking the signs, you don't just see *one* giant space anymore but a collection of details, some fitting together better than others. The details make the space. You began to see details even in the clear desert sky.

So we used the desert. We had sensors on the main routes, on the old Indian trails, on footbridges we put up over ranchers' fences so the wets wouldn't destroy the fencing, and along the river, but not off trail, out in the desert space. Maybe a Libyan terrorist might survive, but anymore no one else, not even an agent, had enough skill to just hightail it across the desert.

Still, some tried, or just panicked and got off the trail. The buzzards would spot them for us. Then again, to me, given the choice of taking on the desert or being locked into a boxcar or a car trunk and breathing gas fumes or stale air until I had no air, I'd choose the desert.

By the time Pat Coomer pulled the truck into the Border Patrol station in Presidio and I pulled in behind him on the motorcycle, the wind had gotten stronger and cooler. The gas signs at the Presidio gas stations swung on their hinges, and trash and tumbleweeds blew down the dirt streets and caught on curbs or picket fences. The starving dogs that wandered over from Ojinaga looked for a place out of the wind to lie down.

The Border Patrol station was a cinder block building surrounded by a high fence, on the juncture between the only two paved streets in town, 170 and 67. During high winds the Border Patrol station caught its share of foam cups, old newspapers, greasy napkins, and tumbleweeds. Several of the starving stray dogs liked to dump over the station's large trash cans and scrounge for food. Even this isolated part of the world, with fewer people than most anyplace in the USA, had its share of people's trash.

As Pat Coomer stepped out of his truck and I walked up to him, two joggers in expensive Gore-Tex jogging suits loped past the station and into the north wind. Pat said, "Crazy Yankee bastards. Running in this kind of weather." I waved to the joggers, our newly hired city administrator, Ben Abrams, and the other "Yankee bastard," Father Jesse Guzmán from St. Margaret Mary's Church. Guzmán and Abrams were as close as we had to yuppies. They were headed for the recently bulldozed track a quarter of a mile north of the station. The high school track team used the rough gravel pit for practice. In this weather, Guzmán and Abrams would be choking on the dust.

Pat opened the back door of the truck to let the wets out; I held open the door to the station, and Consuelo and Arturo led the other man and woman and kids into the Border Patrol station for processing. Pat followed the wets in, but before I went in, I glanced up at Guzmán and Abrams, fighting against the wind.

The station was empty except for the secretary, Carmen Lopez, and Patrol Agent Dede Pate sitting at one of the desks, filling out her reports. Then the door to Major R. C. Kobel's office opened, and R. C., the patrol-agent-in-charge of the Presidio station, looked at the wets filing in. Without looking at me, he said, "Dolph, once you get these guys cleared up, stop by."

We pulled some chairs around a desk next to Dede and had the wets sit around us. "Hey, Carmen," Pat said. "How about some help typing?"

Carmen barely lifted her eyes from her own typing. "I plan to finish this just at quitting time."

"You know what it does to my nails," Pat said. Carmen didn't smile, didn't look up, just kept punching the keys in front of her.

So Pat and I, with Dede looking on, tolerated the stink of these people, took whatever names they decided to give us, checked them against names of people somebody in the country might want detained, filled out the forms to be filed up in Marfa at sector headquarters, signed everything, then looked through the forms for mistakes. Throughout, the woman with the cut calf repeated her refrain, "*Yo no soy pollita. Estoy un política.*"

"Yeah, yeah," Pat mumbled to her.

Arturo courteously answered all our questions. The kids rubbernecked the room, and their mother, looking a bit worried, pulled at one, then the other to keep them seated politely and quietly by her. Maybe she had heard the rumors about kids being kidnapped to be sold to rich, childless gringos.

When it was over, Pat stood and said, "*Hasta mañana.*"

With the wets looking on, I said, "Whoa! Who's gonna escort 'em across the bridge?"

"I got to get home," Pat said as a plea.

I raised my hand to my lips and motioned like I was drinking a beer. "Later?" The two men and Consuelo smiled at me. Then Dede chuckled.

"No," Pat said. "Like to. Goddamn, I need to, but the wife's been bitching. And you know how mean a Mexican woman can get." After four years in Presidio and no transfer, Pat met a local woman with a missing husband. She filed, and Pat married her and moved into her mobile home with her and her three kids. We'd both been up since dawn, so I let Pat get in his pickup and drive home.

As Pat left and let the screen door bounce closed, as Carmen slipped the cover over her typewriter and a sweater over her shoulders, as the Mexicans slumped in their seats and the two kids drifted off to sleep, I stretched my arms, rubbed my eyes, and got ready to beg R. C. Kobel for a transfer.

I heard a chair scoot across the floor, then turned to see Dede almost sitting on my lap. "Dolph," she said. "I hear you found another dead one."

"Yeah," I said.

"Shot?"

"Yeah."

"Scares you, doesn't it?"

"Especially since somebody is getting away with it."

"You going to do anything?"

I squared to look at Dede and smiled. Three weeks before, our newest and youngest agent had found a mule with a hole in his head and drug the body out of some Rio Grande cane and salt cedars.

"What kind of boots did yours have?" I asked.

"What?" Dede stared at me and wrinkled her nose, making her look even younger. "You gonna start working on a Border Patrol GQ?" From beers and lunch with Pat Coomer and me, Dede was getting better with her jokes.

I smiled and said, "No, I'm thinking about going into the desert fashion-consulting business. What about his hair? What do you remember?"

"He had on good boots, no tennis shoes or hand-me-downs. His hair was long, in a ponytail." Dede's eyes started to brighten.

"And so?" I waited.

Five-foot four and small framed, she was the only Presidio agent shorter than me. And like most of the rest of us fifteen agents in Presidio, Dede was single, with no immediate plans to be other than single until she got transferred the hell out of Presidio. Since she had first appeared a year ago and got the male agents whispering about her young body, lines had etched themselves into her eyes and chin and her once long, permed, brunette hair was baked and frizzed and cut into a short, dirty pageboy. I patted her shoulder and kept myself from hugging her. "You get better after you're here ten or fifteen years."

"As old as you," Dede said.

"Come on," I said, and got up and headed toward Major Kobel's door.

"What about them?" Dede jerked her head toward the wets.

"Where are they going to go?" Then I raised my voice. "Consuelo," I said. The woman with the cut in her calf didn't look up. "Consuelo," I said again, and this time, realizing what name she had given herself, she looked up at me. "Watch them," I said. Arturo nodded and smiled.

Dede raised her hand, but before she could knock on R. C.'s door, I opened the door and stepped in. When I walked in, R. C. sucked in on his Lucky Strike, then held it under his desk, but I could still see the smoke around his head and trailing up from under his desk. "No smoking in federal buildings," I said.

"Goddamn you," R. C. said. "This concern for our health is gonna kill some of us old farts."

I walked up to R. C.'s desk and sat across from it. "You hear?"

"Another dead one." Kobel's head swung to Dede. I motioned to the other chair in front of his desk, and Dede sat.

R. C. grabbed a pad on his desk and shoved it toward me. As I tore the paper off the pad, R. C. said, "That's some kind of Mexican Colonel So-and-so, working for the Ministry of Defense of Coahuila on special assignment to Chihuahua to track down some enemy of the state—or some such. Sounds like a crackpot, but he mentioned drug enforcement—not DEA bozos," he added, referring to the Drug Enforcement Agency. We had constant battles with other agencies or other feds over turf.

"Customs or Feebies?" Feebies were the FBI.

"No, Mexican something or other. Maybe he can help you."

"Yeah, wonder what the *mordida* is?" In dealing with Mexican officials, the "bite," a kickback or bribe, was always involved.

"Well, then fuck him," R. C. wrinkled his brow, then looked at Dede. Dede's face remained frozen. She didn't make it to R. C.'s office as often as I did.

"Ever get tired of detaining wetbacks and looking for drugs?" I asked R. C. "Ever want to really track something down?"

"I once caught a Czech, or at least he claimed he was," R. C. said. "He was planning on sneaking into this country by way of Mexico. What a poor dumb, lost, misguided bastard he was." And he told us that Border Patrol story. The R. C. Kobel story, like my getting gut shot, that had worked its way into the Border Patrol lore, was the one about Kobel's favorite horse getting gunned down. Kobel was riding down several wetbacks and cutting across ranchers' land up around Marfa. One rancher, who was feuding with a neighbor, shot at Kobel, but Kobel's horse raised his head and took the bullet between the eyes. Before the horse had even fallen, Kobel had drawn his pistol and put two bullets in the rancher. Legend has it that he walked to the wounded rancher and told him that the second shot was for the horse.

When he finished, R. C. raised his cigarette to his lips and took a drag, looked at Dede, then crushed his cigarette in an ashtray that he pulled out of his drawer. Kobel had been the agent-in-charge for two years. He had put in time at Del Rio, El Paso, and Marfa and wanted to ride a desk and the accompanying salary until he retired. This post was a gift to him for his past services.

"Dede, tell him about the boots," I said.

Dede swung her head between me and Kobel. "Good ones."

"Mine had Red Wings and this." I pulled the vial out of my pocket and held it up between my thumb and forefinger. "Sister Quinn's medicine," I added.

"Crazy bitch," Kobel said.

I put the vial back in my pocket and held up one finger. "One, the guys are dressed alike." I held up my middle finger. "Two, Dede's guy was less than a mile from the river, right?" Dede dutifully nodded. "So?"

Dede looked at me. Kobel said, "Quit being cocky. You're the hot shit senior agent who doesn't knock anymore."

"They're probably both with the same outfit. Probably some bad fuckers with some management problems, so they're shooting employees. But why would they shoot Dede's so close to the river, probably before he could deliver his dope?"

"Go on," Kobel said, but I looked at Dede.

"Because they were finished," Dede said. "They're taking something across from our side."

I smiled at Dede, then turned to Kobel. "Let me free to scout the river. A drug bust would look good for us."

Kobel nodded. "Okay, you want to investigate, go ahead." He looked at Dede, then back at me, and said, "I heard from Nogales."

Dede caught the hint. "I guess you won't need me."

I smiled, and Kobel said, "Thanks, Dede." Dede caught the handle of her pistol on the arm of her chair as she got up. She tilted the handle down and swung her butt to clear the arm of the chair, smiled, and left. "Probationary is up on her in how long?" Kobel asked.

"A year."

"How's she doing?"

"She can hang. What about Nogales?"

"Advanced degree, good record. Definitely supervisory material. The word is you have the inside track for assistant field office supervisor or agent-in-charge."

I leaned back in the chair and smiled. R. C. frowned. "But I've got a different suggestion." He hesitated while I leaned toward him. R. C. continued, "I think you ought to stick around awhile."

"Why should I stay?"

"What's so bad about this place?"

I looked out the window in R. C.'s office. Kobel's gaze followed mine, and we saw one of the stray, starving dogs digging through the trash. I didn't need to say anything, so Kobel did. "Mandatory retirement age is fifty-seven. I've got seven months. Sometimes that seems too long what with goddamn budget cuts, sensitivity training sessions, quadruple forms. Remember when we tried flying those silly ass blimps? Hell, the locals would just call the bad guys across the border when we'd pull 'em down, then the bad guys would fly the drugs over in their planes. Jesus."

R. C. had a way of trailing off. "Your point is?"

R. C. focused on my face. "You take my place."

"Why should I? Why should I stay here?"

"You ever seen Nogales?"

"It resembles America more than this place."

"You want McDonald's hamburgers?"

"I want to be someplace besides the third world."

"Look, you go outside and you ask some Presidio citizen what lawman in the area they can trust. What do they say? Dolph Martinez, goddamn it. They like you here. You know the people, the area. You're the best tracker I have. You know how hard it is to learn that shit? You could train the new people. Look what you've done with Dede."

"Goddamn, R. C., I can die happy now."

"Well, shit." Kobel tried to think. "This place ain't so bad. Great dove hunting."

"I don't like shooting God's defenseless creatures."

"Good climate," R. C. said, and I looked up at him. "In the winter," he added. "Great for golf."

"How far do you have to go to play golf?" I asked. Kobel didn't answer. "Where does your wife live?"

"Alpine," Kobel muttered.

"Where you going to retire?"

"A lake in central Texas." I leaned back in my chair and laced my fingers behind my head. Presidio had no doctor, no drugstores, no paved streets except for the intersecting highways, no dry cleaners; it was a hardship station. You could put in for a transfer after two years, but transfers were slow. I had been here seven years. "You're goddamn right, I want to eat McDonald's hamburgers. I want to speak English more than Spanish."

I started to rise, but R. C. interrupted. "Why the hell are you in the Border Patrol anyway? Why not a lawyer, a politician? You've got a goddamn graduate degree, for Christ's sake."

I stared down at the toe of my boot, then shrugged. "Jobs are tough to come by, especially cushy government jobs."

"Get them wets outta here. It's quitting time," R. C. said, and I pushed myself out of my chair and went back into the station. Dede and the wets were waiting for me.

The sun was setting and making cold shadows when Dede and I loaded the wets back onto one of our vehicles and got them to the crossing station at the new international bridge. We escorted them through customs on our side, then sent them across. Arturo's smile dropped—back in Mexico and no green card from a kindly *la patrulla* agent. The mother carried the sleeping child and pulled the older one by the hand. Her shoulders seemed to droop with the weight of her child. And Consuelo-María limped behind everyone and jerked her head over her shoulder to stare at Dede and me, hoping that maybe we'd call her back across.

"She's not from northern Mexico," Dede said. "Her accent is different. I'd guess Guatemala. She kept saying that she was a political refugee."

"I heard her," I said.

"You think she was lying?"

"Who knows?" I shrugged. "I hope I'm not the one to catch her next time. Let's go home." Home for Dede was a rented house built in the middle of what used to be a gravel street, so that now the unpaved street split at her gravel front yard. For me, home was Cleburne Hot Springs Resort.

Time Bombs

NANCY HERNDON

El Paso, Texas's sprawling desert metropolis, receives less than ten inches of rain a year. This is in marked contrast to Beaumont, on the opposite end of the state, which can expect over fifty inches annually. Yet most of Texas is more like El Paso than Beaumont—perpetually short on water. Nowhere is the situation more critical than in El Paso, which has taken to purchasing tracts of land in neighboring counties—and even across the state line into New Mexico—in an attempt to gain control over more water rights.

El Paso-based mystery writer Nancy Herndon has proven adept at weaving local issues into her plot lines, and the seven novels in her Elena Jarvis series are the best-known mysteries set in El Paso (the city is referred to as "Los Santos" in the books). Herndon's protagonist, detective Elena Jarvis, is often called upon to solve crimes at Herbert Hobart University (HHU), an upscale, somewhat wacky, private college—the university president is a former television evangelist. Herndon also publishes a Texas-based culinary mystery series written under the name Nancy Fairbanks.

In the following excerpt from *Time Bombs*, HHU is targeted by a series of bombings. In a typical mystery, such bombs would be aimed at particular faculty members or at specific buildings. Not in Nancy Herndon's madcap Los Santos. Instead, the target is HHU's sprinkler system. Detective Jarvis takes note of the wasteful use of the precious natural resource, and she concludes that she "could almost sympathize with whoever blew up the watering equipment."

SATURDAY, MAY 18, 11:55 A.M.

Boom!

The first explosion stopped the university president in mid-prayer. Detective Leo Weizell lunged into the aisle and scooped his partner, Elena Jarvis, off the floor, where she had dived, rolling, coming up on all fours. "You saw the mountain lion again, didn't you?" Leo said, hauling her back into her chair.

Shaken, Elena nodded. She'd been having flashbacks and nightmares for over a month—the result of a particularly violent case she and Leo had worked in March. Her friend Sarah Tolland said it was post-traumatic stress and kept recommending clinical psychologists. Elena's lieutenant, who didn't even know about the flashbacks, had suggested, at the time of the mountain lion incident, that she see the stress management company contracted to the Los Santos Police Department, but Elena had hoped the problem would go away if she gave it time.

"That palm tree just blew up," cried President Sunnydale.

"Get hold of yourself," Leo whispered to Elena. "Say, you're not carryin', are you?" He asked the question as if he thought she might go berserk and shoot him.

"Sure," she replied resentfully. "Under two layers of clothes." Having been uncomfortably hot, she now felt chilled and slipped her shaking hands into the sleeves of her academic gown. "I'm fine," she assured him.

Leo was attending Herbert Hobart University's first graduation with his wife, Concepcion, because they had been designated the "university's adopted family," which meant that the Psychology Department had offered to pay the freight on the quintuplets they were expecting. In return an HHU psychologist got the right to study the seven Weizells in their natural habitat.

Elena had just received HHU's first honorary doctorate. What a crock that was! HHU didn't have doctoral programs. She was being rewarded for her "services" to the university, like catching a couple of campus murderers in timely fashion, but mostly for her last case, which the papers had facetiously called the "hot regalia caper."

"Sure, you're fine," said Leo, worry lines lengthening an already long face. "Your lips are blue."

"Well, I'm not fine," hissed his pregnant wife. "I just had a contraction."

"False labor number three?" Leo murmured.

"You'll be sorry if my water breaks in front of this mob of millionaires," Concepcion retorted, dark eyes snapping with the frayed temper of a woman too long and too heavily pregnant.

Once Elena had shaken off the flashback, she felt a stab of apprehension because she doubted that palm trees were given to spontaneous combustion. Several spectators, rich parents undoubtedly, were covered with globs of dirt and bits of palm leaf. Noisy dismay prevailed among the university administrators and faculty, who had, just seconds ago, been heat-dazed and somnolent during the long closing prayer.

Boom!

"That was an oleander bush!" exclaimed Dr. Harley Stanley, vice president for academic affairs. Most of the distinguished party on the stage had risen, craning to see the shower of glossy green leaves and red petals. Could the exploding shrubbery be some weird graduation finale arranged by Hector Montes, the superintendent of buildings and grounds? Elena wondered.

"I just had another contraction," said Concepcion, wincing.

Boom!

Chief Clabb of the university police force rushed to the edge of the stage and cried, "Sir, the sprinkler system seems to be blowing up."

"Our palm trees? Our sprinkler system?" President Sunnydale looked as if he'd just heard Armageddon announced on the loudspeaker system.

Boom!

Three gardenia bushes under the salmon plastic graduation tent burst into a perfumed, green-and-white cloud. Plastered with gardenia petals, the nearby parents tried to escape down the rows toward the center aisle. An art deco tent support tilted, shedding turquoise and gold tiles, causing the salmon-colored ceiling to sag. Turquoise and salmon were the university colors.

The graduating class, bedecked in turquoise academic gowns, all stood up and cheered, flinging their color-coordinated mortarboards into the air.

Idiots, thought Elena.

Boom!

The green-and-rose fragments of four more bushes ballooned majesti-cally into a tattered cloud. Shrieking and cursing, more parents scrambled into the crowded rows.

Without relinquishing the microphone, President Sunnydale fell to his knees and raised his face to heaven—as seen through a transparent plastic ceiling. The tent had been his idea. He'd told Elena at the pregraduation prayer and cocktail brunch that he wanted the parents to be able to admire HHU's beautiful art deco architecture and lush shrubbery set against the stark grandeur of the desert mountain on which the campus was built. "Oh, Lord," the ex-TV evangelist prayed, "if it be thy will—"

"There's another one," gasped Concepcion.

"—spare our palm trees," President Sunnydale beseeched his God.

Boom!

A second palm erupted.

"Spread the mantle of thy divine protection over our shrubbery, oh God of our fathers."

"Are you sure it's not another false alarm?" Elena asked Concepcion, who had gone into labor twice previously without producing any of the five children she was now thought to be carrying.

"Send forth battalions of angels to defend our trees."

Boom!

"How would I know?" said the expectant mother testily. "Leo, I told you I should have stayed home."

"Consider, oh Lord, our sprinkler system," begged Dr. Sunnydale into the microphone. "Without water, how can there be grass? Without grass, how can our students frolic on the greensward?"

"Hey," said Leo, "don't blame me. We need the money, and this was the public acknowledgment that we're going to get it."

Elena was still feeling dazed and shaky from the flashback and all the commotion when her father and mother, Sheriff Ruben Portillo and the beautiful Harmony, climbed the stairs at the side of the stage and made their way toward her. They had insisted on coming down from Chimayo, New Mexico, for Elena's hooding. "You'd better do something about this," advised the sheriff.

"I don't know how to deliver a baby," Elena protested.

"I do," said Harmony. "Are you in labor, dear?" She studied Concep-cion. "Goodness, you look as if you should have delivered a month ago."

Boom!

More petals, leaves, and mud showered the fleeing crowd.

"Our enemies are legion, oh Lord, but we stand steadfast in thy strength." President Sunnydale looked close to tears.

"I'm talkin' about the explosions," said Elena's father.

"The campus police should be dealing with it," Elena replied, lifting a fall of long black hair from her neck. She was sweating because the portable air conditioners that were meant to cool the tent couldn't contend with the rising temperatures of May in the desert. Desperately, she looked around for Chief Clabb. After his initial announcement, he had disappeared. "Of course, they usually run away when things get tough," she mumbled bitterly. Now that she was Detective Dr. Jarvis, she'd probably be expected to deal with every weird thing that happened here at HHU.

"Mom's had five kids," she told Leo's wife, who had groaned again.

"We are beset on all sides, oh Lord, by the enemies of art deco," complained the president.

Boom!

"Let us smite them hip and thigh!"

Wringing his hands, Vice President Harley Stanley bent down and murmured, "I'm not sure this is an architectural protest, sir."

Boom!

"Let us rise like Christian soldiers to defend our green and leafy ramparts."

The tent began to collapse, dropping transparent salmon plastic on the panic-stricken crowd. Pandemonium broke loose, but Elena was still rattled and slow to act. Her father stared at her in surprise, then turned to his wife. "Harmony, you an' Weizell get Miz Weizell out before the ceilin' falls on the stage." They left immediately, Leo and Harmony supporting Concepcion. "*Elena?*" Her father spoke so sharply that he caught her attention. "Start callin' for help." He thrust his cellular phone into her hands. "I'll see what I can do out there."

She blocked out the memory of the big cat's snarl, closed her mind to the savaged corpse in her bedroom, and made her first call—for the fire department and EMS units to take care of the tent and the casualties. At least one person had gone down under those tiled tent posts. She called the Westside Command for crowd-control officers and, last, the bomb squad because, inexplicably, someone had blown up a lot of Herbert Hobart University landscaping. Then she took a deep breath, cursed her hands because they were still shaking, and waded into the melee.

Bordersnakes

JAMES CRUMLEY

In James Crumley's detective novels, the wide-open spaces of the American West are as hard-boiled as any dimly-lit back alley. Crumley is widely regarded as one of America's premier writers, a literary force who happens to write within the mystery genre. Although Crumley is a Texas native, most of his novels are set in Montana, where he has lived on and off since the 1960s. His books have alternated between two protagonists, Milo Milodragovitch and C. W. Sughrue. Both men are hypermasculine Vietnam veterans with a taste for hard drinking, recreational drugs, sardonic humor, and violence.

In 1996, Crumley brought Milodragovitch and Sughrue together for the first time in his novel *Bordersnakes*, as they investigate drug dealing and murder in Texas. Crumley knows the state well. He was born and raised in South Texas, spent part of his childhood in the Texas Hill Country, played college football for the Texas A&I (now Texas A&M–Kingsville) Javelinas, and he held a visiting professorship at the University of Texas–El Paso in the 1980s.

Bordersnakes finds Milodragovitch and Sughrue teaming up to investigate drug smuggling and murder along the Texas-Mexico border. The novel winds its way toward Austin, but it begins with Milodragovitch attempting to locate Sughrue, who has been hiding out in the desolate West Texas wilderness after being shot and left for dead.

Rocky drove me back to the Paso del Norte Hotel and kindly helped me to my suite. We drew some odd looks as we crossed the lobby, but I crossed some palms, and the looks disappeared. We had plenty of help the rest of the way. After that it was all gravy. A house doctor brought codeine and a half-circle of stitches for the corner of my eye. The bellman took my bloody suit off to the cleaners, then fetched coffee for me, a large glass of tequila for my new buddy, and an extra television set to roll beside my king-sized bed so I could see it with my single working eye.

"Thanks again," I said to Rocky as he took his leave. "And tell your little brother that I ain't ever been hit that hard in my whole fucking awful life."

"Shit, man," he said, "everybody tells him that."

I had to laugh. Maybe it was the drugs. A little later, codeine smooth and toweled warm from a hot tub, I slipped naked between cold expensive sheets. I thought about ordering a scotch the size of West Texas, then knew I shouldn't drink it without Sughrue, and wondered where the fuck he had hidden from me. And why.

When I finally found him three weeks later outside a rock-house convenience store in the tiny West Texas town of Fairbairn, we had both changed so much we didn't even recognize each other. But at least I'd found his hiding place.

Earlier that afternoon, five hours on the interstate east of El Paso, I decided to take the scenic route and turned south on a narrow paved strip that wound through the dry, scrub-brush foothills of the Davis Mountains. In spite of the barbed-wire fences flanking the pavement, I couldn't imagine soft-footed steers grazing across the thin grass scattered among sharp rocks. Maybe sheep or goats. But the rusty, four-string barbed-wire fence couldn't hold a goat. Or even the world's dumbest walking mutton.

After thirty minutes on the little highway without seeing a soul—not even a buzzard—I spotted a small herd of longhorns among a patch of thorned brush hopelessly trying to crawl up the genetic ladder toward freedom. When I stopped to stare at the cattle, they stared back, their wild eyes perfectly at home in that reckless landscape, their gaze as rank and rangy as the African breed that began their bloodline. I wondered how the hell those drovers managed to herd these beasts from West Texas to Montana in the 1880s without Cobra gunships.

Then I began to see people: a welder hanging the blade back on a grader that had been scratching a firebreak out of the stony scrub; two Mexican hands greasing a windmill under a sky swept pale, polished blue by the constant wind; an old woman in a tiny Ford Escort running her RFD route, bringing the mail to the scattered, shotgunned mailboxes along the road.

At a Y intersection with an even smaller highway, I had to stop to let a funeral cortege pass, though I couldn't imagine a graveyard in the middle of this nowhere. The next vehicle I met was a pickup that contained three teenage boys with faces painted like clowns under their broad cowboy hats. I don't know what I'd expected in West Texas, but I began to suspect that I had wandered into a fucking Fellini film.

Then came the tourists as I climbed past slopes of juniper and scrub oak, and higher still into the improbable gray rock peaks: a busload of ancients turning into a picnic ground already occupied by several families in vans; a couple of drugstore cowboys drinking beer at a turnout; and a group of hikers who looked like retired college professors. Then I saw the McDonald Observatory rising from the mountain ridge like an escaping moon.

Too weird, I thought, too fucking weird. So I stopped at the next wide spot in the road to collect myself, wondering what I'd done, wondering what the hell I was doing in West Texas.

I had been born and raised in the small western Montana city of Meriwether and, except for my time in the Army, had always lived there. It had taken only a month, but now I owned nothing, just a rented mailbox and a telephone number that rang at an answering service. I had destroyed my past, abandoned my parents' graves, said goodbye to the few friends still alive, then flew to Seattle to buy a new car. I had visions of exotic convertibles, crouched low to the road, faster than death, more surefooted than a Revenue Agent. But now that I could actually afford one, I didn't fit in the little bastards anymore. A Porsche salesman pointed me toward a Cadillac Eldorado Touring Coupe, nearly two tons of Detroit iron driven by three hundred horses out of a thirty-two-valve V-8, a car big enough for my butt and my head, a trunk the size of a small country, and a Northstar engine that nailed my ass into the driver's seat when I stuffed the accelerator into the fire wall. And the Beast held the road in a screaming corner. At least as fast as I cared to push her. But I had to wait a week to get the color I wanted with a sunroof. The salesman tried to sell me a Dark Montana Blue, but I assumed I'd given up sentiment in my middle age, so I waited for Dark Cherry.

That's where the trouble started. In Seattle. Still not drinking, just waiting for the sunroof, I decided that the new ride deserved a new wardrobe. A couple of tweedy blazers, maybe, a pair of cords, maybe new boots. So I dropped into a store a couple of blocks from the Four Seasons, found a tall, elegant lady with a British accent, who sold me five thousand dollars worth of Italian foofaraw, including a two-hundred-fifty-dollar felt hat that she claimed could be pulled through a napkin ring, then nearly fucked me to death. I was so sore driving from Seattle to El Paso not even the eight-way power seat took the strain out of my groin. But it was fun. In my drinking days, I might have married her, lived with her, or tried to love her. But I already had enough ex-wives, ex-roommates, and ex-lovers to last me a lifetime. Oddly enough, I'd taken a vacation from love about the same time I began my long rest from drinking.

But down in this moonscape I decided I'd rested long enough. So I pulled into the next unpaved turnout and dug into my elegant road provisions: I fired up a fancy English cigarette, a Dunhill Red, and cracked a bottle of Mexican ale, Negra Modelo, then stood in that relentless fall wind smoking and drinking like a civilized man, suspecting that soon enough I'd be back to Camel straights and cheap shots of schnapps anchored by cans of Pabst, living like the drunk I'd always been. Or maybe not. Ten years dry and sober without the crutches of cigarettes and meetings—it hadn't been a waste of time, but it hadn't been constant entertainment, either.

All the high-class fixings burned my tongue like fried shit and made me dizzy and reckless. I loved it. But I didn't have another beer. I guess it was a test. I guess I sort of passed.

All I had was an address on the single main street of Fairbairn, a dying town about halfway between Marfa and the Mexican border at Castillo, a town killed by cattle prices and the closure of a military firing range. I drove past the address twice, not believing my own eyes or notes. Once the Dew Drop Inn must have been the best motor court in town. Eight native rock cabins with Spanish tile roofs and tiny garages stood in a shabby half circle around a patio filled with Russian thistle tumbleweeds and ancient dust, and the cabins looked as if they hadn't been occupied since WWII. A small cafe and beer joint perhaps once had adjoined the office. But now a shabby convenience store filled that space. It advertised ICE COLD BEER and HOMEMADE TAMALES, two major West Texas staples, it seemed.

As I parked in front of the store, a darkly brown man stepped out. He looked rope-wiry and rank in a flat-brimmed hat, jeans, and only a vest in spite of the sharp wind. A knife the size of a small sword dangled from his belt. I couldn't see his shadowed eyes, but his mouth pursed as if to spit when he passed my Caddy with the temporary tags. Fucking tourist. Then he climbed into an ancient GMC pickup and rattled away.

Inside the store, blinking against the sudden shade, I paused as the tall blonde behind the counter rang up a candy sale and made change for a couple of young Mexican-American kids. She looked up, her mouth moved as if to ask if she could help, then tears filled her eyes and she rushed around the counter to hug me long and hard, as if I were her long-lost father. She even whispered "Milo" against my shoulder.

Shit, I had driven two thousand miles to be attacked by a woman I had never seen before. But I didn't say anything. My life had always been like that.

After a long moment, the woman realized that I wasn't responding in kind, so she stepped back, wiping her eyes. "Milo," she said, "it's me. Whitney. C. W.'s wife."

"Wife?"

"Whitney. From Meriwether. I used to work for . . . for C. W.'s lawyer friend," she said, then paused. "You know. Solly . . . I guess they aren't exactly friends anymore."

Then I realized who she was. One of Lawyer Rainbolt's endless stream of tall, blonde, perfectly lovely, and damn smart legal secretaries. After Wynona died in a bout of gunfire, for which Sughrue blamed himself, he had split for Texas with her baby boy, Lester. This woman had started dropping into my bar, the Slumgullion, shyly asking about Sughrue, but not often enough to make me remember her name. That woman was just barely visible beneath the face of this one. Her darkly burned face with a fan of hard-sun wrinkles winking white at the corners of her blue eyes looked nothing like the one I remembered. What time couldn't do, Sughrue and the West Texas climate had. Still lovely and surely still smart, even though she *had* married the crazy bastard, her face no longer even vaguely resembled the distant, professional mask I remembered. This was the face of a woman who would kick your ass and give you an hour to draw a crowd.

"Whitney . . ." I said. "I'm sorry, but is that your first or last name?"

In answer, she laughed, bright silver peals that chased the shadows from among the half-empty shelves. "I could tell that you never remembered my name," she said, smiling, then added proudly, "Whitney Peterson . . . well, Sughrue, now," and shook my hand. "I'm so glad you're here. C. W. will be so happy to see you. You just missed him, you know."

I should have recognized the knife, I thought. "I didn't know . . ." I said.

"Oh, we didn't tell anybody," she continued. "We didn't want anybody to know. We did it in the hospital . . ." Then she paused; a shade fell across her face. "I better let him tell you about that," she said quietly. Then she grabbed a tablet off the counter and began to draw. "Let me show you how to find the place. I'd call, but he won't have a telephone in the house." She tore a sheet off the tablet, handed it to me as if it were the winning ticket for a lottery I hadn't entered, then dropped her eyes and added, "When you get out to the trailer, tell him I'm right behind you. Just as soon as I can get Dulcy to relieve me. I'll bring dinner. And tequila. And some more beer. And we'll have an evening of it . . ."

Her wrinkles deepened with sadness, as if she meant to weep again.

"Is there any place to stay in this town?" I asked, to bring her back to this moment.

"Oh, you have to stay with us. You must. The trailer is a double-wide. With an extender. We've got tons of room . . ."

Eventually, I convinced her that unannounced guests deserved to pay for their own space. So I left, loaded down with tamales, ice, and beer, and took a room at the only open motel, the Cuero, named I assumed for the dry creek that skirted the tiny town, and followed her map south and east of town.

The rough mountains had ended north and west of Fairbairn, but they had left a score of rocky echoes trailing into the desert. Scuts of wispy clouds troubled the afternoon sky, flirting with a half-moon rising. On the parched flats between the outcroppings, the desert wind picked up strength, moaned and rattled, shifting even the weight of my new Detroit Iron as I rode south and east, following Whitney's directions, trying not to think about what she had said, the H-word.

Hospitals had already taken enough of my friends. My people had a history of living until somebody killed them. Usually themselves. But Sughrue's mother had died of lung cancer years ago. And his crazy father of a benign brain tumor. So without thinking it, the worst came to mind. If the bastard was dying, I told myself, I wouldn't tell him why I'd come hunting him. No matter what. And I wouldn't cry, either. At least not sober.

I turned onto a dirt track a couple of miles past a pretty little roadside park, stopped to open a wire gap, then eased the Beast down a one-lane track, rutted and rocky, that led between two rusty barbed-wire fences across a flat pasture where a dozen antelope grazed on invisible grass, then through another gap, across another pasture. This one rolling toward the blue mountains beyond. And filled with tiny horses grazing. Those little horses were my last straw. All over again. I grabbed another beer. My second of the day, of the decade. It worked just fine, just wonderful. And I ignored the fucking little horses flittering like gnats at the corner of my eye.

Once through the last gap, I glanced back at the trail of dust I'd left, in spite of driving slowly, as it fled before the ever-rising wind. Then at the road ahead. More of the same. Winding over a couple of small ridges and around another heap of rocks, I found Sughrue's double-wide permanently installed and sided with rough boards nestled in a small depression, as if seeking lee shelter from all the winds that might blow. Some sort of unfinished frame structure stood in front of the trailer and a metal shed behind, with a windmill and horse trough beyond that.

I parked in front, honked the horn into the wind without response, then walked up to the trailer's steps. The frame structure turned out to be a grape arbor of some kind, standing over a patio in progress, Mexican tile set directly on the hard-packed ground. The marker strings hummed in the wind, and the dead vines rattled, almost blotting out the pumping grind of the windmill. I turned back, surveyed the thorny brush—greasewood I guessed from reading western novels—scattered with dwarf mesquite.

A child's voice shouted "Yo!" from the corner of the house, and I turned quickly enough to catch a glimpse of a small figure darting around the corner. Before I could take a step in that direction, though, a brown blur swept from under the steps, a forearm as hard and unforgiving as sun-dried leather locked around my throat, and I could feel the point of a knife blade under my ear. Actually, the point was too sharp to feel. What I felt was the slow trickle of blood down my neck. Another goddamned suit for the cleaners.

A voice hissed, the breath beside my face smelling of dried beef and chilies, tequila and lime and fear, a whisper as roughly soft as a wood rasp in white pine.

"Who the fuck are you, buddy?" it said, then the forearm eased slightly off my throat.

"It's me, you fucking idiot," I gasped. "I gave you that knife."

Everything stopped for a moment. Then released.

"Milo?" Sughrue said as I turned. He slid the twelve-inch blade of the full-sized Ruana Bowie back into its sheath. "What the hell are you doing in those clothes?"

I might have asked the same thing.

It was the guy from the parking lot in front of the Dew Drop Inn. Except he had exchanged his jeans for a loincloth and his hat for a leather string around his forehead holding back the long sun-bleached hair. Up close I could see a puckered scar that divided his ridged abdomen. And Sughrue's blue eyes in this rawhide stranger's face.

The beef had been whittled away, the stocky body now fence-rail thin instead of cornerpost solid, the eyes as wild and shifty as those of the long-horns, the old laugh lines of his face washed out, blown away. When he finally smiled, I thought his face would crack.

"Goddammit," he said, "you got your fucking money." My insane mother had convinced my father to keep my inheritance in trust until I was fifty-three so I wouldn't squander it on wild women, whiskey, and trout streams. As my father had. "You finally got the money." Sughrue hugged me so hard he nearly knocked the breath out of me. "So how is it? Being rich?"

I didn't bother to answer but nodded at the scar. "Your wife said you'd been in the hospital," I said when he turned me loose. I pointed at his scar. I swear he flinched.

"It's nothing," he said quickly.

"Nothing?"

"Had a little trouble up in New Mexico," he said, trying to smile. "Nothing serious. I'm fine. Never been better," he went on as Baby Lester crept quietly around the near corner of the trailer to wrap his brown arms around the corded leg of his adopted father. Baby Lester wasn't a baby anymore. Just a smaller version of Sughrue, silent and wary, and dressed like his foster dad. He would have looked at home on one of the dwarf horses. "This is your Uncle Milo," Sughrue said to Lester, and the small boy shook my hand solemnly. "Why don't you grab us a couple of beers, son?" Sughrue said. "Unless your Uncle Milo is still on the wagon . . ."

"I just fell off today," I admitted as Lester went up the steps to the front door.

As soon as it closed behind the boy, Sughrue turned to me, asking with a wolfish grin that only hardened his icy blue eyes, "How the hell did you find me, old man?"

"I hired a private eye," I said, laughing. The bark that escaped his thin smile didn't exactly resemble laughter. "Just a joke," I explained.

His story about getting shot drifted like the trip he'd made that day through the Rio Grande Valley north of El Paso, back in town after a long, ugly chase to catch a bail jumper, a child molester who had once been a citizen. There was that. And the fear that the bastard would slither through the system, more trouble than he was worth.

But mostly the wandering, afternoon road trip was about Wynona, Baby Lester's mom. Sughrue still blamed himself, though nobody else did. And on his way to see the sunset over the desert, Sughrue stopped for a sixpack in a New Mexican beer joint and somehow got involved in a hassle between the bartender and a group of El Paso Chicanos, led by a tall, loud kid.

Words were exchanged. Then the big kid whipped a cheap, snub-nosed .38 out of his back pocket and snapped a round at the bartender, a loud, stinky pop that smashed an old Coors sign. The second round clipped right between Sughrue's fingers, between the little finger and the ring finger on his right hand, right through the beer can, and into his gut.

In that moment the motes dancing on the shafts of sun shivered with the cloud of gun cotton, wadding, and unexploded powder grains, not to mention the fucking lead, plus the vaporized beer from the murdered can. But by the time Sughrue let this random madness roar through his mind, before he could step forward, the flattened .38 lead had tumbled through the edge of his liver, several loops of gut, and his left kidney, where the spent round died like a lost marble.

Between midnight and sunrise Sughrue stopped talking; we sat on a picnic table at the little rest area just up the road. Stone Corrals, it was called, I learned from the sign as I pissed on it. A short ride from the trailer. Sughrue loved the Beast but couldn't stand to be inside too long. When I walked back to the table, he took up the tale again.

"So they took the kidney and a couple of feet of intestine," he said jauntily, then gunned a beer. "The only telephone number in my wallet was Whitney's." He sounded embarrassed. "The hospital called her. I didn't want to call anybody. I don't know. Maybe I was ashamed. They say it happens that way sometimes. Maybe I wasn't too lucid. I don't fucking know. Anyway, she came down, hung around, and finally said it might cheer both of us up to get married. So we did."

"So what the hell are you doing out here in the middle of nowhere? Playing cowboys and Apaches?"

"I came down this way once," he said softly, "on a job, and I liked the country. It suits my personality." Then he stopped and pointed his finger at me. "You ever realize that you and me, we've always lived close enough to the border to run if we have to?"

"Sounds right," I agreed, and he just let it hang there. "So what's the problem?"

"What the hell are we running from, man? What are we afraid of?" Sughrue paused, then walked away for a moment, hitting on the tequila bottle, then back to the cooler for a beer. He offered me a drink, which I declined. Another test maybe, but maybe I just needed to be a little sober, now. Then Sughrue turned away from me. At first I couldn't hear him, so I moved closer.

". . . all the customers ran, everybody ran, but the *cholos*, the kids, those fuckers dragged me out back to the edge of the irrigation ditch, then the big one stuck the pistol in my ear and pulled the fucking trigger, pulled the fucking trigger with the barrel in my ear . . ."

"I don't understand," I said, quietly.

An easy breeze rattled the stunted trees among the rocks. Stars and a half-moon filled the night sky with enough light to see a small herd of desert white-tailed deer grazing in the shadows across the highway. They raised their soft noses and flickering ears at a rattle of gunfire from the south.

"What the hell is that?" I asked.

"Hollywood blanks," he answered. "Some asshole is rehearsing a western movie around here. On the old pieces of the gunnery range. Down by Castillo. Fuck 'em."

"Fuck 'em?"

"They don't know a thing about gunfire," he said softly.

"Or having a thirty-eight stuck in your ear?"

"You're dead right there, bro."

"What happened?"

"The goddamned firing pin shattered," Sughrue said. "I heard it. Broke like an ice crystal. I still hear it. Then the big guy threw the pistol away."

He was talking but wasn't getting to it. I knew that much. Pushing wouldn't help. It had taken two years and ten thousand drinks to get the story of his Vietnam troubles, particularly the one that nearly got him sent to Leavenworth. I didn't have either the time or the liver for this one.

"Yeah," I said into the silence.

"So I rolled into the irrigation ditch," he said. "The guy who shot me wanted to come after me, but the other guys, they were dressed out and didn't want to fuck up their good clothes. What the hell, they said, I was one dead fucking gringo already.

"I didn't disagree with them, either," he continued. "I floated along, drifting and dreaming. I might still be there, but I bumped into a head gate. Climbed out, walked back to the van, and drove myself to the hospital down in El Paso."

"Nobody picked you up?"

"Drunk, wet, bloody in the middle of the afternoon," he said, "who would pick me up?" Then he looked at me and laughed. "You would, you dumb son of a bitch. Even if you didn't know it was me. Asshole."

"Thanks."

"You're welcome."

It passed for a joke between us. Until he told me what he had been working toward.

"I heard them talking, Milo. I've got just enough border Spanish to understand a little. Somebody hired these fucking guys to kill me," he said flatly. "Some son of a bitch."

"Who?"

"They didn't say and I couldn't think of a soul who'd want to. Still can't."

"What'd the cops say?" I asked.

"Fucking cops," he answered. "Not much. Couldn't find the piece. Told me I was crazy. According to the bartender, the *cholo* was just some drug dealer passing through town. Nobody would dare testify, even if they could find him. And according to the Luna County Sheriff's Department, if I wasn't crazy or drunk or stoned, or all three at once, it was just some hangover from my troubles down here a few years ago."

Sughrue stopped. I knew that sorry story. It had ended where this one began. With the death of Wynona Jones.

"The fucking DEA ran Dottie and Barnstone all the way to Costa Rica, so I didn't have any friends. And all kinds of law, they're still mad at me. If the licensing rules weren't so fucked down here, man, I'd never have gotten a ticket to work.

"So the official stance is that since I'm not dead," Sughrue growled, "it's not their problem. So fuck it."

"And if you're dead? Fuck that, too?"

"Right on, brother," he muttered. "But I ain't dead. And I know the bastards are still looking for me."

Death of a Healing Woman

ALLANA MARTIN

Texas's Big Bend region is only sparsely populated, yet the rugged, starkly beautiful area is the setting for several mysteries. Dallas-based writer Allana Martin has written several books that feature Texana Jones, an amateur sleuth who runs a trading post outside of the fictional town of El Polvo (Spanish for "dust").

The harsh climate and unyielding landscape are on full display in Martin's work, as are the commingled cultures of the Texas-Mexico borderlands. Although the Rio Grande—which often exists here only as a muddy trickle—remains a fortified international boundary, the river also serves as a magnet and unifying feature to the few people who live in this isolated region.

Martin's Texana Jones novels effectively capture many aspects of the local culture, particularly the region's Hispanic influence. Characters express themselves through *dichos* (Mexican American folk sayings) and also participate in the annual Día de los Muertos (Day of the Dead) celebration. In isolated areas with little access to modern medical care, *curanderas*, or folk healers, serve an important function. Here, Texana Jones launches her career as an amateur sleuth after she discovers that the local *curandera* has been murdered in *Death of a Healing Woman*.

We fear death, my friend Maria had told me, so we laugh at it, and adorn it in gaudy colors, and give it shape in the form of macabre candies in order to hide our fear and make death palatable.

It was el Día de los Muertos, the Day of the Dead, and I had brought flowers for the graves of Maria and her husband.

I jammed the marigolds into the vases angrily. I was angry because I had yet to come to terms with their deaths. Angry because I resented Andalon's easy assumption that their murders were a part of the necessary violence of minor drug lords. Angry because I wanted answers. No. I wanted more. I wanted justice. I wanted retribution. I wanted revenge.

To achieve any one of those required that the killer be known, and in the six months since Maria and Bill had been shot at point-blank range, their bodies doused with gasoline and set aflame, neither a hint of the motive for the killings nor the identity of the killer had surfaced.

The odds of my winning the lottery with my dollar-a-week investment were greater than the chances of my tasting sweet revenge. So I told myself to calm down and tried to arrange the bright yellow flowers into more seemly bunches.

Aztec custom specified yellow for adults. I knew that Maria would have approved of this symbolic veneration of her Spanish-Indian ancestry. And Bill would have liked anything that made his wife happy. I touched my fingertips to the cool stones, running them across the incised names: Maria Elena Ortega-Deed, William August Deed.

Something bumped me hard from behind. As I stretched out a hand to steady myself a child squealed, and the weight lifted off my back. I turned my head and saw a young woman holding tightly to the arm of a wriggling little boy. She gave me an apologetic look as she dusted him off and led him back to the family plot.

The small adobe-walled cemetery was crowded with families from both sides of the border. Old men and women, some dressed in somber black, washed the dust from the whitewashed crosses and *sillar* block tombs and rearranged the circles of stones that kept evil spirits at bay. Younger adults pulled weeds, hauled water, painted, and repaired, while their children ran in and out among the graves, excited by the holiday atmosphere and the feast to come, with skull-shaped candies and brightly tinted *pan de muerto*, the sweet bread that would entice the dead back to the living world on this night between the first and second of November.

I got to my feet and stared down at the grave of my best friend. Born on the border and bilingual, Maria and I had shared the giddy secrets of childhood, teenage anxieties, and adult confidences, worries, and joys. I had taken for granted that we would grow old in friendship, would reminisce, and would bore one another with stories about grandchildren. I had assumed too much.

Trying to shake off my blue mood, I took comfort in the explosion of noise and people and color around me. Flowers had been heaped on each grave. Wreaths of mint marigold, coffee cans stuffed with the velvety purple spikes of bush sage, and fragrant bouquets of pineapple sage turned the graves into extravagant altars. Later the cemetery would glow with hundreds of candles lighted for the all-night vigil. Feeling more at peace, I knelt and broke off one of the marigold blossoms and fixed it in a buttonhole of my blouse for remembrance.

"Who's minding the store, Texana?"

I smiled at the soft voice and turned around. Annie Luna's voice always makes me smile. It's so deceptive, with a hint of hesitancy and shyness, which doesn't exist at all in the personality of the strong-minded twenty-five-year-old. Annie is tiny, maybe five-foot-one and ninety pounds. She was wearing jeans and a turquoise shirt. Her waist-length hair had been pulled back and braided in a businesslike fashion. I liked Annie and was actively promoting the growth of a dormant romance between her and Billy Deed, Maria's son.

"Cadillac Charlie is in charge," I explained.

Annie glanced at the Deed graves.

"Billy will like those flowers," she said. The smile on her face did not reach her eyes. A nurse at the VA hospital in San Antonio, Annie had come home to help care for her mother, who was dying slowly of cancer. Annie looked so miserable that I volunteered the information she probably had joined me to get.

"Billy's taking a prisoner to Marfa. He stopped to help a man change a flat. Turned out the man didn't have a spare, a license, or a registration slip for the car. What the poor mule did have was a five-pound bag of marijuana taped under the front bumper. Billy thought he'd make it back for the vigil."

Annie shrugged, trying for uninterest and reminding me how glad I was not to be young and in love with someone I considered the wrong man.

Annie tugged at her braid and changed the subject.

"My father asks if you'd like to share our meal later."

As in all small communities, our knowledge of each other's activities and personal habits is intimate and instant. The Lunas knew that Clay had left early to drive to Sul Ross University to speak at a seminar on controlling rabies in the border counties and that I would be alone for the evening. I appreciated the thoughtfulness of the invitation, but explained to Annie that I'd be away, too.

"I'm going to see Rhea Fair."

Annie cocked her head and dropped her eyes, masking a curiosity she was too polite to show. I saw no reason not to tell her why I was going to see the *curandera*.

"Rhea's a week overdue picking up her supplies. She doesn't buy much at a time, so she should be running out by now. I'm taking a few things out to her."

Annie frowned. "I hope she's not sick." She paused. "I wonder why she didn't send Trinidad."

"He may not be on this side of the river right now," I suggested, though in truth I had wondered the same thing. Trinidad Quiroz had worked for the Fairs when Rhea's husband Jake had been alive, and the old man had remained loyal to the widow. Once a month, Trinidad would drive Rhea in his ancient pickup to get her supplies. White Dog, Rhea's current pet, a mongrel of uneven temperament, rode in the bed of the pickup, pacing from side to side, jumping down to hide underneath as soon as the pickup stopped.

"Mrs. Fair is a good person," Annie said, twisting the end of her braid around her finger. "I hope nothing's wrong."

"I wouldn't worry," I told her. "She had a visitor last week. A young woman. She stopped at the store and bought some beans and bread and asked for directions to the Fair place. That's probably why Rhea hasn't been in to shop for herself." It was general knowledge that the *curandera* never accepted payment for the herbal remedies that she blended and handed out so freely, so many visitors took food as a gift.

"Her reputation as a healing woman must be growing," Annie said. "I hear she's had people come all the way from El Paso for her remedies."

I nodded. "The woman who stopped last week was driving a rental Suburban. She'd gotten it in Alpine." I dug in the pocket of my jeans for my keys. "I'd better get moving."

"If you feel like it, on your way back stop for the vigil," Annie said. "It's my favorite part of the day."

She turned to go back to her family. I headed toward the gates and my pickup, working my way along the crowded aisles and nodding and speaking briefly to old friends.

A few latecomers came in at the gates as I left. I climbed behind the wheel, started the motor, and pulled onto the road. There was no other traffic.

The cemetery sits on a rise at the southeastern tip of El Polvo. Heading northwest, I passed the one-room school and the post office, and then the double line of flat-roofed adobes and the scattering of trailer homes that make up the rest of the town. As I speeded up, a half dozen mutts chased after the pickup, barking in mock ferocity before wheeling back to the shade.

The blacktop lasts only as far as the edge of town; there it turns into a lava-rock surface that has to be driven with a careful hand on the wheel because of the 15 percent grade. The road parallels the Rio Grande as the river snakes its way between Texas and Mexico, a thin line of murky blue bounded by the gray-green of salt cedar.

Five miles farther and the road disappears altogether as the fractured buttes and pinnacles of ancient lava flows close in on either side. The river is diminished here to a shallow humble sheet of water. You can drive across the riverbed to where the road picks up in Mexico, a lifeline connecting distant villages and solitary adobes.

I turned the pickup away from the river crossing and toward the blue of the Chinati Mountains. Ahead, startled by the noise, a roadrunner chasing a lizard leaped over his quarry and lifted off in a low glide.

Mindful of the pickup's shocks, I slowed to a crawl as the track crossed the loose stones of a dry creek and wound on through creosote bush, clumps of yucca, and spikes of sotol. Here and there the rimrock fanned out in waves, and the track climbed steadily.

Three winding miles and two cattleguards farther, I pulled over and parked. The rest of the way had to be made on foot, following a rocky path as it climbed the mesa for a quarter mile. I lifted out the box of tightly packed supplies from the bed of the pickup. I had brought bags of rice and beans, a loaf of bread, two jars of peanut butter and one of jelly, five pounds of coffee, paper towels, and a can of kerosene.

Starting up the path, I almost fell. I had caught my foot in a mesh bag on the ground, the kind illegals often use to carry a jug of water, tins of sardines, and bread. Our section of the river, roughly sixty miles or so, is a trickle of dirty water known only to smugglers, a few ranchers, and a handful of border patrol agents. Illegals, deceived by the ease of getting across the border, and without a compass or any knowledge of the terrain that lies ahead, cross over only to die of snakebite or dehydration or sunstroke in the high desert mountains, their bodies bleached to white bone before they are found months later by cowhands checking for strays.

I shook my foot free of the mesh bag and wished safe journey to the man who had carried it.

Slightly out of breath, I reached the end of the path, a mesa where the land had been cleared of brush and cacti for perhaps an acre. In the center of the clearing stood Rhea Fair's house, built of cottonwood poles chinked with cement and roofed with used tin, so that both the scarce rain and the abundant sunlight leaked through the old nail holes.

I put down the box and stood catching my breath, puzzled by the empty clearing. Where were the rangy hens scratching in the dirt? The wormy goats browsing the edges of the brush? Why no White Dog barking and jumping at the end of his tether? The only living thing I could see was a redtail hawk high above, gliding on the breathy air.

"Rhea," I called.

Keeer-r-r . . . cried the hawk.

Rhea was shy and liked time to make herself tidy before coming to the door, so I waited, turning to face the horizon, expecting to hear her ask me in. The view in front of me was a grand sweep of the river valley across to the sepia hills of Mexico's Sierra Bonita range, but I paid little attention to the vista. Instead, I listened. What I didn't hear worried me. No muted sounds from within the thin-walled house. No bleating of goats from the distant brush. No sound at all save the rush of an immense silence.

The Killer Inside Me

JIM THOMPSON

At his 1977 death, not one of Jim Thompson's books remained in print in the United States. Toiling in the paperback market in the 1940s and 1950s and churning out such titles as *A Swell Looking Babe* and *A Hell of A Woman* did not seem to be the path to a literary legacy. However the 1980s brought Thompson posthumous fame with the reprinting of his novels and the 1985 film version of *The Grifters*.

Thompson was born in Oklahoma but he spent his formative years in Texas in the 1920s after his father launched an unsuccessful career as an oilman. His experiences in Texas had a major impact on his life and writing. As a bellboy at the Hotel Texas in Fort Worth, he did more than ferry suitcases—he sold bootleg whiskey, peddled dope, and procured women for guests. He later hitchhiked to West Texas, where he lived as a hobo, gambler, and pipeliner. It was in the oilfields of West Texas that he acquired his political philosophy through his friendships with the militant "Wobblies" of the Industrial Workers of the World.

Perhaps Thompson's most famous novel, 1952's *The Killer Inside Me* reflects the effects of both the oil boom on an otherwise quiet West Texas town and the grifters—outcasts and psychologically challenged protagonists who inhabit his malevolent world. In lawman Lou Ford he creates his most memorable character, a man whose seemingly straight-laced demeanor masks barely-contained demons within. In a strangely more benign form, Ford returned as a major character in another Thompson West Texas noir, 1957's *Wild Town*.

I'd finished my pie and was having a second cup of coffee when I saw him. The midnight freight had come in a few minutes before, and he was peering in one end of the restaurant window, the end nearest the depot, shading his eyes with his hand and blinking against the light. He saw me watching him, and his face faded back into the shadows. But I knew he was still there. I knew he was waiting. The bums always size me up for an easy mark.

I lit a cigar and slid off my stool. The waitress, a new girl from Dallas, watched as I buttoned my coat. "Why, you don't even carry a gun!" she said, as though she was giving me a piece of news.

"No," I smiled. "No gun, no blackjack, nothing like that. Why should I?"

"But you're a cop—a deputy sheriff, I mean. What if some crook should try to shoot you?"

"We don't have many crooks here in Central City, ma'am," I said. "Anyway, people are people, even when they're a little misguided. You don't hurt them, they won't hurt you. They'll listen to reason."

She shook her head, wide-eyed with awe, and I strolled up to the front. The proprietor shoved back my money and laid a couple of cigars on top of it. He thanked me again for taking his son in hand.

"He's a different boy now, Lou," he said, kind of running his words together like foreigners do. "Stays in nights, gets along fine in school. And always he talks about you—what a good man is Deputy Lou Ford."

"I didn't do anything," I said. "Just talked to him. Showed a little interest. Anyone else could have done as much."

"Only you," he said. "Because you are good, you make others so." He was all ready to sign off with that, but I wasn't. I leaned an elbow on the counter, crossed one foot behind the other and took a long slow drag on my cigar. I liked the guy—as much as I like most people, anyway—but he was too good to let go. Polite, intelligent: guys like that are my meat.

"Well, I tell you," I drawled. "I tell you the way I feel, Max. A man doesn't get any more out of life than what he puts into it."

"Umm," he said, fidgeting. "I guess you're right, Lou."

"I was thinking the other day, Max, and all of a sudden I had the dog-gonedest thought. It came to me out of a clear sky—the boy is father to the man. Just like that. The boy is father to the man."

The smile on his face was getting strained. I could hear his shoes creak as he squirmed. If there's anything worse than a bore, it's a corny bore. But how can you brush off a nice friendly fellow who'd give you his shirt if you asked for it?

"I reckon I should have been a college professor or something like that," I said. "Even when I'm asleep I'm working out problems. Take that heat wave we had a few weeks ago, a lot of people think it's the heat that makes it so hot. But it's not like that, Max. It's not the heat, but the humidity. I'll bet you didn't know that, did you?"

He cleared his throat and muttered something about being wanted in the kitchen. I pretended like I didn't hear him.

"Another thing about the weather," I said. "Everyone talks about it, but no one does anything. But maybe it's better that way. Every cloud has its silver lining, at least that's the way I figure it. I mean, if we didn't have the rain we wouldn't have the rainbows, now would we?"

"Lou . . ."

"Well," I said, "I guess I'd better shove off. I've got quite a bit of getting around to do, and I don't want to rush. Haste makes waste, in my opinion. I like to look before I leap."

That was dragging 'em in by the feet, but I couldn't hold 'em back. Striking at people that way is almost as good as the other, the real way. The way I'd fought to forget—and had almost forgot—until I met her.

I was thinking about her as I stepped out into the cool West Texas night and saw the bum waiting for me.

Central City was founded in 1870, but it never became a city in size until about ten-twelve years ago. It was shipping point for a lot of cattle and a little cotton, and Chester Conway, who was born here, made it headquarters for the Conway Construction Company. But it still wasn't much more than a wide place in a Texas road. Then, the oil boom came, and almost overnight the population jumped to 48,000.

Well, the town had been laid out in a little valley amongst a lot of hills.

There just wasn't any room for the newcomers, so they spread out every which way with their homes and businesses, and now they were scattered across a third of the county. It's not an unusual situation in the oil-boom country—you'll see a lot of cities like ours if you're ever out this way. They don't have any regular city police force, just a constable or two. The sheriff's office handles the policing for both city and county.

We do a pretty good job of it, to our own way of thinking at least. But now and then things get a little out of hand, and we put on a clean-up. It was during a clean-up three months ago that I ran into her.

"Name of Joyce Lakeland," old Bob Maples, the sheriff, told me. "Lives four-five miles out on Derrick Road, just past the old Branch farm house. Got her a nice little cottage up there behind a stand of blackjack trees."

"I think I know the place," I said. "Hustlin' lady, Bob?"

"We-el, I reckon so but she's bein' mighty decent about it. She ain't running it into the ground, and she ain't takin' on no roustabouts or sheepherders. If some of these preachers around town wasn't rompin' on me, I wouldn't bother her a-tall."

I wondered if he was getting some of it, and decided that he wasn't. He wasn't maybe any mental genius, but Bob Maples was straight. "So how shall I handle this Joyce Lakeland?" I said. "Tell her to layoff a while, or to move on?"

"We-el"—he scratched his head, scowling—"I dunno, Lou. Just—well, just go out and size her up, and make your own decision. I know you'll be gentle, as gentle and pleasant as you can be. An' I know you can be firm if you have to. So go on out, an' see how she looks to you. I'll back you up in whatever you want to do."

It was about ten o'clock in the morning when I got there. I pulled the car up into the yard, curving it around so I could swing out easy. The county license plates didn't show, but that wasn't deliberate. It was just the way it had to be.

I eased up on the porch, knocked on the door and stood back, taking off my Stetson.

I was feeling a little uncomfortable. I hardly knew what I was going to say to her. Because maybe we're kind of old-fashioned, but our standards of conduct aren't the same, say, as they are in the east or middle-west. Out here you say yes ma'am and no ma'am to anything with skirts on, anything white, that is. Out here, if you catch a man with his pants down, you apologize . . . even if you have to arrest him afterwards. Out here you're a man, a man and a gentleman, or you aren't anything. And God help you if you're not.

The door opened an inch or two. Then, it opened all the way and she stood looking at me.

"Yes?" she said coldly.

She was wearing sleeping shorts and a wool pullover, her brown hair was as tousled as a lamb's tail, and her unpainted face was drawn with sleep. But none of that mattered. It wouldn't have mattered if she'd crawled out of a hog-wallow wearing a gunnysack. She had that much.

She yawned openly and said "Yes?" again, but I still couldn't speak. I guess I was staring open-mouthed like a country boy. This was three months ago, remember, and I hadn't had the sickness in almost fifteen years. Not since I was fourteen.

She wasn't much over five feet and a hundred pounds, and she looked a little scrawny around the neck and ankles. But that was all right. It was perfectly all right. The good Lord had known just where to put that flesh where it would *really* do some good.

"Oh, my goodness!" She laughed suddenly. "Come on in. I don't make a practice of it this early in the morning, but . . ." She held the screen open and gestured. I went in and she closed it and locked the door again.

"I'm sorry, ma'am," I said, "but—"

"It's all right. But I'll have to have some coffee first. You go on back."

I went down the little hall to the bedroom, listening uneasily as I heard her drawing water for the coffee. I'd acted like a chump. It was going to be hard to be firm with her after a start like this, and something told me I should be. I didn't know why; I still don't. But I knew it right from the beginning. Here was a little lady who got what she wanted, and to hell with the price tag.

Well, hell, though, it was just a feeling. She'd acted all right, and she had a nice quiet little place here. I decided I'd let her ride, for the time being anyhow. Why not? And then I happened to glance into the dresser mirror and I knew why not. I knew I couldn't. The top dresser drawer was open a little, and the mirror was tilted slightly. And hustling ladies are one thing, and hustling ladies with guns are something else.

I took it out of the drawer, a .32 automatic, just as she came in with the coffee tray. Her eyes flashed and she slammed the tray down on a table. "What," she snapped, "are you doing with that?"

I opened my coat and showed her my badge. "Sheriff's office, ma'am. What are *you* doing with it?"

She didn't say anything. She just took her purse off the dresser, opened it and pulled out a permit. It had been issued in Fort Worth, but it was all legal enough. Those things are usually honored from one town to another.

"Satisfied, copper?" she said. "I reckon it's all right, miss," I said. "And my name's Ford, not copper." I gave her a big smile, but I didn't get any back. My hunch about her had been dead right. A minute before she'd been all set to lay, and it probably wouldn't have made any difference if I hadn't had a dime. Now she was set for something else, and whether I was a cop or Christ didn't make any difference either.

I wondered how she'd lived so long. "Jesus!" she jeered. "The nicest looking guy I ever saw and you turn out to be a lousy snooping copper. How much? I don't jazz cops."

I felt my face turning red. "Lady," I said, "that's not very polite. I just came out for a little talk."

"You dumb bastard," she yelled. "I asked you what you wanted."

"Since you put it that way," I said, "I'll tell you. I want you out of Central City by sundown. If I catch you here after that I'll run you in for prostitution."

I slammed on my hat and started for the door. She got in front of me, blocking my way.

"You lousy son-of-a-bitch. You—"

"Don't you call me that," I said. "Don't do it, ma'am."

"I did call you that! And I'll do it again! You're a son-of-a-bitch, bastard, pimp . . ."

I tried to push past her. I had to get out of there. I knew what was going to happen if I didn't get out, and I knew I couldn't let it happen. I might kill her. It might bring *the sickness* back. And even if I didn't and it didn't, I'd be washed up. She'd talk. She'd yell her head off. And people would start thinking, thinking and wondering about that time fifteen years ago.

She slapped me so hard that my ears rang, first on one side then the other. She swung and kept swinging. My hat flew off. I stooped to pick it up, and she slammed her knee under my chin.

I stumbled backward on my heels and sat down on the floor. I heard a mean laugh, then another laugh sort of apologetic. She said, "Gosh, sheriff, I didn't mean to—I—you made me so mad I—I—"

"Sure," I grinned. My vision was clearing and I found my voice again. "Sure, ma'am, I know how it was. Used to get that way myself. Give me a hand, will you?"

"You-you won't hurt me?"

"Me? Aw, naw, ma'am."

"No," she said, and she sounded almost disappointed. "I know you won't. Anyone can see you're too easy-going."

And she came over to me slowly and gave me her hands. I pulled myself up. I held her wrists with one hand and swung. It almost stunned her; I didn't want her completely stunned. I wanted her so she would understand what was happening to her.

"No, baby"—my lips drew back from my teeth. "I'm not going to hurt you. I wouldn't think of hurting you. I'm just going to beat the ass plumb off of you."

I said it, and I meant it and I damned near did.

I jerked the jersey up over her face and tied the end in a knot. I threw her down on the bed, yanked off her sleeping shorts and tied her feet together with them.

I took off my belt and raised it over my head . . .

I don't know how long it was before I stopped, before I came to my senses. All I know is that my arm ached like hell and her rear end was one big bruise, and I was scared crazy—as scared as a man can get and go on living.

I freed her feet and hands, and pulled the jersey off her head. I soaked a towel in cold water and bathed her with it. I poured coffee between her lips. And all the time I was talking, begging her to forgive me, telling her how sorry I was.

I got down on my knees by the bed, and begged and apologized. At last her eyelids fluttered and opened.

"D-don't," she whispered.

"I won't," I said. "Honest to God, ma'am, I won't ever—"

"Don't talk." She brushed her lips against mine. "Don't say you're sorry."

She kissed me again. She began fumbling at my tie, my shirt; starting to undress me after I'd almost skinned her alive.

I went back the next day and the day after that. I kept going back. And it was like a wind had been turned on a dying fire. I began needling people in that dead-pan way—needling 'em as a substitute for something else. I began thinking about settling scores with Chester Conway, of the Conway Construction Company.

I won't say that I hadn't thought of it before. Maybe I'd stayed on in Central City all these years, just in the hopes of getting even. But except for her I don't think I'd ever have done anything. She'd made the old fire burn again. She even showed me how to square with Conway.

She didn't know she was doing it, but she gave me the answer. It was one day, one night rather, about six weeks after we'd met.

"Lou," she said, "I don't want to go on like this. Let's pull out of this crummy town together, just you and I."

"Why, you're crazy!" I said. I said it before I could stop myself.

"You think I'd—I'd—"

"Go on, Lou. Let me hear you say it. Tell me"—she began to drawl—"what a fine ol' family you-all Fords is. Tell me, we-all Fords, ma'am, we wouldn't think of livin' with one of you mizzable ol' whores, ma'am. Us Fords just ain't built that way, ma'am."

That was part of it, a big part. But it wasn't the main thing. I knew she was making me worse; I knew that if I didn't stop soon I'd never be able to. I'd wind up in a cage or the electric chair.

"Say it, Lou. Say it and I'll say something."

"Don't threaten me, baby," I said. "I don't like threats."

"I'm not threatening you. I'm telling you. You think you're too good for me—I'll—I'll—"

"Go on. It's your turn to do the saying."

"I wouldn't want to, Lou, honey, but I'm not going to give you up. Never, never, never. If you're too good for me now, then I'll make it so you won't be."

I kissed her, a long hard kiss. Because baby didn't know it, but baby was dead, and in a way I couldn't have loved her more.

"Well, now, baby," I said, "you've got your bowels in an uproar and all over nothing. I was thinking about the money problem."

"I've got some money. I can get some more. A lot of it."

"Yeah?" "I can, Lou. I know I can! He's crazy about me and he's dumb as hell. I'll bet if his old man thought I was going to marry him, he—"

"Who?" I said. "Who are you talking about, Joyce?"

"Elmer Conway. You know who he is, don't you? Old Chester—"

"Yeah," I said. "Yeah, I know the Conways right well. How do you figure on hookin' 'em?"

We talked it over, lying there on her bed together, and off in the night somewhere a voice seemed to whisper to *forget it, Lou, it's not too late if you stop now.* And I did try, God knows I tried. But right after that, right after the voice, her hand gripped one of mine and kneaded it into her breasts, and she moaned and shivered . . . and so I didn't forget.

"Well," I said, after a time, "I guess we can work it out. The way I see it is, if at first you don't succeed, try, try again."

"Mmm, darling?"

"In other words," I said, "where there's a will there's a way."

She squirmed a little, and then she snickered. "Oh, Lou, you corny so and so! You slay me!"

The street was dark. I was standing a few doors above the cafe, and the bum was standing and looking at me. He was a young fellow, about my age, and he was wearing what must have been a pretty good suit of clothes at one time.

"Well, how about it, bud?" he was saying. "How about it, huh? I've been on a hell of a binge, and by God if I don't get some food pretty soon—"

"Something to warm you up, eh?" I said.

"Yeah, anything at all you can help me with, I'll . . ."

I took the cigar out of my mouth with one hand and made like I was reaching into my pocket with the other. Then, I grabbed his wrist and ground the cigar butt into his palm.

"Jesus, bud!"—He cursed and jerked away from me. "What the hell you tryin' to do?"

I laughed and let him see my badge. "Beat it," I said.

"Sure, bud, sure," he said, and he began backing away. He didn't sound particularly scared or angry, more interested than anything. "But you better watch that stuff, bud. You sure better watch it."

He turned and walked off toward the railroad tracks.

I watched him, feeling sort of sick and shaky, and then I got in my car and headed for the labor temple.

PART 2

AUSTIN AND THE HILL COUNTRY

A Twist at the End

STEVEN SAYLOR

O. Henry, the acclaimed short story writer, was a pseudonym created by William Sydney Porter, who lived in Austin in the late 1800s. While in Austin, Porter married, worked at the General Land Office and as a bank clerk, and founded his own newspaper, *The Rolling Stone*, in 1894. A discrepancy at his bank led to an embezzlement charge, and Porter eventually served three years in federal prison. After his release he moved to New York and began publishing the short stories that made him famous.

Historical mystery fiction is the hallmark of Austin writer Steven Saylor, who is best known for his critically acclaimed series, Roma Sub Rosa, set in the Roman Empire. Saylor's careful research into events, personalities, and settings is also on display in his historical Austin mystery, *A Twist at the End: A Novel of O. Henry*.

Saylor's novel is structured as a series of flashbacks as O. Henry, America's favorite short story writer, is blackmailed by someone attempting to expose his secret past in Austin. O. Henry reflects on his time in Austin, recalling the completion of the new state capitol in 1888. O. Henry was also quite aware of a crime spree that was then terrorizing the city—seven young Austin women were brutally murdered in the 1880s. Saylor's *A Twist at the End* explores this unsolved mystery and O. Henry's possible connections to it.

The lady lies in pieces on the capitol grounds . . .

William Sydney Porter dreams. He lives in New York City now, but in the dream it is almost twenty years ago—back when he still lived in Texas, and worked as a draftsman at the General Land Office in Austin. He could look out the window above his drafting table and watch the tall cranes and the antlike workmen busily constructing the dome on the new state capitol building. It was on a day in February of 1888, not quite noon, when he and Dave set out from the land office and went for a stroll before lunch, and they came upon the lady lying in pieces on the capitol grounds.

In his dream, the lady lies there still.

She lies in four pieces. The most identifiable of these consists of her head, along with her left arm and the uppermost part of her torso. This part of the lady is situated face-up, and except for the separation from the rest of her body she might simply be a woman reclining on her back, staring up at the sky with her left arm thrown above her head, the elbow slightly bent. At the end of this upraised arm, her fingers and thumb are curled and joined as if to grasp something no longer there, some object with a cylindrical handle that has been plucked from her frozen grip.

Her mouth is shut, but her eyes are wide open, staring up at the sky through a winter canopy of naked branches.

Not far away, the lady's disembodied right arm lies against the trunk of a pecan tree. Nearby in the brown grass is another piece consisting of her legs and the lower parts of her anatomy. Next to that lies the bulk of her torso, from midriff to breasts.

Beyond her, up the hillside, looms the new, almost finished capitol building. Its walls of dusky rose granite seem to glow with warmth against the cold blue sky. The lofty central portico of the building and the three-storied wings are virtually complete, but a mass of scaffolding and a convergence of cranes indicate where the workmen, small as insects at such a distance, are still busy completing the dome.

The General Land Office is situated a little to the south and east of the new capitol building, at one corner of the grounds. A homesick German architect designed it before the Civil War. The German allowed for big windows to give the draftsmen plenty of light, and decorated the top with fanciful battlements to make it look a bit like a castle.

That was where William Sydney Porter worked in those days, toiling for hour after hour in a dusty, high-ceilinged office up on the third floor, unrolling maps on big drafting tables, placing glass weights to hold down the corners, using rulers and compasses and pens to calculate the longitude and latitude of various claims. A draftsman saw terrible things at the land office: widows and children who lost homesteads for lack of a proper claim, swindlers who grabbed vast tracts by legal trickery, fools who spent fortunes on worthless treasure maps and stormed into the land office determined to prove that the official surveys had to be wrong. But mostly the work was long and boring and tedious, just the sort of thing that people seem to have in mind when they speak of a "real" job, as in: "Now that you're married and have a baby on the way, you must think of getting a *real* job, Will." And so he had, and that was how he ended up at the land office, drawing lines and circles and scribbling numbers in ledgers, instead of sketching funny pictures and writing clever little poems and stories that nobody wanted to publish.

But in the midst of all that daily tedium there was the blessed oasis called lunch, and on the day he is revisiting in the dream, his friend Dave Shoemaker is treating him to lunch, because Dave has just received a raise in pay from the penny-pinching tyrant who owns the newspaper where Dave works.

In Will Porter's dream, just as it actually happened on that February day in 1888, the two of them descend the little flight of steps from the main entrance of the land office, walk past horses and carriages gathered in the forecourt, then cross the capitol grounds heading for Congress Avenue. Some spots are prettily landscaped, with shrubbery and grass and flower beds. Other areas are scraped or furrowed or piled high with dirt or gravel. Though they do not know it, each step brings them closer to their discovery of the lady who lies in pieces.

Will is in his middle twenties. Dave is not quite thirty. Both are respectably but not ostentatiously dressed, wearing hats, vests, and long winter coats. Each has a mustache; Will's is ginger-colored and Dave's is black. Almost every man had a mustache in those days, or else a beard. Hair on the face was considered a mark of manhood and commanded respect. The older generation who ran things in Austin, men who were old enough to have fought in the Civil War, were given to wearing full, dense beards requiring the expert attentions of a barber. Young men of courting age were more likely to sport mustaches; a woman had to see a man's chin to judge his character.

Will and Dave stroll slowly across the grounds, nodding gravely, like two men discussing a matter of great importance.

"Will," says Dave, "I think you know my feelings on the subject."

"Do I, Dave?"

"Under no circumstances is a tamale a fit thing to put into a man's system in the middle of the day. That goes double for two tamales. Triple for three."

Will raises an eyebrow. "Millions of Mexicans swear by 'em."

"You'll hear me swearing, too, about twenty-four hours from now, if you persuade me to eat a couple of damn tamales for lunch."

Will licks his lips. "Mama Rodriguez makes a mighty fine tamale. She's only a streetcar ride away, down on Nueces across from the lumberyard. My heart was set on it, Dave."

"My stomach is dead set against it. Who's paying for this meal, anyway?"

"Touché, Shoemaker. What about the Iron Front?"

"Too greasy."

"The Blue Front, then?"

"Not greasy enough."

"Salge's Chop House?"

"Too crowded."

"Simon's?"

"Quiet as a graveyard."

"Roach's, then?"

Dave raises an eyebrow. "Never cared for the name."

"David Shoemaker," says Will in some exasperation, "I have just recited the entire list of decent eateries in the city of Austin, Texas, and you've vetoed every one."

Dave brightens. "I suppose the only remaining alternative is to take a liquid lunch down in Guy Town." He pats his vest pocket. "I even have a fresh deck of cards on me! Shall we wend our way down Congress Avenue and see what saloon we come to first?"

Will tugs at his ginger mustache. "You forget, Mr. Shoemaker, that I am now a married man! For me, Guy Town and its bachelor pleasures have retreated behind a veil of mystery."

Their path takes a detour around a high mound of gravel. When they reach the other side, Dave comes to an abrupt stop. He wrinkles his brow. "What on earth . . .?"

Will follows Dave's gaze to see what he's staring at. He steps closer, then steps back, turning his head this way and that, as if seeing the thing from the right angle will explain it. "Not a pretty sight, is it?"

Dave peers at the lady's tight-lipped, blankly staring face. He shakes his head. "I'll say it's not! When did this happen?"

"Don't know."

"Someone should cover her up!"

Will raises an eyebrow. "Don't see why. Decently dressed, ain't she? And it don't look like rain."

Dave nods vaguely. He walks from piece to piece, carefully observing each segment of the lady in turn. "Mr. Gaines at the *Statesman* will want to send a sketch artist," he mutters.

"Can't imagine why," says Will. "She's so very ugly." He walks up to the disembodied torso and gives it a kick. The blow reverberates with a hollow, metallic clang. "I suppose it's the perspective—nobody was ever meant to see this thing so close up. There's something grotesque about such an over-sized specimen of womanhood. What man wouldn't be unnerved at the sight of a woman three times bigger than he is, even if she is all in pieces! Now, at a proper distance—once she's all assembled and welded together and they set her on top of the capitol dome—I suppose everyone will rave about what a beauty she is. But this close up—well, if ever there was a face that could stop a clock . . ."

"She is indeed a harsh-looking lady," Dave agrees. "I suppose no one ever said that Liberty has to be beautiful. Now why do you suppose her left arm is raised up like that? It looks like she's holding on to a cylinder of thin air."

"Really, Dave Shoemaker! She's the Goddess of Liberty, ain't she? I imagine she's supposed to hold a torch of some kind. Or maybe a star."

"Ah, yes. A goddess. That explains why she's all dolled up in robes and drapery. And barefoot!"

Together, they study the various scattered pieces of the statue of the Goddess of Liberty, the crowning monument for the capitol dome. "She received quite a bit of coverage in the *Statesman* when the molds arrived from that catalogue outfit in Chicago," recalls Dave. "There's a foundry in the capitol basement where they cast her out of zinc. The workmen must have lugged her out here early this morning, getting ready to put the pieces together. A mail-order goddess—but from Chicago, not Olympus!"

Will laughs, but feels vaguely apprehensive as he continues to study the pieces of the statue. It's the monstrous scale of the thing, he thinks, and the fact that she's scattered all about, as if she'd been standing here on the capitol grounds minding her own business, doing whatever a goddess of liberty does, and some equally monstrous fellow had come along and chopped her to pieces with a monstrous ax . . .

The same thought seems to occur to Dave at that instant, because they exchange a look and see the same darkness reflected in each other's eyes.

They are thinking of *her*.

They are thinking of all the women who were so brutally murdered in Austin in the long, bizarre sequence of murders still fresh in everyone's memory. They remember one woman in particular. In light of those horrible crimes, it is no laughing matter to come upon a dismembered woman on the capitol grounds, even if she's only a statue made of zinc.

Rock Critic Murders

JESSE SUBLETT

Austin boasts of being the live music capital of the world. It earned this designation largely by being the kind of city where generations of college students decide to stay forever, despite the relative lack of economic opportunities. The city's legions of overeducated and underemployed hipsters were made famous in Richard Linklater's 1991 film *Slacker*.

The rest of America began discovering Austin's charms in the 1980s, and since then the population has boomed, turning the once pleasant mid-sized city into a major metropolis. Austin's slackers have resisted the changes every step of the way, and their battle cry is still heard today: "Keep Austin Weird."

A significant figure in Austin's live music scene is Jesse Sublett, lead singer and bass player for Austin's seminal punk band of the late 1970s, the Skunks. Sublett was still working as a musician when he began writing mystery novels in the 1980s. He has published three novels that feature musician and detective Martin Fender. Tellingly, Martin Fender can't pay his bills as a musician, even in the live music capital of the world. So he earns his living as a skiptracer for a collection agency.

The Rock Critic Murders is the first book in Sublett's Fender series. Here the ambience of Austin's slacker culture and its live music scene are captured amidst the backdrop of an economic boom that is transforming the city.

Austin, Texas, 1984. It was a dull, hot, mid-July Monday with nothing going for it. I was holed up in the small room in my apartment that I used as an office and storeroom for my music gear. Sometimes when I had nothing else to do I just sat in there and stared at my things instead of watching T V.

My bass guitar leaned against an amplifier, ready to play the blues. Maybe I'd get around to changing its strings later, since I'd decided to take the afternoon off from the collection agency where I'd been working part-time as a skiptracer. When gigs got too few and far between, I took it out on people who'd moved without paying their bills, and that was how I paid my own.

I was good at it, but I was better at playing bass and that was what I preferred. I sat there, blowing smoke rings at the instrument, admiring its curves, its hard mystery, watching the smoke fall into lazy tendrils around the body. Knowing that it was an idle beauty, and idle beauties can't stay that way long.

I'd been thinking about True Love. The band I used to play with, not the emotion. I'd heard they were getting back together.

The phone sat there on the corner of the desk, squat, black, and ugly. There was something malignant about it and its silence, just as there was something magical about my musical instruments. Gradually I realized that I was sitting there staring at the machinery of my fate, getting the same feeling you get when you stare at a clock long enough to see the hands move.

I knew that if they hadn't gotten in touch with me by now, I wasn't their first choice. I wasn't the original bass player, and I had no right to expect anything from the old band. And I'd almost talked myself into expecting nothing but a phone call letting me know that I'd be on the guest list. It was a few minutes later, after I'd decided how I would take the news—cordial but coolly distant—when he called.

"Is this Martin Fender, semi-legendary Austin rock and R & B bassist?" asked a voice that was calm and sober. "Fender, as in . . ."

"As in the guitar," I said. "Post-Bogart and pre-synth pop, this is he. Hello, KC." A gig review in a local rag had said all those things about me. I was surprised that anyone would remember, especially the bourbon-chugging guitar player. "It's barely after noon. I'm a little shocked to hear from you so early in the day."

"The day starts a little bit earlier when you stop drinking, Martin. I'm just down the street, having some migas at Dos Hermanos. I was wondering if you could use a gig this weekend."

"Odds are I could," I said.

"It'll be easy money, Martin. You already know the songs . . ."

I looked at the clock again, and the calendar too. I hadn't worked with a guitar player half as good as KC in a long time, but what were the odds he'd still be on the wagon by the weekend?

". . . and this seems to be the year for reunions. I know they might seem corny, but we got a damn good offer. It'll be the grand opening of a new club."

"Those kind of gigs can be loose with things besides cash, KC. They flash a lot of dollars at you and then it turns out they haven't built the stage yet or remembered to get their ad in the paper. Remember when we drove all the way to Brownsville for that rock festival and came back with nothing but a couple of switchblades from Matamoros?"

"Sure do. Nothing like a night in Boystown to take the sting out of getting stiffed by a promoter."

"But as I recall, you woke up in a motel room and she'd only left you a garter belt to remember her by."

"No goodbye note, no wallet, and no shoes. Had to walk two miles to find a pay phone to call you guys to pick me up. Barefoot, in the middle of June."

"August, I believe."

"Probably right, Martin. Anyway, this one's in town. And I'm sitting on a certified check. Your cut would be two grand."

Ten weeks of afternoons at the collection agency. My cut of a dozen fraternity mixers or debutante balls. More than I'd see after thirty or forty midweek one-nighters at the Continental Club or the Black Cat Saloon. And it was the old band.

"What do you say, Martin?"

"What time is sound check?"

He suggested that he come by so he could give me the rest of the details and then I could give him a ride by the Tavern and then home. I said that would be fine.

While I still had the phone in my hand I almost called Ladonna. She would probably be at work, though. The guys she worked with would go, "Was that Martin?" and they would know I hadn't called in over a week, so they'd ask if I was on the road. She would have to say no, and there you go.

"Has it really been five years?" asked the guitarist as we rolled down South 1st with the top down on my banana yellow 1970 Karmann Ghia, caught in the flow of traffic that would sweep us from laid-back South Austin across the Colorado River and on into the heart of the boomtown, if we let it.

"Close enough," I said. He had put on a little weight. He wasn't fat, but the trademark black leather jeans—which had always been tight—and black sleeveless shirt were carrying an extra twenty to thirty pounds. The tiger in the tattoo on his arm looked less likely to spring, and there was an extra fold of skin under the eyes behind the Ray Ban Wayfarers. But he hadn't lost any of the defiant shock of hair that stuck up like stiff black flames, tousled enough to have that look of ambivalent neglect. Nor the ragged fingernails, the hoarse cough, the three-day beard.

"Think you'll remember the songs?" I asked.

"How could I forget? Never stopped playing them. You know that. People never get tired of hearing Al Green, Wilson Pickett, Stax, and Motown. The originals might take a little time, but I can fake what doesn't come back straight away. And the way I remember it, so can you."

When I'd been called in to replace the original bass player, True Love already had a large following throughout the Southwest and a couple of albums on small independent labels, making them enough money to make payments on a van and keep it running. Which was good, since it was on the road the better part of the year. True Love would be pick of the week when we played New York or LA, but the band was never snatched up by a major label and therefore had never, as most people would say, "made it."

"We were the biggest band around here for a good six years," said the guitar operator.

"Legends," I said.

"Ex-legends," he said, lighting another cigarette, "who are going to look like clowns if we don't sound good. I admit I took the gig because of the money, but it's gotta be right. I hope you don't feel too put out by having to spend a week in the country rehearsing—"

"It's got to be right," I agreed, cutting him off. We'd already been through that. He'd given me his scribbled directions out to the ranch house we'd rehearse at all week. Only a beat later, he told me which new club we'd be playing at. I knew the club owner well enough to almost change my mind about taking the gig.

"I know how you feel about Ward, too. He's stiffed me a couple of times and pulled dates out from under me more times than I can count, but like I said, I got the certified check. The money's enough so that I don't mind playing his little game. I guess he figures I'll be less likely to backslide and start guzzling Jack Daniels if we're stuck out in the hills, and you can't blame him for wanting us to do the interview. You could use the publicity just as much as the club can, and I told them we could only give them a half hour since we need to get going."

"We do?"

"Relax, Martin. We'll make it fun."

There must be an interview school somewhere where all prospective music journalists must go before they can practice their trade, and at that school they ingrain upon young impressionable minds the necessity of asking the ten stupidest questions a musician can be asked. When our cub reporter started out with the time-worn "What are your influences?" and then proceeded to stupid questions number two, three, and four, I decided to cut things short and try to sum it all up for the record.

"True Love was a helluva band, one of those bands that believed that the blues is all there is. But we played the blues loud and hard, our own way. Somebody once said that the blues are sad and lonely and kind of raw, the way that freight trains always seem raw and sad and lonely. Well, True Love was raw and sad and lonely as a freight train doing ninety miles an hour. So, one more time, for a couple of hours this weekend, the blues will be all there is, because we'll be firing up that old train. The 123 Club will have state-of-the-art sound and lights and free champagne and *everyone* will be there, including this guitar mangler here, KC, along with Frankie Day on lead vocals and Billy Ludwig on the drums."

"But aren't you looking at this as the start of a new career for the band? A chance to really go for it this time?"

I looked at KC. There was no life in the Novocain face. He could have been a killer, sitting in a windowless room, talking to a hack lawyer about a no-hope appeal. The interviewer fidgeted nervously as the tape rolled in the cassette recorder, preserving the methodical sounds KC made as he dropped another Gitanes out of the box and struck a match for it. He inhaled and deliberately let the smoke roll out across the table after he'd had a lungful.

"We'll see," he said finally.

I had a pretty good idea of how the story would run. It would say something about how it seemed like only yesterday when True Love kept the town's feet tapping and ears ringing. It would wax nostalgic, associating the reunion of the band with better, or, at least, more carefree times. Typical Baby Boom stuff. And it would mention that the original bass player, a guy named Dan Gabriel, had left the band after five years, and that was when they asked me to join. Now Dan Gabriel was a successful real estate hustler with a downtown office, Armani suits, and a secretary who had dutifully taken the messages that KC had left about getting the band back together for one night, messages that could just as well have been dropped in the middle of Town Lake.

The story would have a smattering of song titles, mostly reworkings of R&B classics that sounded good in smoky bars and trendy dives. It probably wouldn't mention KC's drinking and it probably wouldn't mention my hassle with the law last year. Which was OK with me. That kind of publicity we could do without.

When the reporter was gone and it was just the two of us again, the sounds of the restaurant seemed to envelop us, reminding me that we were in the Tavern, one of the loudest places in town. Dishes clattered together in cold, greasy bus trays, waitresses threw orders at the guy flying the deep fryer vats, beepers beeped, voices at other tables talked software and real estate. And all of it was mashed together into one big din.

But the Tavern's abrasive atmosphere went down easy as a frost-covered longneck at a patio barbecue. There was a cool blue neon sign in the window that said something about air conditioning, and a '50s deco clock the size of a truck tire over the bar that made time seem like a friendly thing.

KC had both elbows resting on the checkered oilcloth and seemed to be watching the cars skate by on Lamar Boulevard. The journalist had left a print of a photo with us that was supposed to run with the story. I looked at it.

KC had changed, but I hadn't, not really. I was thinner than he was even then, and, at six feet, a bit taller. My hair was still, at just under thirty, a dark brown that was just this side of black, and the front bit of it still fell over my right eyebrow no matter how often I combed it back. I even had on the same clothes—black Converse All-Stars, skin-tight black jeans, black cotton shirt cinched up with a bolo tie, and the same black, blocky, unvented, thrift-shop jacket with notched lapels that was draped over the back of my chair.

KC noticed me looking at the photo and frowned. "Some of us have changed a bit," he said. I shrugged. "Why don't we seal the deal with a—"

"Water will be fine, or maybe one more cup of coffee," he said. "Go ahead, have a drink, I can take it. I ain't that much of a wimp."

"Just trying to be sensitive."

"Go ahead, have one. I know you could use two or three fingers of scotch after that bullshit," he said, signaling our waitress. She came, coffee pot in hand, serviced KC's cup and scratched my drink order on our ticket.

"Salud," he said, tipping the cup. "I just want you to know, Martin, I'm glad it all came down the way it did. As much as I can't stand the prick, Ward is the only guy in town who can come up with the cash."

"That may be true, KC. But he needs us, too. He's buying nostalgia. He's gotta have a gimmick, and we're it."

"I know. Screw it. It's gonna be mighty trendy, you know, with video monitors everywhere, big screens, multiple levels, after-hours disco, and that New York trip where they make you wait on the wrong side of the velvet rope before they decide if you're cool enough to get in. Not the kinda place I'd hang out."

"It'll need some gimmicks to compete with all the other clubs on 6th Street. Might even run one of his other clubs out of business. What's this one make, four?"

"Yeah," said the guitarist. "But I just want you to know I'm glad it came down this way, even if it means you might have to shake hands with the sonuvabitch afterward. I really wanted you for the gig, even though I was sorta obligated for authenticity's sake to give Gabe a call."

"No big deal," I said, downing my scotch seconds after it was placed in front of me.

"You're a better bass player, anyway."

"Thanks."

"Too damn loud, though."

"Got to be to compete with your shit," I said. I looked for some life in the whiskery mask. There was a little. It was jaded, and it was hoarse, but it would pass for a laugh.

"Ready to give me a ride?"

We walked to my car, and as we got in—careful not to get burned from the door handles or seat belt buckles—I suppose both of us gave a nod or a squinty wink to the object slowly turning on its sixteen-foot pedestal across the street. It was a red and blue and green steel insect almost as big as a VW Beetle, with glass wings and blinking eyes. The bug had been the figurehead for Texterminators Pest Control for more than twenty years. But it was more than just a mascot. It was an old friend that stayed the same in a sea of change, a reminder of the often quirky personality of a town that was prospering and metamorphosing but that still, in many ways, refused to grow up.

We lit up cigarettes as we pulled out. Up the 12th Street hill going into Clarksville, KC went into a coughing fit. Having seen him go through half a pack in less than two hours, I wasn't surprised. Being around him proved that if you wanted to keep your smoking in check you shouldn't give up drinking. Nature abhors a vacuum.

"How'd you quit drinking?" I asked.

"Lorraine. You've met her, haven't you?"

I nodded. I'd met the redhead all right. I'd met her over at their house years before when I'd dropped by to loan him a Howlin' Wolf album. I reminded him.

"Oh yeah. Remind me to give that back. I still have it, don't I? Anyway, it was her idea. She paid for a detox deal. Here we go."

We were in front of his house, a run-down white frame thing with a porch and untended yard, a not uncommon sight in the funky but trendy neighborhood. Lots of musicians, hip professionals, and, as everywhere in Austin, college students, lived there and paid the inflated price for hardwood floors and relaxed atmosphere on the near west side of town. A cedar stood a little too close to the sunset side of the house. That would be the tree that was outside the window of the bedroom, the room with the door I'd opened when I was looking for the bathroom that night.

"Think you can figure out the map?" he asked.

"Yeah. I just need to pack some things and cash a check. You really think it'll take all week?"

"Hell no," he replied, leaning one hand on the open door. "And I wouldn't bother cashing a check unless you need some gas money. You won't need any cash out there. Ward's paying for the groceries."

"All right," I said.

He got out and shut the door. "She's coming, too. It's a big old house, there's plenty of room out there and . . ."

"KC," I interrupted. It was too hot to listen to explanations.

"What?"

"Thanks."

He nodded, flipped his cigarette butt into the street, turned and went inside. I let out the clutch and turned the car around in the narrow road, only once glancing in the rear view mirror at the house where I'd accidentally walked in on the guitar player's girlfriend. I still remember the sight of that tree outside the window on the night of a full moon, framing the standing figure of the girl who looked up at me with those big blue eyes that showed no sign of being startled. Even though she was as naked as you can get.

I set the controls for downtown. Somewhere a dog was barking.

★

So I had a gig. I hauled my watch, a missile-shaped circa 1955 Louvic, over to the jeweler on Congress Avenue and dropped it off. By the time it was repaired, I'd have the money to pay for it. The jeweler loaned me a digital watch. It was as plain and ugly as any digital watch ever was. I doubled back and took the tree-lined drive around the state capitol, nodding at the cranky old men who sat in lawn chairs guarding the bureaucrats' parking and feeding the squirrels that scampered around the elm and pecan trees.

The double-domed granite building was five feet taller than its Washington, D.C., counterpart. Atop it stood a zinc goddess of liberty with a foul expression on a face even a zinc mother couldn't love. Maybe she was unhappy about the pigeon's nest in her right armpit, or about the crack in her shoulder blade. There had been some discussion about giving the lady a makeover, maybe even giving her a new face and slimming down those nineteenth-century thighs, but no one knew how she got up there in the first place eighty years ago and no one knew how to get her down.

I took the avenue back toward the river, keeping an eye out for buildings that might have gone up since the night before. Construction cranes towered over the avenue like surgeons giving it a quadruple bypass. New postmodern monuments were shooting up all over, loud and tall and squeaky clean.

Did the town need any more of these new buildings? Did it need another rock and roll reunion?

Normally I shied away from funerals and reunions and I couldn't figure out which was sadder or more shot through with hypocrisy. Funerals were ostensibly about confronting death and celebrating life. But in the center of the whole thing was a dead body, cold proof that Death had won again.

Reunions were supposed to bring people together, to show that the old war horses were still alive and kicking, still vital. But did they? Reunions brought out the seedy side of rock and roll, as bloated caricatures waddled onstage with roots that had been nurtured in Memphis or the south side of Chicago now slanted towards Vegas. Showing what rock and roll can do to you, when it hasn't done enough *for* you. Half the time the music was so lame you wondered if it had been any good the first time. Bad examples came to mind—the Grass Roots; Crosby, Stills, and Nash; Steppenwolf; the Guess Who.

Reunions. I cringed at being associated with the word, much less the groups that had been doing it. But True Love wasn't like that. We were tough local boys and we were still—all of us except maybe Billy—under thirty. And we played the blues. You could play the blues forever. We weren't going to be a sideshow.

Also, it would be good to see the old crowd of regulars out in force again, wearing the essential Transylvanian black and gravity-defying hairstyles. They were night creatures, people whose days started where other people's days ended, who lived in dumpy houses without central air so they could spend their money on *important* things: records, leather jackets, custom guitars, cool cars, Harley-Davidsons, and sometimes drugs. Lots of times drugs. Some worked day jobs, considering them only temporary, while others got by doing things that were somewhat illegal. These were people with an advanced degree of cool. Many of them had no last names. They weren't in any of the lines of cars idling at the drive-in banks. They weren't wearing hard hats, tying steel on any of the new skyscrapers. They hadn't succumbed to condo fever. Thinking of them brought warmth to my jaded heart. Too bad they'd have to come to one of Ward's clubs to see us.

Maybe the reunion was a good thing. The scene needed a big shot in the arm. Live music was down—more people were staying home, watching their VCRs, playing with their home computers. Spending their disposable income on the back catalogs of old favorites that had just been released on CD. Having babies.

Live music was also down on account of the real estate boom. Because in a city with more live music venues than either LA or Manhattan, things had always centered around a downtown area no more than a couple of miles in diameter. And in that area, skyrocketing land value called for maximum use for maximum profit. High-rises were in and clubs were out. Venues were closing left and right.

Things had always been tough for local live music, though, and it was hard to feel sorry for club owners. Down at the street level, the clubs—as well as booking agencies, studios, and bands—often survived only by bending laws and cutting corners and using money that someone needed to lose. Sometimes the money came from drugs, sometimes it came from someone just trying to avoid a tax bite. I remember one club that was run by men who had connections with a string of sex-oriented clubs out of Houston. When you went downstairs to get paid, they took the cash from a big steel trunk the size of a coffin. There would be four or five guys down there and at least that many guns. You didn't ask where that money had been.

Not that everyone got by with transfusions of illegitimate cash. Some of the clubs were like the town's Old Money—it seemed like they'd always been there and always would be. There were clubs that stayed open even if no one liked them, while some popular spots closed no matter what was done to keep them going. Also, every six months or so a club or a band came up with the right idea and it was a big success. You saw glitter and flash and lines around the block. Bartenders saw their tip jars overflow and club owners saw themselves get fat and happy. It never made sense.

The slippery economy gave the whole business a surreal aura. It made the musicians embarrassingly subservient to the club owners because it made the club owners look like the real magicians. Pulling a club through hard times appeared to be a lot harder than pulling a rabbit out of a hat, maybe even harder than whipping out a blistering lead on a Stratocaster. It wasn't as glamorous, but it was essential, and it certainly held an air of mystery. Mystery can be power and once you have both, look out.

Even if a band was hot, a club owner could make them feel like he was doing them a favor by giving them a gig. And if he cancelled it two days before the date, or didn't pay them after they played, he could shrug and say, Hey, that's the way it goes, isn't it? That's rock and roll.

It didn't help that musicians have a natural tendency to be laid back and naive about business. In Austin, you could generally count on that tendency being doubled or tripled. You don't see many Austin musicians at motivational seminars. To a musician, motivation is a simple thing. Love of music, respect for the icons of the genre. Wishes for fame. The desire to be wanted, loved, adored.

But what motivated a person to be a club owner? The desire to emulate Rick Blaine in *Casablanca*—smart, amoral, and in control? I doubted that. Club owners didn't generally have that kind of class. Nor did the curious assortment of misanthropic bouncers, anti-social bartenders, deaf sound engineers, and mercenary agents who only used pencils, never ink, on their booking calendars. They were a whole subclass of people with a subterranean bottom line. They made things work by being there and running things, but they were in the music business the way cheap hookers were in the love business.

Yeah, they were.

But that was the way it was, and it worked.

Music and the music business. If you only knew one and not the other, you weren't a professional. You were just a fan.

I loved it. I hated it. It was screwed up enough that it could put you off music, and it was run by people that couldn't be put off because they were too weird to do anything else. Those people paid you, or didn't pay you, and even if you didn't care for them, you had to live with them, or you didn't work.

Buck Fever

BEN REHDER

In Texas, hunting is not just a popular sport, it's big business. Hunters pay thousands of dollars for the privilege of killing a trophy buck. Ranchers have responded by managing deer herds for maximum profit by utilizing high fences, nutritional supplements, and selective breeding. Deer seem to be transitioning from wildlife into livestock, and, increasingly, even the hunts themselves are stage-managed, with hunters pre-selecting the very animal they are to shoot.

Ben Rehder is an Austin-based writer who owns a small "ranchette" in the Hill Country west of Austin. Rehder is not only an avid hunter, he is also one of the funniest mystery writers to come out of Texas. His inclination for humor, combined with his knowledge of the hunting culture, is on full display in his series of comic mysteries featuring game warden John Marlin.

In Rehder's first book, *Buck Fever*, Marlin confronts a variety of situations as deer season gets underway—two over-the-top rednecks who view poaching as a birthright, a man disguised as a deer, deer on drugs, and deer in lingerie. While Rehder's oddball characters capture most of the attention, one serious element shines throughout—the importance of deer hunting in the Texas Hill Country.

By the time Red O'Brien finished his thirteenth beer, he could hardly see through his rifle scope. Worse yet, his partner, Billy Don Craddock, was doing a lousy job with the spotlight.

"Dammit, Billy Don, we ain't hunting raccoons," Red barked. "Get that light out of the trees and shine it out in the pastures where it will do me some good."

Billy Don mumbled something unintelligible, kicked some empty beer cans around on the floorboard of Red's old Ford truck, and then belched loudly from way down deep in his three-hundred-pound frame. That was his standard rebuttal anytime Red got a little short with him. The spotlight, meanwhile, continued to illuminate the canopy of a forty-foot Spanish oak.

Red cussed him again and pulled the rifle back in the window. Every time they went on one of these poaching excursions, Red had no idea how he managed to get a clean shot. After all, poaching white-tailed deer was serious business. It called for stealth and grace, wits and guile. It had been apparent to Red for years that Billy Don came up short in all of these departments.

"Turn that friggin' light off and hand me a beer," Red said.

"Don't know what we're doing out here on a night like this anyhow," Billy Don replied as he dug into the ice chest for two fresh Keystones. "Moon ain't up yet. All the big ones will be bedded down till it rises. Any moron knows that."

Red started to say that Billy Don was an excellent reference for gauging what a moron may or may not know. But he thought better of it, being that Billy Don weighed roughly twice what Red did. Not to mention that Billy Don had quite a quick temper after his first twelve-pack.

"Billy Don, let me ask you something. Someone walked into your bedroom shining a light as bright as the sun in your face, what's the first thing you'd do?"

"Guess I'd wag my pecker at 'em," Billy Don said, smiling. He considered himself quite glib.

"Okay," Red said patiently, "then what's the second thing you'd do?"

"I'd get up and see what the hell's going on."

"Damn right!" Red said triumphantly. "Don't matter if the bucks are bedded down or not. Just roust 'em with that light and we'll get a shot. But remember, we won't find any deer up in the treetops."

Billy Don gave a short snort in reply.

Red popped the top on his new beer, revved the Ford, and started on a slow crawl down the quiet county road. Billy Don grabbed the spotlight and leaned out the window, putting some serious strain on the buttons of his overalls, as he shined the light back over the hood of the Ford to Red's left. They had gone about half a mile when Billy Don stirred.

"Over there!"

Red stomped the brakes, causing his Keystone to spill and run down into his crotch. He didn't even notice. Billy Don was spotlighting an oat field a hundred yards away, where two dozen deer grazed. Among them, one of the largest white-tailed bucks either of them had ever seen. "Fuck me nekkid," Red whispered.

"Jesus, Red! Look at that monster."

Red clumsily stuck the .270 Winchester out the window, banging the door frame and the rearview mirror in the process. The deer didn't even look their way. Red raised the rifle and tried to sight in on the trophy buck, but the deer had other things in mind.

While all the other deer were grazing in place, the buck was loping around the oat field in fits and starts, running in circles. He bounced, he jumped, he spun. Red and Billy Don had never seen such peculiar behavior.

"Somethin's wrong with that deer," Billy Don said, using his keen knowledge of animal behavioral patterns.

"Bastard won't hold still! Keep the light on him!" Red said.

"I've got him. Just shoot. Shoot!"

Red was about to risk a wild shot when the buck finally seemed to calm down. Rather than skipping around, it was now walking fast, with its nose low to the ground. The buck approached a large doe partially obscured behind a small cedar tree and, with little ceremony, began to mount her.

Billy Don giggled, the kind of laugh you'd expect from a schoolgirl, not a flannel-clad six-foot-six cedar-chopper. "Why, I do believe it's true love."

Red sensed his chance, took a deep breath, and squeezed the trigger. The rifle bellowed as orange flame leapt out of the muzzle and licked the night, and then all was quiet.

The buck, and the doe of his affections, crumpled to the ground while the other deer scattered into the brush. Seconds passed. And then, to the chagrin of the drunken poachers, the huge buck climbed to his hooves, snorted twice, and took off. The doe remained on the ground.

"Dammit, Red! You missed."

"No way! It was a lung shot. I bet it went all the way through. Grab your wire cutters."

Knowing that a wounded deer can run several hundred yards or more, both men staggered out of the truck, cut their way through the eight-foot deerproof fence, and proceeded over to the oat field.

Each man had a flashlight and was looking feverishly for traces of blood, when they heard a noise.

"What the hell was that?" Billy Don asked.

"Shhh."

Then another sound. A moaning, from the wounded doe lying on the ground.

Billy Don was spooked. "That's weird, Red. Let's get outta here."

Red shined his light on the wounded animal twenty yards away. "Hold on a second. What the hell's wrong with its hide? It looks all loose and . . ." He was about to approach the deer when they both heard something they'd never forget.

The doe clearly said, "Help me."

Without saying a word, both men scrambled back toward the fence. For the first time in his life, Billy Don Craddock actually outran somebody.

Seconds later, the man in the crudely tailored deer costume could hear the tires squealing as the truck sped away.

Just as Red and Billy Don were sprinting like boot-clad track stars, a powerful man was in the middle of a phone call. Unfortunately for the man, Roy Swank, it was hard to judge his importance by looking at him. In fact, he looked a lot like your average pond frog. Round, squat body. Large, glassy eyes. Bulbous lips in front of a thick tongue. And, of course, the neck, or rather, the lack of one. It was as if his head sat directly on his sloping shoulders. His voice was his best feature, deep and charismatic.

Roy Swank had relocated to a large ranch southwest of Johnson City, Texas, five years ago, after a successful (although intentionally anonymous) career lobbying legislators in Austin. The locals who knew or cared what a lobbyist was never really figured out what Swank lobbied for. Few people ever had, because Swank was the type of lobbyist who always conducted business in the shadows of a back room, rarely putting anything down on paper. But he and the entities he represented had the kind of resources and resourcefulness that could sway votes or help introduce new legislation. So when the rumors spread about Swank's retirement, the entire state political system took notice—although there were as many people relieved as disappointed.

After lengthy consideration (his past had to be weighed carefully—life in a county full of political enemies might be rather difficult), Swank purchased a ten-thousand-acre ranch one hour west of Austin. Swank was actually planning on semiretirement; the ranch was a successful cattle operation and he intended to maintain its sizable herd of Red Brangus. He had even kept the former owner on as foreman for a time.

But without the busy schedule of his previous career, Swank became restless. That is, until he rediscovered one of the great passions he enjoyed as a young adult: deer hunting. The hunting bug bit, and it bit hard. He spent the first summer on his new ranch building deer blinds, clearing brush in prime hunting areas, distributing automatic corn and protein feeders, and planting food plots such as oats and rye. It paid off the following season, as Swank harvested a beautiful twelve-point buck with a twenty-two-inch spread that tallied 133 Boone & Crockett points, the scoring standard for judging trophy bucks. Not nearly as large as the world-renowned bucks in South Texas, but a very respectable deer for the Hill Country. Several of his closest associates joined him on the ranch and had comparable success.

Swank, never one to do anything in moderation, decided that his ranch could become one of the most successful hunting operations in Texas. By importing some key breeding stock from South Texas and Mexico, and then following proper game-management techniques, Swank set out to develop a herd of whitetails as large and robust—and with the same jaw-dropping trophy antlers—as their southern brethren.

He had phenomenal success. After all, money was no object, and the laws and restrictions that regulated game importation and relocation melted away under Swank's political clout. After four seasons, not only was his ranch (the Circle S) known throughout the state for trophy deer, he had actually started a lucrative business exporting deer to other ranches around the nation.

Swank was tucked away obliviously in his four-thousand-square-foot ranch house, on the phone to one of his most valued customers, at the same moment Red O'Brien blasted unsuccessfully at a large buck in Swank's remote southern pasture.

"They went out on the trailer today," Swank said in his rich timbre. He was sitting at a large mahogany desk in an immense den. A fire burned in the huge limestone fireplace, despite the warm weather. He cradled the phone with his shoulder as he reached across the desk, grabbed a bottle of expensive scotch and poured himself another glass. "Four of them. But the one you'll be especially interested in is the ten-pointer," Swank said as he went on to describe the "magnificent beast."

Swank grunted a few times, nodding. "Good. Yes, good." Then he hung up. Swank had a habit of never saying good-bye.

By the time he finished his conversation, a man who sounded just like Red O'Brien had already made an anonymous call to 911.

John Marlin, Blanco County's game warden for nineteen years, thought he had seen and heard it all.

There was the hapless roadside poacher who shot an artificial deer eight times before Marlin stepped from his hiding spot and arrested him. The man claimed he thought it was a mountain lion.

There was the boatload of fraternity boys who unsuccessfully tried dynamiting fish in a small lake. They sank their boat and one young Delta Sig lost three fingers. Even after all that, one of the drunk frat boys took a swing at Marlin when he confiscated the illegal fish.

And, of course, there was the granddaddy of all his strange encounters. The hunter who shot a doe one night out of season. That wasn't strange in itself—but when Marlin found the doe on the ground, it was wearing a garter belt and stiletto heels. The poacher had seen Marlin's flashlight and took off, but he left behind a video camera mounted on a tripod, set to catch all of the action.

Even so, when Marlin took this evening's call from Jean, the dispatcher, he had a little trouble believing what he heard. "A deer suit? You've got to be kidding."

"That's what the caller said," Jean replied. "The ambulance is already on the way. And Sheriff Mackey."

"Six miles down Miller Creek Loop?" Marlin was making a mental note.

"Right. Look for the hole in the fence."

Marlin hung up and started to roll out of bed. Louise, still under the sheets, grabbed his arm. "You're not going to leave me hanging, are you?" She pushed out her lower lip in a mock pout. "

"'Fraid so. Duty calls."

Louise was a tall, blonde waitress at the Kountry Kitchen in Blanco. For six months, she and Marlin had enjoyed a series of passionate trysts. No strings attached—an arrangement that suited them both.

Marlin pulled on his khaki pants and his short-sleeved warden's shirt. It was late October, but the evening temperatures still averaged in the low seventies. As he looked for his boots, he told Louise what the dispatcher had reported.

She was equally intrigued. "That's over by the Circle S, right?"

"Yep. Miller Creek Loop is the southern border of the ranch, all the way out to the Pedernales River. From what Jean said, the guy's lying in one of Roy Swank's pastures."

Louise could pick up a trace of sadness in John Marlin's voice. Setting foot on that ranch, even at night, would bring back some bittersweet memories.

"You think Roy will be out there?" Louise asked.

"No idea. Don't really care." Marlin said as he strapped on his holster. Even without his revolver, Marlin was an imposing figure. Just over six foot two, with a broad chest and thick arms. Getting a little thick through the middle in the last few years, but he could still feel the hard muscles underneath. He had short black hair, a square jaw, and eyes that could make a veteran poacher drop a stringer of fish and run.

Marlin bent down to kiss Louise, who let the sheet fall to her waist. She grabbed one of his hands and playfully placed it on her breast.

"Hey, that's not fair," Marlin said softly.

"It's your choice. Roam around in the woods playing lawman, or stay here and write me up for some kind of violation." She put special emphasis on the word "violation."

Marlin smiled. "You know you can stay here if you want." He always offered. She always passed. Just the way they both wanted it.

Louise told him to be careful. Then John Marlin went outside, climbed in his state-issued Dodge Ram pickup, and headed out for the Circle S Ranch.

Ten minutes after John Marlin left, Louise let herself out, locking the door behind her. She got into her ten-year-old Toyota hatchback, checked herself in the mirror, and drove away.

Five minutes after that, a small, wiry man with a handlebar mustache slithered out from the crawl space underneath Marlin's small frame house. Marlin had a pair of floodlights at every corner of his house, so a passerby could have easily spotted the intruder. But the quiet country lane Marlin lived on was sparsely populated, so nobody saw the man.

He started at the front of the house, checking the doors and windows. Finding them all locked, he circled around the house and climbed the four steps to the back door. Standing on the small porch, he turned the knob and gently shoved the door with his shoulder, trying to force it open. No luck. He tried a little harder. The door wouldn't give. Pretty soon, the man began throwing himself against the door.

He stopped and took a breath, hands on his knees. After a minute, he faced the door again. He raised his right Wolverine work boot to waist level and began to kick the door with the bottom of his foot. The wooden porch shook with each blow.

With each kick, the man was backing up a little farther to get maximum force. On what was to be his last effort (whether he intended it that way or not), the man accidentally stepped backward off the porch, windmilling his arms wildly as he tumbled down the stairs. He landed hard, his head bouncing smartly on a large limestone rock in Marlin's rustic backyard. Anyone listening would have said the impact sounded like a shopper thumping a ripe melon.

At 10:15 p.m. on Thursday, October 28, Barney Weaver, Louise's exhusband, lay unconscious at John Marlin's back door.

The first thing John Marlin saw after winding his way down the familiar county road was a gauntlet of deputies' cars, volunteer firefighters' trucks, and two ambulances, one on each side of the road. Pulling through the chain of vehicles, he saw Sheriff Herbert Mackey leaning over the hood of his cruiser, leveling a rifle at the oat field on the Circle S Ranch. A deputy was training a spotlight on a massive white-tailed buck, not fifty yards away, prancing around in the field.

Marlin parked his truck and climbed out. As he approached the crowd surrounding the sheriff, he heard Mackey say, "Gentlemen, you're about to learn something about the fine art of marksmanship."

Several of the men murmured their approval.

"What's up?" Marlin said to the crowd in general.

Bill Tatum, one of the sheriff's deputies, answered. "Got a crazy buck on our hands, John. Wounded, too."

Marlin looked out at the buck. The animal seemed to know that a rifle was being aimed at it. The big deer would run quickly back and forth across the field and then come to an abrupt stop. Then it would bound on all four legs like a kid on a pogo stick. Marlin could occasionally glimpse a thin trail of dark-red blood running down one of the animal's forelegs.

"Looks like a flesh wound to me," Marlin said to nobody in particular. When no one responded, Marlin walked over and stood next to Sheriff Mackey. "Do you really think this is necessary, Herb?"

Marlin knew it bothered Sheriff Mackey when he called him by his abbreviated first name rather than his official title.

Mackey raised his large belly off the hood of his Chevy, spit a stream of tobacco juice at Marlin's feet and said, "Don't see as how I got a choice. Damn buck's gone nuts. Nearly gored us all when we were fetching Trey."

"Trey Sweeney?" Marlin wished someone would tell him the full story.

Bill Tatum spoke up again. "You know about the 911 caller, right? Well, Trey's the one in the deer costume." Tatum nodded toward one of the ambulances just departing. "He took a pretty good hit across the ribs, but he should be all right."

Marlin shook his head and grinned. Trey Sweeney was a state wildlife biologist and Blanco County native. Known for his eccentric behavior, Sweeney had gained national attention when he traveled to Yellowstone Park and holed up for three days with a hibernating black bear. His intention was to prove that the bears are not territorial and will attack only when their cubs or their food supply is threatened. After three days, Trey was certain that his theory was correct. Then the bear, apparently unaware of Trey's presence for the first seventy-two hours, awoke with a yawn, scratched his privates, and tore Trey's right ear off. (The chief reason Trey wore his hair long nowadays.) Trey still counted the whole episode as a victory, maintaining that the bear was only exhibiting post-hibernation playfulness. Nationally recognized wildlife authorities disagreed.

"So what's the story on the buck?" Marlin asked.

"Trey told us it was one of his test deer," Tatum said, referring to the small radio collars Trey had fitted on several deer on the ranch years earlier. The biologist had been conducting an ongoing study on the nocturnal movements of whitetails. "That's all he said. Except for asking us not to shoot it."

The crowd turned toward Sheriff Mackey, still holding his rifle. "That deer is obviously a danger to the community," Mackey said, feeling a little foolish as he looked around the isolated pasture.

Yeah, and he'd look damn good on your living-room wall, Marlin thought.

The sheriff shifted uneasily as the crowd remained silent. Most of the men were hunters and couldn't stand to see a deer killed in such an unsporting manner.

Finally the sheriff asked bitterly, "All right, then. Anyone else got any brilliant ideas?"

"I say we tranquilize him." Marlin said.

"You gotta be kidding. Then what? You gonna play like Sigman Fraud and ask him what's troubling him?" Several of the men smiled.

Marlin started to reply when one of the deputies spoke up. "Sheriff, I got Roy Swank on my cellular."

The sheriff opened his mouth as if to say something, then shuffled over to the deputy's car and grabbed the phone. The men could not hear the ensuing conversation, but Mackey gestured wildly several times. After a couple of moments, the sheriff returned with a tense look on his face.

"You win, smart boy," he said to Marlin. "That's one of Swank's trophies and he don't want it killed."

Marlin tried not to gloat, but he felt a sense of relief. Just being around Sheriff Mackey made him a little edgy. The man was obstinate, obnoxious, and downright rude. More than once they had butted heads over the finer letters of the hunting laws, chiefly because Mackey was one of the county's biggest poachers. Wordlessly, Marlin walked over to his vehicle and reached into the backseat of the extended cab. He took out a hard-sided gun case and removed the tranquilizer rifle inside. After loading it properly, he walked up to the fence, took aim, and made a perfect shot.

Rosemary Remembered

SUSAN WITTIG ALBERT

The Texas Hill Country is a favored destination for tourists, who come not only to enjoy the spring-fed rivers but also the charming towns, such as New Braunfels and Fredericksburg, founded by German immigrants in the nineteenth century. The Hill Country is also a favorite place for Texans to retire. It offers a slower-paced quality of life than the state's major cities, although the influx of new residents to the region has brought many big city issues, such as traffic, urban sprawl, and crime.

Pecan Springs is the fictional Hill Country town inhabited by herbalist-detective China Bayles. The series was created by Susan Wittig Albert, a former English professor and university administrator at Texas State University–San Marcos who left academia in 1985 to write full-time. In addition to her China Bayles series, Albert writes Beatrix Potter mysteries and Victorian mysteries with her husband Bill Albert under the pseudonym Robin Paige. She's also published several nonfiction books.

Albert's protagonist, China Bayles, has retired from a high-powered Houston law firm, yet she retains her feminist sensibilities. Her new home of Pecan Springs incorporates elements of several Hill Country cities—a Germanic cultural influence, a tourist-based industry, and a political schism between pro-growth and pro-conservation movements. In *Rosemary Remembered*, the fourth novel in the series, China Bayles has successfully reinvented herself as the owner of an herb shop, but her life is fractured by a series of murders.

The tourists flock to the century-old stone-and-timber buildings in the center of Pecan Springs like pigeons to a roost. (In fact, the City Council recently built a public potty behind the library to meet their basic needs, a move which is said to have been instigated by Henry Hoffmeister of Hoffmeister's Clothing & Dry Goods, who got tired of providing toilet paper and a flush for the masses.) They come to Pecan Springs not just for scenic beauty but for a nostalgic taste of small-town Texas, which the merchants ladle out liberally. The square is decorated with flags, red-white-and-blue bunting, and posters announcing that the streets will be roped off on Saturday evening for the square dance competition.

This morning, a small group of silver-haired ladies in summery dresses and white shoes were standing on the corner listening to Vera Hooper, the town docent. Wearing a denim skirt and yellow tee shirt hand-painted with green cacti, Vera was extolling the architectural wonders of the Adams County Courthouse, which was constructed a hundred years ago of 160 flatcar loads of pink granite, hauled in from Burnet County by rail. As I passed, Vera pointed across the street to the Sophie Briggs Historical Museum, which features (among other enticements) a dollhouse that once belonged to Lila Trumm, Miss Pecan Springs of 1936, as well as Sophie Briggs's collection of ceramic frogs. The Sophie Briggs Museum is a big draw in our town. It's amazing the interest people can have in ceramic frogs.

The square is the first stop on the Gingerbread Trail. After the ladies have admired the courthouse and availed themselves of the new public potty, they'll board an air-conditioned minibus, the Armadillo Special, and tootle south on Anderson Avenue to admire the fine old Victorian houses that line both sides of the street. Pecan Springs was settled by German immigrants in the 1840s, but the big building boom didn't come until the '90s. That's when the arrival of the railroad brought the money to build the courthouse, the gingerbread Victorians, the Grande Theater, and the Springs Hotel. An opulent era, but I'll bet the residents would have traded it all for central air-conditioning. I'll further bet that Vera Hooper's ladies wouldn't have been so enthusiastic about the Gingerbread Trail if they were required to hoof it, rather than riding the air-conditioned Armadillo Special.

I waved at Vera and headed down Anderson to Chisos Trail and made a right. A few blocks west, I drove into Pecan Park, a recently built development of expensive homes surrounded by synthetic green lawns, unnatural rock terraces, and landscaped garden pools. Pecan Park doesn't have much to do with Pecan Springs. As I drove along I was reminded of the Houston suburb where I used to live: green, serene, and empty. In fact, I'd be willing to bet that very few of the residents were around this morning to enjoy their upscale homes. Most of them probably had to work from before dawn to past dark to make enough money to pay their upscale mortgages.

Rosemary Robbins lived on a winding street a couple of blocks off Chisos Trail. Her house was set well back from the road behind a screen of cedar and yaupon holly, with a carefully arranged clump of purple crepe myrtle and plumy pampas grass surrounded by a bed of flaming red salvia, all heavily mulched with bark chips and without a single weed, compliments of Garcia's Garden Service. A cement drive looped behind the streetside clump of oaks and onto the street again. Through the trees, I could see McQuaid's Blue Beast, sitting sheepishly behind Rosemary's stylish gray Mazda. This was not the neighborhood where a battered old truck felt at home—or a twelve-year-old Datsun, either.

I swung into the drive, parked far enough behind The Beast to give myself maneuvering room, and got out. McQuaid had asked Rosemary to lock the truck and leave the key in the magnetic box under the fender. I wouldn't bother to knock on her door. I'd just get in the truck and drive off. McQuaid and I could pick up my Datsun this evening.

As I stepped out into the heat, the cicadas began a loud metallic drone. Their high-pitched crescendo was counter-pointed by the sardonic clucking of a yellow-billed cuckoo, the bird that Leatha, my mother, called a rain crow. When I hear that sinister clucking, I remember summer afternoons when I was ten, eleven, twelve, reading a book in my favorite tree, Leatha on a chaise lounge beneath me, her gin glass within easy reach. The rain crow is a bad-luck bird, Leatha always said, in her soft Southern drawl. When you hear it, watch out. Warnings like that were her defenses against the random perils of a world over which she had little control. Look for cars. Keep your hand on your purse. Lock the car doors. Don't let him touch you.

Perversely, I left the Datsun unlocked. I walked toward The Beast, wanting not to think of Leatha's warning—or of McQuaid's. Sure, Jacoby was a bad actor, and what he had done to his wife and mother-in-law was enough to curl anyone's hair. But Jacoby could be anywhere, Dallas or Houston or El Paso. Anyway, I reminded myself—or rather, the independent China reminded me—Jacoby wasn't the real issue. I slipped my hand under the fender and took out the magnetic key box. The real issue was a power issue. The real issue was—

No key. Well, no problem. Rosemary had probably left it under the seat. And if the truck was locked, I could knock at the door. Her Mazda was here, so she was still at home.

But the truck wasn't locked. What's more, it wasn't even shut. I pulled the door open and saw her.

Rosemary. On her right side across the vinyl seat, face turned up, empty eyes open, glassy, sightlessly staring. A neat, smooth, black hole under her left cheekbone, the seat under her head rusty with dried blood, furry with flies. Dark blood, like red ink, spattered all over the passenger side of the cab, the dash, the windshield. Blood and bits of something. Bits of the inside of Rosemary's head.

I gagged and stepped back. The cicadas were a hundred buzzing rattlers, the heat a hard, sweaty hand pressing on my head. I grabbed the door to steady myself, then yanked my hand back, hoping I hadn't smudged whatever prints there were.

After a minute I forced myself to look again, but not at Rosemary. The keys were in the ignition, Rosemary's purse on the floor, the wallet visible. A plastic grocery sack beside the purse spilled bars of soap, a carton of milk, a head of cabbage, all polka-dotted with blood. A Handy Jack Dry Cleaners bag full of clothing hung from the hook over the passenger door, blood-spattered. In the back of the truck I could see a gray metal file cabinet and a chair. Groceries, the dry cleaning, used furniture. Ordinary artifacts of ordinary, everyday life.

But for Rosemary Robbins, there was no more ordinary life, no life at all. The brassy rattle of the cicadas was suddenly swallowed up in her stillness. A sour sickness curdled in my throat. I swallowed it down and leaned over her body, clad in expensive beige slacks, creamy silk blouse, paisley scarf, to feel for a pulse at her throat. Nothing. Her skin was cool, her stillness utter, complete, final.

I looked down, feeling her separateness, sensing the absolute distance between us. Who had she been, this woman I had admired but barely known? What had empowered her, brought her pain, brought her peace? What had brought her to this terrible end? And I knew with sad certainty that it was only here, only now, in this last, quiet moment, that Rosemary Robbins could be whatever woman she was. In a little while, she would be the coroner's corpse, the cops' homicide, the DA's murder victim, the media's crime of the hour. Each of us, the living, would dissect her, construct her, imagine her, compose her as it suited our purposes, our needs. It was only in this moment, her death just discovered and not yet acknowledged, that she could be simply and purely herself, whoever she had been. Here, on the sly verge of death, I wished I had known her better.

I stepped back and took a deep breath, coming back to myself. Then I turned away and left the body in peace for the time it took to find a neighbor at home and call 911. When the PSPD showed up, I was beside the truck again, waiting, pacing, collecting observations: the door had been unlatched, the window was rolled up, unbroken, her wallet was still in her purse, there was no sign of a weapon. Unless the gun was out of sight beneath her, she hadn't committed suicide. If she'd been murdered, the killer must have shot her through the open door while she was sitting behind the wheel—last night, probably, just as she got home with her furniture, the groceries, the dry cleaning. I wondered whether she'd known what was about to happen. And wondered *why*, in God's name. Why Rosemary? My eyes, of their own accord, went to the spattered blood, the bits of flesh. Why, why?

The first cop on the scene was a slight, nervous brown-skinned man with large spaniel-brown eyes and a name badge that identified him as Gomez, H. He took one look at the body and ran back to the car to radio for assistance. A few minutes later a second cop arrived, Walker, G., a broad-shouldered woman with a competent jaw, a gritty voice, and a look of twitchy impatience, like a second-string offensive tackle with something to prove—Grace Walker, promoted a couple of months ago from prisoner attendant at the jail to patrol officer. Grace's mother, Sadie Stumb, works at Cavette's Grocery, on the corner of Guadalupe and Green. "That girl," Sadie always tells me proudly, as she rings up my fresh produce, "that Grace, she's goin' far. Ever'body better git outta her way."

Grace looked at Rosemary, then back at me. "Friend of yours?" She turned once again to peer closer. "Sister?"

"Sister?" I was surprised. "What makes you say that?"

Grace raised her heavy eyebrows in a facial shrug. "You look kinda alike. Brown hair, square sorta face."

"Not a sister," I said. "A friend." But that wasn't true, either. Rosemary Robbins and I hadn't been close enough to be friends, except in the most superficial sense. "A business associate, actually," I amended.

I glanced at the still face once again. I hadn't even known Rosemary well enough to know who would be sad, now that she was dead. Who would find the world empty, now that she wasn't in it?

"What kinda business?"

"She was my accountant. She did my taxes, handled my business accounts, stuff like that." I could hear a siren in the distance. More police were on the way.

"Taxes, huh?" Grace moved her shoulder in an economical gesture, expressing understanding. "Maybe somebody didn't get what they thought they had comin', and they took it out on her. I read the other day that accountants are always gettin' threats from people who think they been ripped off. Like lawyers, you know? Lawyers are always gettin' theirselves killed. Somebody just busts into the office and starts shootin'." She sighed and lifted her cap off her head, wiping her sweaty forehead. "Doesn't hardly pay to get ahead, does it?"

The police car pulled up at the curb, and we both turned. If this had been Houston, the vehicle would have been a Mobile Crime Scene Unit, a large white van equipped with state-of-the-art portable forensic technology and manned by a half-dozen criminalists. But this wasn't Houston, and Police Chief Bubba Harris had brought only two uniforms with him. One of them began to loop yellow crime-scene tape across the drive while the other unpacked camera gear. Bubba (his real name is Earl, but not even his mother uses it) conferred with Gomez for a moment, then with Grace Walker, putting them to work. Then he turned to me.

Bubba is in his mid-fifties, with hair going grizzled and a paunch that sags over his hand-tooled Western belt as if the last dozen plates of barbecue are still settling. His gray shirt was wet under the arms, and his unlit cigar—I've never actually seen it lit—was clamped in one corner of his mouth. He growled around it.

"McQuaid's truck, ain't it?"

I wasn't surprised that Bubba recognized The Beast. He and McQuaid, cop and ex-cop, have a fraternal relationship.

"I came to pick it up," I said. "Rosemary borrowed it yesterday evening about six to move some furniture she'd bought—what you see in the back of the truck. McQuaid offered to give her a hand, but she said she could handle it by herself." Typical Rosemary. She was the sort of woman who handled everything by herself. She didn't ask for a thing.

Bubba's heavily jowled face was dark, thick brows pulled down. Like most cops, he doesn't much like lawyers, even ex-lawyers. On the other hand, he likes McQuaid, and the fact that McQuaid likes me complicates the matter somewhat. Over the several years we have known one another, he has grown more tolerant of me.

"Any idea who might've done it?" he asked. "Assumin' she didn't do it to herself."

I shook my head. A flash flared as the photographer did his work. Grace Walker was hunkered down beside the door, dusting for prints. Gomez was beginning a search of the area around the truck. A fourth cop was motioning to a passing motorist who had stopped his car to gawk, directing him to drive on. Bubba turned to the truck and Grace straightened up and stepped aside. He felt rapidly and deftly under the body.

"Doesn't 'pear to be a gun," he said.

"Wouldn't hardly be, I don't reckon," Grace said dryly. "Wound on the left side and the angle the way it is, she'd almost have to hold it in her left hand. It'd be in her lap or on the floor, and it isn't."

Bubba did not seem pleased that a mere female had noticed these things, but he only grunted.

"Had her legs swung partway 'round like she was gettin' out," Grace went on. She was about to say something else, but Bubba turned away. The EMS van had just pulled up at the curb, followed by another car, a green Oldsmobile. Maude Porterfield, justice of the peace, got out of the Olds, conferred with the EMS techs for a minute, then came up the drive toward us, leaning on a cane.

In Texas, the law requires that a JP rule on every suspicious death. This requirement sometimes gives law enforcement officials heartburn, but not when the JP is Judge Porterfield. At seventy-three, she has served the county for forty-two years. Her white hair may be a little thin, but her hearing and her right knee are the only things about her that don't work at an optimum level. In addition to being a JP, she teaches criminal procedure in the seminars conducted by the Texas Justice Court Training Center, headquartered in the Criminal Justice Department at CTSU. Judge Porterfield and I had met at one of the center's social functions and hit it off immediately. As we say in Texas, she don't take no bull.

"Mornin', Earl," she said. "Hot as a pistol." She straightened the shiny belt of her red watermelon-print dress and nodded at me. "Mornin', China. How you been?" Without waiting for my answer, she switched back to Bubba. "Got a problem here, 'pears like."

Bubba plucked his cigar out of his face and raised his voice two notches. The judge wears a hearing aid in her right ear. "Mornin', Judge Porterfield. A shootin's what it is."

The judge, who isn't much more than five feet high, rose on her tiptoes to peer through the open door of the truck. She made a tch-tch noise with her tongue against even white dentures. "Suicide?"

"Murder," Bubba said.

"Domestic violence?"

Bubba looked at me. "The gal was married?"

"Her name is Rosemary Robbins," I said. "She was divorced, or about to be." Rosemary had mentioned the divorce in passing, but hadn't elaborated. Our encounters, while pleasant, had been focused on business and rather hurried. She was always checking her watch, as if she had to get on to another business engagement. It was a restless habit that had reminded me of myself, in my former life. "She was married to Curtis Robbins," I added, offering up the last bit of personal information I had.

Judge Porterfield pulled her sparse white eyebrows together. "Robbins? Manages Miller's Gun and Sporting Goods?"

Gomez came around the truck. "That's him," he said. "Too bad she didn't file a complaint when she had the chance."

"You been out here on a DV, Hector?" Bubba asked.

"Yeah. Back 'round Christmas. She phoned in a complaint, but by the time I got here, she'd decided not to press charges. Usual story."

The judge took a notebook out of her purse, which was red and shiny and shaped like a slice of watermelon. She looked at Gomez, obviously not accepting the "usual story" bit. "What did he say when you questioned him?"

Gomez colored. "He was gone, an' she didn't want me talkin' to him. Said she thought it might make him worse. She didn't want ever'body in town readin' in the paper 'bout her gettin' beat up."

Grace Walker shook her head gloomily. "Everybody'll be readin' about her now."

The judge looked from Grace to me. "She and Robbins have any kids?"

"Not as far as I know," I said. "She had a business. She was a CPA."

"Woman with a business probably doesn't want any kids," Grace remarked sagely.

Bubba gave her a warning look. "This their place?" he asked me.

I shook my head. "I don't think so. I got the impression she lived here alone. Her office is in the back of the house." That much I knew, because we'd met there to go over my tax stuff.

"Mebbe we better take a look at the office, Yer Honor," Bubba said.

Judge Porterfield sighed. "Right, Earl. It'll get us out of this gol-durn heat." She and Bubba walked toward the house.

Gomez blinked. "Earl?"

"She used to teach the chief in Sunday School when he was a kid," Grace said. "Earl's his real name."

"Earl," Gomez mused. "How 'bout that."

Grace turned to me. "You wanta give me your statement now, Miz Bayles?"

Armadillos and Old Lace

KINKY FRIEDMAN

The Texas Hill Country is home to numerous summer camps, where generations of Texas children have frolicked among the scenic hills and clear-running streams. One such place is Echo Hill Ranch, between Kerrville and Medina, which was founded by Tom and Minnie Friedman in the early 1950s. What distinguishes Echo Hill Ranch from other camps is the presence of a singular Texan, one of the Lone Star State's most outlandish personalities—Kinky Friedman.

Kinky Friedman first captured national attention in the 1970s as the lead singer of his own country and western band, Kinky Friedman and his Texas Jewboys. Kinky proved to be an equal opportunity offender, singing outrageously offensive classics such as "They Ain't Making Jews Like Jesus Anymore" and his paean to feminism "Get Your Biscuits in the Oven and Your Buns in the Bed." Friedman also gained attention in the 1980s when he ran for justice of the peace in Kerrville. Then he pledged, "If you elect me your first Jewish justice of the peace, I'll reduce the speed limit from 55 miles per hour to 54.95." Friedman lost that race, but, undeterred, he returned to politics again in 2005, announcing his candidacy for governor of Texas with the slogan, "How Hard Could It Be?"

In the early 1980s, Kinky Friedman began publishing a series of comic mystery novels that feature a C & W musician-turned-detective named, appropriately enough, Kinky Friedman. Most novels revolve around the Greenwich Village neighborhood where Friedman lived at the time. However, his novel *Armadillos and Old Lace* finds Kinky returning to solve a series of murders at his old stomping grounds—his parents' Echo Hill Ranch.

It was late in the afternoon when I finally arrived in San Antonio, but the weather was still hotter than a stolen tamale. It reminded me of my days with the Peace Corps working in the jungles of Borneo as an agricultural extension worker. My job had been to distribute seeds upriver to the natives. In two and a half years, however, the Peace Corps never sent me any seeds. In the end, I had to resort to distributing my own seed upriver, which had some rather unpleasant repercussions. But I loved the tropics and seldom complained about the weather in Texas. Without it, no one would ever be able to start a conversation.

I breezed through the corridor to the gate and on into the terminal past straw cowboy hats, belt buckles as big as license plates, happy Hispanic families. At the Dallas-Fort Worth airport, where I'd gotten off the plane briefly to smoke a cigar, the women all had that blonde, pinched look halfway between Morgan Fairchild and a praying mantis. The men at DFW appeared to have come in on a wing and a prayer themselves.

They'd looked well fed and fairly smarmy, like so many secular Jimmy Swaggarts. At the San Antonio airport the people looked like real Texans. Even the one Hare Krishna had a nice "Y'all" going for him.

Greyhound bus stations, I reflected as I passed long rows of television chairs all individually tuned to "Ironsides," used to tell you a lot about the character of a town. Today, it's airports. All bus stations tell you anymore is the character of the local characters, and there's damn few of them left these days in most places. I wasn't even sure if I was still one myself.

I waited at the baggage claim for a period of time roughly comparable to the length of the Holy Roman Empire.

"What comes around goes around," I said to a man who was dressed as either a pimp or an Aryan golfer.

"True story," he said. "Last time I went to New Jersey the airline sent all my luggage to Las Vegas."

"Sounds like your toilet kit had more fun than you did," I said.

We waited.

Eventually, with suitcase, guitar, and pet carrier in hand, I strolled onto the sun-blinded San Antonio sidewalk like a lost mariachi and gazed around for anybody wearing an Echo Hill T-shirt. The cat gazed around, too. She had not taken the trip very well, apparently, and at the moment, appeared to be pissed off enough to scratch out the eyes of Texas.

If someone is late to meet you in New York it is cause for major stress and consternation. But Texas is close enough to Mexico to have absorbed by some kind of cultural osmosis a healthy sense of *mañana*. In the old days at the ranch, my brother Roger always used to throw any leftover food on anybody's plate out in the backyard. "Somethin'll git it," he'd say.

In the same way, I knew someone would get me. The cat did not seem to share my confidence. She made loud, baleful noises and scratched unpleasantly at the bars of the cage. Several passersby stopped briefly to stare at us.

"Don't make a scene," I said. "We'll be at the ranch in about an hour."

The cat continued making exaggerated mournful moaning noises and clawing at the cage. The new vice president of the Nosey Young Women's Society came by and bent down over the pet carrier.

"Is he being mean to you?" she said to the cat. "Did he make you fly in that little cage?"

"We're both on medication," I said. "We've just returned from a little fact-finding trip to Upper Baboon's Asshole."

She left in a vintage 1937 snit.

I took a cigar out of a looped pocket in my lightweight summer hunting vest, began prenuptial arrangements, and, after all preparations were complete, I fired it up with a kitchen match. Always keeping the tip of the cigar well above the flame. I sat down on a cement bench and, for the next ten minutes or so, I watched the wheels go round, as John Lennon would say. Then I got up and stretched my legs a bit until I was almost vivisected by a Dodge Dart. The bumper sticker on the Dodge, I noticed, read: "Not a Well Woman."

Suddenly, there was a horn honking and somebody yelling "Kinkster!" I gazed over and saw a familiar-looking gray pickup with a familiar-looking smiling head sticking out of it. Both the truck and the head were covered with dust. It was Ben Stroud, a counselor at the ranch.

"You came a little early," said Ben.

"That's what she told me last night," I said, as I put the guitar and suitcase in back and the cat in front and climbed in next to Ben, who was drinking a Yoo-Hoo. Ben was not tall but he was large and loud. In Texas, you had to be large and loud. Even if you were an autistic midget. *Especially* if you were an autistic midget.

"What's new at the ranch?" I asked.

"We're still having borientation, said Ben. "The kids don't arrive for a few more days."

I settled back in the cab and entertained a brief vision of the ranchers, as we called them, arriving in a cloud of dust on chartered buses. The old bell in front of the ranch office would be ringing. A small group of counselors, all wearing Echo Hill T-shirts, would be milling about, waiting for their charges in the afternoon sun. Uncle Tom, my dad, would be bringing the buses in, as always, walking in front of them motioning with his arms in the confident, stylish manner of someone leading a cavalry brigade. Uncle Tom would be wearing a light blue pith helmet that looked as if he borrowed it from someone in a Rudyard Kipling story. Tom, who was much loved and respected by the ranchers, counselors, and me, had a great attachment to tradition. It seemed at times that he borrowed himself from a Rudyard Kipling story.

"Tom's assigned me as his director of external relations," said Ben. "That means I drop the laundry in town every morning and bring back his paper for him."

"Hey," I said, "that was supposed to be my job! Now I'm an unemployed youth."

"Oh, I don't know about that. You'll be helping me out. I think you may be plenty busy with other things, too. Pat Knox called Uncle Tom yesterday. She wants to talk to you. It sounds like some pretty mysterious shit."

Pat Knox was the feisty little justice of the peace in Kerr County who'd beaten me for the job some years ago in a hotly contested campaign. One of the other unsuccessful candidates had chopped up his family collie with a hatchet two weeks before the election. He'd still received eight hundred votes.

"What the hell does Pat Knox want?" I said. "Isn't she busy enough marrying people and going around certifying dead bodies?"

"I think that's what she wants to talk to you about."

"Marrying people?"

"No," said Ben. "Dead bodies."

The truck was zooming along headed west on I-10 through the graceful, gently rolling green hills. In the sky ahead of us, backlit by a brilliant, slowly dying sun, we could see an inordinately large number of buzzards circling. They moved methodically, timelessly, as if imbued with ghastly, fateful purpose.

"You'd be crazy to get involved," said Ben.

"Maybe I am crazy," I said. "You know what Carl Jung said: 'Bring me a sane man and I will cure him.'"

"Maybe," said Ben, "Carl Jung will help us with the laundry."

✪

Halfway to Kerrville along I-10 Ben took a left on a smaller road. The cat and I went through periods of dreamtime as we passed a number of small towns on the way to the ranch. Pipe Creek: so named because a local settler over a hundred years ago ran back into his burning cabin to fetch his favorite pipe after an Indian attack. Bandera: "the Cowboy Capital of the World," where Ben and I stopped at the Old Spanish Trail Restaurant and had dinner in the John Wayne Room. The John Wayne Room's sole motif, other than an old covered wagon used as a salad bar and two defunct pinball machines, was fifty-seven photos, pictures, sketches, and sculptures of John Wayne. This thematic approach led to a rather macho orientation among the regulars, and did not serve particularly well as a digestive aid to the occasional traveling butterfly collector from Teaneck, New Jersey.

I had the Mexican Plate and Ben ordered "The Duke," a chicken fried steak approximately the size and appearance of a yellow-and-white-streaked beach umbrella. Many of our fellow diners wore straw cowboy hats and belt buckles the size of license plates. Possibly they were on their way to the San Antonio airport.

By the time we walked out of the O.S.T., dusk was falling over the old western town. We headed up Highway 16 toward Medina. I offered the cat a few residual pieces of "The Duke," but she demurred.

We rode to Medina in silence. Medina was a very small town that had been dying for over a hundred years and actually seemed to almost thrive on that notion. Sometime back in Old Testament days, it had voted not to serve alcoholic beverages. It was open to some debate whether this policy had caused the town's long decline, or whether it had been responsible for eliciting God's favor in enabling the place to die so successfully for so long.

"Stop for a drink?" I said to Ben.

"You kiddin'? I doubt if they'd even let me recycle my Yoo-Hoo."

I thought briefly of what our longtime friend Earl Buckelew, who'd lived in the area for over seventy years, once said about the place: "Medina is as dry as a popcorn fart."

"This town is so small," I said to the cat, "that if you blink you won't even see it."

The cat blinked.

Medina wasn't there.

We drove a number of miles farther down 16, then took a left and rolled in a cloud of dust across a cattle guard, down a country road, and into the sunset toward Echo Hill. The ranch was set back about two and a half miles from the scenic little highway, but ever since we passed Pipe Creek we'd been in a world that most New Yorkers never got to see. They believed the deer, the jackrabbits, the raccoons, the sun setting the sky on fire in the west, the cypress trees bathing their knees in the little creek, the pale moon shyly peeking over the mountain—they believed these things only really existed in a Disney movie or a children's storybook. I closed my eyes for a moment, turned a page in my mind. When I opened my eyes again everything was still there. Only New York was gone.

We splashed through a water crossing and two more cattle guards, then turned where the sign said Echo Hill Ranch. Ben drove across a small causeway, then deposited me and the cat and our belongings in front of an antique green trailer that looked like it might've once been the object of a failed timeshare arrangement between John Steinbeck and Jack Kerouac. Clearly, it wasn't going anywhere else again, geographically speaking. I felt as much at home as a jet-set gypsy has any right to feel.

I opened the door of the trailer, brushed away a few cobwebs, and turned on a lamp. A happy little raccoon family had apparently been living there over the winter.

"If they want to stay," I said to the cat, "they'll have to pay rent."

The cat said nothing, but it was obvious that she was not amused. In fact, I'd long held a theory that the cat hated every living thing except me. She was ambivalent about me. And that was a nice word for it.

I opened the cage and the cat warily looked out. In a moment she emerged and appeared to gaze in some disgust around the little trailer. It was getting more decrepit every summer, and one of these days even I was going to realize that man can't live on funk alone. The cat stayed a few seconds longer, then shot out the open door like a bottle-rocket.

"What'd you expect," I shouted after her. "A condo?"

She'd be back, I thought. Certain cats and certain women always come back. The trouble is that no man is ever quite certain which ones they are.

I lay down on my bunk to take a quick power nap before going up to the lodge to see Tom and say hello to everybody. Ben had said that Tom was having a borientation meeting with the staff in the dining hall. I figured I might do the same for a while here in the trailer. Orient myself to the sound of crickets instead of traffic. Before I closed my eyes I noticed on the far wall that the large framed pictures of Hank Williams and Mahatma Gandhi were still hanging there side by side. They were a little dusty and off-center, but who wasn't that ever did anything great? They stared down at me and I met their cool gaze. Then I closed my eyes for a moment and, from the afterimages of the two faces, little karmic hummingbirds seemed to fly to my pillow.

When I opened my eyes again Hank was smiling at me with that sad spiritually copyrighted crooked smile and Gandhi's eyes were twinkling like the helpless stars above us all. Just before I fell asleep, I recalled, for some reason, what John Lennon had repeatedly asked the Beatles during their meteoric rise to fame: "Did we pass the audition, boys?"

✪

I woke up from my power nap to find that the cat had not returned. I put on my boots and headed up to the lodge. Across the nighttime Texas skies someone had unrolled a shimmering blanket of stars. I walked up the little hill toward the lights of the lodge. My father was sitting in an ancient red-wood chair on the front lawn, staring into the darkness. He'd made a lot of wishes in seventy years and some of them had come true.

He'd seen thousands of boys and girls grow up here over the years. Many of them had gone away into the grown-up world imbued with an intangible gift my mother, Aunt Min, had called the "Echo Hill Way." The world, in all this time, had not really become a different or a better place. But the world, as most people knew it, stopped at the Echo Hill cattle guard. Here, everybody was somebody. Everybody had fun. Everybody got to first base once in their lives. Many would, no doubt, be picked off later, but at least they'd had a chance.

Many of the early architects of the "Echo Hill Way" were now among the missing and missed. My mother had died in 1985. Uncle Floyd Potter, my high school biology teacher and, for many years, our nature-study man, went to Jesus soon after that. Floyd's wife, Aunt Joan, had helped direct the camp for as long as I could remember. Her birthday, August 18, fell on the same date as Min and Tom's anniversary. They had all been very close. Close as the cottonwoods standing by the river.

Slim, too, had passed, as some colloquially refer to dying. Slim had washed dishes, served the "bug juice," and drank warm Jax beer as he listened to the Astros lose a million ball games on his old radio. Death is always colloquial.

Doc and Aunt Hilda Phelps had been the first to go. They'd always been older, I suppose. Doc was Tom's friend from the air force days who helped Tom and Min start the ranch. Hilda, his Australian wife, had taught hand-icrafts at Echo Hill, and, when I was six years old, had taught me "Waltzing Matilda." For several years I sang the song as "Waltzing with Hilda."

There were many ghosts at Echo Hill, but most of them were friendly. They mixed in quite gracefully with the dust and the campfire smoke and the river and the stars.

Tom was almost all that was left now of the old days. He looked out over the beautiful valley, now quiet except for the horses and the deer. The lights of some of the cabins twinkled merrily. Laughter drifted down from the dining hall, where my sister Marcie was still meeting with some of the counselors. It was hard to believe that within a few days over a hundred kids would be running around the place. It was hard to believe that forty years had gone by and Echo Hill was still the same. Only the names had been changed to protect the innocent.

I opened the gate and walked up the path. Sam, Tom's myopic Jewish shepherd, barked furiously, ran at me, and came within a hair of biting my ass before he recognized me and smiled like a coal-scuttle.

"Sambo!" Tom shouted. "Pick on someone your own size."

"That dog keeps eating like a boar hog," I said as I hugged my father, "we'll have to get him a golf cart."

"Sam's doing fine," said Tom. "Large mammals always put on a little weight in the winter."

Tom would never hear a bad word about Sam. In truth, Sam was a wonderful dog. Tom had gotten him from the pound in the year following my mother's death, and Sam had been a friend indeed. He was a terrific, possibly overzealous watchdog who scared most visitors within an inch of their lives, but he loved children. The only people he hated were teenage boys, people in uniforms, and Mexicans. "What can I say?" Tom had once offered after Sam had chased a Mexican worker onto the roof of the pickup truck. "The dog's a racist."

Tom had put on a little weight himself over the year, adding to an already protuberant abdomen, but he could still whip almost all comers in tennis. Other than an extremely large gut, which he did not recognize he had, he looked very fit and virile.

We talked for a while about the ranch, the staff, the upcoming summer, and, finally, the conversation worked its way around to another matter.

"You got a rather strange message on the machine today from Pat Knox. I still think she did you the greatest favor of your life by keeping you from being elected justice of the peace in Kerrville."

"Yeah," I said. "That could've been ugly. It's a good thing my fellow Kerrverts returned me to the private sector."

"If you'd won that job, what would you have done with it?"

"Pretty much what I'm doing now," I said.

"That's what I was afraid of," said Tom.

I took out a cigar, lopped the butt off, and achieved ignition. I puffed a few easygoing puffs and gazed out over the flat.

"Doesn't the ranch look beautiful?" Tom said.

"Sure does," I said, staring down the quiet, peaceful line of bunkhouses, which appeared to be bracing themselves for an onslaught of shouting, boisterous ranchers. "So what did Pat Knox want?"

"I have no idea," said Tom. "It was strange. She said some things were happening that she didn't understand. She sounded very upset about it. She said she needed to talk to a man of your talents."

"Musical?"

Tom laughed. "Not unless she wants you to perform at somebody's funeral. From her tone, it sounds pretty serious. When she mentioned 'a man of your talents,' I think she must've been referring to some of your forays into crime-solving in New York."

I took a few more thoughtful puffs on the cigar and watched the moon rising over the mountain. "Or," I said, "she may just want me to drop off her laundry."

PART 3

HOUSTON AND THE GULF COAST

Heat from Another Sun

DAVID L. LINDSEY

Houston is not only Texas's largest metropolis but, befitting a port
city, its most multicultural—a "Babel on the Bayou"—where one is as
likely to encounter a turban as a cowboy hat. Houston's Anglo Americans have become a numerical minority in recent years. Among the
fastest-growing ethnic groups are the Vietnamese, who began to arrive following the collapse of South Vietnam in 1975. Houston's Vietnamese population is now the largest in the United States outside of
California, and Vietnamese bookstores, restaurants, street signs, and
radio stations attest to the thriving local culture. In 2004, Houston's
Vietnamese community participated in one of the most shocking election upsets in Texas history, as Vietnamese American businessman
Hubert Vo unseated a seemingly well-entrenched incumbent, a con-
servative Anglo American Republican.

Houston and its polyglot urban landscape are brilliantly mapped
out by Austin novelist David L. Lindsey in his five noir mysteries featuring HPD homicide detective Stuart Haydon. Lindsey has also written several other novels, including the stand-alone suspense novel
Mercy, which is also set in Houston, as well as best-selling international thrillers and psychological suspense books.

Heat from Another Sun, the second book in the Haydon series, in-
volves a mysterious Chinese American journalist, a reclusive multimil-
lionaire with kinky viewing habits, and Salvadoran death squads. As
always, the urbane Haydon's investigation leads him from the posh
enclaves of Houston's elite to the city's immigrant neighborhoods.

Haydon left the Vanden Plas in the parking lot of Brennan's, which was just around the corner from Primo's, and rode with Mooney, who took the department car along Westheimer and then north on Montrose. Allen Parkway was a broad curving boulevard that lay on the southern bank of Buffalo Bayou on the northwestern edge of downtown. On the other side of the bayou was Memorial Drive, and in between the two was a beautiful greenbelt of parks with hike and bike trails that ran from downtown west, and almost all the way to the vast reaches of Memorial Park. Both streets represented the most appealing routes from the skyscrapers toward the ritzy neighborhoods west.

The Allen Parkway Village was a rather attractive name for an unattractive forty-year-old deteriorating public housing project that sat on thirty-seven acres of prime Houston real estate between downtown and, a little farther in the opposite direction, River Oaks. The project was a festering scab on the northern edge of the Fourth Ward, the city's oldest black community, itself sliding deeper into dereliction. The sprawling complex of orange brick apartments was once largely occupied by blacks, but with the first wave of immigrants fleeing Vietnam in 1975 the Village became predominantly Indo-Chinese. Now nearly three thousand Vietnamese lived in the dilapidated warrens of the project.

It had been a year since the Houston Housing Authority had voted to raze the projects, which had been a controversial eyesore longer than some people wanted to remember, and make the land available for development. Being just across the Gulf Freeway from high-dollar downtown real estate, the rotting slum was in a location that was strategically appealing to developers. But it would be still another year before the residents were moved, and in the meantime there was no great interest by the Housing Authority to maintain even minimal repairs to buildings which had for so long sapped the city's coffers and were already hopelessly deteriorated.

Mooney pulled off Allen Parkway into the project's streets, slowly working his way toward the center, toward Hoang's apartment. After a few turns he pulled to the curb.

"We'd better walk from here," he said.

They got out and locked the car. The projects had an unhealthy reputation for gangs of teenagers, who roamed the neighborhood vandalizing and testing their ability to run petty extortion rackets. This was in imitation of a larger, citywide problem within the Asian community, which was the second largest in the nation. The Chinese tongs were well established in Houston's crime world. They were organized and efficient, and their members commanded a fearful respect within the Chinese community. They were known as "the gentlemen." The Vietnamese gangsters, however, required and received no such respect. They were considered little more than thugs and hoodlums by their own people. Their influence was supported solely by the fear they engendered within the community, which effectively sealed the lips of their fellow Vietnamese victims, making police investigation almost impossible. Though their organization differed from the Chinese, it was a potent force. The four or five gangs that dominated the Vietnamese underworld in Houston had direct links to the Oriental syndicates in New Orleans, Los Angeles, and San Francisco.

The two men moved along a potholed street that served both as a parking area and a sidewalk. A series of short straight cement walks ran under a maze of sagging clotheslines and up to the stoops of the apartments. The doors and windows of the apartments were open, and the aroma of Oriental cooking floated in the gummy night air along with the lilting tonal monosyllables of Vietnamese dialects. In the splashes of light that came out of the apartments, Haydon could see that some of the bare front yards had been turned into little plots of vegetable gardens, their small neat rows presenting a sane orderliness in the sad disorderliness of the declining buildings.

They passed two boys smoking on the hood of a car and cut across a yard and between two buildings. They came out next to an abandoned refrigerator and another block of stoops. Mooney ducked under a couple of clotheslines and approached a ragged screen door. A radio was playing, and Dolly and Kenny were singing "Islands in the Stream."

Mooney knocked on the doorframe. A little boy came from the dim interior.

"Hey, buddy. Remember me?" Mooney asked, bending down. The boy grinned broadly. "Your daddy in yet?" The boy nodded and disappeared. "I don't know if this guy's his daddy or not," Mooney said under his breath.

Silently a man appeared at the door.

"Hoang Lam?" Mooney asked. The man nodded. "Good, good," Mooney said grinning. "I'm a friend of old Ricky's. He was supposed to meet me tonight in a taxicab, but he never showed up. Somebody told me you owned the cab and that you might know where Ricky went to."

The man looked at Mooney soberly. The little boy came up and stood beside him, and the man put his arm around his neck.

"Why you try to fool me?" Hoang asked. "I don't have anything to fear from police."

Even in the frail light Haydon could see Mooney's embarrassment.

Mooney took out his shield and showed it to the man. "Okay, you win. How'd you know I was a cop?"

The man's slight shoulders rose and fell, and he smiled faintly.

"You are looking for Mr. Toy? He has my taxicab. That is all I know."

Haydon moved up on the stoop and held out his shield too.

"I'm Detective Haydon, Mr. Hoang. Why does Mr. Toy have your car?"

Hoang pushed open the screen door a little ways and looked up and down the courtyard.

"Come in, please, sirs," he said, and spoke sharply to the little boy, who ran over to the radio and turned it off. The room had only a concrete floor, a sofa, and two wooden chairs. There was a reed mat to one side and several overturned paint buckets used for additional chairs. A hand-painted picture of a tropical moonlight scene hung over the sofa, small and lost on the bare wall.

Hoang motioned for Haydon and Mooney to sit on the wooden chairs. He sat on the sofa, on its edge, and his little boy stood beside him, his dark eyes glued to Mooney.

"We are very poor now," Hoang said matter-of-factly. "But we work very hard and everything is very okay. We will not always be poor."

Mooney squirmed on the chair.

"My family want to be good Houston citizen. We want to help the police. But must be careful. Is my friend Mr. Toy in trouble?"

"We think his life might be in danger," Haydon said. "He's missing. We're trying to find him."

Hoang nodded seriously and looked at them.

"Why did he have your taxi?" Haydon repeated.

"The taxi belong to me, my brother Danh and Du. We drive the taxi in turn, eight hour for each one. The taxi never stop. This very good. Ricky Toy ask me to have my taxicab tonight. He pay more I make driving. That is all."

"When did Mr. Toy get your taxi?"

"One of his girlfriend come and drive it away about three o'clock."

"What was her name?"

"Yue."

"You spoke to her?"

"Oh, yes."

"She didn't say what they were going to do with the taxi?" Mooney asked.

"No."

"Where were you earlier tonight?"

Hoang looked at Mooney with curiosity, then answered. "I borrow car to get my son and friend at Chinatown movie."

"How long have you known Mr. Toy?" Haydon asked.

Hoang's eyes widened as he thought, looking at nothing out the screen door. "One year."

"How did you meet him?"

"I get him at Hobby in taxi. He see I am Vietnamese. He tell me he is there many time. We learn we are in many same place same time. That make us feel like friend. We talk for long time. Now he call me when he want taxi."

"How often is that?"

Hoang smiled. "Mr. Toy don't need taxi. He has two very good car. But sometime he take taxi I think to give me work."

"Where do you take him?" Mooney asked.

"Oh, maybe Chinatown." Hoang was cautious, his eyes floating away.

"Where in Chinatown?"

"Different place. To eat. Other thing."

"Does Ricky Toy go to the illegal gambling clubs there?"

Hoang raised his eyebrows, his eyes diverted. "I think so," he said softly.

"Does he go alone?"

Hoang was very uncomfortable with the questioning now.

"Sometime," he said.

"Do the girls go with him?"

Hoang lifted his shoulders in a half shrug.

"Sometime," he said.

"Both girls?"

This time Hoang just looked at them with no reaction, seeming to be waiting politely for the next question.

"Have you ever seen him with an Anglo, with someone not Asian?"

Hoang shook his head.

"When did you see him last?" Haydon asked.

"One week ago. Yes."

"You took him somewhere?"

"Oh, yes."

"Where?"

"Chinatown."

"Where in Chinatown?"

Hoang shook his head. "No place."

"Was it an old building? A warehouse?"

Hoang nodded. "I think maybe. Yes."

"Was Toy alone?"

"No."

"Who was with him?"

"One of his girlfriend."

"Were they carrying cameras?" Haydon asked.

Hoang's eyebrows went up again. "Oh, yes."

"Do you remember where you took him, Mr. Hoang? Could you find it again?"

"I think so."

"Could you take us there?"

"Tonight?"

"Right now."

Hoang thought about this a moment, then said, "Excuse me." He stood and left the room. Mooney quickly pulled out his wallet and got two dollars, which he handed across to the boy and winked. The boy took the money and looked at him without any change of expression, as if he suspected there was still a catch to it that he didn't understand and that Mooney was just as likely to take the money back again.

"It is very okay," Hoang said, coming back into the room. He had a worried look on his face as if, in fact, it was not very okay at all.

They traveled down Dallas Street and then cut across the southern tip of downtown on Clay until they passed under the Highway 59 expressway and entered Chinatown. Houston's Chinatown did not consist of narrow, densely populated streets and alleyways teeming with people and flashing neon lights like those in San Francisco or New York. Though Houston's Asian population was enormous, like everything else in the city it was spread out. Besides Asian enclaves here and in Allen Parkway Village, there were others along Bissonet near Bellaire, in the Taum-Milam streets area known as Little Vietnam south of downtown, and still another major grouping in Missouri City far south. But Chinatown was the oldest of these enclaves and occupied a topography typical of warehouse districts everywhere, mostly single-story commercial establishments scattered among littered vacant lots and dreary warehouses that once served thriving rail freight activity.

There were two triple-spurred rail sidings surrounded by warehouses in the immediate area between Clay, Dowling, and the expressway. When

Hoang was confronted with the choice of the two locations, he was not sure which of the two had been Toy's destination. They had to cruise through both of them several times before Hoang recognized a landmark and pulled Mooney off the street and onto the crushed-shell driveway of a brick warehouse. It appeared to be abandoned but was directly across from one of the sets of loading docks that flanked each of the three rail spurs. Looking through the windshield from the back seat, Hoang declared that he was sure this was it.

Haydon and Mooney took flashlights from under the seats, and the three men got out of the car and locked it. Haydon and Hoang went to the front door, while Mooney circled the building to see if there was anything immediately suspicious. By the time he got back to the front door, Haydon had gotten a tire tool out of the trunk of the car and wrenched off the padlock that was slipped through the hasp above the doorknob. He pushed the door open, and they went inside.

It was dark except for a cobwebby glow coming through a row of small windows glazed with years of dust and soot near the ceiling on either side of the vast warehouse. The building's flat tar roof had trapped the killing temperatures of the long day's sun, and the heat inside was oppressive. It smelled of wooden skids and shipping crates, of old mortar, yellowed newspapers, and something else.

Haydon turned his flashlight upward, at the bare light bulb hanging from a frazzled wire. A string hung down from the socket. He reached up and pulled it, and a weak yellow light fell on their faces and the stacks and rows of crates. Shadows jittered back and forth from the swinging bulb.

Mooney looked around and took five or six steps away from the light into the warehouse. He turned and looked back.

"Goddamn, Stuart. This is it."

There was an irregular corridor formed by the rows of crates leading farther toward the center of the warehouse. The weak light of the bare bulb penetrated only a short way into it. Haydon flipped on his flashlight again and started into the corridor. There were little narrow aisles branching off in several places, but they were far too small and awkward for half a dozen men to maneuver easily. Haydon stuck to the wide passage as it turned and switched directions. Because the floor of the warehouse was completely covered with packing crates reaching far above his head, Haydon kept his bearings as to his location in the building by shining the light at the ceiling where the walls converged with the roof. Occasionally they would come upon piles of rubbish, strong with the pungent odor of urine, where a transient had bedded down. The deeper they went into the maze of aisles, the more vicious the heat. Sweat pulled at their clothes.

They heard the sound before they actually got to the open space. It was only a faraway whisper at first, almost a remembrance of a sound, but they were aware of it. As they moved on, approaching the end of their search though they were unaware of it, the sound grew distinctive, like a great vibration of millions of small wings.

They rounded the corner at the same moment Haydon identified the odor.

"Blood," he said, and their flashlights lit an open area of unspeakable carnage, great swaths of it working with swarms of black flies, grubbing among themselves to get to the source of attraction. Haydon had never seen so much gore, on the floor and splattered on the packing crates that formed the three-sided cul-de-sac nearly twenty feet square in the center of the warehouse. Inside the cul-de-sac the stench was overwhelming.

"Jesus God," Mooney said. "I don't believe this."

Haydon moved farther into the cul-de-sac. Some of the blood was old and black, and the flies mostly avoided it. But in other areas, on the cement floor especially, such huge quantities had been spilled that large smears of it, though undoubtedly drying in the intense heat of the warehouse, were still attractive to the flies and had been ripe enough for breeding grounds. A moil of waxy maggots worked beneath the rind of glossy black flies.

"What in God's name happened here?" Mooney said. He had taken out a handkerchief and was holding it over his mouth and nose.

Haydon moved the beam of his flashlight to the far side of the cul-de-sac and slowly brought it around, following the seam where the stacks of crates met the floor. The beam was more than halfway around to them when a small object caught Haydon's eye, and he stopped the light on it.

"What's that?" Mooney said. He stepped across in front of Haydon and carefully made his way toward the object, negotiating the irregular verge of the blood. Without thinking, he bent down and reached to pick it up. Even while he was still in the motion of crouching, an uncharacteristic bleat of horror came from his throat as he tried to get away from it, falling hard against the crates. Before he could stand he was retching, coughing, coming at Haydon, getting out of the cul-de-sac.

"Nose," he choked. "Nose." And he pushed past Haydon and an astonished Hoang. They could hear him vomiting in the darkness of the aisle behind them.

Haydon stared at the black object in the center of the beam and, with a peculiarly clinical detachment, observed the actual sensation of a cold breath start between his shoulder blades and creep up the sides of his neck.

Interstate Dreams

NEAL BARRETT, JR.

Houston overtook Los Angeles as America's smoggiest city in 1999.
The air in Houston has become so poisonous that, at times, schoolchildren are kept inside during recess periods. A major contributor
to Houston's air pollution is the exhaust from millions of cars in the
metropolitan area. Predictably, in a state that forswears mass transit,
Houston's traffic congestion is among the worst in the country.

Houston's urban sprawl becomes another outpost in the bizarre
kingdom of Neal Barrett, Jr., an Austin writer whose oeuvre could be
described as "Chicken Fried Magic Realism." Barrett has written several mysteries, science fiction, and fantasy novels, drawing raves from
his writing peers while remaining too little known among the general
public.

Barrett's novel *Interstate Dreams* falls loosely—all Barrett's works
seem to fall loosely—into the category of "caper" novel popularized
by Donald E. Westlake. Here, an army veteran named Dreamer carries a metal plate in his head as a result of a war injury sustained in
Panama. Curiously, Dreamer's malady allows him to see vivid colors
in his head, and to also neutralize all known security devices. This
fact complicates his quiet life as a tropical fish store owner. With the
help of his African American sidekick, Junior Lewis, Dreamer uses his
special powers to recover a stolen object. In the following excerpt, the
two men are setting out on their quest. But first they have to get out of
Houston traffic.

In the burgundy-colored van, the white man smoked and sorted colors in his head. Waited for a neat chromatic fix that might reveal the facts of life. Why cats don't seem to give a shit. Why girls don't like to fish. These would be good things to know, things that might lead to a better life for all.

The black man drove and watched the road. Didn't just *drive* like an ordinary man, like a man going down to the 7-Eleven store. Junior Lewis drove with heart, drove with his soul linked directly to the road. Driving was the second best thing he liked to do.

Dreamer didn't like to drive. He lacked dedication to the wheel, but he understood another man's needs. He liked to sit back and put his feet on the dash and watch Junior Lewis drive. Junior thought stopping off for gas was a pure aggravation, a precious waste of time. He didn't like to stop he liked to go. If a car didn't have to stop for gas, he'd drive straight through past Houston, Kansas, and Fargo, North Dakota, up across the polar ice. Down the other side into Coldass, Russia, tires down to nothing, out of beer and barbecue. Rosy-cheeked girls would crowd around in furry hats. A girl with glacier eyes would say, "Hey, now, what's Junior Lewis doing here?"

Dreamer followed this scenario a mile or maybe two, losing interest fast when the Russian girl wouldn't cash a check. Leaned back and slid down easy in his seat. Watched Houston traffic slug along through the hot oppressive night. Watched the bright sulphur-eyed fish in a hydrocarbon sea. Wondered if a nuke would clear the air. Wondered if a girl in Oklahoma knew his name.

Dreamer watched Junior Lewis drive. Dreamer wished that he was black too. He felt he had a knack for darker skin, in spite of no talent for the dance. Junior had skin black as night. Not your common Hershey bar tone or a high yellow wimpy kind of black, but undiluted Kenya genes. In the stroboscopic light of passing cars, quicksilver washed the hard angles of his face. Dreamer thought it might be a Pharaoh's face, that Junior had likely done Egypt some time. He asked Junior once if Nefertiti rang a bell, if he had a thing for cats. Junior said he didn't know, said he couldn't quite recall.

All this quite coincidental with a Mako Binder sort of off-the-cuff aside the week before, Mako in Dreamer's Austin store to buy a matched pair of Red Devil Cichlids at a fairly hefty price. Mako Binder looking criminally intent in a Panama suit, and somehow spotting Dreamer's wish for greater soul. He said he felt Dreamer would fit right into nigger life. That he might give some thought to basketball. This without malice of any sort at all, simply mobster insight, storing up shit that could turn out useful sometime. Which was how Mako Binder stayed firmly at the top, in a business where retirement meant free fall without a gold watch.

Junior Lewis took a nip from his pint and passed it on, a pint in a brown paper sack.

"I guess not," Dreamer said, though a drink seemed proper at the time.

"Might just settle you some," Junior said.

"I feel I'm settled just fine."

"I see that you are."

"I got a firm handle on my needs. When I want a drink and when I don't."

"That's good."

"A man know his needs, he going to be a happy man."

Junior briefly took his eyes off the road. "What you ought to do, you ought to stop talking like that."

"Like what?"

"Dropping words and letters, then sticking one in that don't belong."

"You do it," Dreamer said.

"That's different, man. I got an ethnic obligation to talk the way I do."

"Well see, that's it. I wish I did too."

"You lay off those *Jefferson* reruns awhile, you're going to be fine."

"I envy you minorities a lot. I feel incomplete."

"I've got this Mes'can friend works down on the Gulf," Junior said. "He can read English okay, but he's got this dyslectic tic he try to read any Mex. Doctors can't find a thing. They maybe going to write him up."

"This is the funny looking dude with one eye."

"Who you thinking about is Raoul. Raoul the man bet Sid Pink he could drive to LA buck naked without getting stopped. Which he did, except Sid tips the law and Raoul is out twenty-five grand and a couple of weeks in jail."

"Sid doesn't much like to lose."

"That is a fact."

Dreamer looked out the window at the soupy primal mix that passed for air. Traffic up ahead disappeared, lost in a deadly yellow veil.

"I wouldn't live in Houston on a bet," Dreamer said. "What you got right here, you got the asshole end of the world."

"Nobody going to argue that."

"You ought to come to Austin, get out of this place."

"That hippie dog life's not for me," Junior said. "I'm your big spending type. I got the need for finer things."

"Jesus," Dreamer said, "where you been, man? Austin isn't like that now, hasn't been fun for thirty years. All the old hippies wearing suits."

"You don't say."

"Come over there, you could eat at Mama Lucy's every night. Eat ribs and sing darky songs. You play any banjo at all?"

"You tell Mama Lucy Junior Lewis says hello. You tell her that. Mama Lucy is one fine lady. There isn't many like her anymore."

"I don't guess I'll do that," Dreamer said. "Wouldn't want her to know I even saw you over here. She finds out I'm using you on something like this, she'll have my ass in a sling."

Junior laughed at that. "Don't have to tell that woman anything. She want to know something, she know."

Junior thought on Mama Lucy, thought about the long night ahead. "You want some more help on this, you got it. I don't have to tell you that."

"You're doing all you need to do, friend."

"Shit, I'm driving, isn't much to that."

"It's enough," Dreamer said, and said it in a way that didn't call for extra talk.

Traffic wasn't bad for Friday night. Slow, but better than the other way, better going out than coming in. Fun-lovers groped for the city's strangled heart, weekday people seeking weekend dreams, seeking joy and release, seeking major aggravation and assault. Dreamer thought about a drink, about the bottle in Junior Lewis's sack. A drink seemed the right thing to do. Alcohol abuse would put the night on hold, muddy up the colors in his head. In the morning he could tell himself he didn't need the money, didn't need it bad.

The thought seemed to carry some doubt, seemed to lack true conviction and accord. Money didn't matter and it did. The money was good, too good this time. When it got that good, there was always a bad reason why.

And that, Dreamer thought, was reason enough to call the whole thing off and have a drink. Drive back to Austin and call Eileen. If she's speaking to him now, they can go and have a steak and a beer. Tell the client in the morning things didn't work out the way they should. They wouldn't like that. They'd figure he was holding them up for extra bucks. But hey, you can't help what other people think. That's the way they are, that's what they're going to do.

Just at that moment, as a plan began to jell, as decision seemed complete, Dreamer looked past Junior at the traffic going south, at the yellow wash of light, at the phosphorescent blur, looked and saw the bottle-green Jag, saw the car stalled out and saw the girl, saw the skinny-butt jeans, saw the cool Madonna eyes, saw the bright sequin halter that would make a fag bullfighter cry.

All this in a wink but enough to let him know that love had struck him blind. Love, passion, and romance. True love paperback style, and, if the present is a mirror of the past, maybe something greater, maybe something bigger than that . . .

"Pull off," Dreamer said, and Junior did.

Junior Lewis had seen the girl too. "We doing Batman and Robin?" he said, and didn't need to ask.

"We just might." Dreamer got out quickly and walked to the back of the van. Junior slid out on Dreamer's side, unwilling to risk awesome injury or death. He read the look in Dreamer's eyes. Found no trace of reason or restraint.

"Man, you don't want to do this," he said. "This is not a cool idea."

"That little girl needs care."

"Not from over here she don't."

"We can't just leave her there, Junior. That amounts to criminal neglect."

"That Batplane'd do it," Junior said.

Dreamer knew Junior was right, but he kept on watching all the same, searching for an answer through the white electric blur, through the whine of passing cars. He saw her in a fast-frame beat, saw her looking at the Jag, saw her staring at the hood. Knew there was nothing under there she cared to see. There was magic in the motor but she didn't have the spell.

The night smelled of chemical abuse, there was poison in the air. Dreamer felt he could love this girl a lot. Take her to his heart, answer all her dreams. And, with cross-traffic love came a sadness of the soul, a little tenor sax, a little moment of regret. He didn't know how this could be. They hadn't known each other long enough to sing the blues.

"Come on," Dreamer said, "let's go. We got to get off this mother and circle back."

Junior shook his head. "We be three whole days just finding an exit, man."

"Well goddamn, we sure have to try." Dreamer started for the van and then stopped. Cross-lane motion caught his eye. The car snaked out of traffic and nosed up sly behind the Jag, a *barrio* Buick set gnat-turd close to the ground, a paint job slick and beetle-black, a Tijuana fresco of green serpent gods and a vaguely Mayan Jesus on the hood, Mary there somewhere, lost amid airbrush crucifixion and tears, possibly a yucca and a rose, all this a Sistine taco work of art and clearly trouble on the run.

"Uh-oh," Junior said, "those Mes'can Americans going to *help* that lovely girl."

"Christ, let's go," Dreamer said, unpleasant visions in his head.

"Time and space against us all the way," Junior said. "That gal have two little babies by the time we get over there, man."

"I don't care, it's better than just sitting here."

"Sittin' here's fine," Junior said. "You stay and watch. Stay cool, think black."

"Do what?" Dreamer watched in extreme irritation as Junior ran back to the van. Maybe Junior Lewis had automatic weapons in the back. Streetsweepers, Uzis, and Stens. He looked across the lane. Fate dropped a snow cone down his back. All the doors of the Buick seemed to spring wide at once, as if the riders might have practiced such a move till they got it down pat.

There were six dark and fragile young men, jack-knife lean, clothing bright as ocean pearls. Some had Apache war paint across their eyes. Some had the look of Inca kings. One wore a Japanese mask. There was ethnic confusion in the night. They walked around the girl, they circled in a quick dance step with pointed toes, with a matador strut, a touch of the palm to slick the hair. Shy winks passed between them now and then. One seemed to parody the next. They paid no attention to the girl, never let her out of sight.

Dreamer spotted the leader of the band right away, and fear and sorrow reached out for him again. The boy was as pretty as the girl. A scar across his cheek only added to his grace. A Michael Jackson face with opal eyes. An angel with a shadow on his soul. He spoke very softly to the girl. He spread his arms wide and looked to God. Dreamer read his smile. With the help of *El Dios*, he would see this girl through trying times. He would take her to his breast, he would keep her from the night. He would show her razor love, but he would never break her heart.

Dreamer wondered if he could make it through the cars. Maybe so and maybe not. Then Junior Lewis came back.

"You take a nap in there or what?"

"Got us some cellular aid," Junior said. "Got some black road knights coming down. They maybe half a mile back."

Dreamer felt relief but not a lot. "They better do it real quick."

"They on the way now."

"I never heard of black knights. I'm pretty sure you had to be white."

"Who said?"

"You can look it up. A black guy couldn't be a knight."

"I don't remember readin' that."

"You probably skipped class. Went down to the fishin' hole."

"Lawdy, we likes to do that."

The boy stood very close. The girl had no place to go. She was feeling the gravity of this, feeling some alarm, feeling the pure and dark convergence of an alien soul. She tried not to let her fears show, but the boy had seen all this before, there was little that the boy didn't know.

The Merc blinked its lights, pulled off the road behind the Buick and the Jag. Two men got out, two Brothers in shades. One had a shiny bald head. One wore a Bogart hat. The man with the hat walked up politely and spoke to the boy. The man had a very winning smile. He looked as if he smiled all the time.

The boy stood his ground. Stayed long enough to hold his pride, long enough to scare the girl again, then he turned and walked away, turned and walked away as if he'd planned this all along.

"She be okay," Junior said.

"What those dudes'll do, they'll keep her for themselves," Dreamer said. "You can bet on that. A white girl's a black man's delight."

"I heard about that," Junior said.

He couldn't get his mind off the girl. He turned around and watched until the Jag disappeared, until love was out of sight, until Junior found a spot and tacked neatly in the flow. Her image burned a hole in Dreamer's heart. Where did she come from, what did she do? How would he ever find her now? Love wouldn't have a chance if they didn't get to know each other, if they didn't sit and talk.

He thought about her hair, he thought about her jeans, he thought about her lips, and her cheerleader thighs. An emotional stew began to simmer in his head. Purity and lust. Tenderness and pain. Joy and regret. He imagined them together. What she said, what he said after that. He yearned to buy her a burger and a beer. A triple-dip cone. A double feature at the drive-in, 1956, a soda and a kiss.

The colors in his head made sounds he didn't like. He pushed them all aside. He didn't want to mess with tints and tones. He wanted to think about *her*, and nothing else at all. Dreamer made a picture in his head. A double-strength sack from the grocery store. He stuffed all the colors in fast, rolled down the window and tossed it outside. Looked and tried to find the girl again and she was gone.

"I saw this thing on *Nova*," Junior said. "They got this Death Star circles out wide around the sun. Goes way out and comes back 'bout every twenty-six million years. Flat wipes everything out. They think it might've done the dinosaurs."

"Is it coming back again?"

"Sure is."

"Fucking figures," Dreamer said.

It is past eight-thirty and still close to ninety-four degrees. Houston chokes beneath a heavy ocher sky. Air superheated from the day rises up to meet the hydrocarbon farts of Subarus, Chevrolets and Saabs, Broncos and Beetles, Fiats and Fords. Phantoms from above meet and mix, join with the wraiths from down below. Chemical remorse from the Houston ship channel, from the dead and turgid waters, clotted and congealed, mingles with the sweat-ghosts of bankers, bakers, bums, and bookmakers, sinks to kiss the vapors of medical waste, bodies dumped in haste, bad breath from winos, bimbos, and girls with broken hearts. Do-do from pit bulls and registered cats, Big Mac sighs and former satiated rats.

Through some emissive law, colors seem to seek their own kind. Yellow and brown and bilious green, a deadly shade of red, all coalesce in a mighty septic pie, in a poison club sandwich nearly half a mile high, a multi-layered dome that masks the city down below, an awesome incandescence in the final light of day.

Beneath the scabrous sky, people scutter this way and that to find a bed or a bar, an all-night movie or an unattended car, anywhere to suck in the chill electric air. Only the truly down and out, people sitting down to a cat-food supper and a single color set, suffer from the stifling heat of night.

Drowned Man's Key

KEN GRISSOM

At the dawn of the twentieth century, Galveston was a major commercial center—the United States' third-busiest port and a leading Texas city. Then came the 1900 hurricane, the worst natural disaster in American history, which swamped the island and left an estimated six thousand people dead. Galveston eventually rebuilt itself, importing tons of sand to raise the island's elevation and fashioning a seventeen-foot-high seawall for protection. But Galveston never recovered its economic position, yielding to Houston and its ship channel as Texas's major port. Galveston has remained a popular tourist destination, however, particularly during Prohibition, when it became a haven for liquor, gambling, prostitution, and organized crime. It was during these years that the island city earned a reputation as "the free state of Galveston."

Galveston is the natural home for John Rodrigue, a roguish salvage boat operator with a fondness for rum and an eye for pretty ladies. Rodrigue is featured in three novels by former *Houston Post* writer Ken Grissom. In *Drowned Man's Key*, Rodrigue is caught up in murder and industrial espionage at the Johnson Space Center. Compounding the tension is a category five hurricane moving in on the Texas coast.

From the hotel parking lot, Rodrigue turned right on NASA Road 1. It was a wide four-lane that ran from the Gulf Freeway eastward toward the bay, bordering the south side of the Johnson Space Center, then skirting the north shore of the lake. Rodrigue's old black Chevy Blazer was one of the few vehicles traveling east, but the oncoming traffic was bumper-to-bumper and crawling. At the first intersection, the signal light was being ignored. A cop in a yellow slicker had stopped the traffic to let cars in from a side street. He looked back in time to give Rodrigue a perfunctory wave.

The road wound past boat dealerships, marinas, restaurants, and condominiums sitting on the lakeshore. In Seabrook, with the wide bay just ahead, Rodrigue turned right onto Highway 146, the old bayside highway that would take him south. He came immediately to a high bridge that spanned the channel connecting Clear Lake with the bay. On the other side was Kemah and the start of Galveston County.

The bridge was relatively new. Before, there had been a drawbridge that held up motorists while sailboats filed in and out of the lake. The new bridge helped the motorists, but it didn't do much to speed up boat traffic. There was still a hundred-year-old railroad trestle crossing the creek below. The trestle was unused and the swing bridge stayed open, but there was room for only two boats to pass, and then only very slowly and very carefully. On sunny weekends, boats were lined up thirty or forty deep on each side, waiting for a turn. Progress, Rodrigue had decided, did not go on like a smooth coat of paint.

On the other side of the bridge, a Galveston County sheriff's car was parked sideways, all but blocking the southbound lanes. Rodrigue stopped and showed his driver's license, and the deputy waved him on. One of the problems with a massive evacuation like this was keeping looters away from the abandoned homes and businesses. They had to assume a resident was on a legitimate errand, but they would keep out all nonresidents.

Rodrigue was stopped twice more on 146, once at Dickinson and again at Texas City. And then after he had merged onto the Gulf Freeway and was approaching the Galveston Causeway, he saw a whole line of emergency vehicles—police and sheriff's cruisers, ambulances, and a fire truck—blocking the freeway. He rumbled to a halt, elbow resting on the open window. A deputy walked up suspiciously. A gust of wind forced him to grab his hat.

"Island's been evacuated, bub."

Rodrigue handed him the license. Looking at the name on it, the deputy's right eyebrow arched in recognition.

"Where ya goin', Rod?" he asked in a friendlier tone. Rodrigue was something of a legend on the island.

"Pick up some stuff at home, and at the yacht basin, then I'm outta here."

"Better get a move on," said the deputy, handing back the license. "We're cleaning everybody off this time—us included. You get hung up, there ain't gonna be nobody to help."

The causeway was a mile and a half long, with a hump in the middle to let the tall inland tugs on the Intracoastal slide under. It spanned an arm of the bay that separated Galveston Island from the mainland. On the east end of the island were ferries that carried traffic across the main ship lane to the Bolivar Peninsula. And on the west end, there was a bridge over San Luis Pass. But whether you went east or west, you would find yourself on a low-lying road right on the Gulf beach—no place to be in a hurricane. Very soon this causeway would be Galveston's only route to safety.

Galveston was a barrier island, the principal geographic feature of the Texas coast. Essentially, they were sandbars that had emerged offshore and become more and more substantial as they moved landward. In an eon or two, they would merge with the land and a new sandbar would rise from the sea. East of Galveston beyond Bolivar Peninsula (an island in the act of merging), the coast began to take on the marshy character of Louisiana. But stringing westward and then southward as the coastline curved were Follet's Island, Matagorda Peninsula, Matagorda Island, San Jose Island, Mustang Island, and Padre Island. In Mexico, the process continued for another hundred and fifty miles, two-thirds of the way to Tampico.

Human history had caught Galveston in its prime, with terrain high enough to support a live oak forest that sheltered inhabitants and anchored the drifting sands. Centuries of Indians sitting in the shade shucking oysters had left shell middens that would later become part of the foundation for the Gulf Freeway. Jean Lafitte built his famous red house and some wharfage for his pirate ships. Then came the Texas Revolution and a flood of settlers from the United States. For a time, Galveston was second only to New Orleans as a Gulf port, but then business interests in Houston got the upper hand and built a ship channel through the bay that routed most commerce past the island.

Now Galveston relied on tourism. Mainly, there was the beach, blue-green water that tumbled onto the khaki sand in rows of gentle breakers. The seawall protecting the city was topped with a broad walkway that linked curio shops, carnival rides, and fishing piers. In between were long stretches of open beach for sunbathing and volleyball and girl watching. A cruise ship docked where the banana boats used to, and the old red-brick warehouses of the harbor district were one by one being turned into Yuppie bistros. The stately Victorian mansions rising from the subtropical vegetation along Broadway attracted old couples with cameras. Fishermen flocked to the yacht basin, where they could book a trip for speckled trout or blue marlin.

The fishermen and other boaters had been the reason Rodrigue had moved to Galveston. There was always a way an enterprising diver could pick up a few bucks around a busy seaport. And a few bucks had been all Rodrigue thought he needed until that last visit from Ann Eller. Now he was a CEO with a forty-five-mile commute to work.

Rodrigue took the 61st Street cutover to Seawall Boulevard. The seawall extended from the eastern tip of the island westward for nearly ten miles. It had been built after an unnamed 1900 hurricane shoved Gulf waters completely over the city, erasing most of what had been built and drowning some six thousand residents.

Past the seawall, the island was lower, with just a narrow strip of land between the Gulf beach and the marshy coves that lined the bay side. Rodrigue drove through several small resort communities until he reached his own, Sea Isle, at the far west end. He backed up the drive and hitched onto his boat trailer.

His house was on the beachfront. Like most houses on the unprotected part of the island, it was built high on piers, so that the house itself served as a carport. Steps up the side took him to a wide deck overlooking the beach.

The angry Gulf caught his attention and drew him to the smooth wooden rail. The tide was already raging and the first line of glinting olive green breakers were crashing way offshore. Rushing shoreward, tumbling, boiling up sand and foam, they produced a monotonous roar that he felt as much as he heard.

Rodrigue had always been soothed by the raging surf, a feeling he only half-understood. Maybe, because his ancestry was so intertwined with the sea, some kind of genetic memory was involved. Certainly, though, he had his own memories. They flooded back into his mind almost like a vision.

The sea had been raging then, too, pounding so hard they could feel it on the damp sand where they sat, watching the sun climb out of the thick storm haze. They were all wet and cold and elated.

Their shrimp boat had capsized and sunk in rough seas and they had clung to a wooden hatch cover half the night, miraculously winding up on a barren stretch of Mexican beach about eighty miles south of Brownsville, Texas.

Sooner or later, Papa would have to think of something to do, but there didn't seem to be any hurry. They just sat in a row—Papa, Uncle Maurice, Reuben with the bad complexion, and him—gazing at the waves, which at first seemed to roar and snap at them like some caged animal denied its meal.

At some point that day, though, the pounding surf lost its malevolence for the young Rodrigue. It was still awesome, but it made him feel good to bask in the harmless violence a few yards away while at the same time soaking up the warmth of the rising sun.

About midmorning, Papa and the others started talking about how to get back to civilization and what they would do when they got back. For them, the euphoria had worn off.

But Rodrigue carried the feeling into adulthood, past many encounters with a frisky sea.

Now, this thundering ocean scared him. Rodrigue was a changed man, no question about it. He shook his head disgustedly and went into the house.

He hurriedly packed a seabag with clothes and hustled it and a few other belongings downstairs. Back in the kitchen, he loaded an ice chest with most of the fresh fruit from the refrigerator, put some canned goods in one cardboard box and the contents of his liquor cabinet—mostly rums of widely varying quality—in another. He put the rest of the contents of the refrigerator into a garbage bag to be chucked, and used the emptiness to give the inside of the fridge a quick scrubbing. At the very least, the electricity would be off for days.

At the *very* least.

He pulled a new fifth of dark Jamaican rum back out of the cardboard box, cracked the lid, and sloshed some of the coffee-colored liquor into a plastic tumbler. He scooped up some ice cubes and found a wedge of lime in the ice chest. Satisfied with the drink, Rodrigue leaned on his breakfast bar and let his gaze drift around the room. The furniture, even the TV, had been here when he moved in. Even the Starving Artists seascapes on the wall, which were pleasing to him, had been hung by the former owner.

Easy come, easy go.

Bay of Sorrows

GAYLORD DOLD

Texas ranks first among all states in toxic and cancerous emissions released into the air. Texas also leads the country in the amount of toxic chemicals discharged into water. The "Golden Triangle," so named by boosters in southeast Texas, includes Beaumont, Port Arthur, and Orange, and is the source of much of this pollution. Once prosperous from oil fields and refineries, the area is now plagued by economic downturns and environmental damage. The refineries' toxic discharges have crippled the local fishing industry, which was also impacted by the arrival of many Vietnamese refugees in the 1970s. These new immigrants, many of whom worked as shrimpers in their native country, began competing with Texans. The situation quickly turned violent, leading to firebombings of Vietnamese shrimp boats and the resurgence of the Ku Klux Klan.

Gaylord Dold is a Kansas-based criminal attorney and a novelist hailed for lyrical prose that transcends genre fiction. In Dold's novel *Bay of Sorrows*, Deputy Sheriff Tom Poole is a Vietnam veteran who must come to terms with his past while investigating the death of a Vietnamese immigrant. Dold effectively captures the racial tensions and the environmental degradation along the upper Texas coast. Here Deputy Sheriff Poole investigates a specific crime scene, while at the same time the author creates a backdrop of a larger crime scene—the environmental degradation of a once-magnificent bay.

Tom *Poole was tired of corpses.* In those days death had become a way of life.

He had been driving north along the Port Arthur highway with the bay behind him, a long, shiny seam of water, heading home after a hard Saturday, when the call came over his radio. Dispatch said there was a dead guy in a fishing shack just down the beach from the old marina. Poole knew where that was, and something—he didn't know what—made him turn east, back toward the ocean. It took some driving around the barren dunes, sumps and oil pits, and tule groves, but he finally found the shack, and the corpse, and now he was waiting on the veranda for the sheriff.

Maybe he was heat-wilted, maybe just tired, but something made him focus on a bright orange gas flare coming from the stack of Port Arthur Oil and Pipe, a lick of flame just across the water. It was being rippled by a breeze whisking in from the bay, and when Poole closed his eyes, concentrating on the smell of the acrid gas, he lost his focus and sensed not the gas but only a dull ache in his head, a stab of pain between his shoulders, as if a knife had been plunged deliberately between the shoulder blade and his arm socket. You can't start thinking this way, he said to himself. *You have to float and relax and allow your feelings to coalesce around an object, make the pain come together on the head of something. Otherwise, it will eat you alive, like what happens to guys on the Jefferson County detective staff, pinheads who walk around with a hard-on for the world. It's only a job. You answer calls down on the Port Arthur highway; you see dead guys in fishing shacks—that's what you do for a living.* Poole knew, deep inside, that it was silly to complain about the things you choose to do, like making a living, but he was wishing just then that he had gone on home and left someone else the job of sitting up with a corpse.

He leaned on a rickety balustrade overlooking a brackish tide pool which led away to reeds and the sump that Port Arthur made of its waste. The palms along the beach were singing in the wind, a silky sound buried under the steady *clump-bump* of the oil tankers, pump engines running as they unloaded into pipelines, engines grinding away in the near background. Standing there, his mind's eye turning through the past like a bore, Poole was returning thirty-five years to a Gulf Coast that didn't exist anymore, except on fancy travel posters, on TV in modern momentary figments like sale items of the imagination that Poole knew happened only in the medium of advertising. Snap your fingers and the past is right there, then fleeing; you never get it.

Poole wanted a cigarette, but he had quit, one of many times. He turned his gaze down the beach toward the highway to Galveston where it ran past Sea Rim State Park, all the worn-out road shacks, fast-food joints now, shit that littered the seafront, with the palms dropping their fronds and the surf turning poisonous. The light, in times past that Poole remembered, would pour in over the bay and the ocean toward the offshore islands in a solid magenta wash, like varnish, and the sea looked emerald green, except when the wind was up or when hurricanes threatened in summer. Then the sea turned oxblood in color, like a pair of shoes that had been shined and then had gotten a layer of dust. When he was a kid, Poole had fished off the jetties down there, piles of rock, taking off his shoes and socks and shirt, leaving them on one of the dunes to get later, taking his casting rod and a box of tackle and a sack lunch to the end of the jetty to fish.

Poole could remember casting his jig and lead weights into the deep pull of the Gulf, letting the whole rig drop to the bottom with the bait, a chunk of mackerel, waiting on the rocks as the spray climbed around him. More than anything, he could remember the pull of a redfish as it hit the rig, down deep, the fish lying on the sand bottom, using the undertow while Poole backed away, setting his drag. Poole thought he could feel the past; his jaws were clenched. Back then . . . the Gulf didn't have a solid string of platforms pumping oil and gas, tankers flowing down to Galveston, up to New Orleans, wind that smelled of gas. Poole caught a lot of fish back then, and sometimes his father would grill the fish in the side yard of their house. Sometimes after his family had eaten, his father would take him to the movies in Beaumont, but that was a long time ago. Now, Poole was all grown up, sitting on a crime scene, baby-sitting an old man who was dead in a fishing shack—gunshot, from what Poole could see.

Suddenly, Poole felt amused by what he was doing, what he had tried to teach himself not to do anymore, which was not to romanticize the past but to keep clear the focus of each emotion so that he could avoid confusing himself with false feeling. More than anything, his past was shrouded with falsehood. It was simple. He had answered a call down on the highway and now he was doing his job. A daughter had found her father dead. She became hysterical, running down the beach, probably screaming bloody hell, and now Poole was waiting for the sheriff, looking around just to make sure the place was secure. He couldn't help it if the old man was stone dead, and Poole couldn't help the fact that his own wife had run away, and he couldn't help it if there weren't as many redfish in the surf as there used to be. Now, Poole was trying to live his life by a few simple rules, feeling that the simpler he made things for his internal life, his psyche, the better off he would be. He was afraid of becoming bitter if he didn't, and maybe even cynical, which Poole had discovered was an occupational hazard.

"Eat shit and die!" his wife had said once when he came home after three days away on police business. She had been drinking Tokay wine and crying, and there had been such a look of lost resentment on her face that Poole felt he couldn't ever change it no matter how hard he tried, nor did he quite know what he would do to change it if he had the chance, or the power, either one. "Eat shit and die!" she screamed, overwhelmed with tears, and Poole had tried to comfort her simply, putting his arms around her, but he had felt like a complete fool because the gesture had seemed false the instant he made it, and he knew he would have been better off not having tried to express an emotion he didn't feel, because people, his wife, Lisa Marie, included, eventually saw through false emotion, thinking you were a liar instead of being, as Poole was, confused and flattened by his life.

The word *corruption* crossed Poole's mind. He began to walk back and forth across the veranda like a caged panther, peering around the sun-shaded corner of the fishing shack, studying the clean line of sand where it curved uphill to the dunes, broken sea grass, and tule. There was a ring of dark brown lumber piled against the side of the shack, and two oil drums were buried in the dune, sides tinged by charcoal fire where fishermen had burned some trash and garbage. The land on the other side of the dunes was gray and beige where oil roads ran through collections of shacks and storage sheds and abandoned oil equipment. It was ramshackle country, and Poole wondered if there was anyone out there, if anyone had seen anything or heard anything. It was so quiet, you'd think a gunshot would have carried a long way.

Some pelicans were flying over San Juan Island and Poole could faintly hear their wings beating against the wind. He could hear the clop of the oil derricks, too, but then the birds folded their wings and plunged down to the surface of the bay, smacking the water with an instantaneous whack, ripping back skyward where others were already disappearing into a ragged mangrove beyond the jetties.

The mangrove was a smudge of green just like the hump of a turtle shell. God, Poole was still remembering. . . . He had once seen a sea turtle that had been hooked by a fisherman on the Port Arthur pier. He could remember the flash of its shell as it rose through the water, foam rolling off its back, its flipper hooked next to the white underbelly, the flipper mottled gray and dangling helplessly out of the water as the turtle struggled against the weight of the line. Poole had watched for a long time while some young boys gathered around the fisherman, urging him to land the turtle, some of them throwing pop cans and cigarette butts at the helpless animal. Poole had pulled his knife and had walked over to the guy with the rod, a kid no more than fifteen years old. There was a rip of silence as Poole handed the knife to the kid, who just stood there silently for a time, until he had finally cut the turtle free as Poole stared right at him. There had been a surge of something electric, and then the turtle was gone to sea.

All the while, Poole knew what the crowd on the pier had been thinking, ruffians in cutoffs and tank tops, hard guys smoking cigarettes, throwing the butts off the pier, watching the butts wash in to the beach. Eat shit and die! Yeah, motherfucker, eat shit and die! The vector of their existence was like the point of many knives, a shiny explosion of intention. And how could Poole's actions have made any difference? And now Poole was looking around a crime scene distractedly, the pelicans re-forming over the mangrove, settling on pilings, all over the rock jetty near the marina store. Poole felt okay about the turtle. He just didn't want good things to have such a high price.

Poole couldn't believe how sharp Mirabelli looked with his blazer and a red power tie, a pair of gray flannel slacks. Even in the heat, he looked as if he had just stepped out of GQ. Mirabelli flicked a fingernail at his suit pocket as if some sand had offended him. "The fuck," he yelled down to Poole, "my kids are playing *Hansel and Gretel* at Children's Theater in Beaumont." He smiled at Poole. "Here the fuck I am on Saturday night."

Poole was on the veranda. He could hear Hernandez moving around in the shack: a sneeze, the click of a shutter as he took some quick photos, then the sharp crackle of the car radio coming in over the wind, which had become steady. Poole walked up the dune path to where Mirabelli had parked his car next to Poole's on the top of the dunes, and he and Mirabelli relaxed against the hood. In the wind, some of the sweat finally cooled away from Poole's body.

"Who offed the old fart?" Mirabelli asked.

Poole had been telling him about the Vietnamese. Poole thought about the question, and when he didn't respond, both men leaned back in the sunshine, listening to Hernandez humming a weird tune down in the shack.

"Maybe the old fart offed himself," Mirabelli said.

The palms were working now, *clickety-click-click* in the wind, like billiard balls on a smooth felt table, and out on the ocean in the blue evening, the oil rigs made a chain up and down the Gulf, so many lights that Poole found himself astonished that there was any open water left between Port Arthur and Galveston. Poole was not surprised to see refuse out on the water, since he was used to seeing the sprawl of plastic suburbs between Spindletop and Beaumont, what had once been scrub creosote and black cotton land. It was phenomenal. Americans killed history as soon as it threatened to exist. Poole wondered if Mirabelli shared his perception in any way, but he doubted it, knowing that Mirabelli lived in Boomtown with his wife and kids, in a brick house that really didn't belong on the Gulf Coast, or anywhere in South Texas, a single-story ranch, some slotted windows at roof level, low ceilings, big heat pumps on concrete in the backyard.

When Poole had married, he and Lisa Marie rented a big house on Laurel Street in Beaumont, in an older neighborhood. The house was run-down in a nice way, with its peeling paint and genteel sagging porch, a breezeway with a good run of wind north to south, and, between the kitchen and the garage, a covered walk with trellis roses and honeysuckle, where Poole used to sit in the evenings and drink ale and listen to ball games on the radio. There were some old oaks that shaded the house in summer, and Poole thought the ten years he had lived there were his happiest times, though later when he thought about it, he realized that his happiness was either relative or utterly imagined—romanticized, at any rate.

Early on in their life together, Poole and Lisa Marie had taken to going to flea markets and antique shops, trying to find old things that fit their idea of what they would share as they got old, shopping for their future by rummaging in the past. They came back with some furniture—overstuffed chairs—and an old-fashioned Zenith tube radio that Poole had insisted on buying even though they couldn't afford it. Their forced effort to create a shared future, instead of sharing one, hadn't worked.

Poole had been to Mirabelli's house in Boomtown once for dinner and he'd never been invited back, probably because he had alienated Mirabelli's wife by going into a premature shell. That had happened, he thought, because of the family feel to the place: the flat beige paint on the walls, the kid noise, the smell of broccoli, and the TV that was playing while they ate. Even now, after all this time and distance, Poole would sometimes buy a twelve-pack and drive over to the house on Laurel Street and sit out in front in his Caprice, drinking the warm beer and smoking cigarettes one after another until his mind shut down, discovering later in the dawn that he had burned his suit coat, dropped some ash on his pants, wondering if he wasn't shutting down too much—turning off entirely was more like it.

"On the way," Mirabelli was saying over the car hood.

"What?" said Poole, startled.

"The ambulance," Mirabelli said, louder, looking at Poole as if he was deaf.

"Sorry," Poole muttered.

Mirabelli had one hand on the hood of his car, his shoe on the fender. Then Mirabelli put his hands on his knees and did a bongo beat, *tap-tap*, unconcerned and relaxed, as though the old Vietnamese down in the shack didn't exist.

"So," Mirabelli said in jazz tone. "The old fart offed himself?"

Poole was not Mirabelli's boss, but he had been in the department longer, and Mirabelli would more than likely do what Poole told him to do, and besides, the implication from Daddy John was that Poole would lead any investigation. While Poole was pondering this fact, he looked up the beach at the marina, where some sailboats were bobbing up and down around a wharf. Dim lights shone inside the bait store and beside the jetty the rocks were black as obsidian. The jetty stuck out fifty yards into the surf. Below him, the fishing shack stood on a spit of land by an estuary that worked its way south to where it became a tidal basin of the Sabine River. Beyond that was some brackish land and a system of swamps and lakes that had been protected from drainage and development by the state parks along the beach. Back to the north, toward Louisiana, the oil roads cut a crazy quilt pattern around the bay. The land was highwater table, brush, and salt-encrusted with mounds of tule, saw grass, then the suburbs with houses like the one Mirabelli lived in.

Poole was trying to think what to say. "I don't know," he managed. "Maybe the old fart did off himself."

Mirabelli was still using his knees as bongos. Poole knew Mirabelli wanted to go home and see his kids in the play, and this knee tapping was a way of diverting his impatience. Poole was sympathetic.

"Work your way back to town on the back roads, would you? Make me a map of the shacks along the way. Maybe I'll knock on some doors in the morning." Poole smiled, splitting the difference with Mirabelli. He didn't want to be anybody's boss around here, but he didn't feel like letting the old Vietnamese go that easily, either. It was funny, Poole thought, talking to Mirabelli, how worked up people get over abstracts like flags, medals, battleships, even ideas, communism, freedom, but how real things never take a strong hold. Some guy sees a dog hit by a car in the street and he turns the other way, heading down to McDonald's for a burger and fries, not wanting to be delayed five minutes. There had been body counts and rocket fire on Walter Cronkite for years, and then some chicken colonel blows a VC away for live TV and everybody goes apeshit. And now the old Vietnamese was turning into an abstraction, this dog in the street.

Mirabelli grinned at Poole. He nodded and hurried around his car, leaving Poole to take Hernandez back to Beaumont when they were through in the shack, unless Hernandez wanted to ride back in the ambulance. Poole hoped Hernandez *would* ride back in the ambulance, not only because he didn't feel like talking right now but because he wanted to be alone on the beach, knowing he was going to have to talk to the old man's daughter soon enough, dreading it, not wanting to add Hernandez to the equation of his personal dissonance.

When Poole had satisfied himself that Mirabelli was going to go over the roads slowly enough to check things out, watching his taillights weave around the dusky horizon, Poole walked down to the shack and told Hernandez he wanted him to start talking with all the fishermen and oil riggers along the beach, telling Hernandez that tomorrow was soon enough, after church, because he knew Hernandez would be going to Mass, especially now that his kid had been killed.

For some reason, Poole felt suddenly calm. He decided that he would walk down the waterline so he could take a closer look at the beach, the dunes, maybe scan the area with his flashlight just to see if somebody had left something lying around, although he thought that there was little chance of that because it was wild down there and the road was made with crushed hard coral and shell. As Poole walked, he could see bottles and cans everywhere in the dunes, and he could see how the humps of sand and sea grass had been leveled by three-wheelers and cycles, by guys in Jeeps who took off over the sand on weekends with their beer and boom boxes. Poole could see behind him that Hernandez had turned on an overhead light in the shack, by now not knowing what more to do, probably feeling badly about being all alone with a dead man.

It was after sunset and the mosquitoes were bad. Poole had a hard time keeping them off his neck. They were driving him crazy. He crossed the beach and went up into the dunes, shining his flashlight around while he walked. This place had once been a broad delta of the Sabine, where the river rushed-out into the sea, but what it was now was a sump, low and marshy, not very pleasant, though once it must have been filled with game. It was like all this peckerwood country, scraped over and left behind.

Poole climbed a hump of saw grass and spotted a house on Sabine Pass. It looked like it was made of stucco, standing on a rise above the river between the Clam Lake canal and culvert, which was navigable all the way to Walker Lake and the Intracoastal. The walking was hard work in the heat and Poole was sweating again inside his suit, feeling the gun belt tight around his waist where his skin was chafed. He felt like a stupid cowboy cop swinging a flashlight around in the half-dark, walking down a barren road. Then before he could see the stucco house again, he went down and up a hillock. When he got back to the top of a dune, he could see the house again, pink cracked stucco with a slab porch, sliding glass doors in back and a boat trailer in the driveway, just behind a pickup truck. There were slot windows near the roof, just like Mirabelli's house in Boomtown, prefab from hardware store kits, hauled in from someplace like Cleveland and planted on Sabine Pass. One side of the house, Poole could tell, was sloping already, downhill toward the beach, the other slipping into the estuary. It was coming apart in the middle, which wouldn't have happened if it had been built of cypress on stilts, the way the bubbas used to build on the Gulf before there were so many people.

Poole walked up the oil road and stood in the driveway of the stucco house, looking at the ocean, realizing that he could hear frogs croaking in the fresh water of the estuary. He looked at the estuary, bright nickel light on the water, and he thought to himself, Yes, these oil rigs are pumping two or three barrels a day now, maybe a little more, maybe not, and five or six hundred gallons of salt water a day along with the oil, which went back down the hole where it came from. So the sand was sinking, and the beach was eroding because of all the jetties, and the marshes were drying up as the salt came to the surface.

Poole walked across the dirt yard and tapped at the front door. He looked, but he couldn't find a bell, and so he knocked again softly and slapped some mosquitoes off his neck. He had his back turned when he heard the door open, and when he turned around, he was surprised to see an older woman with graying hair standing there, not Vietnamese as he expected, but an Anglo with a nice face. Her face was wrinkled with character, as though she had gotten plenty of sun. She looked like a woman of laughter, too, but right now she just looked surprised, a little exhausted, and Poole knew he looked surprised, as well. They stood like two waiters who arrive at the swinging doors with full trays on their shoulders at the same time.

"I hope you're the police," she said.

Poole gave his name, explaining he was with the sheriff's office.

"I'm Adrienne Deveraux," she said. Poole probably looked perplexed, because she added quickly, "I live in one of the beach houses back there." She pointed back north toward the marina, from where Poole had come.

"I walked down," Poole said. "I didn't think anyone lived along that stretch."

"Just us," the woman said, "my husband and I."

She had stepped back into the house and Poole followed her, seeing the woman over his shoulder while she closed the door. Poole looked around and saw a slab patio directly across the living room, through sliding glass. The glass was partly open, but it was hot in the room, so close that Poole could hardly breathe. A fan on the kitchen floor was blowing hot air across the room. To his right, Poole noticed a hallway, which probably led to bedrooms. He was feeling heat-prickly, flashing on the citronella smell, which was strong in the room, and put off by the sound of the sand he was crunching under his shoes on the bare linoleum. Maybe it was a cultural reaction to the smell, the sand, and the hot air blowing along the floor, but whatever it was, he was a long way from blaming the dead Vietnamese for it.

Adrienne Deveraux was saying something. But Poole was busy noticing things, fixing himself on his surroundings as if he were a radar dish, locking in. There was an amplifier in one corner of the room and what he thought was a preamp next to it, and two guitars were piled around a Formica table in the kitchen. The table itself was covered with dirty dishes and ashtrays full of butts. It had the look of a welfare house, but what did that mean? What had Poole expected? You survive, hammered by facticity. There was nothing regular for these Vietnamese fishermen but need. It wasn't as if they were Pilgrims coming over on the *Mayflower*, sitting down one bright fall day with some friendly Indians, passing turkey around. Nothing was that simple anymore. Nowadays, you had to muscle up for everything, and if you didn't have any muscle, you didn't have anything. Even Poole felt that sometimes he didn't have muscle. And look where he was at. What would it be like for these people?

"Tran comes to see me . . ." Adrienne Deveraux was saying, her voice trailing off. Poole was looking at her now, taking his inventory, beginning to be impressed by the bones in her face. He couldn't guess her age, but thought she might be ten years older than Poole. She was telling Poole that the girl was in a back bedroom, pretty broken up still, but through crying, so she thought it might be okay to go on back. Poole nodded, noticing the woman's eyes, then took a long look at the kitchen, which was small and messy. Poole walked out the patio door and looked at the Gulf, where there were tankers and oil rigs, tugs lighted up like computer screens, palms in dim outline on the beach.

When he came back inside, he said, "How do you happen to be here, Mrs. Deveraux?"

"I told you," she said. "Tran came for me. She was down at the shack and came by my house on her way here. I told you, we're friends."

Poole bit his lip. He had been looking and not listening. He could tell he had dropped a notch in the woman's judgment, which was something he regretted.

"We're friends," she repeated, emphasizing the words so that Poole would hear and not ask again.

Poole was about to go back to the bedroom to talk with the girl named Tran when he asked Adrienne Deveraux if she would mind sticking around. He realized down deep that he had a mysterious empathy with the woman, an innate confidence in her he couldn't explain, which troubled him, because he thought it might be something sexual. She was trim and bony, done up in cotton pants with a rope belt, a blue ribbon around the crown of her hair. She looked something like his ex-wife. Maybe that was it, and Poole winced to think that he could still be so affected by the ghost of his Lisa Marie.

Adrienne Deveraux said, "Of course," as if it had been an expected request. But it helped Poole contract back into the flow, because he was beginning to experience the hooch again, the smell of citronella and fish sauce, and when he came back from the bedroom from talking with the girl Tran, he wanted to see something he could fix on that would be familiar.

The girl was down the hall in a bedroom. Poole found her there, sitting on a single bed in the heat, with only a ruffle of air coming through one of the slot windows up near the ceiling. Gray geese on cheap curtains, buff white walls with spackling, some cracks. Poole held out his badge and introduced himself, saying he was sorry but not speaking forcefully the way he knew he should.

PART 4

DALLAS, FORT WORTH, AND THE PANHANDLE

Umbrella Man

DOUG J. SWANSON

Dallas is Texas's best-known city around the world, thanks in part to a prime-time soap opera and the Super Bowl-winning Dallas Cowboys. And then there's the matter of the events of November 22, 1963. Dallas suffers from continual image problems, in part because of the Kennedy assassination, but also because it is a major financial center and has long been derided a place ruled by conspicuous consumption. Dallas does, in fact, boast more retailers per capita than any other U.S. city. "Big D" prides itself on its "can do" spirit and entrepreneurial energy—qualities which have allowed the prairie city to grow, prosper, and attain a world-class status.

Doug J. Swanson, a long-time reporter for the *Dallas Morning News*, understands Big D's civic spirit, its drive for material success. In his series of novels featuring Jack Flippo, a down-and-out lawyer turned private detective, Swanson gets Dallas exactly right. His characters might be motivational speakers, divorce lawyers, or reformed strippers, but they all share one thing in common—a belief that money is the easiest way to make life better. They are on the make, hustling to get their share of Dallas's economic pie. In this regard, despite extravagant differences in class and occupation, each is a model Dallas citizen.

In *Umbrella Man*, Flippo has managed to acquire a "normal" job in a boring law firm. His domestic tranquility is soon shattered, however, when a former acquaintance turns up claiming knowledge of a missing piece of film that promises to solve the mystery of John F. Kennedy's assassination.

The twenty-second day of November came with brilliant sunshine and perfectly clear skies, a beautiful slice of fall in Dallas, Texas. Eddie Nickles said, "Let you in on a little secret, my friend. Snipers love weather like this."

As he spoke, a midnight-blue 1963 Lincoln convertible limousine made its way down Main Street, engine purring, paint glinting in the sunlight. Christ, it was a beautiful car. Two flags rippled from small staffs above the Lincoln's headlights. One was the Stars and Stripes. The other displayed the seal of the President of the United States.

A radio newsman described the scene. Big deep voice, trying to paint a picture for all the listeners: *The crowds are six deep here along the sun-splashed streets of downtown Dallas, a colorful sea of Texans. It's a warm, friendly Lone Star welcome for the President and Mrs. Kennedy.*

"Everybody's happy, everybody's feeling good," Eddie said over the radio cheers. "Especially the dudes with the guns. Notice I said dudes, plural. Notice I—Hey, champ, do me a favor, don't spill no coffee on the upholstery."

The Lincoln moved now toward the old schoolbook depository, a red brick box of a building. The grassy knoll loomed ahead. Eddie glanced at a window on the book depository's sixth floor. He said, "Here's where we get down and get funky. Like the man says, Gentlemen, start your carbines."

From the radio newsman: *President Kennedy's motorcade has entered Dealey Plaza. The President is smiling and waving to the delighted crowd. He seems to be saying something to Mrs. Kennedy.*

"You got that right." Eddie nodded and licked his lips. "He's telling his old lady they should get the hell out of this burg right now."

The Lincoln crept downhill, into the sweeping curve toward the Triple Underpass. Now the radio guy was confused: *There seems to be some problem . . . A sound . . . Could have been a motorcycle backfire . . . Something has gone terribly wrong.*

"Shots fired!" Eddie shouted. "Hear that? Shots fired! The President has been hit! President Kennedy has been—" Eddie broke off his shouting when the Lincoln became hard to control. Saying to himself, the hell is this? He gripped the wheel with both hands and steered the limo toward the curb, like bringing a big boat to dock in rough water.

"You believe this?" Eddie said. "This is nuts. I think we just blew a tire."

The radio newsman was at fever pitch now. Jabbering about gunshots and Secret Service agents and Mrs. Kennedy on the trunk of the car—going full tilt until Eddie pressed the eject button on the Lincoln's tape player. The newsman's voice went silent and a cassette came sliding out. On its label: YOU ARE THERE, DALLAS, NOV. 22, 1963. Copyright 1999 by Edward T. Nickles, Grassy Knoll Productions.

"Goddamn piece-of-garbage used tires." Eddie shifted the Lincoln into park and slammed a hand against the dashboard. "Supposed to be a twenty-thousand-mile guarantee."

Traffic backed up behind the Lincoln. A driver in a delivery truck hit his horn twice. Eddie gave him the finger as he got out of the car and checked the damage. The right front tire was nothing but shredded rubber.

Eddie said, "We're talking lawsuit now." This should have been his biggest day of the year, the anniversary of the JFK rubout. There would be people all over Dealey Plaza—all over the world, it seemed to Eddie—wanting to take the Assassination Re-creation Tour in Eddie's authentic replica of Kennedy's limo. People who would think nothing of paying twenty-five dollars a head while Eddie drove them along the exact presidential death route, playing the *You Are There* tape and providing expert commentary as needed.

"The sons of bitches will not get away with this." Eddie leaned against the hood, his hands flat on the shiny new paint job that still hadn't been paid for. The presidential flag stirred in a light breeze. "These tire company bastards are gonna cough it up big, believe that. Major damages."

From behind him a man's voice said, "Pocklin?"

Eddie turned. The tourist who had been in the back seat of the Lincoln stood on the sidewalk now, still holding his coffee cup. Eddie tried to remember what country the guy was from. All he could come up with was one of those places where they wore leather shorts and yodeled all day.

"Now what?" Eddie said. The tourist set his coffee cup on the sidewalk, unzipped his fanny pack and found one of Eddie's brochures for the Grassy Knoll Experience. He pointed to the section labeled *Exciting Finale*. Eddie had written the text himself: *Join in the exciting thrill of a high-speed dash to Parkland Hospital, where gallant doctors worked feverishly in a vain effort to save the mortally wounded President's life!!!*

"Go now?" the tourist said.

That was the best part of the tour, Eddie had to admit. Doing eighty up Stemmons Freeway, the limo's top down, while the *You Are There* tape gave the sound of a siren over moans and screams. Then roaring into the Parkland entrance and hitting the brakes in front of the emergency room.

Some of the customers liked the Parkland run so much they tipped Eddie a ten-spot. One night it even got him laid, right on the Lincoln's JFK death seat by a thin, bucktoothed girl with a Jacqueline fixation.

"To Pocklin now?" the tourist said.

Eddie pointed to the dead tire. "Hey, ace, you see this? Maybe in Slobovia you drive on a flat. Not in this country."

The tourist frowned and said something about money back. Amazing, Eddie thought. The guy could barely speak English but had the concept of refund down cold.

"Hey, if it was up to me, sure. But refunds are against federal law. Tell you what I'll do, though. Right up the hill here"—Eddie pointed up Elm— "is a place called the Conspiracy Institute. Go up there, say Eddie Nickles sent you, they'll let you in free."

"Say Eddie Neekles sent you."

"In Dallas, Texas, them words is magic."

When he hesitated Eddie told him, "They might even throw in a free T-shirt." That sealed it, and the tourist walked away, leaving Eddie to deal with another problem: No spare tire in the trunk, and not enough ready cash for a tow truck.

A small crowd had gathered near the Lincoln, which happened whenever he brought it anywhere near the assassination site. Eddie got ready for the question somebody was sure to ask: Is that *the* car? If I tell you that, Eddie always answered, the Secret Service will have me *and* you killed.

He found some Grassy Knoll brochures in the glove box and handed them out to the people gawking at the limo. Saying, "Have it up and running in no time, folks. Then you can take the death ride of your life."

An old man with a video camera wandered over. He taped the Lincoln from a couple of angles, finally asking Eddie, "What happened?"

"Somebody sabotaged it. Slit the sidewall."

The old man knelt and studied the flat tire. "Looks like it just wore out to me."

"No, somebody cut it," Eddie said, loud enough for everyone to hear. "Wouldn't be surprised if it was the CIA. Could have been the Cuban mob, they're around." He gazed toward the Triple Underpass. "They don't like what I'm doing out here, I can tell you that, the things Eddie Nickles is uncovering. They don't like it one—Hey, no more pictures. Who you working for anyway? You with the FBI?"

Jack Flippo parked in front of Big Dee's Adult Books & Videos on a hideous stretch of Dallas named Harry Hines Boulevard. Thinking as he got out of his car, the things I do for lust.

Big Dee's filled a windowless building between Stag's Topless Lounge and a discount mattress outlet. Jack opened the door and walked into low-ceilinged, overlit fluorescence and the smell of disinfectant. He saw rows of videotapes arranged by persuasion—traditional, bondage, groups, amateur. Half a dozen male customers wandered the place, hands in pockets, not making eye contact.

Jack found what he was looking for on a shelf along one wall, near the edible underwear and just above a display of picture books called *Hot Knockers & Humongous Butts*. He took four boxes from the shelf and carried them to the cash register. Each contained one life-size blow-up woman, Vinyl Venus, $12.95 apiece. Jack checked his wallet to see if he had enough.

The clerk looked bored, chewing gum. He started to ring up Jack's purchase, then stopped. "For the same price you can get Party Gal and Party Pal. Better grade of plastic."

"Sure." Jack shrugged. "Go for quality. Where do I find them?"

The clerk pointed. "Aisle two. Next to the inflatable sheep."

Jack paid cash and drove toward home with two Party Gals and two Party Pals boxed and bagged on the seat beside him. Traffic was heavy as the late-afternoon light drained away. He called Lola from the car, telling her as soon as she picked up, "Okay, I got what you wanted."

"You're my man," she said.

"Be there soon."

"I'll be waiting."

Lola was twenty-seven, ten years south of Jack, with business cards that identified her as a Next Wave Artistician. Her dark hair had purple and green streaks. There were two silver studs in her nose and a ring in her left eyebrow. Her parents called her Jennifer, but she had renamed herself after hearing the old Kinks song. Lola stayed out of the sun and slept only about four hours a night. She had more tattoos than a merchant seaman.

She had been living with Jack in his East Dallas bungalow for two

months. Lola liked to refer to it as a fact-finding mission among the indig-
enous peoples of the bourgeoisie. Jack would unlock his front door each
evening and call out, "Hi, honey, I'm home." Cracked Lola up every time.

Tonight Lola was in the kitchen. She wore a black shirt, black tights,
black boots and some kind of short-sleeved, knee-length coat, black.
"Johnny Cash just phoned," Jack said, walking in. "He wants his clothes
back."

She kissed him on the cheek and said, "How was your day, dear?" Another joke.

"It was—" Jack stopped. "Something's wrong here. I smell food."

Lola beamed. "Yes, you do."

"You cooked? You're kidding me."

"Special occasion. Just for tonight." Jack opened the oven and saw six
TV dinners bubbling in their trays.

"You want fried chicken," Lola asked him, "or meat loaf?"

Jack chose meat loaf and choked down as much as he could, a couple
of bites. Bland and hard to swallow, just like his new job. He had shuttered
the one-man detective agency known as Flippo Associates. Now he was
drawing a check at the downtown law firm of Lennard & Ratliff, wearing
a dark suit every day: the prodigal attorney, allowed back in the club.

Lola said, "You think you'll like it? That would be cool. Then it becomes
like a daily Stockholm-syndrome hostage thing, you know?"

"No, I don't know. Listen . . ." Jack was ready to give a speech, tell her
what she and her friends, irony-dripping artsy-fartsies straight out of trust
fund land, didn't understand about making a living.

But Lola, pushing back her chair, said, "Pictures, remember? You
promised."

"What? Oh, baby, not tonight. I'm beat. I had a long day cheating widows out of their pensions."

Lola put a box on the table, reminding Jack that her gallery show was
only two weeks away and there was no time to spare, tons of work to do
before then. She cracked open the box and breathed out as if she'd just
glimpsed King Tut's tomb. "Oh . . . awesome."

Jack took a handful of old black-and-white photographs and spread
them on the table. "What are you talking about?"

"These are beautiful. I mean, look at the history here."

Jack didn't see history. All Jack saw was a bunch of old shots of the
Flippo family from when he was a kid. Lola stood behind him, looking
over his shoulder. She said, "I think it's so cool that you grew up in the
sixties."

"Check this one, the old man in a suit and tie. Must have been a wedding or a funeral." He held up a shot of his father: Tall and thin, with a big handle of a nose, just like Jack. "Guarantee you," Jack said, "somewhere outside the frame there's a Pall Mall going and a can of Schlitz making a ring on the coffee table."

Jack remembered a man who had two modes of dress around the house, his jumpsuit from Flippo Bros Welding or his underwear. A man who, if he had a few beers in him, might break wind at the supper table. Then ask while the kids laughed, Somebody hear a spider bark?

"Hey, check this one," Lola said. It was another black-and-white, a little fuzzy and underlit. Jack studied the whole Flippo family: Mom, Dad, big brother Jeff and one gawky teenager with zits and a bad haircut—Jack.

"That's it." Lola reached for it. "That's the one I want."

Jack gazed at his mother's smiling face. "The woman was sad every day of her life."

"It's perfect." Lola took the picture from him and moved into the living room. She began unboxing the Party Gals and Party Pals. Asking Jack, "Aren't you going to help me blow these up?"

He helped for a while, inflating the two plastic women before retreating to the back of the house. Jack took a shower, then looked for something to read, going through a stack of magazines but not finding what he wanted. He checked a drawer of the nightstand and turned up only a dirty sock and a bound copy of Lola's master's thesis, "The Slaughter of Arnold Ziffel: CBS Television's Embrace and Subsequent Abandonment of the 'Rural' Comedy, 1965–1971."

He called out, "What the hell happened to my *Sporting News*?"

"In here," Lola answered.

Jack walked back toward the living room and stopped at the edge. "It's a joke, right?"

Lola swept the room with an open palm. "I'm moving this whole tableau to the gallery. When you walk into my show, this will be the first thing you see."

The blow-up dolls were seated on Jack's furniture. One held a newspaper, one had its face toward the television, one had knitting in its lap and one had its hands inside its pants.

Lola said, "I'm calling them the Nuclear Love Family."

They were dressed in thrift shop clothes and bedroom slippers, and had blond wigs taped to their plastic heads. They dined at fold-up trays holding the TV dinners that Lola had heated up. The picture of Jack's family, now framed, rested on a lamp table.

Jack bent to get his *Sporting News* from the coffee table. "Wait," Lola said. "You can't do that. The magazine is part of the scene."

He sighed and glanced at the clock. Time for working stiffs to get some rest anyway. "Fine," he said. "Now how about something real? Something like you, in bed with me, and all that black shit you're wearing on the floor."

Lola fussed with the wig on one of the Party Gals. "In a minute maybe. I've got some touching up to do."

"Or"—Jack smiled—"we could do it right here on the floor. With the Nuclear Love Family watching."

She turned toward him, gave him a look. "I like that," Lola said. "I really do." She took her coat off and began to push her tights down, keeping her eyes locked on Jack's. Man, she was twisted. Jack loved that about her.

From Jack's driveway there was the sound of a car door slamming. Lola pulled her tights back up. She went to the living room's big picture window and parted the curtains, looking across the front yard. "Wow," she said. "Cool car."

The doorbell rang twice, followed by three quick knocks. "Whoever it is," Jack said, "I'll kill him." He opened the door and stared into the porch light at a face he hadn't thought about lately.

"Hey, Jackie," Eddie Nickles said. "You got a minute for an old friend?"

Prime Suspect

A. W. GRAY

Fort Worth's wealthy elite are responsible for numerous civic achievements, most visibly a world-class museum district that outshines that of any other Texas city. But Fort Worth's millionaires haven't always made such positive contributions, particularly in 1978, when a mansion overlooking the Colonial Country Club became a famous murder site. The gunshots that evening targeted the estranged wife of oil baron T. Cullen Davis. Soon thereafter, Davis became the wealthiest man in America to ever stand trial for murder. He spent millions in his own defense and was eventually acquitted.

Fort Worth author A. W. Gray often paints a cynical portrait of the powerful in his detective novels set in the Dallas/Fort Worth metroplex. (Gray also writes legal thrillers under the pseudonym Sarah Gregory.) In his hard-boiled novels, the establishment, as represented by cops and prosecutors, are often as amoral as the criminals. Gray's protagonists are working-class underdogs caught squarely in the middle, struggling successfully against the odds.

In *Prime Suspect*, Gray takes aim at Fort Worth's upper class. A wealthy woman is murdered in her mansion adjacent to the Colonial Country Club. Gray's protagonist, the aptly-named Lackey, becomes the chief suspect. Lackey is hounded by the cops, but the millionaire husband of the murdered woman experiences no such worries. Two days after his wife is killed, the husband will play a round at the Colonial with famous pro golfer Greg Norman. Such corrupt morals can't endure, of course. Especially in an A. W. Gray novel.

On the Third of June, Nineteen Hundred and Seventy-three, J. Percival Hardin III graduated from Berlyn Academy in Fort Worth, Texas, in the upper third of his class. There were forty-nine graduating seniors. The entire baccalaureate assembly, relatives and all, filled less than half of Landreth Auditorium on the TCU campus while a Van Cliburn protégé played "Pomp and Circumstance" on a concert grand piano. The graduating class had voted to forego the traditional caps and gowns; the men wore plum tuxedos while the female seniors made do with the same formals they planned to wear to the following month's Debutante Ball.

Ross Monroe, whose daughter Marissa was a Berlyn senior, held the post-baccalaureate get-together at his home. The Monroe digs overlooked the seventeenth fairway of Colonial Country Club, and inside the mansion were nine bathrooms and a sixty-foot den. A parlor ensemble from the Fort Worth Symphony provided the music. Percy Hardin got high on Purple Passion, which was grape juice mixed with 180-proof Everclear, and rejoiced over his graduation present from his father, which was a brand-new yellow Grand Prix. He danced every dance save one with Marissa Monroe; the lone dance without Marissa he endured with her mother, Luwanda Monroe the hostess. During a break in the music, Marissa took Percy by the hand and led him outside. The couple strolled along stone pathways through the gardens, talking of college plans while they gazed upon azaleas and impatiens in livid shades of red and yellow and blue, and finally sat down together in the vine-shielded gazebo. There Marissa rewarded Percy with her own graduation present, a blow job which curled his toes into knots.

On the same Sunday, June 3, 1973, and in the same city of Fort Worth, Texas, Lackey No-Middle-Name Ferguson graduated from Richland High, 427th in his class. Lackey's baccalaureate took place in the Tarrant County Convention Center, which boasted the only auditorium in the county large enough for the 736 Richland seniors along with parents, siblings, current wives and husbands of parents, and children of some of the seniors, legitimate and otherwise. The class wore gray caps and gowns rented from Arnold's on the Loop for twenty-six dollars plus a fifty-buck security deposit. The New York Philharmonic Orchestra played "Pomp and Circumstance," though there was quite a lot of static on the convention speakers, and the tape, which was rerecorded from a pirated cassette, lacked a bit in the quality department.

Mr. Hale, the Vice-Principal and Chief Disciplinary Officer at Richland High, called the men of the graduating class aside just prior to the service. "Look, guys," he said, "this may be the end of the line for you, but it's old hat to me. Every year the same shit, so listen up. We've got three thousand people out there, three thousand hardworking folks that came down here to give their little dumplings a send-off, most of them tickled to death 'cause after today they don't have to support you any more. They deserve a nice ceremony. So what I'm saying here is, the first guy I catch playing grab-ass in line, I'm tearing up his diploma and he can just figure on having to fuck with me again next year. Any questions?"

The baccalaureate itself went off pretty smoothly, though Lackey had a hard time accepting his diploma with a straight face after receiving a well-timed goose from Ronnie Ferias just prior to Lackey's walking across the stage. And a secretly pregnant girl named Lucy Martin retired from the service with a bout of morning sickness and had to get her sheepskin by mail. The highlight came shortly after the service ended, when the fathers of the valedictorian and salutatorian went after it with broken beer bottles in the parking lot.

Lackey Ferguson's graduation gifts, which came in the form of cash from uncles and aunts, with ten bucks kicked in by his father, totaled fifty-two dollars. He spent part of the money on a six-pack of Lone Star Beer and the balance at the Jackson Hotel, a whorehouse on South Main.

The following day, while Percy Hardin completed his acceptance letter to Princeton, and while Lackey Ferguson nursed his hangover in the US Army Recruiter's office, the Texas Education Agency entered both young men on a percentage-of-high-school-grads statistics ledger. Aside from their names on the same TEA printout, the two had nothing in common at that point in their lives.

(Note from the editors: Several years later, Lackey Ferguson is the co-owner of a small construction business. He answers a newspaper ad to build a $100,000 bathhouse at Percy and Marissa Hardin's home. Percy then refers Lackey to his own bank to secure a loan for the building materials. Lackey is unsuccessful, and here is returning to the Hardin home to see about getting an advance for the job.)

Lackey Ferguson decided on the way over to J. Percival Hardin's house that he wouldn't like living on the west side. Lackey thought that walking around on the lawn and making sure the gardener wasn't fucking up the rosebushes, or sitting out by the pool and reading the *Wall Street Journal* while Nancy sunned on a raft in her string bikini and drank mint juleps, well, that kind of stuff would be kicks for a while. But if a westside guy wanted to take off his shirt and shoes and lay around watching the ball game, his wife would be all over him about it. Lackey and Nancy had rented a movie, *War of the Roses*, with Michael Douglas and Kathleen Turner, and in the movie Douglas and Turner had been living in a house sort of like the ones in this westside neighborhood. One thing Lackey had noticed (and hadn't mentioned to Nancy for fear she'd start getting ideas) was that Michael Douglas had come to supper in a coat and tie. Duding out for supper was something that could get old in a hurry.

Hardin's home was a ten-minute drive from the bank, down the red-brick paving on Camp Bowie Boulevard with its fancy dress shops and cutesy French pastry restaurants, north on Hulen Street, past clipped lawns the size of polo fields and houses with fountains in their yards, and finally east on a winding, tree-shaded boulevard which offered glimpses of Colonial Country Club. As he pulled his blue and white GMC supercab to the curb in front of Hardin's, Lackey wondered briefly whether Percy Hardin carried his deposits to the bank, or if maybe the worried-looking guy (Graham? Yeah, Merlyn Graham) came over in person to save Hardin the trouble. Lackey couldn't understand why the banker had seemed so worried; it was pretty obvious that Ridglea Bank didn't lend any money to anybody who needed the loan to begin with. If a guy really needed some money he could try and get it from his brother-in-law.

The pickup was spotless and its chrome gleamed like polished sterling. Lackey and Nancy had spent part of Sunday afternoon washing the truck and vacuuming out the inside, taking extra care with the windows to be sure there weren't any smudges; Lackey couldn't afford to show up in search of a contract on the bathhouse in a dirty pickup. Like he'd told Ronnie Ferias, getting the bathhouse job wasn't a matter of life and death, but it was pretty important. Remodeling kitchens and enclosing back porches into extra bedrooms put food on the table and paid the rent, but something like this bathhouse job was pure gravy. Lackey and Nancy had set the date—August 15th—and the westside job would give them a nice honeymoon in San Francisco three months from now. San Francisco was the one place that Nancy had always wanted to go. Lackey had been there when he was in the army, and picturing Nancy strolling along on Fisherman's Wharf with the seabreeze whipping her dark hair made Lackey want to take her. He was going to get this bathhouse job, bank loan or no. He'd just have to figure something out. He climbed down from the pickup and crossed the lawn toward the house.

Hardin lived in a two-story gothic of dark red stone. The house was seventy-five years old if it was a day. During the brief meeting he'd had with the Hardins in their parlor that morning, Lackey had done some looking around. He'd decided that the parlor furniture alone had probably cost more than Lackey and Ronnie had made in the past six months, and the paintings that hung over the mantel were probably good for a couple of years' worth of remodeling jobs. The house appeared enormous as seen from the street; as Lackey drew nearer the structure loomed like Texas Stadium.

He passed the gardener, a Mexican guy in overalls who was clipping a hedge. Lackey nodded and winked, and the gardener smiled. He'd tried talking to the gardener that morning and found that the guy didn't speak any English, which made Lackey wish he'd brought Nancy along. The gardener paused in his hedge-clipping to mop his forehead with a handkerchief. The noon mid-May temperature was nearing ninety degrees, and Lackey decided that he wouldn't take the job as Percy Hardin's gardener unless they'd let him work in his bathing suit.

He went up a stone walkway between twin two-story pointed spires and skirted a fountain on his way to the front porch. The fountain showed thick green plants waving gently beneath the surface of the water, and maybe a thousand trout-sized goldfish that wriggled about and flicked their tails among the leaves.

Percy Hardin waited on the porch. Hardin was fretting about something, pacing back and forth with his hands clasped behind his back. He was a tall, slender blond, wearing baggy navy pants with pockets in the legs, and a blousy pink Remert knit shirt whose hem was snug around his hips. His sleeves hung to his elbows. Nancy watched the fashion pages like a hawk and wanted Lackey to try the oversize look; Lackey personally thought that guys dressed like Percy Hardin looked as though their clothes didn't fit. Lackey climbed the three steps up on the red-stone porch and said hello.

Hardin's lips were thin, and his eyes were hidden behind black sunglasses with silver wire frames. He reached up under his shirt to scratch his ribs, at the same time snapping the fingers of his free hand as he said, "Let's see, you're the . . ."

It took a couple of seconds for Lackey to get it; it had only been two hours since he'd talked to this guy. Finally Lackey said, "Contractor. We talked about the bathhouse you want behind your pool. You sent me over to your bank to talk about interim financing, remember?"

The fingers snapped again. "Sure. Sure, of course. Merlyn Graham fix you up?"

"Well, not exactly. He didn't have the interest rate I was looking for."

"I know just what you mean," Hardin said. "The bastards really stick it to you for money these days. For a hundred thou, though, what the hell. I don't know as I'd be shopping around that much."

"Yeah. Yeah, a lousy hundred," Lackey said. "But all those points, well, it just rubbed me the wrong way is all. Tell you the truth, I got an alternate plan to run by you."

"Hey, I like that. A man that lives by his principles. Look, do you mind? I'm running way late." Hardin went over to lean on a set of golf clubs, Ping Eye irons and woods with fuzzy head covers inside a big pink leather bag like the touring pros had.

Lackey thought, Do I mind what? No, the guy wants to lean on his golf clubs, I don't mind. Percy Hardin seemed a little weird to begin with, and if Hardin wanted to lean on his golf bag, then Lackey Ferguson sure as hell didn't have anything to say about it. "Suit yourself," Lackey said.

"No, I mean"—Hardin flashed a plastic smile—"would you mind carrying these out to the curb for me? My regular help took the day off."

Lackey permitted himself one blink, then decided that if he was going to get this bathhouse job he'd better do what Percy Hardin wanted. Just think of Nancy on Fisherman's Wharf with the wind in her hair. Better yet, picture Nancy without any clothes, that should do the trick. "Sure, no problem," Lackey said. Then he hefted the golf bag and slipped the strap over his shoulder and followed Hardin down the steps and around the fountain. Hardin walked with long strides, his hands swinging loosely by his hips, his head moving slowly from side to side like a guy used to giving orders and having everyone jump when he said the word.

"Wouldn't you know they'd pick this morning to be late," Hardin said. "Fucking *years* I've been trying to get in the group with Norman. Finally I'm in and stand a good chance of missing my practice round."

Lackey wanted to say, Norman who? But he had enough to do carrying the golf clubs, so just struggled along without saying anything. The golf equipment must have weighed seventy-five pounds with all those extra wedges and crap in there, and Lackey wondered whether he could carry the bag for eighteen holes, reading the break on putts and telling Percy Hardin what club to hit. Be a tossup.

"Of course, the real thing's not till Wednesday," Hardin said, "and usually the club's closed on Monday. But NIT week they let us get in extra practice rounds."

Lackey said between huffs and puffs, "I thought the NIT was in Madison Square Garden." He quickened his pace, doing his best to keep up with Hardin as they crossed the yard. The tiff grass was the color of pool-table felt and, Lackey knew, required tons of water in the Texas heat to keep it from burning out.

Hardin stopped and looked around. "Madison . . .? Oh, you're talking about basketball. Hey, pretty funny, I like that. Colonial. Colonial National Invitational, that's what I'm talking about. I'm getting ready for the pro-am. Do you play golf?"

"Yeah, some. Me and Ronnie Ferias and a couple of other guys go out to Rockwood sometimes on Saturday mornings. Say, you'll meet Ronnie if we do the bathhouse. He's my partner."

"Oh. Rockwood Muny," Hardin said, as though he was saying, Oh, what a pile of shit. Which Rockwood was, Lackey supposed, big patches of bare ground in the fairways and greens so bumpy you'd miss a four-footer about half the time. Then Hardin said, "Give me a minute, huh?" and went over to say something to the gardener in Spanish.

Lackey set the bag down; the clubs shifted and made hollow thunking noises. A towel hung from the bag ring, and Lackey used the towel to wipe the sweat from his forehead. Not only was it hot as hell, the humidity must be ninety percent or so, and Lackey decided right then and there that no way would he be a caddy. He was pretty impressed that Hardin could speak Spanish; in fact Lackey himself had thought about taking a night course at Tarrant County Junior College so that he and Nancy could speak Spanish to one another. But on second thought, Hardin's Spanish wasn't lilting and musical like Nancy's; Hardin spoke Spanish like a guy who'd taken the language in school and liked to try it out on Mexican waiters. Lackey decided that if his own Spanish was going to sound like Percy Hardin's, then he'd as soon not learn to speak Spanish at all. Whatever Hardin was saying to the gardener must have been pretty good; the guy stopped clipping the hedge and took off for the corner of the house with a big pass-the-enchiladas grin on his face. Come to think about it, Lackey thought, how come that gardener's not carrying these golf clubs instead of me? At least the guy's getting paid.

When the gardener had disappeared from view, Hardin gave Lackey a come-on motion and continued on his way toward the street. Lackey sighed, shouldered the bag, and took off after Hardin like Gunga Din. Hardin said, "That's one way to keep the help in line. Give them the day off every once in a while, then when you ask 'em for a little extra they don't have any argument." As Lackey was wondering if he was included as one of the help, Hardin paused, hands on hips. "Well, it's about time. About fucking time," Hardin said.

Lackey followed Hardin's gaze. A white Lincoln stretch limo had come abreast of the house and was angling to the curb behind Lackey's pickup. The limo was every bit as spotless as Lackey's truck, and its windows were one-way black. "Yeah," Lackey said. "You'd think people would be more considerate. Listen, about the bathhouse."

Hardin's lips twisted in thought. Then he said, "Oh, yeah, the bathhouse. I thought we had that settled this morning."

"Well, I did, too. But that was before I had the problem at the bank."

Lackey realized that Hardin wasn't really listening; the slender blond guy was in a hurry to make his tee time, and anything as pissant as a hundred-thousand-dollar bathhouse was something he didn't have time to fuck with. The limo's trunk lid sprung open with a metallic *pop*, and a uniformed chauffeur hopped out and hustled to the rear. The backseat window slid down with an electric hum, and a man of about fifty stuck his head outside. He wore a snow white golf shirt and had silver curly hair combed straight back. "I get four strokes a side," he said. Then, glancing at Lackey, "Got you a new man, huh?"

Hardin jerked a thumb in Lackey's direction. "This guy? No, this guy's . . . what's your name again, guy?"

Lackey said, "Huh?" then got it and said quickly, "Lackey Ferguson," and then said to the silver-haired guy, "How you doing?"

"He's here to talk about the bathhouse," Hardin said. "You know, *that* fucking deal."

The silver-haired man climbed out to stand on the curb. "Yeah, a honey-do. 'Honey, do this and honey, do that.' My old lady's wanting a doghouse that some guys wish *they* could live in." In addition to the golf shirt he wore gray slacks, and he was round shouldered with a protruding belly. "Well, listen, Lackey. Slide them sticks over to my man back there. We got tracks to make."

"Hold it," Hardin said. Then, as Lackey was wondering, What sticks? Hardin came over and unzipped one bulky side pocket on the golf bag. He took out a pair of pale pink golf shoes, held them pinched together in one hand and said to Lackey, "Give the clubs to the chauffeur. That's a good man." Then Hardin walked past the silver-haired guy to sit sideways on the limo's back seat and take one sneaker off.

Lackey was beginning to do a slow burn, but thought about the bathhouse job and decided that Percy Hardin was something that he was just going to have to put up with. He lugged the clubs back to the trunk where the chauffeur waited. The chauffeur was a thin guy of about forty who looked as though he knew which side his bread was buttered on. He rolled his eyes at Lackey as he loaded the clubs into the trunk. Lackey went back to stand beside the limo and said to Percy Hardin, "Listen, on the bathhouse deal, I got to have some answers. I hate to push you, but me and my partner got to make some plans."

Hardin paused, then winked at the silver-haired man. "What's to talk about?" Hardin said, then bent over to tie the laces on one golf shoe. On his other foot he wore only a white sock.

"Well," Lackey said, "it's the financing. I'm going to—"

"Wait a minute." Hardin yanked the laces into a bow, then eased his stockinged foot into the other golf shoe. "Let me make sure you get the big picture here. That bathhouse. I don't care about that bathhouse. I don't give a *shit* about that bathhouse. My *wife* wants the bathhouse, not me. I want to play some golf. So what you need to do is, you need to talk to my wife. Okay? Now if you're going to do the job, I'll see you around. Let's get cracking, Sam." Then, as the silver-haired guy climbed into the front seat beside the chauffeur, Hardin swung his legs inside the car and slammed the door. The limo moved slowly and smoothly away from the curb as the rear window beside Hardin hummed and slid upward.

Lackey cupped his hands to his mouth. "Hey. Hey, well, is your wife at home?"

"She was the last time I checked," Hardin said loudly. He disappeared from view as the window closed. The limo picked up speed.

Lackey watched the limo round the corner, then stalked away in the direction of the house. He was pissed, but forced his emotions down to a low boil. Bitching at Hardin's wife wasn't going to help. As he moved between the spires and went around the fountain, Lackey wondered if Percy Hardin was into something crooked. Everyone Lackey knew who did nothing but hang around Rockwood and play golf all the time was either dead broke or dealing dope, and it was a cinch that Hardin wasn't broke. Lackey decided that if he was going to do the bathhouse, he needed to keep his eyes and ears open.

The Sheriff and the Panhandle Murders

D. R. MEREDITH

Agricultural communities are not the usual setting for murder mysteries, which tend to favor more exotic locales. On the surface, the Texas Panhandle seems to offer little in the way of intrigue. A flat, treeless horizon rules the landscape. Waves of prairie grass have long since given way to straight-rowed furrows of wheat, corn, and sugar beets. Irrigation pumps are a constant presence, testifying to the vast underground reservoir, the Ogallala Aquifer, which sustains the farm economy in this arid region.

Yet Amarillo resident D. R. (Doris) Meredith has created three Panhandle-based mystery series, each meticulously researched and showcasing a surprising cultural and geographic diversity. Meredith's series feature reference librarian Megan Clark, attorney John Lloyd Branson, and Texas sheriff Charles Timothy Matthews.

The Sheriff and the Panhandle Murders, Meredith's first book, introduces readers to Sheriff Matthews, a heroic, red-blooded lawman cut out of the archetypal Texas Ranger mold. The setting is fictional Carroll County, a rural farming area that closely resembles Moore County and its seat, Dumas, where Meredith lived at the time. Meredith often finds unique ways to dispatch her victims, making the best possible use of the ingredients afforded by her setting. Here the initial murder is carried out with the aid of a crop duster, which flies low over the victim's pickup truck and douses him with an insecticide. In a later scene, a murder victim is discovered in the community barbecue pit as the town gears up for its annual "Frontier Days" festival. Criminals, even murderers, can occasionally be forgiven. But messing with Texas barbecue, never!

Sheriff Charles Timothy Matthews was born and reared in the urban sprawl of Dallas. Since most natives of Dallas and points south considered the Panhandle to be an area of ignorant cowboys and hick farmers whose drawls were thick enough to plant wheat in, his presence in Crawford County, Texas, was inexplicable to his family and friends.

His law degree didn't necessarily set Charles apart from others but his graduation from Rice University did. Kids from the Panhandle generally attended West Texas State, Texas Tech, or Texas A&M. Rice University is almost as exotic a school as Harvard, except that its graduates are more trusted; after all, Rice is in Houston.

But the single most distinctive aspect of Charles Timothy Matthews was his lack of a nickname. In the Panhandle, nicknames are as common as sagebrush, yucca plants, and grasshoppers. Charles Timothy Matthews was always addressed as "Charles." Persons calling him "Charlie" or "Chuck" were always politely but firmly corrected. He seldom had to correct anyone more than once. There was a certain aura about him that unconsciously impressed everyone that here was a man who meant what he said.

When asked, as he frequently was that first year, why he had chosen Carroll, county seat of Crawford County, as his new home, Charles would smile gently and reply the town seemed to be a fine place to live. No one asked why he had left Dallas in the first place. Enough of the Old West philosophy lingered in Carroll to prevent their asking about his past; a man was still accepted at face value until proven otherwise.

Only his intimate friends knew the truth: Carroll was as far as he could drive from Dallas in one day and still stay in Texas.

"Actually, L. D.," Charles said, slumping deeper into the overstuffed couch, "Carroll had another advantage besides just being a day's drive from Dallas."

"What's that?" asked L. D. Lassiter, Crawford County Attorney and hometown boy.

"Carroll had a liquor store at the edge of town, and I badly needed a drink at that particular time."

"Charles, if the town ever hears you say that, the citizens will tar you with liquid manure, roll you in tumbleweeds, and ride you out of town in a horse trailer," Angie Lassiter said as she appeared from the kitchen with a tray laden with cold cuts, beer, and crackers. Charles grinned at her. "May I depend on you to keep my secret?"

Angie smiled as she set the tray down. "I think I'll just hold that information over your head, Charles, in case I need it to keep you in line. Enjoy yourselves, gentlemen; I'm going to take a nap while the kids are asleep."

Charles reached for a beer and admired Angie's slim legs as she walked out of the room. He felt his usual self-recrimination for wanting his best friend's wife. He often wondered why he tortured himself by spending so much time at L. D.'s house. He would never allow himself to tell her how he felt, yet he couldn't bring himself to stop taking advantage of every opportunity to be around her. The ringing of the telephone interrupted his thoughts, and he unconsciously rose to answer it.

"If it's a divorce client, I'm not here," said L. D., making himself a towering sandwich. "I'm sick and damn tired of people calling me on Sunday to tell me about their marital problems."

"Don't you know a lawyer is a father confessor?" asked Charles.

"Don't tell me! I'm the one who has to listen to them complain about their spouses, and they always insist on telling me more than I want or need to hear. You'd be amazed—"

"Charles, it's for you," Angie interrupted.

"This is the sheriff," he said, his voice lacking the familiar drawl of the region. He leaned against the kitchen wall and crossed one ankle over the other. A frown line appeared between his eyebrows and he straightened up, his fine-featured face assuming its usual stern lines.

"Where did it happen? Okay, tell Meenie I'll be right out." He hung up the phone and turned to L. D., a puzzled expression replacing the frown.

"Some farmer just found Billy Joe Williams's body out on 1283. I need to call the J. P. and get out there. Come with me, L. D.; Meenie thinks there's something funny about this one."

"Meenie would see something criminal about the Second Coming," said L. D., disgust in his voice. "Let me tell Angie where I'm going, and get some shoes on." He padded into the bedroom and Charles could hear his deep voice and Angie's murmured responses. Again he felt a stab of jealousy. "Always want what you can't have, don't you, Charles boy?" he asked himself. He smiled at his own bitterness and, turning, dialed the justice of the peace.

"Sammy, this is Charles. I need a pronouncement from you. A farmer found Billy Joe Williams out on 1283. Looks like a car wreck." Charles cursed silently at the strident voice coming from the phone. "I know it's Sunday afternoon, Sammy, but no one is officially dead until you say so. I'll have a patrol car pick you up. Thanks, Sammy," he said, without waiting to hear any more excuses.

"Damn him," said Charles as they left the house. "Next election, I'm putting up my own candidate for J. P. That man is too lazy to scratch his own fleas."

"Good luck, Charles, as long as the bastard dismisses all his friends' traffic tickets, the office is his for life."

"Don't be too sure; he's never had me after him before." Charles's voice was expressionless, and all the more frightening because of it.

Charles and L. D. got into the beige patrol car with its star-shaped insignia on the door. The make of car varied from year to year, depending on which local dealer got the bid, but the color and insignia never changed. The hum of the air conditioning and the staccato sounds of the police band radio formed a familiar background for their conversation.

"I suppose you will be ladling the beef and beans at the barbecue tomorrow?"

"Of course; it's my service club that sponsors Frontier Days, after all. Besides, it's a good time to see everybody in the county."

"Anyone would think you are running for reelection this year," grinned Charles.

"Anyone with any sense starts running for reelection from the day he is sworn in," said L. D. "You need to remember that, Charles."

"I had enough of political trade-offs and maneuvering in Dallas, L. D., and I found I wasn't very good at it."

"You're a politician; County Sheriff is an elective office," objected L. D.

"But I won't play politics to stay here," snapped Charles, annoyed with the conversation. L. D. had polished the art of small-town politics to a high gloss, but it was one of his friend's accomplishments that Charles didn't admire.

They left the city limits and the air shimmered with the afternoon heat. Fields of maize rippled like green ocean waves as the hot summer wind blew across them. Pivot irrigation systems sprayed water through their aerial pipes, covering over a hundred acres at a time, turning an arid land into some of the most valuable farm property in the world. Charles turned onto Farm Road 1283 and picked up speed. The road was a tunnel between the corn fields that covered hundreds of acres on either side.

"How do you suppose Billy Joe could wreck his pickup out here? There's nothing to hit, and usually the bar ditch isn't deep enough to roll a vehicle," asked L. D.

"I don't know, but Meenie thought something was a little odd," Charles answered. "And if Meenie thinks something is odd, then you can depend on it being true."

Red flashing lights and a small group of people signaled the site of the wreck. Charles parked the patrol car on the shoulder of the road and climbed out. A short, bowlegged man dressed in the Sheriff's Department uniform of beige western-cut pants and shirt detached himself from a small crowd of similarly dressed men that surrounded the battered pickup. Shifting a wad of tobacco from one cheek to the other, the man spat into the bar ditch, hitched up the trousers that threatened to slip off his skinny hips, and walked up to Charles.

"Sheriff, L. D.," Meenie Higgins nodded at each man, rocking back and forth in his boots, thumbs hooked over his belt. "It's a funny one; looks like someone dumped a load of parathion right over his pickup."

"I didn't think spray pilots sprayed insecticides across roads. Was it an accident?" asked Charles, his long legs carrying him down the bar ditch to the pickup.

Meenie spat a stream of tobacco juice onto the asphalt. "If it was, no one reported it. Besides, there's traces of parathion for a hundred yards down the road. Don't generally fly down the middle of the highway sprayin' the stuff. Not too many grasshoppers on asphalt."

"Just a minute, Meenie," said L. D. "Parathion can't kill anyone instantly, unless you held his head down in a tank of the stuff so he would drown."

"L. D.'s right; that chemical won't kill you, leastways not right away. But it sure as hell made him sick," said Meenie. "Looks like he hit his head on the dashboard, too."

Charles squinted through the window at the limp body, noting the vomit-flecked shirt. He looked around the cab of the pickup, and finally asked, "Where's his hat?"

Meenie pushed his own hat to the back of his head, shifted his wad to the other cheek, and accurately struck a grasshopper with a stream of tobacco juice. "Don't know, Sheriff. Never saw old Billy Joe without his hat. Got to be around here somewhere."

"Send someone down the road to see if it can be found. There's evidence on the side of the door that Billy Joe was sick more than once. Maybe he leaned out the window and his hat fell off." Charles rose and dusted off his trousers.

"What's so important about his hat, Charles?" asked L. D. as the two men moved away from the pickup to seek air less pungent with the smell of death and parathion.

"Billy Joe would never drive off and leave his hat. That was a good Stetson he wore, and he couldn't afford another one. No matter how sick he was, even if he had been sick right on top of it, he would never have left it behind." Charles shaded his eyes under his own broad-brimmed hat and looked down the road that seemed to undulate in the oppressive heat.

"Let's talk to that farmer that discovered the wreck. Maybe he noticed something." Charles walked over to a heavy-set man in his middle thirties.

"I'm Sheriff Matthews," said Charles, shaking the man's hand. "When did you discover the wreck?"

"Joe Davis, Sheriff," replied the man. "I was on my way down to my corn field to check the irrigation water. Corn takes a hell of a lot of water. I don't think I'm going to make a dime on that crop, either; it hasn't rained in six weeks, and I've had to irrigate every damn day. My hired hand quit last week, and I've been meeting myself coming and going, just trying to stay even with all the work."

"I'm sure it's difficult," Charles broke in smoothly. He had lived in the Panhandle long enough to learn that a farmer could spend hours discussing the price of irrigation gas, the rising cost of seed, fertilizer, herbicide, and the ridiculously low prices their crops brought in the marketplace. Charles was sympathetic to the family farmer caught in the cost squeeze, but he just didn't have time to listen today.

"Mister Davis, if you would just give me a quick description of what you found," said Charles.

"Well, I found just what you see. The pickup was upside down in the ditch. I looked in and saw Billy Joe. I knew right off he was dead. His eyes were open, and glazed over. I got back in my pickup and drove down to the house and called your office. I didn't see nobody at all."

"What time was this, Mister Davis?" asked Charles.

"About thirty minutes ago," replied the farmer, checking his watch. "Must have been about three o'clock or so."

"Okay, thank you. Go on back to town with my deputy Raul Trujillo and give him a statement."

"Do you mind if I go check my irrigation water first, Sheriff? God knows, I should have done it earlier, but the wife's folks came to dinner, and I was late getting started."

"Go ahead, Mister Davis. Just drop by the office after you finish. And thank you again." Charles watched the man hurry over to his pickup and drive off.

The sound of a siren and flashing lights signaled the approach of another patrol car. It screeched to a halt and an enormous man with a matching belly unfolded himself from the front seat. A well-chewed cigar was clamped between his teeth and a network of tiny veins on his nose and cheeks indicated an excessive fondness for fermented beverages. He took his cigar out of his mouth and picked flecks of tobacco off the protruding lower lip.

"All right, Sheriff, where is this body I have to look at?" Sammy Phillips's voice managed to combine a strident quality with a nasal tone, a combination that immediately set Charles's teeth on edge.

"Right over here. And Sammy, I want an autopsy ordered." Charles's voice and face were expressionless, but their very lack of expression lent him an uncompromising authority.

"Now wait jest a minute, Sheriff. I'm the one who makes that decision. Ain't no sense in spending the county's money for an autopsy on a car wreck victim. Some of you elected officials are always spendin' money like it was water, but not Sammy Phillips, no sir. There ain't gonna be no autopsy when it ain't necessary." Sammy panted with exertion as he climbed down the steep bank of the bar ditch to peer in the window at Billy Joe's body.

"Sammy!" Charles's voice cracked like breaking glass. "There is no visible injury to Billy Joe that could be fatal. When that is the case, the law requires an autopsy to determine the exact cause of death." Charles waited a moment as he and the J. P. exchanged glances, two adversaries preparing for a duel. "I'm sure you don't want the good citizens of Crawford County believing that you are incapable of performing the duties of your office."

Sammy laboriously pulled himself to his feet and stood in front of the sheriff, a whine now becoming evident in his voice. "Now, Sheriff, I told you that I didn't like ordering autopsies for every Tom, Dick, and Harry that gets drunk and piles up his pickup in a bar ditch."

Charles inspected his nails for a moment, then looked at Sammy, a bland expression on his face. "I got an interesting report by teletype the other day, Sammy. It had to do with one of our local citizens, one of our prominent local citizens, being drunk and disorderly in a public bar downstate. You wouldn't know who that prominent citizen was, would you, Sammy?" Charles held up his hand as the J. P.'s face reddened and he seemed ready to explode. "Another interesting thing about that report, Sammy, was the information that the companion of said local citizen was remanded to juvenile court." Charles's voice lowered to a whisper threaded with disgust. "That means the companion was under seventeen, Sammy."

The J. P. pulled a handkerchief out of his pocket and wiped his face, then carefully ran it around the inside lining of his straw Stetson. He cleared his throat noisily, and blew his nose with the same sweat-stained handkerchief. He licked his fleshy lower lip and replaced his hat, setting it squarely on his head. He looked at the cigar held between his fingers as though wondering how it came to be there.

"It seems to me, Sheriff, that the death of that poor boy over there needs further investigation. I'm going to order an autopsy just to satisfy myself." Sammy wiped his face again and climbed back in the patrol car. "Hey, you," he yelled out to one of the deputies, "drive me home." He glared at Charles momentarily, but his eyes shifted away from direct contact with the chilling brown ones of the sheriff.

Charles watched the patrol car reverse direction and head back to town. He didn't regret his tactics with Sammy at all. If his stint in the Dallas District Attorney's office had taught him nothing else, it had taught him to fight politicians on their own terms.

"Raul," Charles motioned to an olive-skinned deputy standing motionless by the side of the road, "get some pictures of the pickup and the body." Raul nodded silently and went to get the field camera from his car. Charles turned as Meenie stepped to his side, holding a Stetson.

"This is it, Sheriff. Found it about a quarter mile down the road. Must have fell off his head when he got sick, and he just drove off and left it. Found some skid marks in the dirt by the side of the road a little farther back. Billy Joe sure wasn't paying much attention to his drivin'." Meenie shifted his tobacco again and turned his head to spit.

"That's kind of strange, too, Sheriff. Ole Billy Joe was a good driver. He never had a ticket in his life; used to brag about it. I guess it was the only thing he ever had to brag about. He wasn't good for much, but he sure could drive."

Charles shifted uncomfortably, feeling the hot sun burning through his sports shirt. He felt the need of some cold beer to wash the dry Panhandle dust out of his mouth. He smiled bitterly to himself. It wasn't the dust that was drying out his mouth and throat, but the familiar fury he always felt in the presence of death, particularly violent, unnecessary death.

"Meenie, you and Raul find out everything you can about Billy Joe. I especially want to know where he was last night and whom he talked to. I want to know what he was doing here. Was he driving to work?"

"Hell, Sheriff, Billy Joe couldn't hold down a job for more than a month at a time. No farmer in his right mind would let him around any machinery; he was too damn careless. None of the ranchers would hire him as a cowboy 'cause he couldn't stay on a horse. Whatever he was doing out here, it sure wasn't drivin' to work." Meenie shifted his tobacco again and spat, striking a beetle crawling along the road.

"Crying shame, Sheriff; Billy Joe never did no harm to anyone. He was kind of a useless human being, but he wasn't bad." Meenie rubbed the stubble on his jaw thoughtfully. He was always trying to cultivate a beard, and would let his whiskers grow until his chin looked like a scraggly pincushion. "What do you think happened, Sheriff?"

"He doesn't appear to be seriously injured from the wreck, and you natives assure me parathion wouldn't kill him." Charles shrugged his shoulders. "I'd say that leaves the case wide open."

Abruptly he turned his back to the wrecked pickup and its pitiful occupant. "Tell the mortician to take the body to Amarillo for an autopsy and find out who was spraying parathion this morning."

"Hell, that could be half the county, Sheriff; everybody's trying to keep the grasshoppers out of their crops."

"Then we'll just question half the county if that's what it takes. Billy Joe Williams might have been shiftless, but he was still worth more than a grasshopper."

PART 5

EAST TEXAS

The Two-Bear Mambo

JOE R. LANSDALE

Deep East Texas has far more in common with the Old South than it does with the rest of the state. Towering pine forests, red clay back-roads, swamps, cotton fields—and lingering racial issues. This region has the highest concentration of African Americans in the state, yet several East Texas towns have populations that are virtually entirely white. One such place is Vidor, which for many years had a Ku Klux Klan bookstore on the main street and hosted a national KKK group. Another East Texas town with a poor racial image is Jasper, where, in 1998, a black man, James Byrd, Jr., was chained to a pickup by three white men and dragged to his death.

East Texas native Joe R. Lansdale explores the consequences of racism and violence in his work, often with offbeat humor. Lansdale is prolific in several categories: mysteries, sci-fi, westerns, fantasy, and horror. His best books are his non-series Southern Gothic noirs: *Cold in July*—a reimagining of the Gold Medal paperbacks of the 1950s with some nasty modern twists; *The Bottoms*—his Edgar Award–winning homage to *To Kill a Mockingbird* set in Depression-era East Texas; and *Freezer Burn*—a Jim Thompson-meets-Flannery O'Connor masterpiece of an incredibly inept robber on the lam with a carnival.

Lansdale's most popular books, however, are found in his mystery series that chronicles the misadventures of the "Odd Couple" of Texas detection, Hap Collins and Leonard Pine. Hap is a white, skirt-chasing good ol' boy while Leonard is black, Republican, and gay. In *The Two-Bear Mambo*, Hap and Leonard travel to fictional Grovetown, where African Americans are most definitely unwelcome.

On the way to Grovetown, Leonard put a Hank Williams cassette in the player and we listened to that. I never got to play what I liked. I wanted to bring some cassettes of my own, but Leonard said it was his car, so we'd listen to his music. He didn't care much for what I liked. Sixties rock and roll.

Even Hank Williams couldn't spoil the beauty of the day, however, and the truth of the matter was, I was really starting to like his music, though I wasn't willing to let Leonard know.

It was cold as an Eskimo's ass in an igloo outhouse, but it was clear and bright and the East Texas woods were dark and soothing. The pines, cold or not, held their green, except for the occasional streaks of rust-colored needles, and the oaks, though leafless, were thick and intertwining, like the bones of some unknown species stacked into an elaborate art arrangement.

We passed a gap in the woods where the pulp wooders had been. It looked like a war zone. The trees were gone for a patch of twenty to thirty acres, and there were deep ruts in the red clay, made by truck tires. Mounds of stumps and limbs had been piled up and burned, leaving ash and lumps, and in some cases huge chunks of wood that had not burned up, but had only been kissed black by fire.

One huge oak tree stump, old enough to have dated to the beginning of the century, had taken on the shape of a knotty skull, as if it were all that was left of some prehistoric animal struck by lightning. Clear cutting, gasoline, and kitchen matches had laid the dinosaurs low. Driven by greed and the need for a satellite dish, pulp wooders had turned beauty to shit, wood to paper, which in turn served to make the bills of money that paid the pulpers who slew the gods in the first place. There was sad irony in all that. Somewhere. May saplings sprout from their graves.

Just past mid-day Hank was singing, for about the fifteenth time, "Why don't you love me like you used to do," when we reached the outskirts of Grovetown. Here the trees were thick and dark and somber. Low rain clouds had formed, turning the bright cold day gray and sad as a widow's thoughts. The charcoal-colored clouds hung over the vast forest on either side of the narrow, cracked highway as if they were puffy cotton hats, leaving only a few rays of sunlight to penetrate them like polished hat pins.

I watched the woods speed by, and thought about what was out there. We were on the edge of the Big Thicket. One of the great forests of the United States, and everything opposite of what the TV and movie viewer thinks Texas is about. The pulp wooders and the lumber companies had certainly raped a lot of it, like most of East Texas, but here there was still plenty of it left. For now.

Out there, in the Thicket, there were swampy stretches, creeks and timber so compact a squirrel couldn't run through it without aid of a machete. The bottoms were brutal. Freezing black slush in the winter, steamy and mosquito-swarmed in the summer, full of fat, poisonous water moccasins, about the most unpleasant snakes in creation.

When I was a child, an uncle of mine, Benny, a man wise to the ways of the woods, had gotten lost in the Thicket for four days. He lived off puddled water and edible roots. He had been one of those contradictory fellas who loved the woods and wildlife, and yet shot everything that wasn't already stuffed, and if the light were to have glinted off the eye of a taxidermied critter, he might have shot that too. He was such a voracious hunter my dad used him as an example of how I ought not be. It was my father's contention, and it's certainly mine, that hunting is not a sport. If the animals could shoot back, then it would be a sport. It is justifiable only for food, and for no other reason. After that, it's just killing for the sake of putting a lid on what still simmers deep in our primitive hearts.

But my Uncle Benny, a big, laughing man who I liked very much, was out late one summer night hunting coons for their pelts. He followed the sounds of his dogs deep into the Thicket, then the sounds went away, and he found that the foliage overhead was so thick he could see neither moon nor stars.

Benny wore a kind of head lamp when he hunted. I don't remember what the stuff was called, carbide, I think, but there were these pellets you put in the headlamp and lit, and they made a little stinky flame that danced out from the headband and made a light. Lots of hunters used them back then.

This headlamp went out and Benny dropped his flashlight while trying to turn it on, and couldn't find it. He spent hours crawling along the ground, but he couldn't locate the flashlight, and he couldn't relight the lamp because he'd gotten his matches wet by stepping waist deep into a hole full of stagnant water.

He finally fell asleep resting against the base of a tree, and was awakened in the night by something huge crashing through the brush. Benny climbed the tree by feel, damn near putting out his eye on a thorn that was part of a wrist-thick crawling vine that was trying to choke the tree out.

In the morning, after a night of squatting on a limb, he came down and found bear tracks. This was before the black bear had been nearly exterminated from the Thicket. In fact, there were still plenty of them in those days, and wild hogs too.

The tracks circled the tree and there were scratch marks where the bear had risen up on its hind legs, perhaps hoping to bring down a treat from overhead. The bear had missed reaching Uncle Benny by less than a foot.

Benny found his flashlight, but it was useless. He had stepped on it in the night, busting out the bulb. Even though it was morning, he found there was no way to truly see the sun because the limbs tangled together overhead and the leaves and pine needles spread out like camouflaging, tinting the daylight brown and green.

All day, as he trekked blindly about, the mosquitoes rose up and over him in black kamikaze squadrons so compact they looked as if they were sheets of close-weave netting. They feasted so often on the thorn scratch over his eye, that eye eventually closed. His lips swelled up thick and tight and his face ballooned. Everywhere he went he wore those mosquitoes like a coat of chain mail.

As the day slogged on, he discovered he had also gotten into poison ivy, and it was spreading over his body, popping up pustules on his feet and hands and face, and the more he scratched, the more it spread, until even his nuts were covered in the stuff. He used to say: "Poison ivy bumps were so thick, it pushed the hair out of my balls."

He told me he hurt so bad, was so lost, so scared, so hungry and thirsty, he actually considered putting the rifle in his mouth and ending it all. Later, that wasn't an option. Crossing through a low-lying area, he discovered what appeared to be a thick covering of leaves was nothing more than slushy swamp, and in the process of grabbing on to the exposed roots of a great willow tree to save himself from drowning, he lost his rifle in the muck.

Eventually he found his way out, but not by true woodcraft. By accident. Or in his words, "By miracle." Benny came upon a gaunt steer, a Hereford/Long Horn mix. It was staggering and its great head hung almost to the ground. It was covered in crusted mud from its hoofs to its massive horns. It had obviously been mired up somewhere, perhaps trying to escape the mosquitoes.

Uncle Benny watched it, and finally it began to move, slow but steady,

and he followed the thorn-torn steer through the thicket, sometimes cling-
ing to its mud-and-shit-coated tail. He clung and followed until it arrived
at the pasture it had escaped from, through a gap in the barbed wire. Uncle
Benny said when that steer finally broke through the briars and limbs and
the light came through the trees and showed him the bright green of the
pasture, it was like the door to heaven had been opened.

When the steer reached the emerald pasture, it bellowed joyfully, staggered, fell, and never rose. Its back legs and hindquarters were swollen
up as if they were made of soaked sponge, and there were wounds that
gurgled pus the color of primeval sin and thick as shaving foam.

Uncle Benny figured the steer had gotten into a whole nest of moccasins, or timber rattlers, and they'd struck it repeatedly. Steer might have
been out there in the Thicket for a week. The fact that it had survived as
long as it had was evidence of the heartiness of the Long Horn strain that
ran through it. It died where it fell.

From there Benny made his way to the highway and found his car. His
hunting dogs never showed up. He went there for a week and called their
names where they had gone in with him, and he drove the back roads
searching, but never a sign. To the best of my knowledge, though he continued to hunt from time to time, Benny never went into the deep woods
again, and the infected eye gave him trouble all his life, until at the age of
sixty-five he had to have it removed and replaced with a cheap glass one.

You don't fuck with the Big Thicket.

Grovetown wasn't much. A few streets, some of them brick, and down on
the square an ancient courthouse and jail, a filling station/grocery store,
and the Grovetown Cafe, and a lot of antique and thrift shops. There were
benches out front of most of the buildings, and you had to figure if it
wasn't Christmas Day and most of those places weren't closed there'd be
old men sitting there, bundled up, talking, smoking, and almost managing
to spit Red Man off the curb.

The filling station/grocery was one of the few places open, and as we
drove past, a tall, thirtyish, handsome, pale-faced guy in a gray shirt,
heavy coat, and gimme cap stood out by one of the pumps with a water
hose, washing down oil and grease in the center of one of the drives. He
stared at us as we drove by, looking like a guy who might wash your windshield, check your tires and oil without having to be asked, just like in the
old days. Then, on the other hand, looks could be deceiving. Guy like that

might piss on your windshield and let the air out of your tires as soon as look at you.

Christ, I was beginning to think like Leonard. Everyone was a scumbag until proven otherwise.

We passed a washateria with a sign painted on the glass. It was faded, but it was defiantly readable. NO COLORED.

Leonard said, "Man, I ain't seen nothing like that since 1970. Jefferson, Texas, I think it was."

We decided we ought to get a room, least for the night until we could get the lay of the land. There were no motels in Grovetown, but there was one old hotel and a boarding house. We checked both for lodging, but they didn't have rooms for us. They claimed to be closed for Christmas. I found this hard to believe. Hotels and boarding houses don't close for holidays, and as for not having rooms, the Hotel Grovetown was so goddamn vacant of life you could almost hear rats farting behind the wainscoting.

At the boarding house, called the Grovetown Inn, there weren't more than three cars in the parking lot, but when we came in together, asked for a room, the proprietors looked at us like we were animated shit piles asking to lie down free on clean white sheets.

Outside the Grovetown Inn, Leonard filled his pipe, said, "No room at the inn, brother. Think it's that shirt you're wearin' they don't like? Personally, I've always felt blue makes you look a little scary."

We drove around awhile. Leonard said, "Have you noted there's no black section of town around here?"

"Yep. I have."

"They haven't even given us black folk a place out next to the city dump, like usual. Or maybe by a sewage plant or a nuclear reactor. I ain't even seen a black person walking around."

"Maybe it's because of the holidays. I haven't seen that many whites walking around. And guess what else? There aren't any more places to stay. We've seen it all."

"I'm hungry. Cafe's open. Let's get something to eat, then figure on what to do next."

"They'll be glad to see us there, Leonard. Why don't I keep things simple for now, get us a couple of sandwiches to go?"

"Hey, I'll tell you now, I'm not going to anyone's back door or stand in a separate line just because I got a better tan than someone else. Get that straight in your head, Hap."

"I'm just wanting things easy. What worries me about you, is I think you like confrontation too much."

"And what worries me about you, Hap, is you don't."

I pulled over in front of the cafe, started to get out. Leonard put a hand on my arm. "You're right. I'm acting like an asshole."

"No argument."

"We're here to find Florida, not have me prove what a badass I am."

"Still, no argument."

"Get us something. We'll eat in the car. I'll give a civil rights speech later. Provided I can get someone to accompany me on guitar."

"I'll just be a minute."

The Grovetown Cafe was not a place you would mistake for a French restaurant. It was overly warm and the walls were decorated with badly painted ceramic birds and squirrels, and there was some of that really bad hillbilly music you hear from time to time but can't quite believe it. It's not even AM radio pop. It only plays in ancient towns with jukeboxes that have glass cases coated gray by oily hands. It's like generic heavy metal and rap. Who listens to this stuff on purpose? It sounds like some kind of joke. The sharp little notes clung to the air and stuck to my head like prickly pear thorns. They went well with the stench of old grease from the kitchen.

I waded through grease and music and found a stool and sat down and waited. From a back booth a couple of guys stared at me. They were in their thirties, healthy-looking, but they had the attitude of men with "back problems" on workdays. It's a mysterious ailment that seems to descend on a large percentage of the redneck population. I couldn't help but think they were drawing a check from somewhere. Some kind of compensation. Maybe they were watching me nervously because they thought I was an insurance man that had caught them without their back braces.

I figured, at night, after a hard day of smoking cigarettes, swigging coffee, and cussin' the niggers and liberals, they'd buy a couple of six-packs, go home and pass out in front of the TV set after beating the wife and kids, a half-eaten bag of generic-brand potato chips clutched to their chests.

Then again, here I was judging people I didn't even know. I was starting to be just like the people I despised. They were probably a couple of nuclear physicists on vacation, stopping in here to soak up the homey atmosphere.

I had to quit judging. Quit being unfair. And I had to face what I was really worked up about. Knowing I'd probably see Florida and have all the old feelings again. And it was cold, and I didn't like it. And I had fewer future prospects than the smallpox virus. In final analysis, I had a hard-on for the world and no place to put it.

I noticed one of the physicists had turned in the booth and the other was leaning out on his side, looking not just at me, but past me. I looked where they were looking, and I could see through the plate glass window, between the fly specks, Leonard's car. He was visible behind the wheel, his head back on the seat dozing.

I began to have those prejudgment thoughts again.

I took a deep breath and let it slide. I tried to remember and paraphrase a comforting Bible verse. "Judge not others, lest ye be judged." Something like that. I also remembered a verse my daddy told me. "You end up havin' to hit some sonofabitch, don't just hit him once, and don't just hit to get his attention."

A fiftyish lady who might have been pretty if she'd had enough energy to hold herself straighter and if her hair wasn't oily and stuck to her cheeks, came out of the back wiping wet flour on her apron. "What can I get you?"

"Couple hamburgers and large coffees to go. Some potato chips."

"It's early for hamburgers," she said.

"I missed breakfast. Got any fried pies?"

"No. We sell some candy at the register. Peanut patties, Tootsie Rolls, Mounds, Snickers, Milky Way. That's it."

"All right. Couple of peanut patties."

"That nigger out there will want more'n a couple of them patties," said one of the men in the back. "A nigger likes a peanut pattie. Next to what a woman's got, and a watermelon, ain't much they like better."

"And loose shoes," said the other fella. "And a warm place to shit."

"Boys," said the woman, "you watch your language in here." I looked at them and smiled sadly. I began to understand why so many clichés persist. Too much truth in them. I gave them a real looksee for the first time.

Big motherfuckers. Not physicists. They looked like human bookends for the Adult Western Novel shelf. Both rednecked and stupid. The one talking almost had a mustache, or maybe he just hadn't quite got shaving down yet. I wished, just once in a while, the guys wanted to harass me or whip my ass would be short. Kind of small. Weak even. In business suits. Yankees. That would make things a little more all right.

Better yet, I wished those dudes would just leave me alone. What was it about me that I was the one always stepped in the doo-doo? If I walked ten miles around a cow lot to keep the manure off my shoes, I'd manage to find a fresh heap of dog shit to put my foot in.

"Better give me a couple creams to go with that coffee," I told the lady.

"Nigger working for you?" said the other man. This one was not a bad-looking guy, but he had a tavern tumor that was threatening the buttons on his paisley shirt, and a kind of smirk like he'd been corn-holing your wife and she'd told him to tell you so.

The lady said, "Boys, y'all ought to go hang out somewhere else." Then to me: "I'll just be a minute. You want those well-done, don't you?"

I spoke so only she could hear. "Actually, I'd like them about as quick as I can get them."

She smiled. "They don't mean no harm. They just don't like niggers."

"Ah."

Now I felt better. I glanced out at Leonard. He was really snoozing. In fact, he might have been hibernating. Great. Here I was with the hippo twins, and the Smartest Nigger in the World was tucked in for the winter.

The boys came over and sat on stools on either side of me.

"I ain't seen you before," said Paisley Shirt.

"Well," I said, "I don't get through here much. Buy you fellas some coffee?"

"Naw," said the other one. "We've had coffee."

"Lots of it," said Paisley Shirt.

"I don't know about you," I said, "but lots of coffee makes me nervous. In fact, maybe I shouldn't have got coffee with my lunch. I've had too much this morning already."

"You look a little nervous," said Paisley Shirt. "Maybe you ought to give up coffee altogether."

"I just might," I said.

"Me and my brother," said Paisley Shirt, "we don't have trouble with coffee. We don't have trouble with beer, wine, or whiskey."

"What about Christmas ants?" I said. "You got Christmas ant trouble, I know two guys you ought to meet."

"Christmas ants?" said Bad Mustache.

The woman called from the back then. Her voice was a little halfhearted, like she was calling a dog she figured had gotten run over. "Y'all go back and sit down, now."

"We're all right, Mama," said Paisley Shirt.

"Mama?" I said.

"Uh huh," said Bad Mustache. "What's this about Christmas ants?"

"Little bastards are serious trouble where I come from," I said. "You think fire ants are hell, you get into some of them Christmas ants, well, those buggers won't never let go."

"I ain't never heard of no Christmas ants," said Paisley Shirt.

"Neither had most anybody else in LaBorde until yesterday," I said. "But you'll read about it in the papers today or tomorrow, see it on the news.

They're epidemic there. Brought in from Mexico, they think. In a crate of bananas. Or a shipment of cigars. They're deadly dudes, these Christmas ants."

"Wait a minute," said Bad Mustache. "Is that like them ants in that movie where they take over this plantation and this guy—"

"Charlton Heston," I said.

"Yeah, I guess . . . you've seen it?"

"Yep," I said. "And that's exactly what I'm talking about. But that was only a picture. They couldn't show it the way it is. I tell you, LaBorde's a mess. I think the loss of life is in the hundreds. Maybe the thousands by now. The guy in the car, Doctor Pine. He's from the government. World's expert on Christmas ants. One reason he's passed out is he's been up all night battling them. He lost."

"A nigger expert?" said Paisley. "There's your goddamn problem."

"I don't know," I said. "He had some good ideas, but the ants were too entrenched. I'll be honest with you. I work for the city there. Water Department. We were the first to catch on to the epidemic. Lots of people don't give us credit. They don't think much of the Water Department, but they don't know the things we see. Alligators. Snakes. Christmas ants. You can't drown those little bastards. The Christmas ants, I mean. And you better not have a banana, or some kind of fruit in your house. They track to the stuff like a pig to corn. Anyway, what I was saying is this. I'm not going back. Dr. Pine out there wants to go back, and he can if he wants, but not me. The ants have gotten too goddamn big for this cowboy."

"They grow?" said Paisley Shirt.

I smiled. "Look, it's not a science-fiction movie. It's not like they're ten feet tall. That's bullshit. They only get about the size of a rat. Some of them do, I mean. Most of them, they're more mouse or mole size."

"Naw," said Bad Mustache. "You're pulling our dicks."

"I wouldn't think of pulling your dick," I said. "Listen here, I wouldn't have believed it either had I not been there. These ants, they don't get that big in their own environment. But they thrive here. No one knew that until this week. What they've discovered, and it's something no one would have suspected, is that the tropical weather was keeping them small. They get a little cold snap, bam, they're big as rodents. It has something to do with the way they eat and the way their metabolism deals with the natural sugars and starches in human flesh."

"Human flesh?" Bad Mustache said.

"Uh huh," I said. "It's not a horror movie where they swarm someone and eat every inch of skin off of them. But they leave bad bites. And they can cause death, and have. Like I said, in the hundreds."

"They bite you to death?" said Bad Mustache.

"I'm a little sketchy on if it's the bite or the poisons in their system that kills humans. They do take a lot of meat with them, though. Actually, you'd have to get Dr. Pine to explain it to you."

"Wow!" said Paisley Shirt.

"Wow, indeed," I said.

"But why do you call them Christmas ants?" Bad Mustache asked.

"Again, you got me. I'm no ant expert. Maybe because they were discovered around Christmastime. That's what I figure."

The lady came out with my hamburgers.

"LaBorde," said Paisley Shirt. "That's not that far from here."

"No it isn't," I said. I got up, went over to the register, and called back to them. "I wouldn't alarm myself. I'd just be alert. Watch the ground. Especially at sunset and sunrise. That's when they like to travel."

The lady took my money at the register. She said, "Those boys are so dumb, I sometimes think maybe my kids were switched at birth, and they gave me these two jackasses. All they know is what they see on the TV."

"Maybe they ought to watch the educational channel. Last night they had a great *National Geographic* special on bears. I tell you, it tantalized me to the point I couldn't sleep afterwards."

"I like a good nature program myself," she said.

I got my change, and started out. Paisley Shirt said, "Hey, you said there were two guys we ought to meet."

"Well," I said, "I meant you would have liked them. They're back in LaBorde. Or were. But, you know . . . the ants."

"You been jacking with us, ain't you?" said Paisley Shirt.

"There's lots of people who've ignored the facts of scientific research," I said. "All of it to their detriment. Believe what you want, it's nothing to me. It's not my job to educate the masses. I work for the Water Department. But I will say this. I'm proud of that. I don't care what anyone else thinks about the Water Department. I'm proud."

I went out to the car and got in. I shook Leonard. He came around slowly and looked at me.

"Man, I sort of passed out."

"Let's go." Leonard started the car as the brothers came out of the cafe, stood on the sidewalk and looked at us. Leonard watched them a moment, backed out and drove off.

"Trouble?" he asked.

"No. But I will say this. It's not every day you can actually step into a science-fiction episode of *The Andy Griffith Show* by way of *Deliverance*."

Gone Fishin'

WALTER MOSLEY

Walter Mosley is the creator of Ezekiel "Easy" Rawlins, the nation's best-known African American detective since Chester Himes' "Coffin" Ed Johnson and "Grave Digger" Jones in the 1950s. Just as Himes earlier portrayed Harlem's culture in his detective novels, Mosley chronicles Los Angeles's African American culture from the 1940s to the 1960s.

Easy Rawlins solves mysteries with the help of his violence-prone best friend, Raymond "Mouse" Alexander, and each of Mosley's novels explores the complicated relationship between the two men. In 1997, Mosley created a "prequel" to the Easy Rawlins series, *Gone Fishin'*, which is set in 1939 and retraces the pair's Texas roots. Soon after this time, America would see a great migration—millions of black Americans would move from the South to urban centers in the North, Midwest, and West Coast. Easy and Mouse are among those who will join the exodus.

In *Gone Fishin'*, Mouse has convinced nineteen-year-old Easy to give up his job in Houston and "borrow" a '36 Ford for a road trip to fictional Pariah, a swampy town in East Texas where Mouse hopes to collect some money. Along the way, they pick up a pair of troubled hitchhikers and encounter a voodoo priestess in the tangled thickets of East Texas. The menacing aura offers hints of the trouble that awaits Easy and Mouse farther down the road.

It was still dark when we made it down to Lucinda Greg's house. She was Otum Chenier's girlfriend. I warmed up the engine while Mouse changed clothes and made lunch inside. He came out in gray pants and a gray shirt, work clothes that fit him like dress clothes.

When we drove off it was still way before dawn. Mouse was sleeping against the passenger door and I was driving with the few feeble lights of Houston behind us. It was going to be a warm day but the air still held a light chill of night. I wanted to sing but I didn't because Mouse wouldn't have understood my feelings about magic and the morning. So I just drove quietly, happy on that flat Texas road.

People don't understand southern Texas. They think that the land there is ugly and flat. They take their opinion about the land and put it on the people—but they're wrong on both counts. If they could see Texas in the early dawn like I saw it that day they would know a Texas that is full of potential from the smallest rock to the oldest woman on the farm.

The road wasn't paved or landscaped. On either side there were dense shrubs and bushes with knotty pines and cherry and pear trees scattered here and there. I was especially aware of the magnolias, their flowers looking like white faces staring down from shadow.

They say it's like a desert down there, and they're right—at least sometimes. There are stretches of land that have hardly anything growing, but even then it's no simple story. Texas is made up of every kind of soil; there's red clay and gray sod and fertile brown, shipped in or strained over by poor farmers trying to make the land work. That earth gives you the feeling of confidence because it's so much and so different and, mainly, because it's got the patience to be there not ever having to look for a better place.

But there's no such thing as a desert down near the Gulf. The rains come to make bayous and swamps and feed every kind of animal and bird and varmint.

As the night disappeared the last foxes and opossums made their way to shelter. Animals everywhere were vanishing with the shadows; field mice and some deer, foxes, rabbits, and skunk.

"I'ma show you how t'fish while we down here, Ease."

I jumped when Mouse spoke.

"Man, ain't nuthin' you could tell me. I been droppin' my line in the water since before I could talk."

"That's all right," he said with a sneer. "But I show you how the master fish."

He took a fried egg sandwich from a brown paper sack and tore it in half.

"Here you go."

We were both quiet as the sun filled in the land with light. To me it was like the world was growing and I was happy to be on that road.

After a while I asked Mouse how it was that he happened to get Otum's car just when he needed a ride.

Mouse smiled and looked humble. "You know Otum's a Cajun, an' them Cajuns is fam'ly down to the bone. They'd kill over a insult to their blood that normal folks like you an' me would just laugh at. An' Otum is a real Cajun. That's a fact."

Mouse knew how to tell you a story. It was like he was singing a song and the words were notes going up and down the scales, even rhyming when it was right. He'd turn phrases that I wanted to use myself but it seemed that I couldn't ever get the timing right. Sometimes what he said fit so perfectly I couldn't ever find the right time to say it again.

". . . I always known that a message from his momma would light a fire under Otum. An' puttin' out fires is my especiality." We laughed at that. "So that night I come home from. Galveston I stayed over at Lucinda's, for a weddin' gift she said. I thought 'bout how she take care'a Otum's car an' how they got a phone down at that beauty shop she work for . . ."

Mouse smiled with all his teeth and put his foot against the dashboard so he could sit back comfortably, "You know once Otum got that message from Lucinda he knew he couldn't take his car down there. The bayou ain't no place t'drive no good car. So Lucinda tole him that you would start it up for him and look in on it every once an' a while."

"Me?"

"Well, yeah, it had t'be you, Easy. I cain't drive no car. Anyway, Otum never did trust me too much."

✪

We had been going southeast for close to two hours when we saw two people with thumbs out on the road. A big young man and a girl, maybe fifteen, with a healthy chest and smile.

"Pull on over, Ease," Mouse said. "Let's pick 'em up."

"You know 'em?" I asked as we passed by.

"Uh-uh, but oppu'tunity is ev'rywhere an' I ain't passin' up no bets."

"Man, you don't know what they's up to. They could be robbers fo'all you know."

"If they is then this here gonna be they last stand."

I shifted the clutch down and put on the brake.

As soon as we stopped, Mouse was out with the door open and the seat folded up. He waved at the couple and they came running. The boy was dragging a duffel bag that was bigger than his girlfriend.

"Come on!" Mouse shouted. "Jump in the back wit' me, man. 'Cause Easy got all kindsa dirty rags back here an' you don't want no girl in that."

"That's all right. We sit together," the young man said in a gruff tone.

"Uh-uh, Clifton," the girl complained in a high voice. "I don't wanna get filthy! Go'on an sit back there wit' him. You can still see me."

Mouse smiled and gestured for the boy to get in. Clifton did as he was asked to do, but he wasn't happy about it.

I could see in his face that Clifton hadn't had a happy day in his life. His jaw was set and his eyes were hard but he couldn't have been over seventeen. He was what Mouse called "a truly poor man." Someone who doesn't have a thing and is so mad about it that he isn't likely to ever get anything.

"Where you-all goin'?" I asked.

"Down t'N'Orleans," the girl said. She looked in my eyes to see how surprised and jealous I'd be. She had a wide face and a forehead that sloped back. Her eyes were so far apart it looked as if she couldn't focus both of them on the same thing. Her look was careless and lazy, and I looked away before I got myself into trouble.

(Note from the editors: Mouse soon learns that Clifton and Ernestine are on the run from the police because Clifton has savagely beaten a man competing for Ernestine's affections. Mouse convinces them to see a friend of his, Momma Jo, who he says can help them escape from the law. Easy takes the turnoff to Rag Bayou and follows a rough road.)

A mist of gnats and mosquitoes swarmed along the road. Mouse was shouting over the whining cicadas, "Turn down there, Easy! . . . That's it! . . . Take a lef'! . . ." The path was so rutted that I worried about breaking an axle—and I knew Otum loved that car more than his whole Cajun family.

"You can stop it right here, man!" Mouse yelled at last.

"We in the middle'a the road, fool! I gotta park."

"Okay." He shrugged. "But Otum ain't gonna like his Ford knee deep in swamp."

"But we cain't leave it in the road. What they gonna do when they come drivin' down here?"

Mouse laughed. "Man who gonna drive down here but a fool?"

I wished I had an answer to that. I pulled the car as far over to the side of the road as I could, and hoped that there was enough space in case some other fool decided to drive by.

"Com'on, Clifton, you safe fo' the first time since you laid that boy down," Mouse said.

"Hey, man." Clifton put up his hands. "Keep it quiet."

Mouse smiled and followed Ernestine out of the car door. Clifton went too.

But I stayed in the car putting on my heavy shirt and pulling my cotton cap down to my ears.

Mouse leaned in the window and said, "What you doin', Easy?"

"It's them bugs," I said. "Just one mosquito in a room will bite me twenty times and every bite swells up into a hump on my skin, and every hump itches me until I scratch it hard enough to draw blood. I hate bugs."

"You just too sweet an' sensitive," Mouse said. "All I gotta do is wave my hand in front'a my face once or twice and the bugs leave me be. An' if anything bite me he ain't never gonna bite nuthin' else."

I came out finally. Mouse slapped my shoulder and said, "Right this way, honey boy."

We walked into a wall of vines and baby bamboo. It was reedy and mulchy and thick with gnats. It was hot too. Ernestine squealed every time a frog jumped or one of those bright red swamp birds got startled and croaked its hoarse swampsong. I was sweating heavy in all those clothes and still getting bites on my face and hands.

"How far is it?" I yelled over the cicadas.

"It's up here, Ease."

"How far?"

"I'ont rightly know, man." He smiled and let go of a bamboo stalk.

"What you mean you don't know?" I had to duck down to keep the bamboo from hitting me in the face.

"Ole Momma Jo's a witch, an' witch houses on out here is like boats." He made his voice sound ghostly. "Floatin' on the bayou."

He didn't believe in that voodoo stuff, but Clifton and Ernestine got quiet and looked around as if they expected to see Baron Samedi looking out from under his skull mask.

"You can tell you gettin' close t'Momma's when the cicadas stop singin' an' the mosquitoes die down," Mouse said.

I thought he was still trying to scare us, but after a while there came a sweet woodburnt scent. Soon after that the whining of the cicadas receded and the ground became firmer. We came to a clearing and Mouse said, "Here we is," but all I saw was a stand of stunted pear trees with a big avocado rising up behind them.

"She live in the open?" Clifton asked.

A cloud shifted and the sun shone between two pear trunks. A light glinted from the trees. Mouse whistled a shrill warbled note and in a while the door came open.

It was a house hidden by trees way out there.

The house was a shock, but it was the woman standing there that scared me.

She was tall, way over six feet, wearing a short, light blue dress that was old and faded. Over her dress was a wide white apron; her jet-black skin shone against those pale colors so brightly that I winced when I first saw her. She was strongly built with wide shoulders and big strong legs.

When she strode toward us I noticed the cudgel in her broad fist. For the first time in my life I felt the roots of my hair tingle. She came to within three strides of us and pushed her handsome face forward like something wild sniffing at strangers. There was no sympathy in her face. Ernestine jumped behind Clifton and I took a step back.

Then she smiled. Big pure yellow teeth that were all there and healthy. "Raymond!" The swamp behind us got even quieter. "Raymond, boy it's good, good to see you." She lifted Mouse by his shoulders and hugged him to her big bosom.

"Mmmmmmmmmmmmm-mm, it's good." She put him down and beamed on him like a smiling black sun. "Raymond," she said. "It's been too long, honey."

Raymond is Mouse's real name, but nobody except EttaMae called him that.

"Jo, I brung you some store-bought." He held out the sack that still had two fifths of Johnnie Walker. "An' some guests." He waved his hand at us.

Momma Jo's teeth went away but she was still smiling when she asked, "These friends?"

"Oh yeah, Momma. This here is Easy Rawlins. He's my best friend. An' these chirren is the victims of a po-lice hunt. They in love too."

She took the sack and said, "Com'on then, let's get in."

We followed her in between the trees into the house, passing from day into night. The room was dark like nighttime because the sun couldn't make it through the leaves to her windows. It was a big room lit by oil lanterns. The floor was cool soil that was swept and dry. The whole place was cool as if the trees soaked up all the swamp heat. In a corner two small armadillos were snuffling over corncobs and above them was a pure white cat, its hair standing on end as it hissed at us.

Funny as a Dead Relative

SUSAN ROGERS COOPER

In Southeast Texas, the lure of high-paying refinery jobs attracted numerous immigrants from neighboring Louisiana beginning in the early twentieth century. As a result, this corner of the state has acquired a vibrant Cajun culture, one that makes its distinctive presence felt in the food, music, and community festivals.

Texas novelist Susan Rogers Cooper has created a series of mysteries that feature Cajun stand-up comic Kimmie Kruse, who hails from Port Arthur. This region can also be considered coastal Texas, but in this novel, with its emphasis on the inland Cajuns, Port Arthur qualifies as "East Texas." Susan Rogers Cooper is also the author of two other mystery series: one with an Oklahoma sheriff and another with a Central Texas romance writer. In all of her work, Cooper displays a comic touch that leavens the seriousness of her murder plots.

In *Funny as a Dead Relative*, comedienne Kimmie Kruse returns to Port Arthur to care for her grandfather, Paw-Paw, after his release from the hospital. Her time at Paw-Paw's house allows Kimmie to reconnect with her family roots, particularly in her grandfather's photo homage to the oil industry that brought the family to Texas from Louisiana in the first place. But all is not bliss, however, as a cousin of Kimmie's is stung to death by wasps at a family picnic. Everyone is convinced that it's an accident. But Kimmie, correctly, suspects otherwise.

Paw-Paw directed me out of St. Mary's Hospital parking lot, right on Ninth Avenue, then left on Gulfway. We stayed on Gulfway through Port Arthur, through the Groves, and then, when Gulfway turns into Highway 87, headed toward the city of Orange. The huge Fina refinery was on our left, with a canal and marshland between it and the highway. To the right of the highway was more marshland, which eventually led to the Gulf of Mexico. As we got to the old Rainbow Bridge that spanned the Neches River, about halfway between Port Arthur and Orange, Paw-Paw directed me to turn off the highway, going under the bridge.

It had been almost ten years since I'd been out to the little fishing shack (or camp, as they called them down here) where Paw-Paw had moved after being kicked out of Me-Maw's house. Back then it had just been a bunch of disreputable old cabins hugging the river. Things had changed a bit. A large restaurant now sat at the curve going into the area under the Rainbow Bridge. A marina harboring homemade shrimp boats, cabin cruisers, sailboats, and dilapidated houseboats ringed the cove in front of the restaurant which the road skirted. Inland from the marina was a large area of huge cages, inside which were tall, strange-looking birds.

"An emu farm," Paw-Paw said when I asked.

"You're kidding. Emus?"

"They going for fifteen thousand dollars a pair. Big business. Don't ask me why."

We drove past the marina, emu farm, and restaurant, over a cattle guard and off the paved road onto a crushed-oyster-shell road, leading us down under the bridge where Paw-Paw lived. I noticed a few new houses—nicer ones built on stilts, but the old ones I remembered were still there—the trailer with the built-on front lean-to covered with telephone transformers and obscured by junk; a small trailer with a shed over it for the safety of the boat. I remember Paw-Paw once telling me that the trailer roof had started to leak and, instead of fixing it, the owner had built an extension of the shed over the top of the trailer for shelter. Naturally, the better-built shelter was for the boat.

There were a few businesses in the Rainbow Marina now too, a boat lift, an electronics shop, a boat supply, a bait shop in a trailer.

Paw-Paw's house was right next to a Scenic Cruiser bus, its tires deflated and gray from age, grass growing up to the undercarriage. Paw-Paw's house was a real-live tar-paper shack. A small wooden porch had been pasted on to the front and leaned precariously to the left. The small yard in front of the house had two peacocks pecking aimlessly at the weeds that grew there.

Paw-Paw rolled his window down and yelled, "Scat!" at the peacocks, who looked up, then went on with their business. "I tole that Bartone Skaggs keep them peacocks out my yard! They shit ever'where! And they meaner than sin. Watch where you walk, girl, and don' rile 'em."

I unloaded Paw-Paw and his one scrawny bag and helped him work his way on crutches up the rickety porch and into the house. There was no lock on the door; it would have been a waste of good money, since the doorframe and the door had but a passing acquaintance with each other. The shack was two rooms: a living room/dining room/kitchen and a bedroom/bathroom. I had been in Paw-Paw's house on many occasions, but never for more than a few moments. Usually, when visiting the family, we would stay with Me-Maw in the Groves and drive out to see Paw-Paw under the bridge, picking him up at his house and taking him to dinner in the suburbs or to a movie or whatever. It suddenly hit me that I was actually going to have to sleep in this shack. Excuse me, camp.

The larger of the two rooms was neat and tidy, with a worn sofa and equally worn easy chair. A coffee table and a small TV on a metal stand rounded out the living-room area. An unfinished wood table and two chairs stood in a corner next to a sink, a small refrigerator, and an apartment-sized stove.

I took Paw-Paw's bag into the other room, the bedroom, and took quick note of just what my job of "Paw-Paw sitting" was going to entail. There really wasn't a bathroom. There was an old wooden commode with a pot that slid in and out underneath it. There was also a large galvanized steel washtub sitting under a spigot-and-hose contraption coming in from the window. That, I realized, was the bathtub. I had never wanted to be a nurse—I especially had never wanted to be a nurse in the early-nineteenth century. The bedroom consisted of—other than the antiquated bathroom facilities—a twin-sized iron bed and a dresser. I helped Paw-Paw down on the bed and said I'd go check out the kitchen for dinner. Instead I went into the living room, threw myself on the sprung couch, and cried.

"You hear the one about lil' Judice da Cajun?" Paw-Paw asked between bites of Kentucky Fried Chicken.

"No, and I don't want to," I said. I was being decidedly ungracious. I didn't want to hear any stupid Cajun jokes. I didn't want to feel guilty about serving KFC instead of a four-course Cajun dinner. I didn't want to sleep on the couch. I didn't want to do my business and then carry it outside. I didn't want to bathe in a washtub. And I just plain didn't want to be there. It was hot, humid, and the smell of the marsh and the river and the refinery was enough to give me flu symptoms: headache, nausea, and the urge to get the hell out of Dodge.

"Big Maurice come upon lil' Judice holding his hands over his ears real hard and big Maurice he say, 'Hey, lil' Judice, what you doin'?' And lil' Judice he say, 'Tryin' to hold on to a thought,'" Paw-Paw said, and laughed like an idiot.

I glared at him.

"Girl, you got no sense a humor," Paw-Paw said. "Don' see how you be a comedian, no. You tell me a joke you so dam' funny, yeah?"

"I don't feel like telling jokes," I said.

Paw-Paw put his chicken down on his plate and stood up with the help of his crutches. "Girl, I don' need you help. I been takin' care myself thirty-five year, I think I can do that a lil' bit longer. You go on back wherever you suppose to be. I take care myself, I tell you that!"

"Paw-Paw, don't be silly, you have a broken leg—"

"I don' need charity an' I don' need you actin' like me and mine ain't good nuff for you! You go on back wherever you suppose to be!"

"Paw-Paw!"

He went into the bedroom and slammed the door. I fell back in my chair and tried to think of alternatives. I could move him into Me-Maw's house.

But only over her dead body.

I could get him transported somehow to Austin, schlep him up the stairs to my garage apartment . . . forget that noise. My parents' house! I could get him to Austin somehow. I had the key to their house and, after all, it was my mother's turn to be taking care of him anyway! Great idea.

Then I remembered Will. Will was in Port Arthur. Will was hurt, grieving, troubled. Will needed me. Or so I hoped.

Paw-Paw needed me. I felt sorry for both of them. I'm not the kind of person one would wish for in need. I am not particularly sympathetic, empathetic, or handy in a crisis. I never wanted to grow up to be a nurse, a teacher, or even a mother. I'm not the nurturing sort.

I knew those things about myself. I knew I wasn't Florence Nightingale, or even Nurse Ratchett. And I also knew above all else that I needed to go to the bathroom. Paw-Paw was in the room where the john was, and after his grand exit I didn't think he'd be particularly gracious about me barging in and asking him to leave.

I looked out the small window at the back of the shack toward the river. To the right of the shack was a smaller shack—with a quarter-moon cut into the door. I figured it beat the hell out of squatting in the front yard with the peacocks.

I opened the rickety back door and jumped to the ground, as Paw-Paw hadn't seen fit, for some reason, to put in a step, and walked toward the outhouse. Just as I got there the door opened and out stepped a man of about eighty, smaller than I, zipping his fly as he walked. He smiled and bowed his head several times toward me. I smiled and bowed back. He was Asian; Vietnamese, I assumed. Great, I thought, a communal outhouse. But need being what it was, I went in anyway.

I didn't see Paw-Paw the rest of that evening, and spent part of the time studying his walls—something I hadn't done since I was a little girl. Looking at Paw-Paw's walls brought back my love for him, my bond with him.

One whole wall of Paw-Paw's shack was covered with framed photographs—but not the kind Me-Maw had; not photos of children and grandchildren and great-grandchildren. Paw-Paw's photos were about Port Arthur, his adopted home, and made me remember why I was where I was at that moment.

One was a tall, thin framed shot of the Spindletop Gusher that blew on January 10, 1901. This was the gusher that caused Port Arthur to become one of the greatest oil-refining centers in the world. Back when there was still oil to refine. The picture next to it was of Spindletop one year after the first gusher blew—a picture of mile upon mile of oil derricks. I remember Paw-Paw telling me, when I was little, with awe in his voice, that one hundred thousand barrels of oil a day were produced there.

Then there was a picture of Pleasure Island in its heyday, a strip of land between Port Arthur and the Gulf of Mexico—Port Arthur's answer to Coney Island. I used to love to look at those pictures when I was little, at the people in their funny clothes and silly bathing costumes, and pretend that I could go back to that time.

But the last pictures were the ones that always fascinated me. The pictures of the Texas City blast. An oil-refinery town like Port Arthur, Texas City is located between Houston and Galveston, and the force of the blast that day, back in 1947, when chemicals aboard a ship docked in the canal exploded, could be felt as far as Port Arthur, over one hundred miles away. The kinship with that town so far away wasn't just that some of the same companies that populated Port Arthur had refineries there; and it wasn't just because a few people from Port Arthur were there that day and lost their lives; and it wasn't because the blast, seventy-five miles away, was so strong it shook buildings in Port Arthur and the residents, Me-Maw and Paw-Paw included, could stand outside and see the blaze when they looked to the southwest.

No, the connection was the brotherhood. It was a refinery town, just like Port Arthur. A place that relied on oil and oilmen to make the livings of those who resided there. And a place that knew, like Port Arthur did, and still does, that one day this could happen. One day hell could rain down upon the town and take away everything. Everyone in Port Arthur, just like everyone in Texas City and every other refinery town in this country and elsewhere, knew he lived twenty-four hours a day, seven days a week, with a living, breathing monster that was stilled only if everyone always did his job—and did it correctly.

There's something horribly fascinating about that kind of destruction, and I remember as a child staring at those pictures for hours: at a torn-apart house with a huge hole in the front yard where a piece of the propeller shaft from a ship had buried itself in the ground almost a mile from the explosion site; at homes with blazing fires and black smoke billowing in the background. The accounts of the dead and dying rose to twelve hundred in some reports.

Paw-Paw had worked in the Texas Company refinery for almost fifty years, and oil and what it wrought were close to his heart, as his picture gallery showed.

I finally turned my back on Paw-Paw's gallery and lay down on the couch, spending a fitful night trying to sleep on the old relic.

The next morning I woke up with my monthly friend. I cleaned up at the kitchen sink, sank down into the couch and pouted. How was I supposed to deal with the needs of my monthly with no proper bathroom facilities? How come, in 1992, I was stuck in a bad imitation of *God's Little Acre*?

I heard Paw-Paw stirring in the other room, but didn't feel quite up to doing anything about it. I sat huddled on the sofa feeling sorry for myself.

When Paw-Paw hobbled in on his crutches, heading for the kitchen area and his coffeepot, I said, "Paw-Paw, we have to do something. I can't live like this—with an outhouse! Maybe we should move you to a motel."

"Outhouse?" Paw-Paw said. He looked out the window toward the quarter-moon receptacle. "You been using Ho's outhouse?"

"What?"

"Why you do that, girl?"

"You were in the bedroom . . ."

"So? Why you not use this?" he asked, walking to a door in the kitchen area and opening it. I followed and looked in—at the loveliest bathroom I'd ever seen. It had a bathtub, a sink, and the most beautiful white porcelain flush commode in the world.

"Paw-Paw, it's a bathroom!"

He said, "Pooey!" shook his head, and moved into the living-room area, sitting down on the old armchair. "You think I don't got a bathroom? You ever come visit me for more than three minute at a time, you see I got a bathroom. I built it my own self back five year ago. I got a kitchen too. I even drive a car when my leg ain't broke! What you think, I some kinda rube?"

"Excuse me," I said, heading in and closing the door.

When I came out I made coffee silently and silently poured him a cup of the strongest coffee I'd ever made.

Paw-Paw took a sip and spit it back into the cup. "You always make dishwater, girl?" He handed me the coffee pot, got up and walked into the kitchen indicating that I should follow. Once there he had me pour the entire pot down the sink. "I see now we gonna have some troubles, yeah? You don' even know how to make coffee, girl, what you mama teach you, eh?" He looked at me standing in the living room. "Well," he said, motioning toward me with his head. "Get over here. I teach you to make coffee Cajun-style, yeah?"

PART 6

SAN ANTONIO AND SOUTH TEXAS

Death on the River Walk

CAROLYN HART

San Antonio's Paseo del Rio, or River Walk, has become one of Texas's best-known tourist attractions, rivaling even the Alamo as a San Antonio icon. The river meanders quietly alongside tree-shaded restaurants, exuding European charm and ambience. But all is not what it appears. Few visitors ever realize that the San Antonio River itself is mostly a dry channel, thanks to overpumping from the aquifer that feeds the headsprings. The "river" that now flows through downtown San Antonio is actually well water, supplemented by generous portions of treated wastewater. Here, amidst the manufactured deception of unassuming tourists, lies the perfect setting for a murder mystery.

While the River Walk often makes cameo appearances in San Antonio-based novels, it is Carolyn Hart who gives the Paseo del Rio the star billing in her book, *Death on the River Walk*. Hart is a nationally known mystery writer based in Oklahoma City, and she has published dozens of novels. In 1993, she launched a new series featuring retired journalist Henrie O'Dwyer Collins. "Henrie O," as she is known to her friends and fans, solves cases that seem to always require trips to favored vacation destinations such as Bermuda and Hawaii.

In *Death on the River Walk*, Henrie O searches for a young woman who disappeared while working at one of the area's upscale shops. Hart's readers have come to expect a certain level of travel writing in her novels, and Hart does not disappoint here as she sets the stage for this San Antonio-based Henrie O mystery.

San Antonio's River Walk is a place where dreams have been made and broken. It would be easy to dismiss today's River Walk as a commercial lure, but the river, sweet product of artesian springs, made life possible ten thousand years ago, when the land knew the occasional nomadic Indian, and the water still makes life possible, though its function is as different now as a present-day shopkeeper from a hunter and gatherer. Today's River Walk, the creation of visionary architect Robert Hugman, hosts lodging, shops, restaurants, and romance, drawing an unceasing flow of visitors who seek a glamorous respite from the everyday world.

If any city represents the glory of Texas, it is San Antonio, where Spaniards, Indians, cowboys, and European immigrants created a multilayered culture unlike that of any other city. The mission San Antonio de Valero was founded May 1, 1718, the result of a missionary journey made by Father Antonio de San Buenaventura Olivares in 1709. Fifteen Spanish families from the Canary Islands arrived in 1731 to establish near the mission the town of San Fernando de Béxar, which became the town of San Antonio. In 1794, the mission was turned into a fort staffed by a Spanish cavalry company named for the town from which it came, San Jose y Santiago del Alamo. The fort became known by the cavalry name, shortened to Alamo. After Mexico achieved independence from Spain, Mexican armies and Texas colonists struggled for control of Texas. In a passage of arms celebrated forever in Texas, the 180 defenders of the Alamo refused to surrender and died to a man after a thirteen-day siege that ended March 6, 1836. Eventually, San Antonio, the heart of Texas, became a part of the United States and the lovely city by the river drew immigrants from Europe, especially Germans. San Antonio remains unlike any other American city. Some cities have elements of San Antonio's intertwined culture, but none match it for sheer exuberance and colorful individuality, permeated by Hispanic grace, German industry, and Southern gentility.

The River Walk is modern San Antonio's heart, attracting well over a million visitors a year, just as the flowing waters in earlier years attracted, in turn, nomadic Indians, Spanish friars, and German immigrants.

I sat at an outside table and sipped iced tea and looked across the placid green water, water that once ran red with blood. In the aftermath of the battle for the Alamo, Mayor Ruiz burned the bodies of the defenders. Charged with interring the bodies of Santa Ana's slain, the mayor buried as many as he could and dumped the rest into the river.

Today a barge glided past, the passengers smiling, taking pictures, welcoming the brief escape from the sun as they passed beneath the occasional arched stone bridges. I shaded my eyes. In a moment, I would cross the near bridge, my goal the three-story stucco building directly opposite. The river is bordered by wide sidewalks. Stone walls serve as the river's banks as it meanders through the city. The restaurants and shops on the River Walk are the first floor of buildings that open to the downtown streets on their second floor.

The breeze rustled tall cottonwoods. Sunlight striking through shifting leaves made filigree patterns on the buildings and the stone walk. Some of the buildings looked very old and some startlingly modern. The stuccoed structure directly opposite was old, the walls probably a foot or so thick. But the curved glass windows that provided a magnificent display area were a renovation. The shining shop windows contrasted oddly with the ornate iron grillwork of the second-floor balconies, each with blue pots holding bright red canna lilies. A white wooden sign hung from an iron post. Gilt letters announced simply: "Tesoros." At one corner of the building hung another sign: "La Mariposa." An arrow pointed up the stone stairs. A glistening monarch butterfly was painted hovering above the arrow. Gilt letters beneath proclaimed: "The River Walk's Oldest Bed & Breakfast."

A silver bell rang a sweet clear tone whenever the ornate carved green door of Tesoros opened. Customers were casually but expensively dressed. As I watched, a young man appeared in one of the windows, arranging a display of pottery. I caught quick glimpses of him, his face in shadow-shining dark hair, a fashionable goatee perfectly trimmed, deft movements. An older man walked slowly around the corner of the building, carrying a pail and a squeegee. His shoulders were bowed, his eyes downcast. The windows looked quite clean, but he walked at a deliberate pace to the near window, carefully put down his pail, then slowly began to wash the sparkling glass. I spent half an hour at the cafe, taking the time to consider how I should approach the store. Sometimes frankness can be effective. Sometimes it can be foolish. I knew nothing about Tesoros, about the people who owned it, about Iris Chavez's job there; In the years when

I was a reporter, I prepared exhaustively for interviews, reading every bit of material I could discover about my subject. But I'd had no idea when I drove toward San Antonio that I would have any need for knowledge about the store where Gina's granddaughter worked, other than its location. But when I telephoned and asked for Iris Chavez, the connection was broken. That was surely odd. Yet, during this short observation, I'd seen nothing remarkable about the store or its clientele, nothing that could even hint at why one of its employees had disappeared. If she had.

I finished my tea, left a bill on the table, and strolled to the bridge. I stopped at the top of the bridge and looked at the green water and at the occasional palms and lacy ferns and bright flowers that promised a never-ending summer. The river curved lazily around a bend, creating an intimate pocket of stores and people enjoying a lovely Sunday afternoon in September. It was hard to connect this holiday picture with the shabby little apartment and Iris's disarranged belongings and the blinking red light on the telephone answering machine, signaling calls for reassurance and calls where no one spoke.

When I reached the front of the store, I glanced in the first window, the window even now being meticulously scrubbed by the stooped man who seemed oblivious both to its cleanliness and to the constant mill of pedestrians behind him.

I've looked in many shop windows in far distant countries. I'm not a shopper. I have no desire to own treasures of any kind. But I appreciate beauty, even beauty priced beyond the reach of most and certainly beyond my reach.

A magnificent glazed pottery jar dominated the display. Stylized birds, flowers, and palms in gold and black glistened against a finely hatched background. Two glazed plates were to the left of the jar. One featured a woman villager, her hat filled with fruit, and the second a man gathering up the fruits of harvest while his donkey rested. On the right of the jar were two dramatic dinner plates with greenish and gold peacocks and flower motifs against a tomato-red background.

A card announced in calligraphic script: "Tlaquepaque style, glazed pottery from the state of Jalisco."

The other window was as bright with color as a field of Texas wildflowers. The young man, arms folded, studied his arrangement of a dozen or so clay banks. The banks were created to hold coins, but now it would take a fistful of dollars to buy them. I especially liked the orange lion and pink polka-dotted pig.

This card announced: "Santa Cruz de las Huertas, 1920–1930."

The silvery bell sang as I opened the door. I still wasn't sure how to proceed, whether to be direct or oblique. Whatever I did, I hoped I made the right choice. I'd found nothing in Iris's apartment to lead me to her. This store was my last hope. I stepped inside to coolness and quiet, to a sense of serenity. Classical guitar music played softly. The wall on my right held a striking Rivera mural, a surging crowd, yet each face distinct, the whole vibrating with passion, protest, and pride.

I saw only one customer, a slim blonde with ash-fine hair drawn back in a chignon, who waited by the front counter. The woman behind the cash register was ringing up the purchase, a wooden bas-relief of a farmer leading a donkey laden with corn-filled baskets.

I wandered among the display islands, slabs cut from big tree trunks that had been dried and glazed. The shiny, rocklike platforms sat on wrought-iron supports. Spotlights inset in the ceiling highlighted each display. There was a glorious diversity: three-dimensional clay figures including a set of Mexican presidents by the celebrated Panduro family, Talavera tiles, flower-decorated bowls by Enrique Ventosa. Several wall cabinets held ornate silver pieces, trays, candlesticks, pitchers. A bookcase contained Day of the Dead representations, including a skeleton poking his head out of a rocket ship. I wandered among the islands and knew that I was indeed in the presence of treasures. It was the same sensation I felt on a visit to a grand museum. It would take weeks to appreciate the collection here, a lifetime to understand the many kinds of art.

I paused at a display of carved wooden animals from Oaxaca. If I were a tourist, here for pleasure, these works would tempt me. The brightly colored animal figures—pink giraffes, spotted rhinos, lemon tigers—spoke of a world of unleashed imagination, the artist's ebullient recognition that the pulse of life is more than is ever seen by the eye alone, that the spirit of joy colors every reality.

The flip of that coin reminded me that behind light there is dark, that I could not accept the serenity and beauty of this room as the totality of this place.

The Last King of Texas

RICK RIORDAN

San Antonio's West Side is the center of the city's Mexican American population, and it thrives with community spirit despite a long history of poverty. One problem affecting the West Side, however, has been the rise of street gangs, many of which rely on the drug trade for income. San Antonio officials have often been reluctant to address the issue for fear of drawing adverse publicity in a city that relies heavily on tourist dollars.

Rick Riordan has received mystery's "Triple Crown"—the Edgar, Anthony, and Shamus Awards—for his series of San Antonio-based mystery novels. Although Rick Riordan grew up in north San Antonio's posh Alamo Heights district, he adroitly portrays Mexican Americans from the West Side, writing without affectation or condescension. Riordan often explores San Antonio's out-of-the-way destinations, offering a funky view of the city that few tourists ever see.

Riordan's protagonist is private investigator Tres Navarre, a Tai Chi expert with a Ph.D. in medieval literature and an enchilada-eating cat. In *The Last King of Texas*, Navarre accepts a temporary appointment as a medieval studies professor at the University of Texas at San Antonio. The position came open after the previous occupant was murdered. It doesn't take long for Tres to be targeted, too. In the following excerpt, his investigation of murder and heroin smuggling leads him to a cantina favored by gangbangers on the city's West Side.

Drifting along the sidewalk in front of police headquarters was the usual parade of undesirables—cons, thugs, derelicts, undercovers pretending to be derelicts, derelicts pretending to be undercovers pretending to be derelicts.

They collected here each evening for many reasons but hung around for only one. They knew as surely as those little white birds hopping around on the crocodile's back that their very proximity to the mouth of the beast made them safe.

Patrol cars were parked along West Nueva. Inside the barbed wire of the parking lot, in a circle of floodlight, five detectives in crisp white shirts and ties and side arms were having a smoke. Outside the fence a couple of cut-loose dealers were trading plea-bargain stories.

I walked across Nueva to the Dolorosa parking lot, got in the VW, and pulled onto Santa Rosa, heading north. I made the turn onto Commerce by El Mercado, then passed underneath I-10—over the Commerce Street Bridge, into the gloomy asphalt and stucco and railroad track wasteland of the West Side.

Ahead of me, the sunset faded to an afterglow behind palm trees and Spanish billboards. Turquoise and pink walls of icehouses and bail bond offices lost their color. On the broken sidewalks, men in tattered jeans and checkered shirts milled around, their faces drawn from an unsuccessful day of waiting, their eyes examining each car in the fading hope that someone might slow down and offer them work.

I turned north on Zarzamora and found the place where Jeremiah Brandon had died a mile and a half up, squatting between two muddy vacant lots just past Waverly. Patches of blue stucco had flaked off its walls, but the name was still visible in a single red floodlight—POCO MAS—stenciled between two air-conditioner units that hung precariously from the front windows.

The building was tall in front, short in back, with side walls that dropped in sections like a ziggurat. Tejano music seeped through the hammered tin doorway.

Two pickup trucks, a white Chevy van, and an old Ford Galaxie were parked in the gravel front lot. I pulled the VW around the side, into the mud between a Camry with flat tires and a LeBaron with a busted windshield, and hoped I hadn't just discovered the La Brea tar pit of automobiles.

The rest of the block was lined with closed *tiendas* and burglar-barred homes. Crisscrossed telephone lines and pecan tree branches sliced up the sky. The only real light came from the end of the block across the street— the Church of Our Lady of the Mount. Its Moorish, yellow-capped spires were brutally lit, a dark bronze Jesus glaring down from on high at the Poco Mas. Jesus was holding aloft a circle of metal that looked suspiciously like a master's whip. Or perhaps a hubcap rim.

At the entrance to the cantina, I was greeted by a warm blast of air that smelled like an old man's closet—leather and mothballs, stale cologne, dried sweat, and liquor. Inside, the rafters glinted with Christmas ornaments. Staple-gunned along the walls were decades of calendars showing off Corvettes with bras and women without. The jukebox cranked out Selena's "*Quiero*" just loud enough to drown casual conversation and the creaking my boots must've made on the warped floor planks.

I got a momentary, disapproving once-over from the patrons at the three center tables. The men were hard-faced Latinos, most in their forties, with black cowboy hats and steel-toed boots. The few women were overweight and trying hard to pretend otherwise—tight red dresses and red hose, peroxide hair, large bosoms, and chunky faces heavily caked with foundation and rouge designed for Anglo complexions. Long neck beer bottles and scraps of bookie numbers littered the pink and white Formica.

On a raised platform in back were two booths, one empty, one occupied by a cluster of young *locos*—bandannas claiming their gang colors, white tank tops, baggy jeans laced with chains, scruffy day beards. One had a Raiders jacket. Another had a porkpie hat and a pretty young Latina on his lap. The girl and I locked eyes long enough for Porkpie to notice and scowl.

Then I recognized someone else. Hector Mara, Zeta Sanchez's ex-brother-in-law, was talking to another man at the bar.

Mara wore white shorts and Nikes and a black Spurs tunic that said ROBINSON. His egg-brown scalp reflected the beer lights.

Mara's friend was thinner, taller, maybe thirty years old, with a wiry build and a high hairline that made his thin face into a valentine. He had a silver cross earring and black-painted fingernails, a black trench coat and leather boots laced halfway up his calves. He'd either been reading too much Anne Rice or was on his way to a *bandido* Renaissance festival.

A line of empty beer bottles stood in front of the two men. Mara's face was illuminated by the little glowing screen of a palm-held computer, which he kept referring to as he spoke to the vampire, like they were going over numbers.

I climbed onto the third bar stool next to Mara, and spoke to the bartender loud enough to be heard over Selena. *"Cerveza, por favor."*

Mara and the vampire stopped talking.

The bartender scowled at me. His face was puffy with age, his hair reduced to silver grease marks over his ears. "Eh?"

"Beer."

He squinted past me suspiciously, as if checking for my reinforcements. Hector Mara just stared at me. Huge loops of armhole showed off his well-muscled shoulders, swirls of tattoos on his upper arms, thick tufts of underarm hair. He had an old gunshot scar like a starburst just above his left knee. The vampire stared at me, too. He clicked his black fingernails against the bar. Friendly crowd.

"Unless you've got a special tonight," I told the bartender. "Manhattan, maybe?"

The bartender reached into his cooler, opened a bottle, then plunked a Budweiser in front of me.

"Or beer is fine," I said.

"Eh?"

I made the "okay" sign, dropped two dollars on the counter. Without hesitating, the old man got out a second beer and plunked it next to the first.

I was tempted to put down a twenty and see what he'd do. Instead I slid one of the Buds toward Hector Mara.

"Maybe your friend could go commune with the night for a few minutes?" I suggested.

Mara's face was designed for perpetual anger—eyes pinched, nose flared, mouth clamped into a scowl. "I know you?"

"I saw Zeta today."

Mara and the vampire exchanged looks. The vampire studied my face one more time, memorizing it, then detached himself from the bar. He flicked his fingers coward the *cholos* in the back booth and they all lifted their chins. The vampire walked out.

I watched him get into the white Chevy van and drive away.

"Yo, gringo," Hector Mara said. "You got any idea who you just offended?"

"None. Much more fun that way. Although if I was guessing, I'd say it was Chich Gutierrez, your business partner."

Mara's eye twitched. "Who the fuck are you?"

"I was at that party you threw yesterday out on Green Road. The one where Zeta blew a hole in the deputy."

Mara's eyes drifted down to my boots, then made their way back up my rumpled dress clothes, my face, my uncombed hair.

"You ain't a cop," he decided.

"No."

"Then fuck off." He pushed the beer back toward me and returned to his PalmPilot, started tapping on the screen with a little black stylus. On the jukebox, Selena segued into Shelly Lares.

I looked at the bartender. "*Dónde está* the famous spot?"

"Eh?"

"The place where Zeta Sanchez killed Jeremiah Brandon."

The bartender waved his hands adamantly. "No, no. New management."

He said it like a foreign phrase he'd been trained to speak in an emergency.

Mara pointed over his shoulder with the stylus. "Second booth, gringo. The one that's always empty."

The bartender mumbled halfheartedly about the change of management, then retreated to his liquor display and began turning the bottles label-out.

"The D.A.'s going to prosecute," I told Mara.

"Big surprise."

"They figure ten to ninety-nine for shooting the deputy, life for Aaron Brandon's murder, maybe federal charges for the bomb blast. Quick and easy. That's before they even consider the Old Man's murder case from '93."

"*Hijo de puta* like you gonna love that."

"And who am I?"

A stripe of green neon drifted across Mara's forehead as he turned toward me. His eyes burned with loathing. "Reporter. Got to let those nervous gringos see the right headline, huh? *Mexican Convicted for Alamo Heights Murder.*"

I pulled out one of my Erainya Manos Agency cards, slid it across the counter. "What if I thought Sanchez was framed?"

Mara's bad-ass expression melted as soon as he saw the card. He looked from it to me. "The guy in the Panama hat."

"George Bertón."

Mara pushed the card away, then leaned far enough toward me so I could smell the beer on his breath.

"I told your friend," he hissed. "I said I'd think about it. All right? Don't push me."

I tried to stay poker-faced. It wasn't easy.

"Sure," I said. "I was just in the neighborhood. Thought I'd check back."

Mara sniffed disdainfully. He gestured toward the back of the room and the screen of his PalmPilot flashed like mercury. "You see the locos in the corner? No, man, I don't mean *look* at them. They'll think you want trouble. Those are Chich's boys. His younger set. You think I'm going to sit here and talk friendly with them watching us, you're crazy."

"Make small talk. Were you in this place the night Jeremiah Brandon got shot?"

"I—" Hector looked down at the bar. "No. I missed it. Most righteous thing that ever happened in this place."

"I can understand why you'd think that."

"Oh, you can."

"The old man had an affair with your sister."

"Affair, shit. Raped, used, sent Sandra away when she was so shamed and scared there wasn't no choice. Like a whole bunch of girls before her. I never even saw her—not a good-bye, nothing."

"Hard."

"You don't know about hard. Now you need to leave."

"Tell me about Sandra."

Hector Mara hefted his PalmPilot. "I got a salvage yard to manage, gringo. Books to balance. Don't help when the fucking police keep me tied up the whole day, neither. Why don't you leave me alone?"

Hector tried to ignore me. He started writing. I drank my beer. Behind us, Shelly Lares sang about her broken *corazón*.

"Was Sandra happy married to Sanchez?"

Hector's PalmPilot clattered on the bar. "*Chíngate*. What the fuck you want, man? Why do you care?"

"I like annoying you, Hector. It's so easy."

Hector stared at me.

I pointed my bottle at him and fired off a round.

"You fucking insane, gringo."

"Tell me about your sister and I'll leave."

Hector glanced across the room. The men at the tables were bragging about greyhound races. One of the *locos* at the back booth laughed and the pretty Latina squealed in protest. They didn't seem to be paying us much mind.

Hector Mara curled his large brown fingers into his palm one at a time. Tattoos of swords and snakes on his inner arm rippled. "You want the story? I claimed a rival set to Zeta Sanchez when I was fourteen. Chich Gutierrez, he was one of my older *vatos*. We were a shitty little set but we thought we were bad. Then one night Zeta and some of his homeboys cornered me at the Courts, said I could die or switch claims. If I switched, I could tell them where to shoot me."

"Your leg," I guessed.

He nodded, traced his fingers over the scar tissue above his knee.

"I did that for one reason, man. I looked at Sanchez and I knew he had the kind of rep I needed for me, my family. Once I was down with Zeta, I got respect. My kid sister Sandra got respect. People left her alone. That was important to me, gringo. Real important."

Hector looked at me to see how I was taking the story so far, maybe to see if the gringo was laughing at him inside.

Apparently I passed the test.

"Sandra wanted to be a poet," Hector said. "You believe that? She never claimed no girl posses when we lived in the Courts. Couldn't stand up for herself. Me claiming Sanchez was all that saved her. Then when we were about sixteen, our mom got busted for dealing. Me and Sandra moved out to my grandmother's place."

"The property on Green Road."

Mara nodded. "For a couple of years I had this stupid idea maybe Sandra was going to make it. Farm life. New school. Perfect for her. She never got into trouble. Made it all the way through high school. Even started college before Zeta got interested in her, you know—in a new way. Zeta decided it was a good match."

"And was it?" Hector turned his beer bottle in a slow circle.

"Zeta was old-fashioned. Didn't want his wife going to college. But he was good to Sandra. Looked out for her."

"You believe that?"

More silence. "She and Zeta would've worked things out, wasn't for the Brandons. After the Old Man caught her, she didn't have no choice but to take his money and run. Sanchez would've killed her for what she did, her fault or not. But, man—it could've been different for her. She almost made it out."

"And you?"

"What about me?"

"Did you make it out?"

Hector smiled sourly. He dabbed his finger in the circle of sweat at the base of his beer, smeared a line of water away from the bottle. "I'm a man. Ain't the same for me."

"You decided to keep living on your grandmother's property. Those chickens in the coop, the garden—those things require maintenance. Somebody cares about that place."

"Go home, gringo. Quit while you're ahead."

"Zeta's gun—the gold revolver. He left it with you."

The sour smile faded. "Say what?"

"The gun didn't go south with Zeta. He should've ditched it, but for some reason he couldn't throwaway that gift from Jeremiah Brandon. He left the gun in San Antonio with somebody—I'm guessing you. The fact that police found it near Aaron Brandon's house is important. You see?"

Mara's eyes darkened to a dangerous shade. "Be careful, gringo."

"'Cause the thing is, Hector, if somebody was to frame Zeta, you'd be in a good position to do it. What with Zeta staying at your place and all, and you doing business with Sanchez's old rival Chich."

"I told your friend in the goddamn Panama hat—"

"Yeah, I know. You told George you'd think about it. All I'm saying is maybe you should think a little harder. Let us hear from you."

Hector studied me for another stanza of Shelly Lares, then reassembled his cold smile. "You'll hear from me, gringo. Now *lo siento*, eh? I got to do this now to keep appearances."

Then he got up and pushed me off my stool as hard as he could. I went toppling backward and on the way down managed to connect just about every part of my body with something hard and wooden. I landed with the seat of the stool in my gut, my left leg laced through the spokes. The floor was sticky. A beer bottle cap was pressed into my palm.

Mara stood over me. The crowd was silent, waiting for a fight.

Mara disappointed them.

"Be cool to the homies, gringo," he told me. "Stick around. See how long before they drag you out with the trash."

He grabbed his PalmPilot and walked toward the exit, the old gunshot wound making his gait only slightly stiff. The *locos* in the corner laughed at my expense.

I got up, dusted myself off.

In the reflection of the hammered tin, I watched Hector Mara getting into his old Ford Galaxie and pulling out of the lot.

When someone humiliates you in a bar, you don't really have a choice.

You've got to sit back down and finish your drink, just to prove you can. So I did.

I listened to another Shelly Lares tune. I thought about George Bertón, tried to remind myself that George was a big boy who knew what he was doing, and he'd just yell at me for interfering if I called him now. I thought about Hector Mara's initiation to Zeta Sanchez's set until my leg started to ache. I looked at the little red circle the beer bottle cap had bitten into my palm and thought about a hundred other places I would rather be than the Poco Más.

Then another round of laughter erupted at the *locos*' table in the back and I decided I might as well add insult to injury.

I grabbed the Budweiser that Hector Mara had refused and went to talk to a girl I knew.

The Case of the Hook-billed Kites

J. S. BORTHWICK

To a growing number of eco-tourists, Texas is known less for its cowboys and cattle than it is for its birds. Texas lies along major migratory flyways, and nearly 600 bird species have been documented in the state. The Lower Rio Grande Valley, situated along the Texas-Mexico border at the southern tip of the state, is a prime destination for these tourists, as it represents the northernmost range of many tropical bird species. Although nearly all of the Valley's original riparian forest has been cleared for agriculture, several wildlife refuges have been established in recent years, attracting birds and birders alike.

A group of New Englanders travels to the Valley in J. S. Borthwick's *The Case of the Hook-billed Kites*. This novel is the first in a series featuring Sarah Deane, an academician from Maine who teams up with Dr. Alex McKenzie to solve murder mysteries. Here, Sarah comes to fictional Doña Clara National Wildlife Refuge at the urging of her boyfriend, Philip—who is kept off-stage in the novel, for reasons that become clear as the plot unfolds. The other birders will learn that Philip scored a coup by sighting of a pair of hook-billed kites—tropical birds rarely seen north of the Rio Grande. But Philip had little time to celebrate his accomplishment, because someone strangled him to death with his own binocular strap.

Sarah had expected Texas to surprise her, to bare its chest and say, "I am the Lone Star State." She had hummed the "Streets of Laredo" while packing back in Boston, but as Alex turned the car south onto U.S. 77 and the landscape began unrolling, she felt let down. It seemed quite ordinary, farm country on a wide scale. Here and there a windmill stood by a water trough, cattle dotted a grazing stretch, a cluster of farm buildings broke the expanse, and now and then a line of pumping jacks appeared, moving up and down like hammer-headed robots.

Even with the car window open, the air was stifling, and Sarah felt heavy-eyed and sleepy. She tried to count the tank cars on a siding and then to read the message on a historical marker, but she could only make out the first line before they drove past. Something about Zachary Taylor and a march to the Rio Grande. He was the one, she remembered, who wore old straw hats and died after drinking cold milk and eating raspberries—or was it cherries? What was he doing marching to the border? It was all a long time ago. Sarah yawned. Even Philip seemed a long time ago. And far away. Not a real person, just a commitment of time and place. That's what flying did to you; it cut connections.

Sarah tried to conjure up Philip as she had last seen him, standing in the drive next to her apartment in Boston. It had snowed hard all that Sunday morning, and Philip was brushing the snow from his car before the drive back to Maryland. She had stood at the door and watched because she had a cold and Philip had ordered her not to come out. He had kissed her goodbye cautiously, just a light touch of a mustache across her forehead. Sarah closed her eyes and blotted out Texas. She could see Philip in his new tan coat pulling up the alpaca-lined hood over his fair hair. She saw him brushing the snow, working methodically with the wind from the rear to the front of the car, and then waving to her with a flourish of the long-handled brush. She remembered thinking that, even with the snow blowing puffs around him, he seemed competent, decisive. His car started at once. It always did. Philip saw to things like carburetors and batteries, and he spoke seriously to Sarah on the subject of "proper maintenance" because her old vw never started without a struggle.

"We're making progress," said Alex. "Three towns gone through while you were daydreaming. Clarkswood, Driscoll, and Bishop."

Sarah looked over at Alex and nodded. She had forgotten all about him in researching Philip. At the airport, Alex had seemed almost a stranger, although she had known him about ten months. But in Boston she had always seen him in the insulating presence of friends, of Philip. She studied his face. Older than she remembered. From the side view it seemed to be all corners and planes, no curves, and the dark hair was cut shorter than was fashionable with Sarah's male friends. The eyes were set deep under heavy brows. Genus Heathcliff, she decided. But she saw that the long uncompromising mouth was relieved by a humorous lift at the corners, and one thing about Heathcliff, as far as humor went, he was a dead loss. She suspected that Alex could be sardonic. Genus Mr. Rochester, perhaps. Not, said Sarah severely to herself, types that interest me. Thank heavens she had gotten over that Byronic nonsense long ago. In a mood of clinical detachment, Sarah shifted her attention to Alex's hands—square, nails short, scrubbed, a mark of his profession.

"Look," said Alex, pointing ahead to a huge sign reading "WELCOME TO KINGSVILLE," over which was suspended the bleached skull of a cow. "You're in Texas, Sarah. Now, shall we hit the side roads for variety? Look for some birds. What's your schedule?"

"I'm not meeting Philip at any particular time. He said that he might not even make it for dinner—he's checking out a couple of refuges for the students' trips. But I'd like to make it by five-thirty . . . to clean up, take a swim."

"Fine. After we get through the King Ranch, we'll turn off and wander around and still have you in the swimming pool before dark."

Alex was aware of Sarah sitting next to him, her left knee, her shoulder, only eight inches away. But, he thought, she might as well be in a glass case. I could be any taxi driver that happened along, while she hangs in waiting for Philip. With an effort, Alex turned his attention back to the road and silently pointed out to Sarah the wildflowers showing by the side of the road: clusters of cream, lemon, blue, wine, coral—phlox, storksbill, bluebonnets, star violets, scarlet paintbrush. Sarah smiled and turned her thoughts again to Philip.

Old Village squats near the center of the Doña Clara. The broken-down buildings, crumbled walls, and rusted iron railings are of negligible interest to the historical archaeologist; the village dates only from the 1870s and was abandoned in the 1950s. A condominium scheme was defeated by a conservation bloc, which subsequently established the refuge itself, and now the village is one of the favorite stopping places, perhaps because there is always something to sit on.

"Thank God," said Constance Goldsmith, collapsing on what was either a step or an overturned gravestone. "I've had it."

"I see an eastern yellow coral snake," said Nina Goldsmith, hopping in a circle around her aunt.

"That's the fifth coral snake you've seen," said Mrs. Goldsmith without moving. "See if you can find a python."

"This heat is murder," said Lois Bailey, sitting down next to her sister-in-law. "Major Foster's still looking for those groove-billed things."

"Anis. Groove-billed anis. Here's the picture." Mrs. Goldsmith opened her guide. "Ugly, aren't they? I hope," she added wearily, "he doesn't find them. My feet are going to explode."

It was past four, the temperature had gone to 88 degrees, the dust had settled, and the air was heavy. The Hamburg Club had hiked long and hard, sighting birds and swatting bugs. Bird lists had lengthened, necks were stiff with craning, and hiking, boots pinched. Enthusiasm had quieted, and most were grateful for a respite.

Two college students sat on a brick wall and puzzled over their lists; next to them sat Mrs. Milton van Hoek, who for her first birding trip wore an Inverness cape and was bitterly regretting it. She was now slumped like a collapsed tweed mushroom on the edge of a ruined well. Nearby was Mrs. Enid Plummer, consort of Waldo, who called Mrs. van Hoek "dearie," and was placidly readjusting a strap on her husband's pith helmet. Others sat, leaned, looked for ticks.

A kiskadee flycatcher swooped from a branch and disappeared, rattling his noisy "kiss-kee-dee," but only two heads turned. Everyone was an old Texas birder now, and this was the sixth kiskadee. The tour members chattered: "How can you tell if you've got chiggers?" "Are you using the new Peterson?" "You can just unscrew a tick. Counterclockwise." "It's the same bird, but one has a black crest—you can't count two. They're both tits." (Here Nina Goldsmith giggled and poked her elbow into the rib of an aunt.)

"Now, people," interrupted Waldo Plummer, who in his reclaimed pith helmet looked like someone pausing in his search for the source of the Nile, "we must trust the A.O.U. for species nomenclature."

"Goodness, what's an A.O.U.?" asked Mrs. van Hoek in a stifled voice from around her cape.

"That's the American Ornithologists Union. They settle species debates," said Jeff Goldsmith with the air of a tenured professor informing a freshman. "The black-crested titmouse and the tufted titmouse hybridize, so they're the same species."

"Jeffrey is correct," said Mr. Plummer, "but now we must all be silent. Major Foster is trying to find an anis for us."

"He moves quietly for such a big man," observed Lois Bailey.

Jeff rounded on his aunt. "Any good ornithologist moves quietly. Only stupid people make a lot of noise and talk all the time." Lois Bailey and Constance Goldsmith sighed in concert. Not for the first time did they regret their invitation to take their niece and nephew on the Texas tour. Jeff, of course, was an avid birder, but an impatient one. Thirteen was an uneasy age, and the difference in years and what Miss Austen might have called "habits of address" made social moments distinctly sticky. As for nine-year-old Nina, she was overheated and bored stiff.

"It's time for the motel and the swimming pool," said Mrs. Bailey, and she wiped her forehead, leaving a wide streak of dirt.

Major Foster reappeared on the brink of the group and held up a hand for attention. "Can't see hide nor hair of those anis, but we'll try again tomorrow. Now, folks, it's after four, and I'm goin' to check out some other trails for new arrivals. Eduardo will drive you to Lupine Lake where there's a photo blind. Then he'll take those folks dyin' of heat to Progreso for a milkshake or a cone. For those that stay, I suggest goin' around Lupine Lake or Dodder Circle over by East Lake—they're both close to the Visitors Center. Don't go off'n your own. We've been havin' a mite of trouble here on the border.

Partners in Crime

ROLANDO HINOJOSA

Rolando Hinojosa is widely recognized as Texas's preeminent chronicler of Mexican American culture and is not primarily known as a mystery writer. But in his novels that make up the *Klail City Death Trip* series, Hinojosa uses the patterns of the crime novel to portray life in the Lower Rio Grande Valley.

The Valley carries a notorious reputation for "boss rule" and political corruption that dates back to the nineteenth century. Political machines often served the interests of the Anglo business class while manipulating Hispanic voters and doing little on behalf of the region's predominantly Mexican American population. In his series of novels, Hinojosa examines political power in the Valley: how irrigation water is allocated, how land titles are maintained (or mishandled), which businesses get county contracts.

Hinojosa's novels rarely employ a single narrator, and instead present different "witnesses," each with different viewpoints. As in real life, some witnesses are more reliable than others. Hinojosa leaves it to the reader to sort things out. This "postmodern" style confuses some readers and thrills others—hence the abundance of academic scholarship devoted to Hinojosa's work. As far as crime fiction goes, Hinojosa's narrative style offers an exact parallel to the methodology employed in police procedurals—detectives must sift through differing accounts as they develop some sense of where the truth lies.

A note, folded and scotch-taped to the telephone dial; he could hardly miss it, and it contained no surprise, either: "Oakland 3, Reds 1. I now owe you $20." It was signed C.

The C stood for Culley Donovan, his partner and chief of detectives for the Belken County Homicide Squad.

Rafe Buenrostro smiled, opened a side drawer on his desk, and slid that IOU along with the others signed by Donovan during that October 1972 World Series.

It had been a cool October in Oakland and Cincinnati, but it was a hot one in The Valley, in Klail City, Belken County, Texas. It was also a dry October, and the hot weather would continue as it usually did until Christmas or until the first norther came rumbling down from the Panhandle. But, until that happened: no rain. Besides, the hurricane season had been declared officially over by the U.S. Weather Service office in Jonesville-on-the-Rio. And that was that.

Rafe Buenrostro looked at his watch; the glass was scratched somewhat, but he could read the time plainly enough: 1:10 p.m. Now, if he could log in two uninterrupted hours of typing, he'd have his preliminary report ready for the District Attorney's office, and he could then begin his weekend fishing with a clean slate.

It had been a stupid murder, he thought. And here he was, six hours after it happened, putting it down on paper; and not through a particularly enterprising piece of detective work, for that matter. Fell on his lap, as it were.

An idiotic murder, he thought. And then, not for the first time in the last eleven years, "Most of them are."

He shook his head again, and he began laying his notes in some semblance of order next to the typewriter. He was about to type the report when Culley Donovan came in.

"Pitching'll do it every time, Buster Brown."

Buenrostro looked up, grinned at him, and went back to his notes.

"Damndest relief pitching I've ever seen," said Donovan. He drew two ten-dollar notes from his wallet and put them in the coffee drawer, alongside the IOUs.

"I hope you and Dorson enjoy the coffee; that's hardearned money in there."

Rafe Buenrostro laughed this time as he centered the form sheet.

Donovan: "You know, you don't know the first thing about baseball, and here you've got me twenty bucks in the hole."

And then: "Is that the Billings thing?"

Nod.

"Tell you what, I'll handle the telephone calls while you get that report in; you got your gear ready, Rafe? You packed and everything?"

"Sure am; as soon as I get this out of the way, I expect to be doing some saltwater fishing out on the Gulf. How's that sound?"

Culley Donovan nodded and said, "I'll tell you how it sounds, it sounds a whole hell of a lot better than Sam Dorson's cackle when he sees the twenty bucks."

Sam Dorson was another member of the Belken County Homicide Squad. Of what Harvey Bollinger, the District Attorney, was pleased to call *his* Homicide Squad.

The trouble with that *his* of Bollinger's was that Sheriff Wallace "Big Foot" Parkinson disagreed—in public—with the District Attorney. This particular bone of contention had been going on for years, as long as Rafe Buenrostro could remember. He was now thirty-seven years old, and he had been on the force for eleven years.

For accounting and inventory purposes, the Belken County Homicide Squad consisted of five men, five desks, four waste paper baskets, three typewriters, three telephones, one clothes rack, and Sam Dorson's long bench. Dorson had pushed it into the office one morning without any explanation, and there it remained in front of his desk.

There were also eighteen filing cabinets in the long room and other office supplies all of which, then, were paid for out of Bollinger's and Parkinson's budgets.

An opinion had been sought from the state's Attorney General, and that splendid officer concluded on the side of what his Opinion Committee called *obvious logic*, a strange phrase in the law, by the way. The Opinion Committee further determined that the Homicide Squad (five men, five desks, etc.) was responsible to the two county entities by virtue (another strange word in the law) of a shared budget responsibility.

And that, too, was that.

Joe Molden and Peter Hauer rounded out the five-man unit; both had transferred from Grand Theft-Larceny to the Homicide Squad in April of that year.

Hauer was called Young Mr. Hauer by Sam Dorson, for reasons best known to Dorson, and if there was resentment on the part of Hauer, he didn't show it. At least not in public.

Joe Molden, also in his early thirties, believed he had a strike against him from the very start: he was Sheriff Parkinson's nephew, and despite assurances by Donovan of impartiality and fairness, Molden usually felt insecure and unwanted. Buenrostro and Dorson thought Molden had no reason to feel that way, but there it was.

The Squad managed to solve the relatively few county cases handled in the course of every fiscal year; the secret to much of this was plain, plodding work. And, county murders were fewer and not as frequent when compared to the murders committed within the jurisdiction of each of the Valley's small towns and cities. The second ingredient that led to the solving of cases was dedication to detail, to the job at hand, and to the amassing of hard facts which would then be translated into evidence. Nothing fancy about it.

The Squad had most recently worked on a murder on one of the nearby farms. It was a case of incest, murder, and suicide. All five members of Homicide had agreed that the case "had been a bitch," but as usual in this type of case, the newspapers were not told of the incest.

The reporters, who had not been allowed in the room, who had not seen the room—a usual procedure of Donovan's—wrote several pages on the blood-filled room, the bodies, of an unknown intruder, of strange writings on the walls (there were none), and on the ghastly scene of the double murder. That last part was correct.

It had been a double murder, and it had been a sad one, too: a seventeen-year-old had shot his fourteen-year-old sister and himself on a bright Easter Sunday afternoon in their parents' bedroom.

The murder earlier that October morning had happened exactly five-hundred feet outside the Klail City city limits, and the distance made it a county crime.

And, where the crime had been committed was an interesting piece of business, too: the site was a gaudily-painted, cheaply-built, two-story apartment building constructed out of hollow cement blocks, which the absentee owner proudly called Rio Largo: A Complex for Young Marrieds. The first floor was known as Rio Largo I and the second as Rio Largo II. There had been plans for Rio Largo III and IV and for V and VI, too, as well as plans for an outdoor theater, maid service, and resident plumbers and electricians; all of this was still on the drawing boards and in someone's imagination other than that of the owner who had gone on to bigger and better things. As it were.

The five-hundred feet location was no accident. The two to three hundred souls who lived there did not vote in city elections, did not, then, pay city taxes, but then neither did the forward-thinking developer of Rio Largo I and II.

The Young Marrieds did have a minor inconvenience: since R.L. I and II were outside the city limits, the Klail City Fire Department could not be called upon for assistance. No, this wasn't exactly true. The FD *could* be called upon, but would not respond, such calls being outside of its jurisdiction.

Most of the tenants held low to mid-level jobs in various Valley and Klail City businesses and accepted the shoddy plumbing, wiring, and construction uncomplainingly. But then, they were just as quick to move out as they were to move in. A halfway house, then.

Rafe Buenrostro continued his typing amid fitful stops and starts as he fiddled with the ribbon which would jump out of its holding bar from time to time. A stupid murder, he muttered, for the third or fourth time, as he attempted to bring a sense of order to a senseless occurrence.

It had begun as one of those harmless domestic disputes, so called. Husband I had a girlfriend who also had a husband. Husband I also had a wife, of course, and it was she who accosted the girlfriend, before two witnesses, in the laundry room of the apartment building. A regular punch-up.

Husband II was bringing in some additional laundry for his loving wife when he saw her being pummeled by Wife I. Husband II separated them and upon learning the reasons for the fracas, flattened his straying spouse, ran to their room, grabbed a gun, and went on the hunt.

Result: The building superintendent, in no way connected, was splattered by three slugs from a nasty-looking .38 S & W Master.

The super had been repairing a bathroom leak in Husband I's apartment and was walking out of the apartment when Husband II unloaded on him. A case of mistaken identity: Husband I, thirtyish and six-feet tall; the super, in his fifties, stood five-feet four inches tall.

Idiots.

Husband I, at poolside, heard the screaming and yelling, and ran for the laundry room. When he heard the shots, however, he sprinted across the parking lot, jumped in his VW, drove the twenty miles to Jonesville at top speed, parked the car in a shopping mall lot, ran across the International Bridge of Amity (El puente internacional de la amistad) to Barrones, Tamaulipas.

Damned fool. Within a few minutes of the shooting, the two women made up on the spot; they also had a good cry, and then Wife I drove her newly-found friend to Small's Medical Clinic where they swore to stand by their mates.

The bonds of friendship.

Husband II, in the meantime, had called an attorney in Klail City who promptly advised his client to turn himself in to the arresting officer. He, the attorney, would then meet his client at Judge Hearn's court. Rafe Buenrostro had taken the telephone call from an excited neighbor who proceeded to report three, possibly four, murders at Rio Largo II.

County Patrolman Rudi Schranz accompanied Lt. Buenrostro who instructed Schranz to arrest Husband II (Andrew Billings) on suspicion of murder and to present him before Municipal Court Judge Robert E. Lee Hearn for arraignment and hearing.

The photographer and the lab personnel arrived within minutes of Buenrostro; thirty-six photographs were taken for evidentiary proof and the various rooms were then powdered for prints.

Husband II handed the gun to Lt. Buenrostro who then tagged it and placed it in a plastic bag.

The victim, too, was identified and tagged and then driven to River Delta Mortuary, Inc., as per contract with the Belken County Commissioners Court. The owner of the mortuary was a brother-in-law to the County Judge and this, too, was no accident.

A search of the victim's room revealed three open cartons of cigarettes: Camels, Pall Malls, and some filter-tipped Delicados. Buenrostro found two picture albums of old-time movie stars: Banky, Bara, Bow, Naldi, Negri, Swanson, etc. . . . A grocery bag stuffed in the bottom of a laundry hamper revealed a small Kodak camera and thirteen envelopes containing two-hundred and thirty-five prints of youngsters ranging from six to fourteen years of age; the youngsters were naked and stared rather gloomily at the camera.

There were other personal effects in the superintendent's room: two pairs of brown shoes, two pairs of khaki pants, two blue chambray shirts, one dress shirt, five pairs of socks, an Army web belt, two new and unused nylon shorts in plastic bags, as well as two grimy jockey straps draped over the shower rod. Buenrostro found some assorted toilet articles in shoeboxes which contained two boxes of unused Sheik condoms and a plastic wallet. The identity card was made out to J. Thos. West; this proved to be the name of the superintendent as identified by the nameplate on his bloody khaki shirt.

The wallet was empty save for some more pictures of young children similar to those found in the hamper.

The two laundry room witnesses and four other apartment residents were cooperative, although none "actually saw the shooting, sir," but all of whom "heard the shots, yessir."

How many shots?

One. Two. Three. Four. Five. Six. Seven.

Names of Husbands I and II and their wives?

Phillips, I think. Brown; no, not Brown. Something like that, though. Can't recall just now. Don't know.

Typical.

A thorough search of the apartment cleared this up, of course.

Rafe Buenrostro telephoned the Mexican counterpart across the Rio Grande. Within twenty minutes, Captain Lisandro Gómez Solís reported that one Perry Pylant had been picked up at Alfonso Fong's China Doll Club rather "drunk and somewhat disruptive of the public order." (The last phrase covered everything from arson to spitting on the brick sidewalks.) Señor Pylant, said Gómez Solís, was then escorted to the Jonesville side, warned not to recross the bridge and held there until he was picked up by the Jonesville police who, in turn, had already called the Belken County Patrol; Perry Pylant was held as a material witness and his car impounded for storage by Lone Star Salvage and Garage.

Patrolman Schranz drove to Jonesville, took a preliminary statement and drove the witness to the Klail City Court House. A second statement was then taken; since no charges were filed, the witness Pylant was released.

What arrangements he made to take his car out of storage were up to Mr. Pylant.

Husband II, Andrew Billings, had his bond set at $25,000 by Judge Hearn; Billings's attorney was accompanied by a friend who made bond. And so, Billings's attorney and both wives drove back together to Rio Largo II after the arraignment.

Assholes.

PART 7

SMALL TOWN TEXAS

Winning Can Be Murder

BILL CRIDER

"Friday night lights" are a Texas phenomenon. High school football fans are intensely devoted to their local teams, and civic pride is often measured by gridiron fortunes. Team mascots can function as expressions of the community's surroundings, as evidenced by the Pampa Harvesters, Columbia Roughnecks, Robstown Cotton Pickers, Port Isabel Tarpons, Dickinson Gators, Winters Blizzards, Crystal City Javelinas, Knippa Rockcrushers, and—somewhat comically—the Cuero Gobblers.

Native Texan Bill Crider was born and raised in Mexia (home of the Blackcats) and is among Texas's most prolific writers. Crider has published non-series mysteries, westerns, young adult novels, and three Texas-based mystery series: one is set on a college campus (Crider is a professor and administrator at Alvin Community College) and another features a Galveston-based private eye. Crider's longest-running Texas series features a Dr. Pepper-swilling sheriff, Dan Rhodes, who lives in fictional Clearview.

In his Dan Rhodes novels, Crider captures the ambience of small town Texas, including the great passion for high school football. In *Winning Can Be Murder*, the Clearview Catamounts are enjoying their best shot at going to the state championship since the fabled 1949 season. But then the team's offensive coach is murdered, and Sheriff Rhodes is under pressure to solve the crime before the next big game.

On certain late-fall evenings in most small Texas towns, Sheriff Dan Rhodes thought, you could actually smell football in the air. It smelled like the first cool days of the season and burning leaves and popcorn and roasted peanuts and leather.

You could hear it, too. You could hear the bands tuning up in the grandstand and then playing "Them Basses" and "March Grandioso" and the school fight song. You could hear the play-by-play announcer's echoing voice reminding everyone to make a trip to the concession stand sponsored by the Band Boosters Club for a refreshing soft drink before the game.

And of course you could see it. You could see the dust motes drifting through the headlights of the last cars arriving at the field, and you could see the haze of yellow light that hung over the field itself, often the only place in town where any lights were on, because everyone was at the game.

Some people said that high school football was almost as important as religion to people in Texas, but Rhodes knew better. It was *more* important. People just didn't want to admit it.

Rhodes, however, didn't think that Billy Graham at the height of his powers—or even a tag-team duo of Graham and Billy Sunday—could have filled the high school stadiums in every city and town in Texas for ten weeks every fall; not for fifty or sixty years in a row. But high school football could. And did. It didn't matter whether the home team had a winning record. The crowds came out just the same.

On this particular fall evening, practically everyone in Clearview, and for that matter in most of Blacklin County, with the exception of the sheriff, was riding the wave of the kind of elation that comes to small towns only occasionally in their history—when the high school team is headed for the state play-offs.

Winning a state championship meant something to a town. You could tell when you saw the signs erected at the city limits of every community whose team had won one. Some of the school colors on the signs were faded by time, the metal flecked with rust, but the signs themselves were still there:

WELCOME TO MEXIA

HOME OF THE MEXIA BLACKCATS!

TEXAS HIGH SCHOOL STATE 3-A FOOTBALL CHAMPIONS 1988!

A state championship was something which, up until this year, people in Clearview had only dreamed of. The Clearview High team had never won one. A team had come close once, in 1949, and people still talked about it at Lee's drugstore on Saturday mornings, where the town's biggest fans met the coaches for coffee and hashed over the previous evening's game. They remembered the players' names, their numbers, and all the ways in which the big game had gone wrong for Clearview.

The game had been played somewhere in the Texas Panhandle, and while Rhodes had once known quite well the name of the winning school, he could no longer recall it. He had been too young to go to the game, but his father had gone and had talked about what happened for weeks afterward. Clearview had lost, fifty-four to seven.

"When those Panhandle boys ran out on the field," he'd said, "I thought they were going to kill our boys."

"You don't mean that," Rhodes's mother said. "You shouldn't exaggerate so much."

She had been standing at the stove, Rhodes recalled, wearing a white apron with blue stitching as she fried chicken in a heavy iron skillet.

"I do mean it," his father said. "I really thought they were going to kill our boys."

Rhodes's father always came into the kitchen to talk to his wife while supper was being prepared. Sometimes they listened to "One Man's Family" on the radio, but mostly they talked.

"They were so big," he went on, "they made our boys look like peewee leaguers. I swear there were two or three of 'em that looked like they were thirty years old. Every one of them probably has to shave twice a day with an Eversharp Schick."

Rhodes's mother turned over a piece of chicken in the skillet with a long two-pronged fork. Grease popped and hissed.

"It'll be a long time before we get that far in the play-offs again," Rhodes's father said, shaking his head. "A long, long time."

It had been longer than anyone had really thought, more than forty years, but it looked as if the time had come at last: the time for Clearview to erase the memory of a humiliation that had lasted for generations.

Which explained why everyone in town, everyone in the whole county, was elated.

Except Rhodes. To the sheriff, the fact that the Clearview Catamounts had won every district game except the last, the one that was being played this evening, meant something quite different—especially on a Friday night.

It meant minors consuming alcoholic beverages; it meant too many arrests for DWI; it meant gambling, often enough right out in the open, in the parking lot near the stadium; it meant fights at every club in town; it meant making sure that the rivalries on the field didn't spill across the sidelines, onto the benches and into the stands; and it meant pulling his deputies in from patrol on Friday nights so they could police the area.

It also meant a considerable bit of worry about something that, so far as Rhodes knew, had never happened anywhere in Texas. If anyone wanted to burglarize on a large scale, a Friday night like this one would be the perfect time. There probably were more deserted homes in most small towns than there were occupied ones.

In fact, Rhodes wondered why whole towns hadn't been looted before now. Even the stores and banks were practically begging to be robbed. Maybe it hadn't happened, he thought, because all the crooks were football fans, too. They were probably at the games.

(Note from the editors: Clearview won its game with a controversial last-second touchdown, followed by a successful two-point attempt. The game was marred by an on-field riot, during which Clearview's assistant coach, Brady Meredith, threw a punch at the team's head coach.)

Rhodes could remember a time when the Clearview business district would have been humming on the Saturday morning after a game, but that had been a long time ago, before Wal-Mart had been built on the outskirts of town.

Now most of the downtown businesses were quiet, many of them practically deserted. The only real signs of life were outside the stores, where the Clearview cheerleaders were busy washing last week's spirit slogans from the windows and replacing them with new ones.

One window they hadn't gotten to yet depicted some kind of dog— which, Rhodes supposed, represented the Garton mascot—impaled on a spit above a roaring fire. Under the flames the words GRILL THE GREY-HOUNDS were painted in blue and gold. It wasn't going to be easy to top that one.

Rhodes was headed to Billy Lee's drugstore, the only place that had a crowd of any kind inside. That was because Lee's was the gathering spot for an informal group known as the Catamount Club, composed of the team's biggest boosters, mostly local businessmen who had been waiting for years for something like the previous evening's game. The membership had varied over time, but some of the men had been coming to the drugstore for decades.

They were in the back of the shop when Rhodes arrived, sitting around a rickety wooden table that was located just to the left of the high counter that separated the pharmacy from the rest of the store. There were cigarette burns on the edge of the table, but they weren't recent. None of the men smoked now, though several of them had in the past. There was a thirty-cup coffeepot on a smaller table, and each of the Catamount Clubbers had his own mug with his name painted on it in blue and gold.

Ron Tandy, a real estate agent, was the leader of the group. He had been one of the founding members, and he was one of the few people in town who still remembered Rhodes's Will-o'-the-Wisp days. He had a fringe of white hair around his head, watery blue eyes, and smooth pink cheeks. The other men at the table were Tom Fannin, who owned a couple of convenience stores; Gerald Bonny, a lawyer; Jimmy Bedlow, who managed Bedlow's Department Store; and Clyde Ballinger, the director of Clearview's largest funeral home. Jerry Tabor wasn't there, though Rhodes knew he was a regular.

Billy Lee, the owner of the drugstore, oversaw the whole thing from behind the counter. He never had much to say, but he heard everything that went on.

The center of attention was, of course, Jasper Knowles, and Rhodes arrived just in time to hear Tandy ask him what was on everyone's mind. "Why did Meredith take that punch at you, Coach?"

"Yeah, what was that all about?" Tom Fannin asked. Fannin was about forty, his hair just beginning to go gray at the temples.

Clyde Ballinger looked up and saw Rhodes. "Wait a minute, fellas. Here's the law. You want some coffee, Sheriff?"

Rhodes declined. He wasn't a coffee drinker. He preferred Dr. Pepper at any time of the day or night.

"Well, pull up a chair," Ballinger said. "You might be interested in this."

Rhodes sat down and waited for Knowles to answer. The coach looked uncomfortable. He took a sip of coffee and looked around at the group of men at the table.

"I don't know much about it," he finally said.

"You don't expect us to believe that," Bedlow said. "You were there. You were the one he took a swing at."

Bedlow was a snappy dresser, even on Saturday morning, but then he managed a department store. He was wearing a pair of gray no-iron Dockers, black Rockport loafers with tassels, and a white shirt with a button-down collar. Most of the other men had on jeans and casual shirts, except for Ballinger, who was wearing a suit. He was always wearing a suit. Rhodes sometimes wondered if he slept in one.

"You might as well believe it," Knowles said. "It was sort of crazy down there."

"What do you mean, crazy?" Gerald Bonny asked, as if he expected Knowles to supply some kind of legally acceptable definition.

"I mean crazy," Knowles said, setting his cup on the table. "Brady was acting crazy, and then he tried to hit me."

"There's crazy, and then there's crazy," Tandy said. "We still don't know what you mean."

"I mean Brady didn't seem to know what the hell was goin' on out there. Maybe it was all the excitement, or maybe he just lost it, but he was tryin' to get me to send in the kickin' team."

There was a moment of stunned silence as the men absorbed the enormity of what Knowles had said.

Billy Lee leaned over the pharmacy counter and broke the silence. "You mean he wanted to kick the point instead of going for two when we were behind in penetrations? But that's crazy!"

"That's what I've been tryin' to tell you!" Knowles looked around the table. "And that's why he punched me, I guess. I wouldn't call for the kicker. I was goin' for the two all the way. Maybe Brady thought I was goin' to lose the game for us. Maybe he thought *we* were ahead in penetrations, but he should've known better. Frankie was keepin' the stats, and he had it all down."

Frankie was Knowles's son, the third-string quarterback. He was a fixture on the bench. He always carried a clipboard, and he never got into the games.

"So Brady punched you because he thought you were going to lose the game," Clyde Ballinger said. "I guess that makes sense."

"Maybe it does," Bedlow said. "But I'm not so sure. Where is Brady, anyway? He's usually here on Saturdays."

"Maybe he was embarrassed," Tandy said. "I damn sure would be if I'd pulled a stunt like that. You going to fire his ass, Coach?"

"Well, I don't know about that," Knowles said. "Brady's a good man with an offense. If he apologizes, I guess there's no harm done. Lord knows, there's been times when I wanted to throw a punch at him when some play he sent in didn't work."

"But you never did," Ballinger said. "Did you?"

"Lord no. I wouldn't do a thing like that."

"And that's the point," Ballinger said. "Brady should've known better."

Knowles wasn't so sure. "Like I said, we'll have to talk it over. I expect he'll apologize, and then we'll see."

"What about that fight after Jay Kelton tackled that Garton kid?" Fannin asked. "I heard on the radio station when I was coming over here that the Garton coaches are really hacked off about their player gettin' kicked out of the game. They say Kelton should've been kicked out, too. They say they're gonna get some kinda restrainin' order and then sue to have the refs' decision overturned and get their boys in the district game instead of us."

Rhodes hadn't heard that little bit of news, and apparently no one else had, either.

"Those coaches ought to be ashamed," Gerald Bonny said. "Taking something like that to court. The game's supposed to be played on the field, not in a courtroom."

"Right," Fannin said. "A courtroom's where you get those million-dollar whiplash lawsuits."

Bonny was insulted. "I don't do that kind of work."

"If those Garton coaches take us to court, are you going to represent our side of things?" Bedlow asked him.

"Damn right. That's different. I won't charge a dime. You can count on me, Coach."

"A lawyer taking a case for free?" Ballinger said. "Now I've heard everything."

The phone in the pharmacy rang, and Lee answered it. He listened a second and said, "It's for you, Sheriff."

Rhodes got up and went to the counter. Lee handed him the phone. It was Hack Jensen. "You better get over here, Sheriff," he said. "We got us a little trouble."

"What kind of trouble?"

"Buddy Reynolds has found a dead man. Says it's Brady Meredith."

"I'm on my way."

Hot Enough to Kill

PAULA BOYD

Larry McMurtry, Texas's preeminent novelist, grew up in the small town of Archer City, near Wichita Falls, and he knows full well the importance of the local Dairy Queen. In his memoir *Walter Benjamin at the Dairy Queen*, McMurtry observes that "if there were places in west Texas where stories might sometimes be told, those places would be the local Dairy Queens."

Comic mystery novelist Paula Boyd was raised in Holliday, Texas, just down the road from McMurtry's Archer City. The area is known for its intense summer heat, and the state's record high, 120 degrees, was recorded nearby at Seymour in 1936. Boyd moved long ago to the cool of Colorado. Since then, she has published two novels featuring an amateur detective, Jolene Jackson, who lives in Colorado but occasionally returns to her Texas hometown, the fictional Kickapoo, to solve murder mysteries. In addition to dealing with her eccentric 72-year-old mother, Jolene must also contend with the omnipresent Texas heat.

In *Hot Enough to Kill*, the first book in the series, the mayor of Kickapoo, BigJohn (one word) Bennett, has been murdered. BigJohn just happens to have been the boyfriend of Jolene's mother, Lucille, who becomes the chief suspect. As Jolene attempts to clear her mother's name, her detective work takes her, naturally, to the town's information exchange—the local Dairy Queen.

When Mother called about the shooting, I'd been grateful I wasn't tied to a real job. The Denver area newspapers and I have an understanding that I'll send them a feature story when it suits me and they'll send me a minuscule check on a similar schedule. I have a slightly better arrangement with a couple of magazines, but none of it requires that I call in sick or fill out a form for vacation time.

And the kids aren't a panic-inducing travel issue anymore either. Usually. Being reduced to nothing but a long distance ATM machine for the college-interred offspring does have its good points.

So, unfettered and feeling a surge of importance that someone really needed me, as opposed to say, my PIN number, I'd saddled up the white horse—or more accurately, the blue Tahoe—and came charging down from the Rockies to rescue my mother.

For the first few hours of the journey, I felt really noble, heroic even. Lady Knight Jo Jackson on her journey to aid the fair queen in her hour of need. It was a large leap, but it kept me driving.

My grandiose self-image began to wilt around one a.m. when I, the would-be knight in shining armor, had to stop for my fourth Big Gulp of Dr. Pepper and stoically threw it on my face instead of drinking it so I could stay awake.

About the time I hit Amarillo—and the serious heat—I was thoroughly disenchanted with the whole notion of charging anything except the cost of a room at the nearest Hilton.

Two hours later, when I checked my messages on the cell phone and learned of my mother's incarceration, I chucked the cavalier attitude completely and went into survival mode. Embracing my dark mood, I told my sensible self good-bye and moved fully into my Kickapoo mindset.

Being of sound and logical mind in Kickapoo, Texas, is neither understood nor appreciated. It is a scientific fact that if you stay too long, your brain begins to feel like it's being sucked right out of your head. I'd learned this the hard way after returning from an enlightening four years at the University of Texas at Austin.

All aglow with youthful idealism, the cold hard truth hit me right smack in the chest while I was dutifully applying for a job at my hometown newspaper. The editor never noticed the As on my transcript, but he did notice my breasts and offered me the job on the spot. His enthusiasm lit up his face as brilliantly as a neon sign flashing "dirty old man." I ran far and fast, and I only come back to this part of the world when I have to. And this time, I definitely had to.

So, here I am, back in my old room, too tired to sleep and too wired to stop thinking about the past, the present, and the screwball mingling of the two.

Somehow it always feels like I'm stepping back in time when I come here. Maybe it has something to do with walking into a 1920s farmhouse and being hit with 1970s décor that throws me off center. Or maybe it's the fact that the farmhouse sits not on a farm but on four city lots at the fringes of a town that isn't more than a blink in the road. Or it could be much simpler: Mother's house, Mother's rules.

I ran my hand over my old, scratchy blue velvet headboard, then stared at the spongy, glitter-flecked ceiling overhead, the kind that sends clumps of white stuff down when you touch it, the kind that a kid can imagine all sort of shapes or monsters in. My room. But not. A kid's room. The kid I had been—and still felt like whenever I was here. No matter how old I get, when I'm in this house, I will always be the child. And I don't care what anybody says, feeling like you're twelve again is not a dream come true. Then again, neither is having to be the adult and collect your mother from the county jail.

I stretched out on the bed and tried to think of something besides bad old memories or bad new memories in the making. The fact that Mother was out of jail and technically off the hook was fine as far as it went. Problem was, it didn't go very far. Even in my sleep-deprived state, I was very well aware that my mother knew something about last night's murder that I didn't. Call it intuition or call it history repeating itself, but I had a very firm hunch that my mother wasn't telling me everything there was to tell about the mayor and/or his murder. Lucille's "if you don't ask, I don't tell" policy had always been a sore spot with my father and me, primarily because it was only a one-way street. Lucille's. What she was hiding this time and how bad it might be were the logical extrapolations, but outlining the possibilities was beyond my abilities at the moment.

What I did know was that Mayor John "BigJohn" Bennett had been shot in the chest with a shotgun while sitting in his den, reclining in his easy chair, feet propped up, television tuned to the station with the preacher who never sleeps. The shot shattered a window and still hit its mark. Messy, but effective. I knew these interesting tidbits because, well, Jerry Don Parker really is a good friend.

Since we parted ways in high school about twenty-five years ago, Jerry's managed to forgive me for a lot of things, childish things, like throwing a bottle at him for leaning entirely too far into Rhonda Davenport's car, kissing half the football team to make him jealous, and, most especially, for not marrying him. Actually, he never held any of it against me. Ever. He even came to my wedding—and smiled. It was more than I ever did for him, and I've always regretted it.

But now, things were different. For one, we were both divorced. Eight years for me, eight months for Jerry. That we both finally wound up single again at the same time did not go unnoticed by either of us. We didn't get too starry-eyed though, having to discuss murder, mayhem, and my mother's release from captivity.

I rubbed my hands across my eyes and yawned, wondering for about the fifty-third time what Lucille was hiding from her only child. I couldn't put my finger on it, but something was wrong with the whole scenario—wrong beyond the fact that a man had been sent to the great beyond by a shotgun. This was Kickapoo, Texas, after all.

And then, that funny feeling that had been nagging at me since last night gelled into a hard, thick ball.

With more energy than I thought I possessed, I jumped up off the bed and ran to the back bedroom.

My adrenaline zinging, I swung open the closet door, shoved aside the off-season clothes and saw exactly what I'd feared: a crescent-shaped indention in the carpet where my dad's shotgun had always been.

"Mother!"

"Yes, Jolene, I suppose I could have mentioned it, but I didn't see the point in confusing things. The gun is around here somewhere. I probably just moved it and forgot where I put it."

"Don't even start singing that song," I said as sarcastically as I could manage, considering the incredulity muddling my brain. "Your memory is better than mine and we both know it. Where's the damn shotgun?"

Lucille straightened her shoulders. "Now, there's no call for such language. If I knew where the gun was, I'd tell you. You don't have to curse at me."

I rolled my eyes and paced again. My mother could say any four-letter word she pleased, but I couldn't. Just like old times. If I didn't have worse problems I'd have pointed it out to her. But I did have worse problems. "When did you notice the gun missing?"

She shifted in her chair. "I guess it was a couple of weeks ago. I didn't think much about it." She paused and glared at me. "I am getting older, Jolene, and it isn't impossible that I moved it and forgot about it."

She was right. I've done exactly what she described on more than one occasion, and I'm three decades shy of seventy-two. Still, I knew my mother. "You've already torn the house apart looking for it, haven't you?"

Lucille tightened her lips, which was as good as a booming "yes" in Lucillese. "The gun's not here," she said, rather tersely. "And I have no idea what happened to it. Nobody's been here except Merline, Agnes, and . . ."

"BigJohn?" I finished for her, lilting my voice upward as if I actually needed her to answer the question, which of course I did not.

"Well, he never went snooping in my closets. And I know he didn't take the gun. Why would he?"

Yeah, why? It made no sense that I could see either, but then that was just par for the course. "I have to call Jerry."

"Well, you don't have to," she said in a superior tone. "But you will. I suppose I should have told you." She shook her head and clicked her nails on the Formica butcher block dining table. "This is certainly going to cause a stir."

I started to make some smart-ass comment like "you think?" but instead grabbed the phone and wagged the receiver at her. "I ought to make you call him. He knew you weren't telling him everything, just like I did."

I punched my finger into the rotary dial hole over the number one and began the tedious process of contacting the Bowman County sheriff's department via long distance and pulse dialing.

When Jerry Don Parker's husky Texas drawl resonated over the phone lines, I completely forgot why I'd called. I was not proud of the fact that at forty-three-years-old, I could still be frozen to the spot with my tongue tied in a knot simply by the sound of his voice. I think I might have managed to mumble "It's Jo" or something equally clever, while I mentally slapped myself into acting semi-mature.

"Hey, Jo," he said, voice rumbling in ways it just ought not. "Where are we going for lunch or do I have to wait and find a fancy place for dinner?"

Food. Just the thing to clear the brain. Fancy dinner. He remembered.

In my younger days, I had a reputation for being a lot of things, none of them cheap. I did eventually rebel from the beauty queen mentality, but I never lost my love of nice things. Besides, I spent too many years at McDonald's when the kids were little, and this was steak country. Visions of a thick, juicy filet mignon danced in my head and my mouth watered in sympathy, but I pushed aside my fantasies as best I could and said, "I'm afraid we might have to postpone our personal business for a while."

"Aw, Jo, what has your mother done now?"

As I said, Jerry is quite astute. "She hasn't done anything specific, at least that I know of, but I do have a problem. After my dad died, Mother insisted I take all of Dad's guns home with me to Colorado. I took most of them, but not all. I left one."

He groaned again. "Tell me it wasn't a shotgun."

"JC Higgins 12 gauge."

"Damn."

"It gets better."

"I can't wait to hear how," he said, none too cheerily.

"It's missing."

He let out a very long and weary sigh. "I'll be right there."

I had a good half-hour before Jerry could get from Bowman City to Kickapoo, so I hopped in the car and headed to the local gathering place and official information dissemination center, aka the Dairy Queen. If Lucille wasn't going to be forthcoming with her knowledge, perhaps some of the fine folks at the DQ would. What I wanted to find out, I wasn't exactly sure, but I did want to get a feel for mood in the community. If I happened to stumble on a few little juicy details regarding my mother or the mayor, well, so be it. I could feel the reporter in me clawing its way up, but I tried to ignore it. I wasn't going to get involved, really, I was just going to ask a few questions and see if I got the same story Lucille was telling.

The DQ is located at the opposite end of town from my mother's house, which means it took me almost three minutes to get there, the speed limit being only thirty.

The place was packed, oil field pickups and big sedans lining the parking lot like matchbox toys in an overstuffed case. I was a little taken aback by the crowd. Even though I hadn't lived here in twenty-five years, I figured a good seventy-eight percent of Kickapoo's residents would recognize me immediately since I really haven't changed that much since high school, if you don't count the attitude and the wrinkles.

I wasn't all that excited about being the outsider walking into the local scene, but I forced myself out of the Tahoe and up to the front of the restaurant.

With a bravado I really didn't feel, I swung open the door and marched inside like I owned the place. Standard Texan behavior, but I've been gone a long time and am sorely out of practice.

The DQ clientele might not have been impressed with my entrance, but my mere presence zipped their lips in a hurry and there was enough neck craning to keep the drop-by doctor busy for a month of Sundays, or Tuesdays as the case happened to be.

As I waved to the crowd, which had become as quiet as Mrs. Stegal's eighth grade English class where breathing was a felony offense, it occurred to me that these folks might think I didn't know about the scene that had transpired earlier in the day. Maybe they thought I'd come here looking for Lucille. I smiled just a little at the thought, and was sorely tempted to see which one of them would get elected to tell me the bad news. But I'm really not the sadistic bitch my ex-husband claims—at least I'm not that way all the time—so I decided to let them off easy.

"Mother's home now and doing fine," I said, smiling to the gawkers. "The sheriff only wanted her to answer a few questions. Everything's just fine."

Whispers, sighs, and mumblings twittered through the group.

I turned to the young clerk behind the counter, who was looking exceptionally confused, being one of twenty-two percent who had no clue who I was and obviously didn't care. Getting right to the point, I said, "Two chicken baskets to go, both with iced tea."

As she jotted down the order, I figured I was obligated to make small talk. After all, if I wanted these people to talk to me, I needed to fit in. "You know," I said, very chummy-like, "where I live, you just can't depend on getting a decent glass of iced tea. Half the time it's been there for days or they make it in the same pot they make the coffee. Sure nice to get a fresh glass here."

Clerk Jimmie Sue (I read her name tag) was quickly thinking I had lost my mind. To confirm the fact, I stuck out my hand and invited her to shake. Women in Texas don't shake hands as a general rule, unless they're passing out Mary Kay cosmetic samples.

Jimmie Sue gamely put her pudgy fingers in mine and tried to smile even though her cheeks were redder than the basket of ripe beefsteak tomatoes sitting behind the counter.

"I'm Jo Jackson, Lucille's daughter," I said, which widened her dark eyes in shock.

Jimmie Sue's hand slipped away. "Oh, my, I'm so sorry. What happened, why, it was just awful," she said, hanging onto the last word for a good six seconds so it came out sounding something like aaawwwwffuuulll. "Mrs. Jackson was mighty upset, no question. She doing okay now?"

My mother, okay? This girl was obviously new in town. To my knowledge, Lucille Jackson hadn't admitted to being okay but three times in her entire life, and all of those were times she really wasn't. "She's doing fine," I said, a real honey-sweet tone to my voice. "The whole thing's been upsetting, of course, but she'll pull through."

"Well, that's good to hear," Jimmie Sue said, putting the lid on a big Styrofoam cup of fresh iced tea. "Corrine was just fixing to call down and check on her."

I didn't know who Corrine was, but I smiled anyway. And just for the record, "fixing to" is a completely proper phrase in Texas. Essential even, particularly when used to string out getting to the actual point of the matter. I nodded to Jimmie Sue. "Lucille's just fine, and I'm sure she'll be up to visiting tomorrow."

Before I had to make up an answer for why Lucille wasn't up to it today, I took my tea and strolled toward to the biggest table of men. I am somewhat of an incongruity around here, you see. I give the illusion of being a cute little sweet thing, just like womenfolk are meant to be, but that only goes so far. Then the mouth opens and confuses the image. It is not something I have completely outgrown.

You could almost hear the eyebrows popping upward as I stepped up behind one of the men sitting around the table and rested a hand on the back of his chair. You see, segregation of the sexes is alive and well at the Kickapoo DQ, and public co-mingling is generally frowned upon. With a quick glance around the table, I recognized a few of my Dad's old friends. This was probably as good a place as any to get the real scoop—if they'd talk to me, me being both an outsider and a female. This was, after all, blatant co-mingling. I am just a scandal waiting to happen.

"So, gentlemen," I said, purring with what I hoped was just the right mix of authority and female manipulation, "what on earth happened down here last night?"

"How's the weather up in Colorado?" said a man I vaguely recalled as working at the Gulf filling station back when there was one. "Heard it was awful hot up there in Denver, almost as hot as it has been around here."

Yeah, right, and that's snow out there sizzling on the asphalt. I kept my unseemly comments to myself and smiled beguilingly at them. Rather than point out that the man had blatantly ignored my question, I played weather girl. "I live up in the mountains so it's not too terribly hot. It was actually forty-eight degrees when I left my house last night." I paused for a moment to let them wonder whether I was lying about the temperature. I wasn't.

"When Mother called me about the shooting, I just threw some things in the car and headed down here as fast as I could. She sounded awfully upset. Then when the sheriff called me this morning on my cell phone, well, I guess y'all know all about that," I said sweetly. I was warmed up and talking Texan with the best of them now, although the mewing vixen thing was wearing a bit thin. "I just can't believe what happened," I said, all breathy and gooey. "I just can't imagine who'd want to kill dear Mr. Bennett, can you?"

Instantly, the men who'd been drawn in by my sultry voice and innocent eyes became immensely interested in their coffee cups. What had gone wrong? I'd had them going. I knew I had. My ego was just starting to turn black and blue from the figurative beating when I felt a not-so-symbolic whack on my shoulder.

I turned to see a little gray-haired woman with steely eyes and a black dress ready to whack me again with her hand. Yet another of the twenty-two percent, I presumed. I might have to revise my popularity figures.

"I know who you are, girlie," the old woman said, a shrill quiver in her voice. "You better be watching what trouble you're a stirring up in this town. We're a God-fearing bunch and it was the devil's own hand that pulled the trigger on that gun. It's hussies like you and that slut mother of yours that invites the devil in. Brother Bennett was an elder in the church and pillar of this community. His death will not go for naught."

The woman was shaking, and frankly, so was I. I've never been attacked by a wiry, granny-type with fireballs in her eyes. I glanced around the table and was not surprised to see everyone staring. No one has ever accused me of knowing the best thing to say or do at any given time, but most folks know I'll do something. Actually, they expect it. I did not want to disappoint my fans.

I turned fully toward her and looked her straight in the eye, which I could do because she was about my same height of 5′4″. She looked about as friendly as a caged cougar, but then I'm no shrinking violet myself. "I'll have you know, Madam," I said in my no-nonsense voice, "it's hussies like us that give biddies like you something to gossip about."

The groaning at the table told me no one was impressed with my performance. Well, fine, I could do better. I scooted closer until my nose was almost touching hers. "Are you ill or something?"

She stepped back, confusion hopping around with the balls of fire shooting from her eyes. "I'm fine. You're the one who's sick. You and that tramp mother of yours."

Tramp, slut, hussies. . . . The words threw up big red flags. Could this be my mother's nemesis, the little church lady who wanted the mayor for herself, and harassed my mother like a jealous teenager? Surely there couldn't be two of these types running loose in this little place. "Oh, my," I said, drawling sweetly. "You must be Old Bony Butt."

Snickers and chuckles rippled through the DQ like a finely swirled Pecan Cluster Blizzard. Apparently my mother's pet name for the witch was common knowledge. I felt a little burst of pride at my mother's dealings with this lunatic, and I couldn't help but smile.

As Bony Butt sputtered in outrage, I put on a nice fake smile and once again reverted to my youthful training. "Perhaps we should step aside and speak in private, Miz Fossy, or do you prefer Ethel?" She scowled but backed away from the table and toward a relatively open corner of the room.

She started working her jaw like she was chewing up her words, ready to spew them forth. I beat her to the punch. "Look, lady," I said, glad to speak my own language again. "My mother has a record of every single hang-up call you've made to her house. There's this clever little box you hook up to the phone that shows the name and telephone number of the caller. Just flashes the information about the call right up on the little screen, then keeps a record of it as well. Absolutely amazing." I was lying through my teeth about this, considering my mother still has rotary dial telephones and will never ever have Caller ID, although she thinks it sounds kind of nice.

"Oh, and let's not forget about the pious hate mail you sent. Don't you watch TV, Ethel? Cut and paste newsprint letters would have been better than longhand. And let's talk about gloves, Ethel. Hides the fingerprints."

You could almost see her twisting up tighter and tighter, and I kept my eyes glued to her, waiting for her to snap. "You know, Ethel, if you're going to be any good at this harassment stuff, you need to take a class or something."

Bony Butt twitched this way and that, looking on the verge of bursting a blood vessel. "You don't scare me," she said, her eyes narrowing to vicious little slits. "I'm a God-fearing servant of the Lord and He will protect me from the likes of you and that lust-crazed mother of yours. Repent or feel the fires of Hell on your heathen flesh."

Wow, this lady would be a hoot to hang around with. I started to tell her I was quite proud to be a heathen if that was the exact opposite of what she was, but decided a pop quiz might be more fun. "So where were you when Mayor Bennett was killed?"

Her mouth dropped open for a second, then started working up and down like a dying fish. "That is none of your business, and what makes you think you can ask me anything?"

I shrugged. "I guess I just figured if you were willing to harass my mother for seeing Mister Bennett that you might be willing to go a little further to split them up." I surprised myself by sort of insinuating this woman might have killed the mayor, but with that card played, I couldn't quit. "Mother thought you wanted him for yourself."

She stood there for a second, just glaring at me, then seemed to drift a little. "I knew nothing good would come of it, him sniffing around her," she said, almost calmly. "I warned him time and again how he was making a mistake with that woman. I begged him to repent. We'd prayed about it, and with my help he found the strength to stop seeing her. He was a fine, fine man, but he was weak. So weak."

I waited a few beats to see if she had anything else to say, but the glazed look was fading quickly, and with it, my window of opportunity, if you could call it that. I debated asking her another question, but since one didn't present itself, I said, "Miz Fossy, I would really appreciate it if you left my mother alone. She's done nothing to harm you, and now with Mister Bennett gone, there's really nothing to be mad at her about. Judge not—"

"Don't you dare quote the Bible to me!"

Yes, that was definitely a bad decision on my part. Very bad. Try to speak a foreign language to fit in with the natives and that's what happens. "Listen, there's really no need for—"

"I know my Bible frontwards and backwards and I understand the teachings well. I do the Lord's work and I'll not be dragged down by heathens such as you. There's only two kinds of people in this world, those that walk with the Lord and those that walk with Satan." She glared at me, apparently waiting for either a Christian testimonial or an admission that I worshipped the devil. She was getting neither. Her view of the world was kind of interesting, though, all black and white, with no gray areas at all. Dealing in predetermined absolutes certainly would cut down on the decision-making process. Good or bad, cut and dried. Which is why I wound up in the "bad" category, I supposed, guilt by association. I smiled at the thought. Oh, that evil mother of mine. Another warm fuzzy of pride puffed up my chest. I started to give her yet another explicit directive to stay away from my mother, but her face was red, her eyes bugged, her veins pulsing, and I was seriously worried about her having an honest to goodness stroke.

"Okay, Miz Fossy, just take a deep breath and try to calm down. No need in getting yourself so upset."

Her hands shook as she clasped them together and held them up before her. I greatly feared she was going to fall to her knees and start praying for my soul, so I made a show of digging in my jean pockets, fully knowing there was nothing there but a couple of bucks, car keys and lint. "I just know I've got some of those worts in here somewhere."

She paused out of curiosity, and I hoped that meant she was going to remain standing. "Now, I'm not trying to butt my nose in where it doesn't belong, Ethel, but you look pretty stressed out and there's some stuff that could help you a lot. Ever heard of St. John's wort?" I didn't wait for her to answer. "Absolutely amazing. Really helps take the edge off those emotional surges."

Ethel was still looking a little confused, so I added, "Comes in capsules. Regular doses could make you a whole new woman."

"Why, you . . . you . . . dope pusher!" she shrieked as she spun on her heel and scurried away.

As the door closed behind her, I turned toward the crowd, figuring I'd better explain that I wasn't trying to get Ethel Fossy hooked on drugs. "I only suggested she try some St. John's wort for her nervous condition."

I waited for a nod of recognition that even one person had a clue what I was talking about. It did not come. "St. John's wort. W-o-r-t, not wart. It's an herbal mood enhancer that's been popular in Europe for years. Just catching on over here." They all still looked bewildered. "You buy it at Wal-Mart. Like Prozac without a prescription. Works wonders."

As they stewed on my latest revelation, I grabbed my carefully packed chicken baskets and large iced teas. I made a beeline for the front door and hurried outside before anybody asked me if I had any of the wonder pills. I did. A big industrial-sized bottle. It was part of my Kickapoo emergency kit, but I wasn't sharing. I had my own nervous condition to worry about, and the churning in my stomach told me I was going to need every single capsule I could get my hands on.

I hurried to my car, wondering exactly what I had accomplished other than procuring a decent supper. I wanted to ask questions, but then again I didn't. At some point I either had to pony up and get busy finding out what was going on, or just leave the state. Oddly, leaving wasn't looking so appealing at the moment. Getting some answers was.

Do Unto Others

JEFF ABBOTT

Religious conservatives in Texas have enjoyed great success at censoring textbooks published for schoolchildren. Thanks to their influence, book publishers have had to delete references to events happening "millions of years ago," instead writing "in the distant past" so as not to conflict with biblical time lines. Sex education has been a particular target, which is unfortunate considering that Texas has the nation's second-highest teen pregnancy rate.

Fundamentalists have been less successful in their attacks on Texas's public libraries, although it's not for lack of effort. The Texas Library Association publishes an *Intellectual Freedom Handbook* that provides guidance for local libraries on how to handle visits from censors. So far, libraries have been holding the line.

Small-town librarian and amateur detective Jordan Poteet is the star of Jeff Abbott's mysteries, set in fictional Mirabeau (based on Smithville). Abbott is one of the rare male mystery writers who pens small-town cozies. In addition to the Jordan Poteet books, Abbott also writes a much grittier series featuring a justice of the peace set on the Texas coast.

In *Do Unto Others*, which won an Agatha Award for Best First Novel, Jordan Poteet has just returned to his hometown to care for his mother, who is suffering from Alzheimer's. Jordan is installed as the town's head librarian but he quickly faces a challenge when a religious fanatic demands that he remove a D. H. Lawrence book from the library. Several townsfolk witness the angry confrontation, which doesn't make Jordan Poteet look very innocent when the woman is later found bludgeoned to death at the library.

It was really rude of Beta Harcher to argue with me right before she got killed. Downright inconsiderate if you want my opinion. The woman acted like she had a toll-free line to Jesus, so you'd think she would have had forewarning of her fate. Plus she went on her tirade in front of folks, which caused me all sorts of grief later. Fortunately I'm not a man to complain about the lack of trump cards that life deals you.

The day she died was a typically humid, sunny spring day in central Texas. I'd been running an errand and I was in a cussing mood when I got back to the library. You see, coming back from the pharmacy, where I'd bought Mama's medicine, I'd tripped over a damn baseball bat some kid had left in the small ballpark next to the library—and I'd nearly planted my face in the grass. I picked up the bat, looking around for a batless kid, but didn't see the owner. I figured whatever little Billy Joe or Bobby Jack had lost his equipment would come wailing about it soon enough, so I took the bat inside.

The Mirabeau public library was its usual hub of activity. Shelves of dusty, unread books made a place scintillate. I walked in, nodded to some of the regulars, winked at a couple of the pretty ladies, and dumped the bat into my little office behind the checkout counter. I surveyed the library.

In Mirabeau, three's literally a crowd, so we had ourselves a horde that morning. Old men sat in the periodical section, slowly scanning the papers and frowning over progress. A couple of book-minded youths from the high school fed their spring break reading habits in the science fiction section. In the most distant corner of the library, the gossipy ladies of the Eula Mae Quiff Literary Society (led by the one and only Eula Mae herself) quietly pretended to discuss the latest offerings in romance literature while chatting about their neighbors. All in all, a quiet group, idling away several hours in the coolness of the books and avoiding the smothering spring humidity.

I'm not usually found at the checkout counter, but since I didn't have a staff I didn't have much choice. The last chief librarian, the much-loved

Miss Eugenia Pollard, had died three months earlier; and her staff had departed for greener pastures. One had taken a job as chief librarian in nearby Bavary; the other had gone off to be a country singer in Houston. I, of course, was the one left warbling the blues—although their departures had left the job available for me. My assistant, Candace Tully, was only half-time and was at a dentist's appointment this afternoon.

The only advantage was I didn't have a staff continually pointing out how everything had been done under the golden touch of Miss Eugenia. My own library experience had been ten years earlier, working part-time in college at the Fondren Library at Rice University; so I'd brought a certain . . . flexibility to the work. *Flexible* meaning that I often didn't know what the hell I was doing and just rolled with the punches.

Fending off my desire for a cigarette with a wad of Juicy Fruit gum, I sat behind the counter and unfolded my many folders. One was of résumés and applications for my unfilled staff; one was a grant request I was working on to the U.S. Department of Education to get money for a literacy program; another folder held the layout for our monthly newsletter (much of it devoted to children's activities); and the last contained a request from the mayor (my boss) to take a look at the Library Rules and Policy, since Miss Eugenia hadn't updated that particular document since Reconstruction. I attacked the résumés first; the sooner I got help, the much less stressful my days would be.

It was the Juicy Fruit that caused the commotion. Beta Harcher resented folks sinning right in front of her. And since I was chewing gum and not reading religious literature, I raised Beta's ire.

I knew she was standing there for a full minute, waiting for me to look at her, so I kept my eyes lowered. It didn't work.

"Mr. Poteet!" she snapped, not bothering to modulate her voice. That irritates me. After all, it is a library. I try to keep the noise down, even if most of my patrons are hard of hearing. I'm a librarian now (although not by training, and my respect for the profession has grown by leaps and bounds).

I looked up at her. She was in her early forties—but carrying all the sins and worries of her neighbors had aged her. Once she might have had a delicate, doll-like face; now lines of worry and pinched anger marred her forehead and cheeks. Shots of gray streaked her thick dark hair. I'd wondered what kind of body might be lurking below her frumpy clothes. It was hard to tell beneath the dark, shapeless jackets and the Bible she constantly clutched to her bosom. Her blue eyes gleamed with shiny, repressed indignation. I suspected her righteousness was going to be all over me like white on rice.

I popped my gum and picked up the book stamp, as though I expected Beta to actually check out a book instead of lighting a bonfire underneath one. I saw the hardback novel Beta held in her quavering hand.

"Goodness, Miz Harcher." I smiled my public relations smile. "I didn't know you liked English literature."

"This isn't literature, mister. This book is obscene."

"*Women in Love* by D. H. Lawrence? Oh, Miz Harcher, that's a classic." I gently tried to take the book from her hands, but she wouldn't let go. She didn't want to miss a chance to wrestle with Satan.

"Classic smut, you mean." She slapped a familiar piece of paper on the counter. The last sixteen times she'd done this, I'd sighed. Now I fumed.

"What's this?" I asked, all innocence.

"Another Request for Reconsideration of Material." Beta smiled. I glanced at the form; she had filled one out for Lawrence's *Women in Love*. Just as she had for books by Mark Twain, Jay McInerney, Raymond Chandler, Nathaniel Hawthorne, Alice Walker, and others.

We're open-minded folks in the New South, no matter what the media might have you believe. If you object to something in the Mirabeau library, you can fill out one of these requests for reconsideration. We didn't get them often; at least we hadn't until Beta went on her empty-the-shelves campaign. I scanned her latest report, written in her creepy thin handwriting; no, she admitted she hadn't read the whole book ("it liked to make me gag, so I couldn't finish the Godless trash"); her estimation of the main idea of the material was innovative ("promote sex outside of marriage"); and in her judgment the book would have a deleterious effect on the youth of Mirabeau ("it's liable to make them want to fornicate before they get halfway through").

I leaned back in my chair. I'd had enough of this harassment.

"Look, Miz Harcher . . ."

"I know my rights, Jordan Poteet. Talking to you isn't going to satisfy my complaint. You got to call a meeting of the Materials Review Committee."

I groaned. If someone files a request, and I can't resolve the problem, I have to call a meeting of the MRC, which consists of me (naturally), the chairman of the library board, and another member of the board. Beta had demanded sixteen meetings thus far and hadn't gotten one book off the shelves. I decided to try polite reason with her.

"Miz Harcher, no one considers Lawrence obscene these days. Why, you can go to the big universities in Austin and College Station and they teach him there."

This academic recommendation didn't sway Beta Harcher. She flipped open the book to a passage of dire sin she'd marked with her bony, blame-pointing finger. She lectured me like she was calling fire down to the pulpit.

"Not to mention that the title itself suggests unnatural acts, but listen to this: 'The thought of love, marriage, and children, and a life lived together, in the horrible privacy of domestic and'"—here she puckered her sour face—"'connubial satisfaction, was repulsive.'" She glared at me. "This book is antifamily."

I sighed. Miz Harcher hadn't consulted Noah Webster on what connubial meant, but it sounded decadent enough to warrant her attention.

Her harangue riveted everybody. I could see Old Man Renfro and my other elderly regulars look up from their reading. Eula Mae Quiff and her groupies watched, more interested in local passions than those described in the bodice rippers they discussed. Gaston Leach stuck his head out from behind the science-fiction stack, ogling the scene through his bottle-thick lenses. Ruth Wills, a local nurse, glanced up from the card catalog. Biggest crowd in the Mirabeau library in three days. Beta loved an audience. I'd seen her poking around the shelves the past couple of days, sniffing out depravity, and now she'd made her move.

"And you know chewing gum's not allowed in the library, Jordy Poteet!" Beta Harcher added, taking on all transgressions in her immediate vicinity.

"I'm trying to quit smoking," I explained, hoping for a little mercy. "And as the librarian, I allow what I like in this library." I tried to puff out a bubble to piss her off, but Juicy Fruit's not built for blowing.

"The city council might argue with that." Beta shook the offending volume of Lawrence in my face.

"If the city councilors want to fire me, they can. *Women in Love* is not obscene, Miz Harcher."

She pulled out her big censorship gun. "Oh, really, Mr. Poteet? I think the God-fearing folks of Mirabeau'd like to know what else goes on in this book." She leaned her face close to mine and I could smell her unpleasant breath. Probably chewing brimstone as a mint.

"Men. Wrestling in the nude together." She enunciated the words carefully, making sure I understood their import.

"Yes, the two men in the book wrestle. It shows their friendship," I explained patiently. "They don't have sex." My twentieth-century Brit Lit professor surely would've found Beta a challenging pupil. "Why don't you really read the book, Miz Harcher? You might find it interesting."

"I don't have time for such smut."

"No," I said, knowing that folks were watching, "but you do have time to come in here, make a scene, disturb the other patrons, and in general make a nuisance of yourself."

"I don't appreciate your tone, Jordy Poteet." She set her lips tightly, glaring at me.

"And I don't appreciate yours, Miz Harcher." I had grown tired of her stunts since my victory over her two months ago at a library board meeting. I stood, hoping to look tough at my height of six feet two. I didn't think it'd work; I've been told repeatedly that my blond hair and green eyes make me look too boyish to scare anyone but infants. "I'll remind you that you were thrown off the library board because of your censorship stance. If you don't want to read the book, don't read it. No one is hog-tying you down and forcing you to read Mr. Lawrence. But don't expect you can come into this library and dictate to others what's available to them. This tactic of continually filing complaints—"

"This trash undermines people's souls."

"Good God, Miz—"

"Don't you take our Lord's name in vain!" she shrieked. You could have heard a page turn in the silence, but no one in the library was reading anymore. Not with Beta's soul-saving floor show playing.

"Hardly anyone checks out that book." I lowered my voice rather than lowering myself to her level. "Very few souls are at risk." I hated all the eyes that were suddenly on me. I'd felt that way ever since I'd come home to Mirabeau and I still wasn't comfortable with it. I can't stand pity. "Maybe we can step into my office and discuss this Request for Reconsideration."

I considered that a perfectly reasonable suggestion. So I was awfully surprised when she slapped me. With *Women in Love*.

She belted that book right across my face. Not a love tap, but an honest-to-God blow. And Jesus made that woman strong. My head whipped around and the ceiling lights flared in my eyes. I felt my lip split and there was a wetness on my nose that I was sure was blood. The carpet felt rough against my hands and I realized I was kneeling on the floor, knocked clear out of my chair. I saw my wad of gum stuck on my office door. I glanced up at Beta Harcher; she smiled, as pleased with herself as a child with a new toy. Her eyes were two shiny pebbles, cold and stony.

Screams erupted from the Eula Mae Quiffers. Gaston Leach ducked back into the space operas and fantasy novels. Old Man Renfro creaked out of his chair, arthritically trying to hurry to my defense. Ruth Wills beat him to it. She ran over and grabbed Beta's arm.

"Let me go!" Beta squawked, as though Ruth were a demon wresting her from the Lord's work. Ruth pulled the book from Beta's clutches and tossed it on the counter. "I think you'd better go, Bait-Eye. You've caused enough trouble."

The look Beta gave Ruth Wills held pure venom. "You watch your mouth, missy. You're a sinner, too. You have no right—"

"You've just assaulted Mr. Poteet," Ruth interrupted coolly. "In front of witnesses." I like Ruth; she's one of Mirabeau's nicest residents. She's also a lovely brunette with a figure a boy could doze against and die happy. "He could press charges against you, and no one here would blame him."

"You better leave, Beta." Eula Mae Quiff herself had come up behind them, keeping the younger Ruth as a buffer between her and our local zealot. Eula Mae is fond of bead necklaces and she nervously fingered one of the several around her throat as she watched Beta.

"That smut he's offering our young's no better than that trash you write, Eula Mae," Beta snarled. "All that sex—and women living independently from God's plan."

"My fans judge it otherwise," Eula Mae sniffed. She swirled her colorful, robelike dress to emphasize her point. I thought she might take a bow.

"God's the final judge." Beta stared down at me like a dog eyeing a pork chop. "I'll close this pit of lies. God will help me."

"Beta, stop it!" An unexpected ally had appeared: Tamma Hufnagel, the Baptist minister's wife. She had come up behind Eula Mae. Beta was one of their flock but Tamma's young face looked pained. "This is not the way to conduct our Lord's work—"

"Hush!" Beta ordered. Poor Tamma clammed up abruptly.

Back on my feet, I grabbed a tissue and wiped the blood from my nose and mouth. I poked at my nose experimentally; it didn't shift into a new shape, so I decided it wasn't broken. I was still in shock that this woman had whacked me. She looked so harmless until she opened her ornery mouth. Why couldn't she have assaulted me with a nice thin book—say *Of Mice and Men*?

"No, the final judge is over in the courthouse." I reached for the phone. "You get out and lay off the library, or I'll call Junebug Moncrief and have your God-fearing self hauled into jail." I couldn't resist, and I should've. "You think St. Peter'll be impressed with your having a record when you approach those pearly gates? He might just put you on the down elevator."

"You're burning in hell, not me," Beta announced, pulling away from Ruth's grasp. She straightened with righteous dignity. "I'll leave, although I'm not afraid to go to jail. I have the Lord's work to do today." She cast a baleful eye over the stunned silent faces in the library. "Y'all remember that. I have the Lord's work to do."

I wondered if I was the only one on Beta's holy hit list. I leaned across the counter and jabbed my finger in her face, tempting her to take a bite. "Fine, you poor misguided woman. Go make trouble for someone else. This may be a public facility, but you are damned unwelcome here. If you bother me, or anyone at the library again, I will press charges."

"You can't punish me. You judge me not. Though God is judging *you*." Her voice hardened, and it amazes me still that there could be so much spite in that frumpy form. "He's judging you, Mr. Know-It-All Jordy Poteet. That's why your mother is the way she is—"

"You shut up!" I yelled. "Get out!" Dead silence in the stacks. Those dark, deadened eyes stared into mine. I fought back a sudden, primitive urge to spit in her face. Yes, I do have a bad temper and Beta saw she'd gone too far. She didn't flinch away, but Ruth hustled her out into the spring heat. I could hear Beta protesting the whole way, threatening Ruth with various fundamentalist punishments. I could only imagine what special levels of Gehenna she reserved for me.

I slumped into my chair. My hands shook. I was ten years younger and a foot taller than Beta Harcher, but her words rattled me more than her punch. I admit it: I could've throttled her—just for a moment—when she made that crack about my mother. Whack me with books all you like, but leave my family alone.

The bleeding stopped, but I kept dabbing my nostrils with the tissue. The blue-haired crowd headed straight for me, gabbing with their henhouse tongues. The Eula Mae Quiffers examined me carefully and, assured that I was okay, offered their opinions on Beta.

"She's addled," said one lady.

"Poor dear just takes the Bible too literally," opined a more pious woman who had not been battered with a book recently.

"I can't believe she struck you," added another, disappointed that my nose was intact.

"What a bitch," Eula Mae commented. She's the closest thing to a celebrity Mirabeau has—a romance novelist known to her fans by the nom de plume Jocelyn Lushe. I have nothing against romances—I could probably use one in my life—but Eula Mae gets inordinate amounts of local adoration for her prose. I can only take so many heaving bosoms and smoldering loins per page, and Eula Mae isn't big on setting limits.

Mousy Tamma Hufnagel watched me carefully. "Miz Harcher's upset about being kicked off the library board, Jordy. She's just awful tetchy about civic morals. She means well."

"No, she doesn't, Mrs. Hufnagel," I answered. "She's a lunatic and they're usually not concerned with the public good." I watched Ruth come back into the library, without Beta. "I could just kill that old biddy."

"Don't you listen to Beta Harcher, Jordy." Dorcas Witherspoon, one of my mother's friends, took my hand. "She's a bitter fool. She's unhappy, so she wants everyone to be that way. We don't care if you keep smutty books. You know all I read here is the Houston paper for 'Hints from Heloise.'"

"Please, ladies, I'm fine," I assured them. I sighed. "I guess Mrs. Hufnagel's right; Beta's just mad she got kicked off the library board. She'll just find someone else in Mirabeau to terrorize."

That, unfortunately, didn't happen. The good Lord decided, I suppose, that He needed Beta Harcher at His right hand a far sight earlier than any of us reckoned.

Agatite

CLAY REYNOLDS

One of the more disquieting aspects of a dying small town is futility. Futility in finding good people for leadership positions in government, commerce, religion, and education; futility of aspirations for the community itself to grow in size, culture, or opportunity. Young people escape by leaving town as soon as possible, returning only rarely and reluctantly. In the plains of North Texas, this seemingly inevitable destiny is made all the more painful by a harsh climate and geography that conspire to make life uncomfortable for all who remain behind.

Clay Reynolds was born and raised in Quanah, a small town between Wichita Falls and Amarillo. Reynolds is a noted writer, literary critic, and the winner of several awards for his fiction. He has taught at Lamar University, the University of North Texas, and the University of Texas at Dallas. Reynolds has published three novels set in Agatite, a fictional town that shares many qualities with his native Quanah.

In this excerpt from *Agatite*, Reynolds provides a withering portrait of the dissolution of a small Texas town. Once-promising fortunes have blown away and the inevitable crumbling has set in. Fatigue and resignation hang in the air, even as race and class divisions remain inflexible. Some look to violence as a way out of despair. The discovery of a murdered woman in an outhouse symbolizes something far beyond one individual death.

In the Old West, when a man's destiny was open to whatever chances he could or would take, Agatite, Texas, sprang up on the north central plains as a major railhead and agricultural and ranching center. Over the years it remained prosperous while smaller communities around it died or were blown away and never rebuilt. When cattle, cotton, and oil were still being discovered everywhere else, the fertile Greenbelt soil of the Red River Valley yielded wheat and soybeans to add to the wealth of the barons already rich in horned, black, and white gold. Even though the Depression and the Dustbowl ruin of the plains took its toll in Sandhill County, almost everyone believed that those who picked up and moved to California were only the weak ones, those who lacked the whatever the hell it took to fight the weather, the banks, or anything else that stood in the way of prosperity.

Along with prosperity, of course, came what the respectable folks in town called the "undesirable element," for farming and ranching and oil wells brought with them the vulgar cowboys and drifters, roughnecks and wheaties, field niggers and mestizos, all of whom from time to time haunted the midnight alleys and streets and just as often populated the town's jails.

Once boasting almost ten thousand souls, Agatite now barely sustained half that number. Aside from the banker, the odd small businessman or insurance agent, the local law officers, and the handful of successful ranchers who had moved into town to live in brick homes, the populace was mostly made up of old people waiting to die and young people waiting to get the hell out. The railhead had moved away from Agatite, northeast to Tulsa, and also shut down were the two small clothing factories that once operated in the city because of the railroad's accessibility. Agricultural goods, now using long-haul trucking that came right out to the farm or ranch to pick up crops or livestock for market, were only rarely stored in the dozen or so elevators or the enormous stockyard near the tracks in town, and the cotton gin that marked the town's skyline along with the Sandhill Hotel and the city water tower had also been left to rust and neglect with the reduced demand for cotton in a world clothed by synthetic fabrics. The gypsum mine and mill, once boasted to be the world's largest, was running at only three-quarters production level, since the slump in the nation's demand for wallboard had put a cramp in business. To the old-timers who thought about it, and only a few did, the town seemed worn out, used up.

The land around Agatite was also used up. All that wasn't completely useless for crops or grazing had been bought up by a small number of enterprising farmers and ranchers, and all the oil that was pumped from it went off to Houston companies that sent in an occasional geologist to live for a year or two but put very little else into the community.

With Fort Worth far to the southeast, Abilene to the south, and Amarillo stretching just as far to the northwest, the small town nostalgically remembered when it had been called the "Jewel of the Plains," fighting an all-out range war with Pease City, five miles away, for the right to be the seat of Sandhill County. Once it had been a stopover for aspiring governors and senators; even foreign dignitaries had paused there, and once, Teddy Roosevelt himself had whistle-stopped through and made a resounding speech from the presidential train in front of the depot. Now the town was merely a scar widening the stretch of blacktop bypass known as U.S. 287, noted chiefly as being the center of the last dry county before northbound travelers reached the Oklahoma border.

Tourists coming from any direction groaned when they sighted the city limits, noting with disgust that it was typical of any of the small towns that dotted north central Texas: dirty, small, dying. Greasy oil and dirt mixed with red clay and gypsum in the streets to form a kind of dustiness that even a rare spring day's stillness could not lighten or disperse. Travelers would move quickly through the main street of the hamlet, hardly slowing down for the blinking yellow light that marked the exact center of town, and they usually slowed again, considering briefly the dirt-encrusted Dairy Mart on the outskirts, across from the equally wind-battered and weathered motel The Four Seasons, across U.S. 287, and they would wonder if anything between Agatite and Amarillo or Fort Worth, Abilene, or Lawton could possibly be less appealing and whether they should just wait until they arrived at one of those more inviting metropolises.

Long before the railhead had removed to Tulsa and trains meant more than something to interrupt the flow of traffic on Main Street, time and progress had stopped in Agatite, and in some ways, the clock seemed to run backward. Except for a new Texaco or Gulf sign, a banker's new Oldsmobile or a rancher's new pickup, the TV antennae, and other small changes, there was little indication that the town was aware that men had walked on the moon, that hearts were transplanted, or that war had become unpopular. Old men fought older wars in the Goodyear tire store's air-conditioned waiting room, the domino parlor, or, on cool days, on benches placed strategically around the downtown area. And when they ran out of war stories, they replayed high school football games, compared the current team to the one that had actually won a state championship in 1966, and speculated on the worth of the nine and ten-year-old boys scrimmaging on the playgrounds around the elementary school.

The WPA provided the town with a park, a football stadium, a post office, a city hall, and a county courthouse, where a broken statue of a Confederate infantryman stood guard, staring toward the empty streets of Agatite day and night. The Women's Club had erected a sign near the highway years before, but the merciless climate that brought winters with below-zero readings and summers with one-hundred-ten temperatures, both whipped by a vigorous wind from the Caprock, had swept by it so often that even the most alert tourist had trouble discovering that AGATITE IS A BIRD SANCTUARY.

The swirl of white dust had not quite settled around the sheriff's big black Buick cruiser when Able Newsome climbed out and stood up straight. He didn't much like the Buick, since it forced him to have to readjust his pistol belt and straw hat every time he got in or out of it, and he was particularly aggravated by the dusty, all-weather street that was already settling on his copper-colored boots.

August heat hit him squarely in the face as he walked through the dust up to the door of the Hoolian Barbershop, and the fabric of his shirt quickly gave up the cool from the cruiser's air conditioner and began to moisten with sweat. The dust made little puffs as he moved off the road that passed for a street across a bed of red ants toward the concrete porch of the shop, and he automatically cast a wary eye into the weeds alongside the ditch for snakes.

Outside the shop, in spite of the heat, a small knot of men stood. Able recognized most of them by face if not by name right away. There was Mel Stephens, the barber, and Ray Clifford, still wearing his barber's apron with small clipped hairs stuck to it. Apparently he had actually been in the shop for a haircut for a change instead of the infamous three G's—Gossip, Guzzle, and Goof-off—for which the small establishment was widely known.

Ever since Able's childhood, Mel had been the barber in Hoolian, and his shop had become one of the two remaining businesses in the small country community that once had flourished in an age before automobiles made travel into such municipalities as Agatite practical. All that remained of Hoolian now was the old barbershop and a combination garage and feed store on what used to be a street corner a block away. In fact, the other two men, whose names escaped Able for the moment, were probably from there, he judged, noting that one wore greasy overalls and the other carried a large socket wrench in one hand.

The Hoolian Barbershop was an institution in Sandhill County, even though Hoolian had ceased to exist sometime before World War II. The three or four stone or adobe buildings that remained were boarded up and in a state of advanced decay, and the one or two houses that hadn't been moved into Agatite in one or two pieces were falling down and choked by weeds and ant beds. As a functioning business, the barbershop was more of a gathering place than a hair-cutting establishment. Mel kept cold drinks on hand and a full rack of pornographic magazines. Anyone who stopped by could count on a game of dominos, checkers, or the latest gossip from around the county. His business was more talk than cut—everyone knew it—and it was regarded with suspicious eyes by the ladies of the county just as it was jealously guarded in its integrity by the men who frequented it as a place to escape the college kids, communists, and other riffraff the government suffered to exist in the world. It was also a place where a man could get an illegal drink in a dry county, although that was the best-known secret around. Even Able knew it and looked the other way. After all, it wasn't hurting anybody, and people had been drinking at Mel's a lot longer than he'd been sheriff.

In order to keep solvent, Mel had to start cutting the hair of the migrant farm workers, mostly Mexican Americans, mestizos, who moved through the county from time to time. The two shops in Agatite wouldn't let them in the door as the workers reportedly had lice and greased their hair so much. Even the one black shop wouldn't take the Mexican Americans, but Melvin kept a special set of scissors and combs under a purple fluorescent light that was guaranteed to purify, and on Friday mornings and some Wednesdays he would take them if they could get off work and if there were no white customers ahead of them—or behind them, for that matter.

No one particularly liked the idea of the dark-skinned men coming into the Hoolian Barbershop, but Mel made the situation easier on his regulars by instituting a set of rules for the mestizos. They had to wait out on the porch, regardless of the weather. They paid double what the white customers paid, and if they needed to go to the rest room, they had to use the outside johnny behind the shop.

The johnny was anything but inviting. Stuck forty feet behind the back wall of the barbershop in a patch of Johnson grass, tumbleweeds, and red ant beds, it challenged even the most desperate individual's resolve not to unzip and piss in public. Wasps and hornets buzzed around the tin roof, and the path was so narrow and cramped by high grass and weeds that even the dullest imagination had no problem envisioning eight-foot rattlers lying in wait on either side.

Mel did nothing to clean or maintain the facility in any way, and the stench from the trench underneath was discernible from fifteen feet, even though no one could remember anyone using it in years. Mel had installed a commode in a storage closet in the back of the shop some ten years before. But it was strictly reserved for his white patrons, particularly those he knew. He had hand-lettered an "Out of Order" sign, which permanently dangled from the closet door's knob, and while Ray and others who dropped by for conversation ignored it, the sign directed other, less desirable clientele to the filthy johnny out back. It was a standing joke among Mel's regulars. Most of the Hispanic patrons avoided it by waiting until they got home or, if their needs were particularly strong, by heading for the outcroppings of mesquite in the pasture beyond the small outhouse.

On this particular August morning, however, a young Mexican lad had come into the shop and was immediately sent out to the porch to wait until Mel completed the finishing touches on Ray's diminishing locks. After a bit, the boy stuck his head indoors and asked permission to use the toilet, but Mel had shaken his head and hooked his thumb out the back window of the shop toward the johnny. "Not working, ameego," he had said, while Ray giggled like an like an idiot. "Have to use the crapper."

A few minutes passed while Mel and Ray exchanged jokes about mescans, and suddenly the boy burst back into the shop's door, screaming breathlessly in Spanish and half pulling and half pushing Ray and Mel out the door and in the direction of the johnny.

Two minutes later Mel called Able Newsome. Hoolian is only about a fifteen-minute drive from Agatite, and Able made it in normal time. He didn't know what was going on out there, but he figured it wasn't too serious, in spite of the loud, confused phone call from Mel. The old barber wouldn't say why he wanted the sheriff to come, only that he'd better come quick, and in the background Able could hear someone shouting in Spanish and Ray yelling for him to "speak English, goddamnit."

So when Able Newsome arrived and approached the men in front of the shop, he wasn't in too good a mood. He envisioned his lunch being spoiled by this stupid country drive in the heat to fix some squabble between Mel and the mestizos, and he looked with less than his usual tolerant feeling toward the small brown boy squatting on the concrete porch of the shop. "So what's up this time," he asked in general. "What is it, Mel?"

The whole group exploded in explanation at once, and Able almost had to scream to get them to talk one at a time. Finally he got the information he sought.

"Who found it?" he asked the boy.

"I did," the youngster answered, dusting off his trousers which were conspicuously cleaner than Ray's or any of the others standing around him. "I went in, and there she was. I slammed the door . . ." He trailed off.

"You know her?" He directed the question at Mel, noting that the boy looked scared and sick, but Able felt instinctively that the youth was worried because he had unwittingly stepped into a white man's mess and figured, all things being equal, he would be blamed. The men were all quiet, watching both Mel and the boy as they shuffled around.

"Well?" Able repeated the question and glanced at them each in turn.

"How the hell should I know?" Mel shouted at Able, then realized how loud his voice was and lowered it. "I didn't stand there and study her none, for Chrissake!"

Ray shook his head slowly. "It's pretty bad, Able, pretty goddamn bad."

Able shifted his weight and took a deep breath of the superheated air around the shop. He felt sweat running from under his arms down his sides. "Did you call an ambulance?" he asked.

"Ambulance?" Mel shouted, and started to guffaw, then caught himself. "You go take a look, Able!" he demanded, moving his hand up to wipe his mouth. "She ain't needed an ambulance in quite a while. You go take a look."

Able stood looking around the faces of the group of men, pivoting his body and holding his hand on the butt of the holstered .44. He realized that they were all waiting for him to go and look. And why didn't he? That was his job, wasn't it? He also realized that from the garbled accounts of what was waiting for him to look at, he didn't want to. He knew he would rather do almost anything than go back there and look into the outhouse. But he also knew that he had to go and look. And he had to do it right then.

Sweat ran down the side of his face and he could feel the wetness of his shirt under his arms. He stood one minute more, listening to the traffic over on U.S. 287, to a dog barking like hell someplace, sounds of cicada, grasshoppers, his own breathing, his own heart beating.

He had seen plenty of death in Korea. Lately, he had been finding more and more old people who had died or killed themselves in houses remotely placed around the country. He remembered the old lady who had been dead and whose dog he had shot. She had been there for three days when he burst into the front door. She had been on the floor, near the telephone, reaching for it when her heart burst. And he had seen car wreck victims, victims of violence of practically every kind, inflicted with all sorts of weapons. But something in him didn't want to see what was in Mel's outhouse.

His eyes moved around the group once more, and he swallowed hard. His mouth was dry, and he wished he could ask Mel for a sip of some of the whiskey he knew the old barber kept in the back room, but he also knew Mel would deny having any, and the whole group would be shocked at Able's breach of county etiquette. The dog in the distance stopped barking, and Able wondered why. Then, without a conscious command from his brain, he found himself walking around the side of the shop toward the overgrown path that led to the johnny in the back.

The four men and the boy hung back a little. Able paused where the path to the outhouse entered the weeds and turned on them. "You men wait here," he said, pointing briefly at Mel, noting that Ray had a pint bottle sticking conspicuously from under his barber's apron.

"Don't worry, Able," Ray snickered. "We ain't gonna look again."

"Then shut up," Able ordered, madder at himself for sounding angry than he was at these buffoons who were lollygagging around, waiting to see what his reaction would be. "You two, go on home, unless you got business here or know something about this," he said to the two mechanics who were standing behind Mel and Ray. They slunk off around the side of the shop.

Able turned to face the path again. The door hung at an odd angle, probably a result of the boy's slamming it shut. It was slightly open, revealing nothing of the interior. The grasshopper sounds increased as he became aware of the white-hot heat from the noonday sun, the breathlessness in the atmosphere. Somewhere the dog, or a different dog, had begun barking again, a rasping, frantic bark that indicated that it had discovered an interloper in its territory, maybe a prairie dog, snake, or other dog. Maybe a man. Able rested his hand on his pistol butt again, then quickly withdrew it, not wanting to gain more snickering comments from the country hicks behind him.

Fear overcame him and he fought it back with difficulty, noting that his stomach was heaving already in anticipation of what he was about to see. He felt a knot forming in his throat, and his tongue felt like an old, dry rope, fruitlessly attempting to wet his lips. Finally he stepped onto the path, instinctively looking for snakes and listening for the warning rattle that would blessedly postpone the task at hand, but none came.

The grasshopper sounds ceased abruptly as his legs brushed the tumbleweeds and cactus and Johnson grass strands, and he set his jaw, walking as deliberately as he could toward the outhouse door.

The smell hit him from about fifteen feet, and he involuntarily reeled back from it, recognizing it immediately from the battlegrounds he had walked on. It was the smell of carrion, of death, of rotting human tissue, or corpse, bloated, bursting, exploding at a touch.

Awful as it was, it gave him an eerie feeling of familiar comfort, and the fear receded. He felt he could deal with what was beyond the door of the johnny now. It was going to be bad, he knew, but at least it was familiar. There wouldn't be anything there he hadn't seen before. More quickly now, he moved to the outhouse door and grabbed it to open it.

The weeds and overgrowth resisted his moving the door to a fully open position. He looked down to see what he could do to make it clear the strands of vegetation that had wound around the rotten bottom of the jam. He pushed harder, and the door came completely off its hinges in his hands, and his attention shifted to prevent falling over with it into the tumbleweeds. He dropped it into the weeds in a cloud of dust and splinters, and then automatically, before he thought about what he was doing, he looked up, into the outhouse's interior.

"Jesus Christ on a crutch!" he said, drawing air in through clenched teeth. "Bleeding Jesus Christ on a goddamn crutch."

PART 8

END OF THE ROAD

The Red Scream

MARY WILLIS WALKER

One of Texas's more dubious distinctions is being at the forefront of state sanctioned executions. Although the legendary electric chair, Ol' Sparky, has been retired to a Huntsville museum and replaced with the "more humane" lethal injection, the death house located at "the Walls" in Huntsville manages to convey a pervasive sense of dread, even when unoccupied. The feeling is appropriate for a place where criminals receive society's ultimate punishment.

Mary Willis Walker, an Austin novelist, chillingly portrays death row's atmosphere in this excerpt from *The Red Scream*, the first of three award-winning novels about Molly Cates, a crime reporter for the fictional magazine, *Lone Star Monthly*. Here, Cates is covering the case of serial killer Louie Bronk when she discovers evidence that might prove his innocence of the murder for which he is being executed. Despite her abhorrence of the killer, her sense of justice obliges her to follow through and ultimately uncover the truth.

The character of Louie Bronk is loosely based on Henry Lee Lucas, the notorious "I-35 Killer" in the 1980s. Lucas exaggerated the number of crimes he committed in his quest for notoriety, and his confessions proved to be very convenient for some police departments anxious to clear their backlogs of unsolved murders. After evidence came to light absolving Lucas in some of the cases, then governor George W. Bush commuted Lucas's death sentence to life without parole. In *The Red Scream*, Louie Bronk will receive no such reprieve.

She gave herself the first hour, from Austin to Caldwell, for listening to Willie Nelson and letting her mind float. Some loose easy time for thinking about Grady and how sweet it would be to get home tonight and find him there, in her bed, and press up against his back and sleep for ten delicious hours while the norther rattled the windows.

Her hour was up when she hit Caldwell. She switched off the tape player and tried to focus on the problem of how she was going to write this story. One thing was sure: it couldn't be just the usual execution story. She'd read plenty of accounts of death-row procedures. She knew exactly what had happened to Louie on this, his last day. Early this morning they had transferred him and his possessions. They had driven him, shackled and cuffed, the fourteen miles from the Ellis Unit to the Walls Unit inside the city limits of Huntsville, where the law mandated executions should take place. There his guards had passed the buck and turned him over to new guards, who had locked him in a holding cell on the old death row a few yards from the execution chamber.

That cell was barred and reinforced with fine mesh so visitors couldn't pass him any contraband—no tranquilizers, no drugs, no poisons to cheat the state of its duty. Two guards had been posted near the cell all day and the chaplain, in this case Sister Addie, had sat with him, outside the cell. He could have visitors, as many as he wanted, but no contact visits were allowed. In Louie's case it didn't matter. There was no one who wanted contact—no family, no friends. His three remaining sisters wanted nothing to do with him.

He had been asked what he wanted for his last meal—it could be anything, so long as they had it on hand in the kitchen.

Sometime during the day the warden had come to see him to talk about arrangements—the disposition of his worldly goods and the disposal of his body. The thought made Molly's stomach contract. And this, for a murder she was absolutely convinced he didn't commit. The only true elements in the account she'd written of Tiny McFarland's death were that it happened on the morning of July 9, 1982, and that Tiny was shot dead. But not by Louie Bronk. By someone else—someone Tiny knew, someone she loved, someone in her family.

She was rich. She was married. She was a mother. She liked to take chances. She was promiscuous. All those things may have contributed. Plus that one other ingredient that all murder victims shared: she got unlucky.

Molly had started the story in her dreams two nights ago. Now she struggled to flesh it out.

Tiny McFarland, dressed in a white linen sheath and high heels, had cut an armful of red gladioli from her garden. On the way back to the house, she'd run into a lover. A lover in the garage. David Serrano—young, attractive, hot-blooded, available. She had dropped the flowers so her hands were free for a lover's purposes. The big garage door must have been closed; lovers require some privacy. Little Alison was asleep and no one else was home, so it wasn't such a big chance to take.

At this point the story got difficult.

First Molly thought it through with David killing Tiny in a jealous rage over someone else, a new lover maybe, or Tiny's desire to end the affair.

Then she envisioned Charlie coming home, using the automatic door opener and finding them there. Nightmare time.

She could see Stuart coming home early and finding them there and killing his mother in some sort of Oedipal rage.

Or even Alison, a nervous girl with great possessiveness toward the men in her life, coming on them and panicking, thinking someone was being hurt. No. She was only a little girl—eleven years old.

Or Mark. Maybe he was infatuated with Tiny. Maybe he'd spied on some of her trysts; he had a history of that. Maybe he was getting revenge on Charlie.

One thing was clear: whoever did it had a clever idea that worked better than he could possibly have foreseen; he'd been reading the paper about the Scalper and decided to make the murder look like just another Scalper killing. What a thrill it must have been when Bronk actually confessed to it. Of course, Frank Purcell had fed him some information, she felt sure, but that must have been after Louie had already confessed.

As for the recent murders, surely David had been killed over what he knew about Tiny's death. He had gotten too nervous and was about to tell it all. Georgia—well, that just got too complicated for her at this late hour. Time was running out.

When Molly pulled into Huntsville, the whole town was dark and buttoned up—just after 11 p.m. on a Monday night in a small East Texas town. She was thirty minutes early and so tense that she found herself craving a greasy cheeseburger even though she'd given them up a year before. A beer might help, too. She drove around a little and didn't see anything open, so she abandoned the idea. Anyway, executions, like surgery and some crime scenes, were probably done best on an empty stomach.

What she really needed was a walk, to get the kinks out of her legs after three hours of driving.

She parked the truck across from the big modern Walker County courthouse on the town square. It was well lighted and there were several sheriff's deputy cars parked on the street—a good place to walk. She slipped on her tennis shoes, laced them tight, and did four circuits of the square, increasing her speed each time, until she was nearly running. When she finished, she felt even tenser and more keyed up than she had when she began. She felt as if the volume of blood in her body were building up, pressing from the inside. God, that sounded like one of Louie's poems.

She got her notebook and pen out of the truck and changed from tennis shoes to a pair of black suede loafers, under the notion that it was inappropriate to wear tennis shoes to an execution; her Aunt Harriet would certainly approve of that notion. Then she headed toward the prison, an easy five-block walk.

She passed the bus station and walked through the incongruously pleasant residential area that surrounded the old prison. It was a lovely neighborhood with handsome Victorian houses and a scattering of more modest but well-kept frame bungalows, green lawns, and flowerbeds.

She'd never been here at night before and as she neared the prison she was awestruck. Against the dark sky, the massive forty-foot-high brick walls, washed in white security lights, loomed over everything. The inmates, and everybody else in Texas, called this place "the Walls." The oldest structure in the Texas prison system, it reminded Molly of a medieval walled town. Inside, on 140 acres, was a nearly self-sufficient world: a textile mill, a machine shop, cell blocks, a chapel, school rooms, an exercise yard, kitchens, garden plots, even an arena for the annual prison rodeo. And, of course, there was also that small separate structure in the northwest corner—the death house, the one place in the prison she had not yet seen.

As she approached, Molly remembered back about a year ago, when she was doing a piece on sex offenders. She had been sitting on the low wall across the street from the prison, waiting to interview Timothy Coffee who was being released after serving thirteen years for several aggravated rapes. That day they had been doing a mass release, because the number of inmates had gone over the court-set limit. One hundred twenty-five men were being released early, before their terms were up. As she waited, they emerged in groups from a small side door. All were dressed identically in the pastel long-sleeved shirts and work pants they were issued on release. Each group did the same thing: the men walked until they were a few yards past the prison wall, and then suddenly they started running. At first, they jogged slowly. Then they picked up speed. They ran as if the devil were chasing them, down the street, down to the bus station.

Molly stopped. The memory made her want to turn and run. There was nothing to stop her, nothing making her go through with this. She could run back to her truck, lock the doors, put the cruise control on sixty-five, and hightail it back home, as if the devil were in pursuit.

She stood rooted to the sidewalk.

Ahead of her, a tiny cluster of demonstrators was gathered near the front door of the prison. A pretty pathetic demonstration—five people dressed in black, holding candles and chanting in low voices words Molly could not make out.

She looked at her watch. It was already past eleven-thirty. Almost time. She started walking again, reluctantly, one foot in front of the other, feeling herself pulled forward by whatever force it was that kept her in motion, doing what she did. It was habit maybe. Habit and curiosity. The curiosity spurred her on to look for the most grotesque things she could find, and habit made her keep on doing it. Appetite for violence and death. Just like the buzzards she'd watched from Charlie McFarland's house.

She passed the demonstrators without a word to them and headed toward the flat-topped, two-story administrative building across the street from the prison. The rosebushes that lined the walk were perfectly pruned and mulched. There was no better maintenance anywhere in Texas than in and around the prison buildings, she thought. And tonight the execution would be exactly like that—a neat and well-maintained death.

Her chest tightened as she walked up the stairs—just the usual pre-Louie jitters, she told herself. *Relax. You don't even have to talk to him tonight; your only job is to watch him die.* It was something just to be gotten over. In four hours she'd be home in bed.

All the lights on the first floor of the administration building blazed. No doubt executions required administrative overtime; it was probably even in the budget. Molly headed down the hall to Darryl Jones's office, where the witnesses had been told to gather. When family or friends of the condemned were attending, they gathered separately, in the basement. But there was no family or friends for Louie Bronk. As she approached the door, she heard the murmur of voices, low, but with an undertone of excitement. The vultures were gathering for the kill, and she had chosen to join them. She was one of them.

The director of public information for the Texas Department of Criminal Justice, Darryl Jones, was in charge of dealing with the press, so Molly had met him often before. He hurried to the door of his office to greet her, like the host of a party, a very subdued party. A tall, slender black man with the profile of a movie star, Darryl gave her the full impact of his splendid smile. "Molly Cates," he exclaimed, "have you come to expose us?"

She smiled up at him. "Darryl, anytime you want to expose yourself I'll be front and center. But I don't really think it would be appropriate right now, do you?" Oh-oh, she thought, crime scene humor slipping out. She was going to have to watch herself.

Darryl gave a perfunctory laugh. "Well, you know everybody?" He gestured into the room. Fifteen people, more than she'd expected, stood talking in groups. Clustered around Stan Heffernan stood six reporters, leaning forward trying to hear what he was saying. Molly recognized Judith Simpson from the *American-Patriot* and a man whose name she couldn't recall from the Associated Press. Stuart McFarland, dressed in a dark suit and tie, stood in the corner drinking coffee out of a foam cup and talking to Tanya Klein.

"Who are the men over there in front of the window?" Molly asked, indicating a group of five men.

"The tall man in the three-piece suit is Tom Robeson, chief of the enforcement division of the attorney general's office. The fat guy with the cowboy hat is Rider Kelinsky, the state prison director, my big boss. The others are just TDCJ brass, no one special."

"Why are they all here?"

"Some of them, like Tom and Rider, have to be. The others, well, they just like coming." Darryl grinned at her. "We could solve our cash flow problems by selling tickets to these damn things if they'd let us. Hey, I've got to make a call, Molly. Why don't you help yourself to a cup of coffee over there." He pointed to a credenza against the wall where a Thermos, some cups, and a plate of cookies sat on a tray. "It'll be another few minutes." He walked off.

Molly looked around the room again. Alison McFarland was not there, which gave her a tiny pinch of misgiving. But there was still time.

She should get out her notebook like a good writer and go interview the various officials, but she couldn't face it tonight—the low droning male voices, the righteous indignation about recidivism and federal court interference, the outrages of Ruiz vs. Collins—she'd heard it all before. She wanted something she hadn't heard. She wished Addie Dodgin were here to talk to.

When she saw Tanya Klein turn to talk to one of the reporters, Molly walked up to Stuart. "Have a good day off?" she asked him.

He reached up to adjust the perfect knot in his tie. "Actually, yes. It makes me realize that the rest of the world doesn't have to work every minute. Yes. A fine day. How about you?"

"Oh, I tried to write and couldn't. I should have taken the day off, too. Have you seen Alison?"

He scowled. "No." He looked at his watch. "She'll be here, though. Mark was going to drive her so she'll make it on time. I talked to her at noon to check." He paused. "She told me about what you said this morning." " Oh?"

"I wish you hadn't done that, today of all days. She was pretty upset. I hope you won't harp on this tonight and make it worse."

"You mean I shouldn't harp on the fact that a man is being executed for something he didn't do? I shouldn't harp on it because it might upset your sister? Stuart, I don't want to upset you or Alison. I know this is a hard time for you both, but the person who really killed your mother may be the one who killed your stepmother and David Serrano. Doesn't that worry you?"

His face darkened. "This is all crackpot theory, Mrs. Cates—your theory. You're the only one who thinks this. Alison told me what you said about Louie Bronk and that damn car. If there were any truth to it, the people investigating at the time would have found it. Or his lawyer. You're not helping matters by interfering here. You're not qualified. Leave this to the law enforcement people."

Molly felt her combativeness rising but she swallowed it down. This man did not need any additional problems right now. "I can certainly see your point," she said.

He nodded, held up his coffee cup, and said, "Excuse me."

Molly watched him walk to the credenza and pour himself another cup of coffee. Then he leaned against the wall and began eating Oreo cookies off the tray. He popped one after another in his mouth, staring off into space while he chewed.

Molly looked around and saw Tanya Klein standing alone. When Molly approached her, Tanya took a step back and frowned. She doesn't trust me any more than I trust her, Molly thought, and I don't trust her at all.

"What's happening?" she asked.

"The Supreme Court denied our last petition for a Writ of Certiorari a few hours ago. Louie Bronk is history."

"Have you seen him?" Molly asked.

"Yes. Right after we got word, I went to tell him."

"How'd he take it?"

"Like a trooper. I hear you went to see the governor this morning."

Molly nodded. Tanya arched a dark eyebrow. "Oh, well. We never had a chance with this one. There are some others coming up, though, that are real cases."

Molly tried to fight down the irritation she felt. It was so unjustified. This was a woman who worked hard in an impossible job that rarely allowed any victories. They were on the same side, opposed to the death penalty. They should be natural allies. But Molly's suspicions had been brewing and now they were bubbling over. "Tanya," Molly said abruptly, "do you know the McFarlands?"

"Well, you just saw me talking to Stuart," Tanya said with a shrug.

"Yes. But do you know Charlie, the patriarch? Ever talk to him about the Bronk case?"

Tanya looked at Molly through narrowing eyes.

"Have you?" Molly asked, her voice more aggressive than she'd intended. "Ever give him any information about what Louie was telling you?"

Tanya's face tightened in anger.

"Maybe about the car he junked in Fort Worth?" Molly was on a roll now and couldn't stop if she'd wanted to. "Ever get any contributions from him for the Center?"

Tanya's nostrils constricted and she shook her head, clearly not in answer to Molly's question but in dismissal, as if Molly were a fly buzzing around her head. She turned and walked out of the room.

Wow, Molly thought, I am really on the warpath tonight. But she had hit a nerve there. Suddenly she felt better. Some of the tension had dissipated. A few more fights and she'd feel almost human. She poured herself a cup of coffee even though she had a rule about never drinking it after noon. What the hell.

A few minutes later, Alison McFarland entered the room. She had dressed up. She wore a long brown skirt and clean white blouse, dangly earrings, and she'd washed her hair. When she saw Stuart, still leaning against the wall gobbling cookies, she made a beeline for him and put her arm through his as if she needed to hold herself up. He stiffened and pulled back slightly. Molly was close enough to hear Stuart say, "You clean up good. You ought to do it more often."

"Yeah, I know. What happens now?" his sister asked.

"Damned if I know," he said. "I wish they'd get on with it."

"I'm so nervous, I'm afraid I'll have to pee right in the middle of it."

"Why don't you take care of that now, Al?" Stuart said, his mouth grim.

Alison left the room. Molly watched her leave and decided she should go to the bathroom, too. Why pass up a chance?

In the ladies' room, Alison was leaning over the sink staring into the mirror. She didn't turn when Molly entered, but gave a tiny smile into the mirror. "Hi, Mrs. Cates."

"Hi, Alison. I don't know about you, but I'm as nervous as a cat. Makes my bladder kind of chancy."

Alison straightened and turned to face Molly. "You know what I hope?"

"What?"

"That in his last words he'll do the right thing and own up to it, settle all your doubts."

"I can't imagine that," Molly said, "but there's no telling with Louie."

When they got back to the office, Darryl Jones was standing in the door saying, "All right, folks. If you're ready, let's walk across the street."

They all filed out, two by two. Alison grabbed her brother's arm and walked pressed up against his side. Stan fell in silently next to Molly. "I hear you went to see the governor this morning," he said as they crossed the street.

"Word does get around," she said.

At the front door of the prison, the demonstrators came to life. They picked up placards and raised their voices. "Execute justice," they chanted, "not people!" No one, including Molly, acknowledged their presence.

The brass hand railing up the steps to the prison door gleamed, as if it had just been polished for a big party. And the whole thing did have a party feel—the undercurrent of excitement and anticipation. It was concealed under a somber facade, but it was there.

Inside the door several of the men wearing Stetsons stopped to check their sidearms at a caged-in desk.

They filed into the visitors' lounge. There an assistant warden and a few other officials from TDCJ waited. The only one Molly recognized was Steve Demaris from the Ellis Unit.

There are so many of us here, Molly thought—wardens and assistants and reporters and witnesses and elected officials—because this way no one is responsible. Safety in numbers. This is all an exercise in passing the buck.

"Ladies," Darryl Jones said, after they'd all gotten inside, "please leave your handbags in here. They'll be safe. Officer Steck will be staying here with them. Members of the press, you are allowed to take into the chamber only a pen and notebook. We are required now to search you for recording devices. Bear with us, please, so we can get this done right quick."

Three young corrections officers began to search them.

Quickly, routinely, they moved from person to person. When it was Molly's turn she lifted her hands so the guard could feel her pockets. "'Scuse me, ma'am," he said as he patted Molly's jacket pockets and the back of her pants.

They stood around for several minutes. Molly looked at her watch, staring at the face until it was exactly twelve. Just like New Year's Eve, standing around waiting for midnight. Waiting, but not to be kissed.

When she looked up, Molly was surprised to see that, somewhere along the way, Frank Purcell had joined the group. He was wearing a Stetson and boots instead of the business clothes she'd seen him in before. When he saw her staring, he nodded.

Alison still clung to Stuart's arm. He looked as if he'd like to be anywhere but where he was.

The phone rang.

Darryl Jones picked it up and listened. He nodded, then said, "It's time."

He led the way through the visitors' room, out a door, down a long corridor, then outside into the night air. The temperature had fallen. Molly wrapped her arms around herself for the brief walk down a cement path to a small freestanding brick building.

The second Molly stepped inside and got hit with the dank odor of ancient dungeons, she felt herself falling backward to another century. She kept her arms wrapped across her chest. The chill. She'd never felt this before. It was as if this place, this killing place, had absorbed into its walls and floor and bars all the terror and death that had passed through. It seemed to be present now, all hundred fifty years of it swirling around her head. This is what Addie meant when she talked about this place. She had called it "corrupted air."

This could not be happening. This was 1993, the year of Our Lord 1993, September. An enlightened age, an age of computers and faxes. It was not an age where people were put to death in cold damp prisons. But this was real. They were here, a group of people gathered behind brick walls at midnight to enact an ancient ritual. To try to cure the tidal wave of violent crime by making one blood sacrifice.

They passed by the eight tiny, empty gray cells of what had been the old death row, before the state of Texas had outgrown it. In the cell nearest the door, the one reinforced with tight mesh, stood three cardboard boxes. Probably Louie's stuff, all packed up. Her chest ached.

Darryl Jones waited at the door until they all gathered. Then he shepherded them into the chamber. It was a small brick room, very brightly lighted and painted an intense cobalt-blue, the kind of garish color you saw on walls in Mexico. The room was empty, no chairs, no distractions, nothing. Molly found herself blinking and wishing the fluorescent lights were not so intense.

Bars painted the same color of blue separated this room from the execution chamber a few feet away. A white curtain was drawn back so they could see through the bars a tableau so strange that the only thing she could think of was a Halloween haunted house where she'd once taken Jo Beth. A gurney was bolted to the floor. On it Louie lay strapped down, his thin arms extended. He was dressed in an immaculate white prison uniform and shiny black shoes. His hair had been trimmed since she had seen him four days ago and he was freshly shaved. The state of Texas had spiffed Louie up for the party.

His scrawny bare arms were stretched out and strapped down at the wrists. IV tubes ran from both arms and disappeared into a tiny square hole in the wall, next to a one-way mirror. The slack pale skin with its network of crinkled blue tattoos looked like some grotesque illustration from an anatomy text. Like skin and limbs and veins long dead. Yes, Molly was suddenly certain that his arms were already dead. So now it was too late to go back. The only humane thing was to go ahead and kill the rest of his body. She tried to swallow but her mouth was utterly dry. God, she was losing her mind. What if she wrote all this? Richard would be convinced she had gone mad. So would everyone else. She forced her eyes away from the dead arms.

At Louie's head stood the warden of the Walls Unit, dressed in a dark business suit and paisley tie instead of his usual tan Western outfit. He, too, had dressed up for company. In a sudden lapse of memory, Molly couldn't quite dredge up his name. She wasn't doing very well. Here she was, the star crime reporter for *Lone Star Monthly*, and she'd forgotten her notebook. Furthermore, she had no idea where the real story was, where it started or where it would end, what she would write, or whether she would write anything at all. Her legs felt rubbery and her stomach so hot and churning she was grateful she hadn't put anything in it.

Sister Addie stood at Louie's side, holding his right hand. She wore the same pastel house dress she'd worn when Molly had first met her, and draped over her shoulders was the ugly pink and brown afghan she'd been knitting for Louie. Her head was bent down to his and they were talking in low voices, but when the group filed in, Louie looked away from her and turned his head toward the witnesses on the other side of the bars. His eyes darted and stopped on Molly. He gave her a slight nod. She nodded back and tried to smile. Instead her mouth fell open, as if she'd just got a shot of Novocain and lost control, or as if she were about to let out a scream.

The door on Louie's side of the bars opened. John Desmond, the state prison director, entered. "Warden," he said in a deep voice, "you may proceed."

The warden turned to Louie. "Do you have a last statement to make?"

Louie glanced quickly up at Sister Addie. Then he turned his head toward the witnesses but kept his eyes fixed on a spot above their heads. In a quavery, whiny voice, he said, "I want to say I'm sorry for the things I done. I want to thank my sister Carmen-Marie who's not here but she's been real nice to me in the past and I wish I'd been a better brother." He paused and ran his tongue over his thin lips. Molly thought she saw him blink once, as if to force back a tear.

"And Molly Cates," he continued, "who tried to help. I left you something." His chest rose and sank several times. "Thanks. Mostly, I want to thank Sister Adeline Dodgin for sticking by me and trying to show me the way to salvation. The only good thing I leave behind in this world is my poems."

He'd spoken the last words rapid-fire and now he had to take a breath. "Oh," he said, as if he'd just remembered something important, "I forgive everyone who's involved with this. Jesus forgives us all. We are forgiven."

He rolled his head on the gurney so that he was looking up at Addie. She smiled down at him, looking directly into his eyes. The room was absolutely silent. Then as if she had received a signal, though Molly couldn't discern any movement on Louie's part, Addie looked at the warden and nodded. The warden stepped back and nodded to the one-way mirror in the wall where the tubes from Louie's arm led. "We are ready," he said.

Death seemed instantaneous.

Louie took a deep breath, his eyes opened wide in surprise, he coughed twice and was still. If she had blinked she'd have missed it.

The only sound was the scratching of pens as the journalists wrote on their pads.

The door in the execution chamber opened. A man in a white coat entered, carrying a stethoscope. He leaned over Louie and put the stethoscope to his chest. Then he stood up and looked at his watch. "Twelve-fourteen," he said, and walked out.

Louie lay still, his eyes wide open.

Molly looked around, feeling confused. That was it? As easy as that? Life hadn't even resisted. There was no fight, no scream, nothing to mark it. The line between being alive and being dead was so narrow it was almost imperceptible.

That's something Louie must have known, she realized—known better than anyone. A bullet or a knife in the right place and it was done. Quicker than a blink. No big deal. Happens all the time.

Buck Fever: A Blanco County, Texas Novel by Ben Rehder, copyright 2002 by Ben Rehder and reprinted with permission of St. Martin's Press, L.L.C.

Agatite by Clay Reynolds, copyright 1986 by Clay Reynolds. Used by permission of the author.

The Last King of Texas by Rick Riordan, copyright 2000 by Rick Riordan. Used by permission of Bantam Books, a division of Random House, Inc.

El Camino del Rio by Jim Sanderson, copyright 1998 by Jim Sanderson. Reprinted by permission of the University of New Mexico Press.

A Twist at the End by Steven Saylor, copyright 2000 by Steven Saylor. Reprinted with the permission of Simon & Schuster Adult Publishing Group.

Rock Critic Murders by Jesse Sublett, copyright 1990 by Jesse Sublett. Used by permission of the author.

Umbrella Man by Doug J. Swanson, copyright 1999 by Doug J. Swanson. Used by permission of the author.

The Killer Inside Me by Jim Thompson, originally published by Lion Books in 1952 as a paperback original. Reprinted by permission of e-reads.com

The Red Scream by Mary Willis Walker, copyright 1994 by Mary Willis Walker. Used by permission of Doubleday, a division of Random House, Inc.